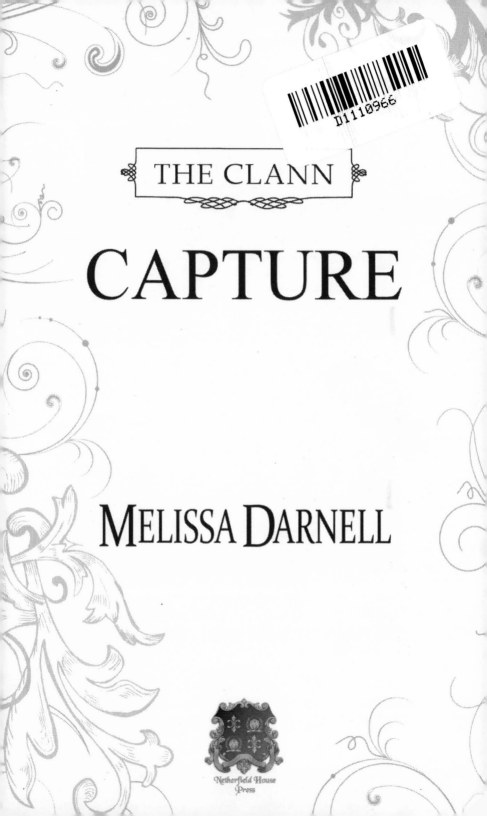

THE CLANN

CAPTURE

MELISSA DARNELL

Netherfield House
Press

Published by Netherfield House Press
www.NetherfieldHousePress.com

ISBN: 978-1-935649-21-2

Graphics Credits:
Cover design by Melissa Darnell.
Male cover model: Hunter Darnell
Female cover model: SavannahAnn McMillan
Background cover photo used with permission from kr-
2y-51-3k at DeviantArt.com.

Also by Melissa Darnell:

Adult:

Homecoming

THE CLANN SERIES:
Dance with Darkness

New Adult:

Guilty

MIDNIGHT GIRLS SERIES:
Scent of Evil
Scent of Revenge
Scent of Rain

Young Adult:

The Last Firefly

THE CLANN SERIES:
Crave
Covet
Consume
Capture

"Darnell has a unique ability to draw her reader into her world. Her imagery is fantastic. Her characters are so real, it's easy to forget they're imaginary. Their struggles are heartbreaking and their love is toe curling."

—*Julie Anne Lindsey, Musings from the Slush Pile review for The Clann Series #2: Covet*

"Covet takes you on one big emotional rollercoaster ride. I loved every minute of it! I didn't think it would top Crave, but Darnell pulled it off. Needless to say, Darnell is on auto buy for me and this series is definitely one of my favorites. I have a lot of books that are my favorite, but when asked for recommendations, this series is one that always comes to mind."

—*Damaris, Good Choice Reading review for The Clann Series #2: Covet*

"Author Melissa Darnell has created characters that are not only like-able, but stay with you well past the pages."

—*Teresa, The Duchess Mommy Reads review for The Clann Series #1: Crave*

"Melissa Darnell has a way of making you feel the emotions right along with the characters and it's brilliant."

—*Jenna, Shortie Says review for The Clann Series #1: Crave*

CHAPTER 1

Friday, November 20th
Tarah

Everyone remembers where they were when the second U.S. civil war began. And how simply it started, with just two big bangs out of nowhere. And how it ended up setting the whole world on fire eventually.

Only minutes before it all began to fall apart, I was standing outside Mr. Sherman's senior World History class with my friend Aimee, her obnoxious boyfriend Gary, and his two usual mindless sidekicks. I was trying my hardest not to lose yet another set of friendships in my life. But lately it wasn't going too well.

"Come on, Tarah, you said yourself this guy used to be your best friend," Aimee whined, clutching Gary's upper arm. "How could he possibly say no to you?"

"'Used to be' being the operative term here," I said. "I haven't even spoken to Hayden Shepherd in years. And now you want me to just go up to him and tell him to—"

"Just to come to a meeting with us, is all," Aimee said.

"It's not that big a deal. He'll probably love it! You always have fun with us, right? Why wouldn't he?"

Why wouldn't he?

A hundred reasons raced through my mind...

Reason #1: Because he's Hayden Shepherd, only surviving son of the most conservative United States senator ever, and his father would kill him if Hayden was even seen with us in public, much less caught in the woods with us at one of our meetings.

Reason #2: Because we were best friends for six years, and then I went and destroyed that friendship with my big mouth.

Reason #3: And because of Reason #2, he probably hates my guts now.

I opened my mouth to list these reasons along with a whole bunch of others to her. But I never got the chance.

"Aim, let it go already," Gary said before I could speak, his thick, dark eyebrows dipping still lower over equally dark eyes. "Hayden's never going to speak to anyone like us, much less actually help us. He's a rich kid, a one percenter from birth. He's never going to help someone unless there's something in it for him."

"That's totally unfair," I found myself blurting out. "Hayden's not like that. Money's got nothing to do with who he is."

"Oh yeah?" Gary turned those dark eyes on me. "If Hayden's such a great guy, then why is his best friend Kyle Kingsley?"

I didn't have an answer for that one. Hayden had replaced me with Kyle the Vile as soon as I stopped hanging out with Hayden and his brother in junior high. Hayden's choice in replacement best friend didn't make any more sense to me now than it had back then.

"What about that night in the woods?" Aimee insisted, her voice dropping to a hushed murmur. "Hayden was the only one who survived. So he has to know something that can help us too."

Crossing his arms over his chest, Gary growled, making the flow of traffic edge further away from us as students hurried past on their way to class. "Why do we keep having this argument? I've told you, the only reason Hayden could have survived was because he caused all those deaths in the first place! Which is just another reason why we've got no business even considering asking for his help. Which, like I've also said a thousand times before, we *don't need*. All we need is a little more practice and—"

"And we're going to end up getting ourselves killed," I muttered, unable to stop myself though I knew how Gary would react.

He didn't disappoint. "No thanks to *your* help," he snarled. "You know, if you've got such a problem with the way I'm running things, you don't have to come to the meetings."

His implied threat to kick me out of the group hit its target, and I flinched in spite of my best efforts not to. Even if I didn't exactly fit in among them and could barely stand Gary and his stupid sidekicks, Aimee and the others in our group were the only friends I had now. If I lost them, I would be truly alone in this school.

"Hey, she's not the one suggesting we get help!" Aimee ducked out from beneath Gary's arm so she could step closer to me. "This was *my* idea, remember? And none of us are trying to replace you as leader, so relax already. We're just looking for a few tips from someone who might have the answers we need to keep us safe."

"And you really think a mass murderer like *Shepherd* is going to help us out?" Gary smirked, his tone making the question rhetorical.

I knew he was baiting me just to get a rise out of me. But I still couldn't keep my lips zipped. "Stop calling him that. That's a crappy rumor, and you know it. If Hayden actually caused all those deaths, even his dad couldn't have saved him." No one had enough money or political clout to get out of killing that many people. Not even the Shepherds. "Besides, why would he kill his brother too?"

I had to fight to keep my voice from wobbling on that last part.

"Obviously because he lost control," Gary said.

My back teeth ground together hard enough to hurt the muscles in my jaw. I took a step closer to Gary. "You don't know him. Hayden's a good guy. And he adored his older brother. There's no way he would have killed Damon, not even by accident." Not Hayden. And especially not in those woods, *our* woods. The Hayden I'd once known had slain dragons, not innocents.

Unfortunately that was the exact moment the subject of our debate chose to walk around the corner of the hallway where we were standing. And the dark scowl on his face didn't exactly make him look innocent of murder.

I froze.

A muscle in Hayden's jaw clenched into a hard knot as he circled around us and disappeared into the classroom behind me.

Had he heard us talking about him?

"You don't think *that guy* is a killer?" Gary hissed, leaning forward into my face and stabbing a finger in the air in Hayden's direction. "Then obviously you're letting your little school girl crush on him totally delude you. He's a murderer, Tarah, plain and simple. Everyone knows it but you. Don't let his money and family name blind you to the truth."

"I'm not!" I had to fight not to shout the words as the blood roared into my head with all the unexpected force of a tidal wave after a dam wall breaks. How *dare* Gary accuse me of being so shallow? I had never cared about Hayden's family name or money.

"Really?" Gary stared at me, disbelief written all over his

face. "Then if he's so innocent, tell me just what do you think happened in those woods that night?"

I sighed and held my tablet tighter against my chest. "I...don't know."

Aimee turned to Gary. "Oh, get off her back about it, Gary. Nobody knows what really happened except for Hayden. But she has a good point. Too many people died that night. If Hayden was responsible, all the money and political pull in the world couldn't have covered it up."

She took a deep breath, then reached down to take her boyfriend's hand. "Look, what if everyone else died that night because they were experimenting like us and they made one mistake too many? We could end up just like them. Dead. Maybe Hayden didn't die because he was watching from a safe distance. Or maybe he knew something that protected him. Either way, we owe it to ourselves and each other to at least see if he could help us stop the same thing from happening to us." She swallowed hard, her pale white throat working with the effort. "I know you don't like it. But we need him. Please give her a chance to try and talk him into coming. It'll only be for one meeting."

Seconds ticked by as Gary stared at me, his jaw muscles repeatedly knotting then relaxing. Finally he shrugged one shoulder. "Whatever. I've got to get to class."

Aimee shot me a quick smile. "Good luck! Call me later and tell me what he said, okay?" Without waiting for my reply, she took off at a jog down the hall to catch up with Gary and his buddies, her thick boots' rubber soles clomping against the shiny, overly waxed linoleum.

Blowing out a long breath, I ducked into history class just as the tardy bell rang.

Hayden was already in his desk directly behind mine, his long, normally stretched out legs cramped up beneath his own desk for a change. As if he didn't want to risk coming into contact with me as I walked past him. He didn't look up as I hurried into my seat then got ready for class, waking up my school-assigned tablet and detaching its metal stylus from its side edge. Several clicks added to the buzzing of the fluorescent lights overhead as everyone turned on their tablets then tapped the screens with their styluses to start their audio recordings of the upcoming lecture.

If only we had known what was about to happen in a few short minutes, we would have held up our tablets, aimed the built-in cameras at the front of the room, and started video recordings instead so that we could capture every single visual detail along with the sounds of history in the making for later generations to try and understand what that earth-shaking moment was like.

But we thought it was just another school day like all the others that had come before it. And having to listen to Mr. Sherman's boring lectures again was bad enough without also having to see just how boring his delivery style was. So we started audio recordings, unknowingly adding to that day's countless other audio recordings and videos shot from cell phone cameras, security cameras, and home television DVRs set to record daytime soap opera shows— ensuring that this infamous day would become the most widely captured day ever in human history.

In those final minutes of peace, Mr. Sherman's voice began its usual droning lecture from where he'd perched on a stool at the front of the room. And with my tablet recording the lecture for me to reference later at home, I thought I was free to zone out.

I needed a way to bring up what would surely be the world's most awkward conversation ever with the guy sitting in the desk behind me.

Or maybe I was overthinking it. Maybe it wouldn't be awkward at all. Heck, maybe Hayden actually didn't even care about the past anymore, and it was only me and my stupid guilt that was blowing it all out of proportion. Maybe he'd be happy to come to a meeting and help out.

I closed my eyes and rubbed at the pounding that had begun in my temples. Yeah right. Even if Hayden didn't remember or care about how our friendship had ended, there was no way he was going to happily agree to come to a meeting with a bunch of Goths in the woods at night. Especially after losing his only brother in another area of those same woods.

Unable to help myself, I risked a look back over my shoulder.

Hunched over his desk, Hayden's piercing blue eyes looked up at me from beneath their heavy fringe of brown lashes and the thick, sun-streaked brown hair that flopped across his forehead and eyebrows. As usual, he was in serious need of a haircut. Some things never changed.

His eyes narrowed, his jaw muscles knotting up at the sides of his face, as he returned my stare.

Then again, some things definitely had changed. And not for the better.

I turned to face the front of the room again, swallowing hard. Either he'd heard us talking about him before class today, or he was still holding a grudge against me for messing up everything we'd once shared together.

A knot formed in my throat, making it hard to breathe. Once, I would have been able to know at a glance exactly what Hayden was thinking, even to the point of being able to finish his sentences. But too much time and distance had made his mind a complete mystery to me. He was no longer the guy I'd once known.

Maybe the rumors about him and all those deaths were true, and he *was* capable of the unthinkable. People changed, and not always for the better.

But in my heart, I just couldn't accept the rumors. People couldn't change *that* much.

Could they?

A quick, loud double rap at our classroom's door made me jump. My stylus clattered to the floor.

The door opened, and Principal Thomas stepped inside.

Frowning, Mr. Sherman stood up and circled around the rows of desks, his loafers making tiny squeaks against the linoleum floor, until he joined the principal. They stood there together for several minutes, their murmurs too low for me to hear clearly two rows away.

Hayden's desk creaked behind me, all but begging me to turn and sneak another glance at him. But this time I was able to resist the urge, because even though I couldn't hear exactly what the teacher and principal were saying, I could at least tell that it was about something major. Just the fact that the principal had come to deliver a message personally instead of using the intercom system was a big clue. And then there was the way they were acting, both of them pale and frowning, the rhythm of their low mutters fast and clipped. Principal Thomas' hands made quick, stabbing gestures every time it was his turn to say something. At one point, Mr. Sherman froze for a few seconds before jamming a hand through his thinning hair. When his hand dropped to his side again, his hair stuck up in little rows of tufts like dead brown grass pushed over by a flash flood.

What was going on?

Then they both turned to look at me. No, not at me. At *Hayden*.

Hayden

All thoughts of the tiny, cinnamon-colored freckle just below the glossy black of Tarah's hairline slid right out of my mind as Mr. Sherman took a step in my direction, his face set into a pale scowl that promised nothing but trouble for me.

My body froze while my mind raced.

Whatever it was, I didn't do it. Not this time.

My next thought was that Dad was going to *kill* me if I'd somehow created another mess for him to have to clean up.

Had Kyle and the other guys from the basketball team finally made good on their plans to steal the Raiders statue from the school's roof? I *told* them it was a dumb idea.

Knowing them, they'd probably gotten caught then lied and said I was the mastermind behind the whole idiotic plan.

If I got busted for their stupidity, I would seriously make Kyle wish he was dead. If I survived my father's fury first.

I turned to my left to look at the most likely suspect for clues, raising my eyebrows in silent question. But Kyle shrugged and shook his head, apparently as in the dark as I was.

Principal Thomas stopped Mr. Sherman with a hand on his shoulder. "Jim, you might as well show everyone at once."

Mr. Sherman hesitated then changed direction towards the classroom's flatscreen TV mounted in the upper corner by the dry erase board. He turned it on, found a news channel and hesitated again.

Looking back over his shoulder at us, he said, "Class, I've got some bad news. Something's happening in Washington, D.C. We're about to see history being made."

I had one last second to feel relief as I realized I wasn't in trouble here.

Then Mr. Sherman turned up the volume so we could hear the news station's anchorwoman, who was in the middle of a breaking news alert.

"...if you are just now joining us, to recap, about ten minutes ago there was some type of massive explosion outside the northwest side of the White House, where President McFadden was scheduled to give a speech that would address the rising anger and frustrations over the long continuing high unemployment rate and the ever widening financial gap between the top one percenters and the rest of the country."

The view on the screen changed to show a huge black cloud of smoke blocking almost the entire west wing of the White House. The cloud extended across the lawn and out into the street, where fire trucks and ambulances were parked and emergency workers led sobbing, soot-covered people away from the area. Every few seconds, the wind shifted the cloud enough to reveal glimpses of the White House lawn, which looked like a giant meteor had crashed into it.

The anchorwoman continued. "The explosion occurred just minutes after the start of today's scheduled press conference in the Rose Garden which, as you can see from the live footage, is now covered in smoke and flames. We're still not sure exactly what caused the explosion. We have heard from witnesses at the scene that it did not appear to be an airplane or other type of aerial attack, but we have received no official report yet to confirm or deny this. We're taking you live now to Jennifer Armstrang, a witness who saw the explosion. Jennifer, are you there?"

"Yes, I'm here!" the witness gasped. There was a loud crackle, probably from interference in the satellite signal to her cell phone.

"Can you tell us what you saw?"

"I was down the street a couple of blocks from the White House, and at first there was just the sound of the protesters outside yelling in the street. And then out of nowhere there was this loud boom that shook the whole street, and people screaming everywhere, and thick smoke started pouring in all directions."

"Jennifer, did you see any kind of airplane or helicopter in the area before the explosion?" the anchorwoman asked.

"No! There was nothing in the sky, no sounds of jet engines or anything like that. Just the sound of the protesters yelling outside the White House fence."

There was a pause before the anchorwoman replied. "Okay, thank you, Jennifer. Please stay on the line if you can and we'll check back with you in a minute. Viewers, we have just received some video from a surveillance camera that had a view of the explosion. We're going to play it for you now. If you have small children watching with you, please be advised that the following could be disturbing to them."

Apparently Principal Thomas and Mr. Sherman both felt our class was old enough to handle it, because neither of them made a move towards the TV as if to turn it off or change the channel.

The live view was shifted to the left side of the TV screen so a new, smoke-free view could be displayed on the right. The new video footage showed the White House in the distance and how before the blast the street in front of it had been filled with a huge crowd that had gathered outside the White House's wrought iron fence with signs protesting the super rich top one percent. Keeping the protesters away from the White House fence was a double line of police dressed all in black, each one holding a huge plastic shield in one hand and a black baton in the other.

The constant movement of the protesters made the single unmoving man at the center of that crowd stand out like an island in the middle of a storm-whipped lake. Also unlike everyone surrounding him, this protester was silent. He held no sign, his arms down by his sides instead of waving a fist or banner in the air. He simply stared with narrowed eyes set within a red face aimed towards the Rose Garden and the president, who was a tiny figure still speaking from behind a podium in the far off distance. The protester's perfect stillness made it hard to look away from him.

Then he broke that stillness by raising both his hands straight up into the air like a preacher praying to the heavens above. The video filled with red, followed by two seconds of static.

It took me a second to remember the anchorwoman had said it was a video of the White House explosion. Which meant most of those people I'd just watched were more than likely either hurt or dead.

The split screen switched back to a single live view of the smoke outside the White House, and the anchorwoman continued speaking. "As previously stated, we do not yet have any official reports, nor do we have any idea of the total number of injuries or fatalities. We will of course keep you posted with any and all updates as we receive them from White House officials as well as the area hospitals. Until then, we can only speculate as to what might have caused this terrible tragedy. While it seems that an aerial attack might be ruled out, some witnesses at the scene have suggested that the explosion sounded like a bomb going off. Witnesses are also reporting that the blast appeared to extend all the way to the garden of the White House, where it is unknown if the president and others at the press conference were injured—"

Silence for a few seconds while the anchorwoman paused, then her voice returned. "Okay, we've just received word that an emergency press conference is starting. We're taking you live to that conference now."

The view on the TV screen changed again. This time a man in a black military uniform with a lot of colorful badges on the left side of his chest stood before the White House seal, which hung against a wall of navy-colored curtains. At the bottom of the screen the news station listed the man's name as General Bridley.

He cleared his throat then began. "Ladies and gentlemen, the initial reports have been confirmed. At one thirty-two p.m. today an explosion from an as yet undetermined cause occurred outside the perimeter of the White House fence. The blast extended to the Rose Garden where the president was fatally injured."

In the silence of my classroom, someone's stylus fell with a sharp crack onto their desktop then rolled off onto the floor. Two rows away to my right, someone else whispered, "holy crap."

The general continued. "President McFadden was determined as fatally injured beyond all possible resuscitation at the scene of the incident. As the rescue efforts continue, we still do not have an exact count of how many others were also injured or killed—"

"They didn't even *try* to save him?" some girl whimpered. "Why wouldn't they at least try to save the president?"

"The blast must have blown off his head or something," Kyle muttered.

It was as if Kyle's comment slapped the entire room back into consciousness again. All around me, the class exploded in complete mayhem. Girls burst into tears and covered their faces, many reaching across seat backs or aisles to hug each other. Most of the guys sat frozen in their desks, some shaking their heads in disbelief.

"It's another 9/11!" Kyle said, looking ready to tear off the wooden top from his desk with his bare hands. "I can't believe this. The terrorists got us again! We ought to nuke them. Nuke them now and show them what happens when you mess with us."

Mr. Sherman yelled at us all to quiet down. It took a couple of minutes till everybody finally settled down enough so we could hear the general as he went on to outline how the vice president, cabinet, and the speaker of the house had all been taken to a secure location during this emergency transition of national leadership.

Suddenly, the screen's view split again, the general muted on the right as the news anchorwoman broke in on the left.

"Viewers, we apologize for the interruption, but we've just received more alarming news. Flight 3233, an airbus coming in on approach to Ronald Reagan National Airport just miles from the White House, has also exploded. The explosion occurred approximately three minutes ago while the plane was preparing to land at the airport. We do not yet know if these two incidents are related."

The news station switched her side of the screen to a view of a huge passenger jet as it exploded in a fiery ball in mid air.

Several students gasped again, and the room broke out into more chaos.

But like the silent protester on TV, I sat frozen in my chair, unable to speak or breathe deeply as the rage and tears flowed all around me.

My dad, Senator Shepherd, was in D.C. today in session with the rest of Congress. If this was all some kind of attack on Washington D.C....

Screw the rules against cell phone use during class. This was a family emergency.

My desk rocked hard as I fumbled for my cell phone in my pocket. Kyle stopped yelling with the others long enough to notice my desk's weird movement. He scowled at me with an eyebrow raised as if to ask "what's up with your desk?" I ignored him, searching my phone's Contacts folder for my dad's work numbers instead.

While I waited for the call to go through to my dad's office, Tarah twisted in her seat to watch me. As usual, the contrast of her dark eyes in that thin, too pale face surrounded by all that long, thick black hair managed to hit me in the gut. And right now, stuck here a thousand miles from D.C. with no news about my dad, I really needed the distraction.

Nothing about Tarah made sense to me lately. Like now...of all the girls in our class, she was the only one who wasn't falling apart, in spite of how breakable her long, skinny arms and legs always made her seem. While those watchful eyes of hers were as wide with shock as everyone else's, hers were still dry. And she only watched me, making no move to reach out to me or anyone else around her for emotional support.

She was a mystery I'd spent years trying to understand. And I was running out of time to figure out the answer before graduation.

The answering machine in Dad's office finally picked up. I ended the call without bothering to leave a message.

In the background, I heard the anchorwoman on TV continue. "Okay, they're telling me that we now have a cell phone video taken by one of Flight 3233's passengers minutes before the plane's demise. Apparently the person who recorded this was also streaming it live to the internet at the time it was taken."

The teacher and several students shushed everyone else so we could hear, a few girls' quiet sobs in the background around us adding to the nightmarish feel that this couldn't really be happening.

The new video showed an airplane cabin filled with passengers. A high pitched female voice, coming from what sounded like inches behind the cell phone, said, "Oh my God. I hope I'm getting this. I'm on a plane flying over Washington D.C. right now, and if you can see this, there's a huge fire in the city. It...it looks like part of the White House just blew up!"

The girl holding the cell phone pushed it closer to a

nearby window, where way off in the distance you could just make out a huge rolling ball of black smoke rising up from the ground, partially blocking out the familiar dome and columns of the White House across the Potomac River.

Someone else in the background of the video said, "Everyone, please, for your own safety turn off all electronic devices." The flight attendant apparently.

Distracted, I looked down at my own phone again. Where was the number for Frank, Dad's aide? Wait, there it was. I hit the Send button to make the call, held the phone to my ear, then glanced back up at the TV.

"Hey, mister, are you okay?" Cell phone girl asked someone not yet visible in the video.

She turned the phone's camera to show a man seated between her and the window. The camera was shaky at first, making it hard to see a lot of detail. Then her hand steadied so we could see how the man's face was beet red all over as he turned away towards the window, his breathing fast and harsh as his upper body rocked forward and back.

"My baby brother. He's gone!" he murmured as tears rolled down his cheeks.

"Your brother was down there?" Cell phone girl asked. A hand appeared from behind the phone to touch the man's shirt sleeve in comfort. "Oh my God, I'm so sorry. But maybe he wasn't hurt. He could still be okay—"

The man shook his head. "He's gone. I know it. I should have been there to stop him. But I was too late, and now all those people..."

"Ma'am, please, your phone," the flight attendant said off-camera.

Cell phone girl ignored her. "Your *brother* blew up the White House?"

"He didn't mean to!" the man in the window seat

shouted. "I know he didn't. He probably just lost control again. But what do you expect when the descendants keep punishing us for being outcasts?" He paused, his eyes widening. "Oh God. An attack on the president... And the Clann will see it and know... They're going to come for all of us now, aren't they? They'll never let the outcasts keep our abilities outside the Clann now. They'll hunt us down and strip us of our powers, or worse, *kill* us just to keep their precious secrets!"

"Sir..." The flight attendant again. "Sir, I'm going to have to ask you to calm down or else the air marshal—"

"It's too late to calm down," the man said. "Don't you get it? My brother's dead, I'm dead, we're *all* dead once they start hunting us!" He jabbed a finger, its nail black with dirt around the edges, at the glass window. His eyes narrowed a second. Then he grabbed the cell phone and began to scream at it, "Outcasts, take back the power that was rightfully yours from birth! The Clann has no right to hog all the money and power in this country just because we don't want to play by their rules anymore. Stand up, end the lies and show the world what you really can do! Make it so that *everyone* knows about the Clann so that we can all share the wealth equally again. It's not the one percenters who are our enemy, it's the Clann hiding behind their masks and controlling everything from the shadows. Help each other, help yourselves, band together so we outcasts are too strong for them to wipe us out or deny what is ours anymore!"

In the background the flight attendant shouted for help. A man in plain clothes shoved past the holder of the cell phone camera, attempting to grab the nutcase by the window and drag him out into the aisle.

"Don't be afraid, outcasts!" the man continued to shout. "There's more of us than them now...thousands, maybe even millions! If we stick together, they can't wipe us out—"

The air marshal managed to flip the man face down in the aisle, apparently knocking the wind out of him because he stopped shouting with a loud "oomph". The cell phone must have fallen out of his hand, because the video's view flipped around for a few seconds before its owner picked it up, righted it once more and began a fast running commentary on the mid-flight arrest.

But I could no longer hear the girl on the video. All I could hear were the echoes of what the man had shouted.

The Clann...

Outcasts...

Descendants...

Where had I heard those phrases used together before? And why did they make my heart pound?

Suddenly the memory of a hard hand gripping my upper arm made me flinch and freeze in my desk.

You are never to discuss the Clann or anything else you just heard, the memory of a voice echoed through my mind. *Do you hear me, Hayden? Promise me!*

I must have been really young when it happened, because I couldn't even fully remember the moment beyond that one bit of shouting and the feeling of that hand on my arm. But I recognized that voice. How could I not? Dad had yelled at me hundreds of times over the years when I screwed up, which was way too often.

But why would he get so upset about my overhearing *those* specific terms? What did they even mean, and where would I have heard them before?

Frowning, I glanced down at my desk, saw my phone still in my hand, and remembered something else. There were way more important things to focus on right now instead of some lunatic terrorist's ravings on TV. Dad. I had to get a hold of Dad and make sure he was okay.

Dad's aide wasn't answering. Time to try reaching Dad directly. He didn't usually have his phone on while

Congress was in session, but I'd run out of other options. I started to hit Send, but my shaking fingers, normally able to pass a spinning basketball from tip to tip without fail, fumbled and nearly dropped the too small gadget.

Calm down, Shepherd, I told myself.

After a few deep breaths, I managed to dial the number, only to hear yet another recording, this one tell me the lines were busy and to try again later. I slammed a finger on the End button to stop the call, then hit Send to redial.

And then the sound of an explosion on TV made my head jerk up again in time to see the screen go red then fill with static. Just like the video of the White House explosion.

Thankfully my muttered curse was lost beneath the louder reactions of everyone else in the room. Even Tarah turned back towards the front of the room to see what had happened.

"Hayden Shepherd," Principal Thomas called out from the doorway. Was he yelling at me about my phone? We weren't supposed to have them out during class.

Though I hadn't moved, my desk wobbled again, nearly dumping me out onto the carpet. In my ear, the same recording told me my call couldn't go through to Dad.

Gotta calm down quick before someone notices.

I looked over at the principal. He jerked his head towards the open door and the hall beyond.

Maybe he had news about Dad. Someone from Dad's office might have called the school.

I jumped to my feet and joined him at the door.

"Did someone call you or...?" I asked as we stepped into the hall and he shut the classroom door behind us.

"No, not yet. But under the circumstances, I assumed you'd need to be excused early." He gestured down the long hall towards the front entrance, and we headed that way.

"Right. Thanks. I'm trying to reach my dad now, but I haven't been able to get through yet."

I hit Send again to redial, and finally the phone began to ring. Once. Twice. Three times.

"Hayden," Dad answered.

I had to stop walking. "Dad! Are you all right? Where are you?"

"I'm okay. They're moving us to a secure location."

"Is this a terrorist attack? I just saw on the news that the White House and a plane blew up in D.C. Were y'all hit too?"

"No, we're all okay here. It could be another terrorist attack. We just don't know yet."

"Are you coming home?" My voice echoed in the empty hall, bouncing off the walls of red lockers and slippery, freshly mopped linoleum floors.

"As soon as I can, son."

"They're saying…the president—"

"I know, son. I know. It's going to be an organizational nightmare around here for awhile." He sighed, and I could practically see him running a hand through his hair, its once black color died silver for years now to help add to his image of experience and wisdom. When he spoke again, he sounded more steady and sure. More like a Shepherd. "Listen, go home and take care of your mother for me, all right? She's going to be upset."

"That's an understatement." Mom was a first class worry wart. But she'd had reason to over the last few months. First my brother Damon. Now Dad…

I could hear the hint of a smile in his voice as he said, "Exactly. So try to keep her calm for me. Let her know I'm safe and I'll call with updates as often as I can."

"All right, Dad." I hesitated. "Be careful, okay?"

"I will."

Principal Thomas had already signed me out of school.

So I headed straight home, and as expected Mom was a mess. As soon as I opened the front door, she lunged off the lower steps of the staircase and ran across the foyer into my arms. It was like catching a panicking bird.

"It's okay, Mom. He's safe. I talked to him."

Leaning back, she opened her mouth as if to argue, froze with wide eyes, then buried her face in her hands. "I thought this was all over." Her words came out in a muffled whisper.

At the time, I thought she was referring to the 9/11 terrorist attacks on Washington D.C. And once again I wished my older brother were here. Damon had always been the funny one, always quick with a joke or just the right thing to say to make everyone around him calm down and lighten up.

Except for on the one night that had mattered the most to him.

After a couple of minutes, I managed to get Mom calmed down enough so we could go sit in the entertainment room. While we waited by the phone for hours that night and watched the news for updates, Mom stayed pale, her eyes red and swollen, her hands trembling hard enough to make her heavy rings clink against each other. It didn't help that the airports were shut down for the next two days. Dad's phone calls didn't help calm her down much either. She wouldn't until he was home safe.

In the days of waiting that followed, it seemed like I said and thought the same things over and over.

If Damon were here...

"Everything's going to be all right, Mom," was what I said, trying my best to sound strong and confident.

But I had no idea then how wrong I was. Nothing was all right. It hadn't been since Damon died, and it wouldn't be okay again for a long time to come, despite Dad's finally coming home safely a week later.

That day's explosions, which had resulted in the president's and hundreds of others' deaths, was just the beginning. From that moment on, none of our lives would ever be the same.

CHAPTER 2

***

Sunday, November 22nd
Tarah

"Tarah, hurry up, it's on!" Dad yelled from the living room.

"Okay, okay, I'm coming," I yelled back, rolling my eyes at the dish towel as I dried my hands. A few days ago, Dad been interviewed by my parents' favorite show, *20/20*. Ever since, he'd been as eager to see it air tonight as a little kid waiting for Christmas morning.

Dad had paused the show's beginning so we wouldn't miss a single second of it while I got settled into the black leather armchair beside the loveseat he and Mom had curled up together on. Frozen on the flatscreen TV was an all too familiar image of a silver rhombus divided vertically into two, the show's logo. We watched the show every weekend, no excuses allowed. My parents believed its ever-changing lineup of interviews with politicians, celebrities, and rebel leaders was the perfect choice for weekly family time because, as Mom liked to say, "it inspired deep, intelligent debate relevant to our times."

Which would be fine if that debate didn't usually turn

into near shout fests between my always practical, psychology PhD-wielding mother and my theoretical science professor father.

Maybe if I'd been smart enough, I could have played mediator and kept things calmer around here, like my older brother Jeremy used to do before he hightailed it off to college and then various war-torn countries in the name of modern journalism. Unfortunately, not only had Jeremy gotten all the book smarts from our parents, but he'd also taken all the peacekeeping skills with him, leaving me alone here to watch our parents go at it every Sunday night like a couple of seasoned lawyers in a courtroom without a judge. When you added in my mother's hot Latin temper and my father's equally hair trigger Scottish ancestry, it was a wonder they'd stayed married a year, much less twenty-six.

Tucking my bare feet up in the chair's seat with me, I wrapped my arms around my legs and rested my chin on my knees.

Just a little while longer, I told myself. In a few short months after graduation, I would follow in Jeremy's footsteps, making the best escape possible in this overly educated household...I would run away to some far off college to get a degree in journalism, get a job that required me to live overseas somewhere, and then weekly family night with all its "thrilling debate" would become a thing of the past.

Seeing that we were all settled in and ready, Dad hit the Play button on the remote.

"Tonight we're talking with Simon Phillips," the young but silver-haired reporter began, his voice smooth and even. "Simon Phillips is the father of Eli and Caleb Phillips, who government officials earlier this week implicated as the suicide bombers behind the White House and Flight 3233 explosions that left 347 people, including President McFadden, dead."

I sat up straighter, making the leather beneath me creak. Okay, now *this* was interesting. It wasn't every day that the father of a presidential assassin was interviewed on TV. "Dad, you didn't say this was about—"

"Because I didn't know," Dad replied, leaning forward. "They never said this was the focus of the episode when they interviewed me. They just asked me about my research."

The camera view switched from the *20/20* reporter to a man in a button-down flannel shirt and jeans. Both men sat facing each other in matching dark brown armchairs in what looked like a dimly lit hotel room somewhere. Though Simon had probably been cleaned up for the interview, the makeup and low lighting still couldn't hide the gaunt shadows on his cheeks or the trembling of his weathered hands now clasped in his lap.

"Simon, why have you agreed to do this interview?" the reporter asked.

"To clear my family's name, of course. Everyone wants to make out like my boys were terrorists or something. But they weren't. They were good, hard working, honest Americans. They just tried to bring some honor and respectability and equality back to the outcasts and lost control of their abilities."

"Their...abilities?"

Simon nodded. "You see, you only think that each country's government runs the show there. But the truth is, all over this world right this very second it's really the Clann who are secretly the master puppeteers, and they have been for a long, long time."

"The Clann?" the reporter repeated in encouragement. "Tell me about this Clann. Is this in any way related to the Ku Klux Klann?"

"Lord, no! It's Clann spelled with a C and two N's. It's Gaelic Irish for 'family' or 'descendant'. The Clann is a huge group of families that began in Ireland and formed together around the time of the druids so they could safely work together to develop their powers, or what you might call special abilities."

"So it's a religious organization."

"No, because you see, there ain't no worshipping pagan gods in the Clann. At least not for as long as any of them can now remember. We all have our own individual choices of religious beliefs to follow."

"I see." You could tell from the reporter's tone that he really didn't. "And these special abilities you mentioned?"

"They start showing up when a descendant hits puberty, and then you've got to be trained up on how to control it all. Or at least that's what my grandpa told me when my abilities started showing."

The reporter frowned. "Wait. So you're saying everything you just told us about this so-called organization is just something you heard about from your grandfather?"

"Well, yeah. I had to hear about it secondhand from him because my family are all outcasts." At the reporter's slow blink, Simon added, "My grandpa left the Clann when he was a teen. He didn't want no part of any of it, and once you know how to control the power, you can decide to leave the Clann if you want. But it's permanent, and once you're out, so's all your kin from then on. Your choice cuts off the rest of your whole bloodline, and you're not even supposed to tell them anything about it."

The reporter cleared his throat. "Mmm hmm. Okay, so what happens when you leave the Clann? Do they strip you of these...uh, abilities?"

Simon shook his head. "Your abilities are supposed to be like a muscle. Once you learn to control them, you can decide not to use them anymore and then they atrophy. The Clann elders thought that also meant your heirs would be born without any abilities. But they were wrong."

"So now you're saying there are hundreds—"

"Thousands," Simon corrected him. "Maybe even millions."

"Okay, so you're claiming there are now thousands or even millions of these outcasts running around with special abilities and they don't even know it?"

"Yep."

"Then why haven't we heard about these abilities before?"

"Oh you have. Circus show performers, traveling magicians—the real kind, not just those fancy illusionist types—even as far back as Merlin in the days of King Arthur and Camelot. Stories about us have been a part of humankind's history for ages."

The reporter gave one long, slow blink and sat back in his chair. His eyelids lowered halfway, as if he were looking down at his notes in his lap either in desperate search of some way to save this doomed interview, or maybe out of boredom. Finally after a long pause he sighed. "Mr. Phillips, you called my producers because you claimed you could reveal the truth behind what happened in Washington D.C., not to discuss fairytales and fantasies—"

Simon's eyes narrowed as he grabbed the armrests on his chair and leaned forward. "Fairytales and fantasies! You think I'm *lying*? Fine, I'll prove it to you! Here!"

Simon held up his left hand, and a ball of fire the size of a grapefruit erupted on his open palm.

"Holy—!" Dad gasped, making me jump.

On TV the camera wobbled, making the view shake for a second as the reporter jumped out of his chair and yelled for a fire extinguisher. The sound of running footsteps broke out in the background of the video as the camera person fought to refocus the camera on Simon.

At our house, Dad fumbled with and then dropped the remote.

"Seen enough?" Simon barked at the reporter.

The reporter nodded quickly.

Simon stared at the fire on his palm and the flame went out with a poof of smoke. "And that's why I told you guys to turn off the smoke alarm in here."

"I knew it," Dad whispered, rewinding the show to the point where the flame burst into life on Simon's hand then playing it again in slow motion. He did it twice more then paused the show. "Haven't I been saying it for years now? I told you these abilities were out there!" He rubbed a hand over his mouth, his gaze glued to the TV. "Oh man, the physics that's got to be behind that... What I wouldn't give to have him in my lab for a few tests!"

I bit my lip and tried to look shocked too, like I never watched a whole bunch of my friends doing some variation of this exact same thing nearly every weekend in the woods.

He should see them call down lightning. That would *really* freak him out.

My only question was...how the heck was Simon controlling his abilities so well?

Mom paused in the doorway to the dining room, full popcorn bowl in hand, and sighed. "This guy's still on? You two do realize that fireball in his hand is completely fake, right? Chris Angel and that Damon Blade kid were pulling stunts like that on TV years ago!"

"You mean David Blaine," I automatically corrected her.

Mom waved off the correction. "Whatever. The point is it's obviously a trick, and an old one at that. I can't believe they've stooped this low just for ratings! Whatever happened to hard hitting journalism? If Jeremy were here—"

"If Jeremy were here, he'd have the good sense to know when to be quiet and watch history being made!" Dad muttered as Mom flopped onto the sofa beside him. "This show's producers never would have put on a simple parlor trick. This is real."

Mom rolled her eyes then stuffed a handful of popcorn into her mouth and glared at the TV.

Dad pressed Play on the remote.

As everyone both on TV and at my own house settled down again for the rest of the interview, the reporter's voice said, "As you can see, Simon's display of abilities was more than a little shocking to everyone who was present at this interview. But I and the producers of this show can all attest that this was *not* CGI effects, nor was it any kind of illusion or trickery that we could detect."

They replayed in slow motion the fire as it erupted in Simon's palm. "As far as we can tell, this was a real display of spontaneous combustion that Simon Phillips seemed to have total control over. Furthermore, his hand sustained absolutely no injuries from the fire."

The interview continued with the reporter asking, "How did you just do that? That was magic, right?"

Simon nodded. "But like I said, it's not like the magic you see in the movies where you've got to call on some pagan god's name or sacrifice a chicken. It's more like working with energy and willpower, though I expect science will figure out a much better explanation for it all someday. Especially if all the descendants and outcasts finally come out of hiding once and for all and let the world accept us for who we really are."

The reporter glanced down at his notes. "A transcript from that airplane video taken moments before its explosion over D.C. shows your eldest son saying, and I quote, 'It's not the one percenters who are our enemy, it's the Clann hiding behind their masks and controlling everything from the shadows.' What do you think he meant by that?"

"Simple. Like I said, it's really the Clann who are controlling everything behind the scenes. They've got their greedy little fingers into everything, and they make sure all that money generated in Washington funnels right back into their pockets to keep them sitting pretty while the rest of us, outcasts and regular citizens alike, starve to death. My boys believe..." He stopped, swallowed hard and started again. "My boys believed same as me that if this country knew the real truth about who was in power, we'd all be working together to make things equal again."

"So you're saying this nation's top one percent are all—"

"No, of course not! But a good portion of them are Clann. And a sizeable chunk of the rest of them have their friendly ties with the Clann to thank for their riches too. The Clann pays its secret supporters well. It also makes sure its outcasts don't suceed financially."

The reporter frowned. "Do you have some evidence to support this? Some sort of paper trail or something?"

Simon scowled. "No. But all you have to do is look at how consistently my family's crops have had to struggle year after year, even in seasons and areas where everyone else's are doing fine. They clearly put the curse on us when my grandpa left them, and we've been feeling the sting of it ever since. If not for our abilities to conjure up a few rainstorms and drying winds at the right times every year, we would have gone bankrupt ten times over before now."

"Rainstorms, winds and fire..." the reporter murmured with a small smile. "That sounds amazing. What else can a descendant or outcast do?"

Simon slowly smiled. "The real question is what can't we do? And that all depends on the individual...what bloodlines they're from, how hard and often they train, their level of determination, and whether they work alone or with others. It doesn't always have to be a conscious thing, either. For example..." He leaned forward again. "In Iowa we have some pretty long winters. My eldest, Eli, was something of a history buff as a hobby and liked to spend those long, cooped up months studying world historical events. And he noticed a kind of pattern developing."

A pattern.

My breath caught in my chest. Slowly, carefully I slid to the edge of the armchair, my heart pounding in my ears so loud and fast it was hard to hear the TV. "Turn it up, Dad," I muttered.

Simon continued, now several levels louder. "If you take a look at the news, especially ever since the creation of the Internet, you might see what he did...a kind of cause and strange effect happening all over the world between mankind when it gets riled up over something and nature's response. And I don't mean global warming."

It was all I could do not to nod. But remembering Mom was in the room with me, I just barely managed to hold myself still.

"Meaning...what exactly?" the reporter asked. "Are you implying that the Clann is somehow actually *causing* natural disasters on our planet?"

Simon hesitated. "Well, see, that's the thing my boys and I could never quite agree on, as to whether it was the Clann doing it on purpose or..."

"Or...?" the reporter coaxed when Simon paused again.

"Or...if it's the outcasts doing it by accident. Because not all of us know what we are and what we can do and just how dangerous we can be. If so, if we are the ones behind it, then it's even more important that the walls between the Clann and the outcasts come down once and for all so the outcasts can be identified, educated about who they are, and trained up in how to control what they can do. For the sake of everyone on this planet."

Finally my dad's face and shoulders appeared on the TV screen.

The reporter's voice said, "To try and understand the possible science behind Simon Phillips' abilities, we spoke with Sterling Williams, PhD, professor of human genetics at the University of Texas at Tyler, who has written several widely referenced articles on the possible future evolution of the human species. Dr. Williams, in one of your articles you stated that you believed humans might currently be in the process of evolving to exhibit special abilities someday. Do you still feel this is true?"

The recording of my dad on TV said, "Absolutely. All species of life are constantly evolving to better suit the changing climate and environment in which they reside, and the human species is no different. In the case of the development of special human abilities, I believe it's more likely that we'd only see the evolution of these new abilities within a few segments of the population based on their geographical location, genetic characteristics, and their family's predisposition towards exhibiting certain…anomalies, if you will. And of course that evolutionary reaction would probably depend on what kind of exposure they had and how long that exposure lasted to a wide array of environmental factors."

"What sort of environmental factors are we talking about here?" the reporter asked, still off screen.

The televised version Dad let out a heavy sigh. "Where do I begin? It all comes down to—"

But in my living room Dad suddenly shut off the TV. As Mom tried to protest, he shook his head. "No, no, absolutely not. There's no need to hear my reply now, because they've made me look like an idiot. I went on and on about how pollution and fracking and genetically modified organisms in our food and groundwater could be inhibiting human's evolutionary capabilities, when all along what they really wanted from me was what I just said. That new abilities in humans could show up in certain genetically predisposed family lines." With a heavy sigh and a grim set to his mouth, Dad dropped the remote onto the table at his elbow. "What a waste of my time. I spent hours showing those people charts and graphs and countless pages of research!"

I bit my lower lip. I could just imagine the tidal wave of data Dad had probably poured onto them. The first time he introduced anyone to his theories, it was always a bit like being swallowed whole by a whale...overwhelming and way too much to comprehend at first. I'd been working with him on delivering his supporting evidence for his ideas in easier-to-swallow bite-sized chunks. But he'd been this way for decades before I came along. I doubted the transformation would happen overnight.

Then I thought of my own mountain of evidence hidden in my closet.

I was halfway across the room before I even realized I'd decided to stand up.

"Tarah?" Mom said. "Is everything okay? This show didn't...upset you, did it, hon?"

Her voice had slipped into that careful psychiatrist tone calculated to both soothe and get me to spill my innermost thoughts and feelings.

But I'd fallen for that trick once before and learned the consequences of telling her my secrets.

I turned to face her with a smile pasted on my lips. "Nope, I'm good, Mom. Just going to get caught up on some homework, is all. Sorry about your interview, Dad."

Mom's gaze searched my face for several long seconds, checking for signs I was lying, before she finally nodded.

Dad caught my eye before I could turn away. He cocked his head an inch to the side in silent question.

But I shook my head. Mom's quick dismissal tonight of Simon's abilities as nothing more than a hoax made it clear she still hadn't changed. Her inflexible mind just couldn't wrap itself around the idea that there might be more to human capabilities than she could fathom. So it would be

34 MELISSA DARNELL

pointless to push this issue with her again. If we tried, it would only lead to a lot of yelling and Dad sleeping on the couch and all of us going through yet another long round of family therapy sessions with one of her peers. And I'd already had more than enough therapy to last a lifetime.

I gave Dad a sad smile then made my escape.

In my room with my door safely shut and locked behind me, I walked over to my closet then hesitated, my hands resting on the bifold doors' plastic knobs.

There is no such thing as magic, Tarah, my mother's often repeated argument echoed through my thoughts. *That's just your father's crazy love for fantasy books stirring up your imagination.*

I slid the doors open then used both my arms to shove back the clothing that hung inside, parting them to reveal my own "research lab" of sorts...two black framed bulletin boards I'd secretly had Jeremy screw into the closet's back wall for me before he left home. Mom never saw them since I'd been doing my own laundry for years now. Which was a very good thing, because if she'd seen these, she really would have insisted on more family therapy sessions.

The boards were covered with news articles printed off from the internet, each one held in place by clear plastic push pins. Around each push pin, a red string looped and stretched, connecting causes with their events throughout history. Taken at a glance, anyone else might see only a crazy, tangled up mess of a spider web. Unless they took the time to see the dates I'd circled in red ink on each news article.

But what alway drew my focus and made my heart hammer like crazy was the *length* of time that stretched between each historical cause and effect event.

It was getting progressively shorter.

Tonight wasn't the first time I'd heard about the Clann. East Texas was full of rumors about it. In fact, just a half hour's drive from Tyler was a mid sized town called

Jacksonville, which was rumored to be the Clann's headquarters and full of all kinds of strange people and even stranger things going on. A few years ago, Jacksonville had even been nearly destroyed by what locals claimed to be some sort of Clann civil war, though the news had blamed it on gang violence instead.

Until tonight, I'd always thought it was the Clann who should be blamed for the rising disastrous pattern of cause and effect tragedies. I'd never considered the possibility that the Clann might have outcast members who could be behind it all.

Simon's theory made sense, though. In fact, it was the *only* thing that made sense. I'd never been able to find a good motive for the Clann to cause all those disasters. Why create so much chaos and pain and death and loss and risk bringing attention to themselves in the process?

But untrained outcasts could easily be making things happen worldwide accidentally without even realizing the power they were wielding against their fellow humans. Especially if certain events in the news managed to stir them up collectively and lead them to feeling a kind of group negativity in the same direction at around the same time.

The question was...if the outcasts learned what they could do, would this stop the cause and effect pattern?

Or would it only make things worse?

Monday, November 23rd
Hayden

Kyle slammed his tray down beside me on the table the next day in the cafeteria. Everyone at our table looked up.

"What's up with you today?" I asked around a mouthful of pizza while Kyle flopped into the plastic chair beside me.

He looked at me like I was some kind of alien.

"Seriously? You don't watch the news, do you?"

I shrugged. "Sometimes. Why, did I miss something new?"

Kyle's girlfriend Becky, captain of the Raiderettes Varsity Cheer Squad, laughed at me and shook her head. Her short, curly red ponytail with its extra shellacking of hair products never budged beneath its crisp red and black bow. "Uh, yeah. The father of those D.C. terrorists is claiming he's some kind of real life Merlin."

I froze. "You're joking."

"Nope," Kyle replied. "It was on TV last night, and Yahoo's been running news features on it ever since."

Someone bumped into the back of my chair, but I barely felt it. "You mean like he's saying he can make broomsticks dance and turn lead into gold?"

Becky jumped in again. "No, like real stuff. He made a ball of fire appear right there on his open hand in front of the cameras and freaked the reporter right out of his chair. And he claims that's how his sons blew up the president and that airplane. That they just lost control or something."

"Yeah, and now there are hundred of people on YouTube claiming they're outcasts from some group called the Clann, and posting videos supposedly showing what they can do," Kyle hissed.

There was that term again...*the Clann*. Goose bumps raced down my arms.

"They have to be making it all up though. Right?" Becky asked.

An uneasy silence formed at our table.

"That reporter ought to be jailed for not helping the police catch Simon during the interview," Kyle said, glaring at the empty center of our table's fake wood grain laminate. "He was right there! Now he's out running around on the loose somewhere. Isn't there some law about aiding and bedding a wanted criminal?"

"Abetting," I corrected him even as the pizza turned into cardboard in my mouth. "And since the dad's not being directly blamed for the D.C. explosions, technically I think the reporter wasn't really aiding a wanted criminal. But even if he was, why are you so ticked off about it?"

Kyle scowled. "Dude, think about it! What if there's more outcasts and descendants out there running things from behind the scenes like he claims? What if these freaks are all around us, and we don't even know it?"

A couple of guys at our table nodded in agreement.

What if one of those freaks was sitting beside you right now?

The thought made my mouth twitch. "Okay, so what if they are?"

Kyle stared at me. "We'd have no idea what they could do to us. Blow us all up in a second, like the D.C. bomber brothers."

"Or drown us inside a building," someone else suggested.

"Or read our minds and rob our bank accounts," Kyle added.

"Exactly!" Becky said.

I couldn't decide whether to laugh or feel sorry for them. Or just feel sick with worry. "Y'all are really that worked up about this?"

"Everyone should be," Becky replied. "Look at what these so-called outcasts have already done! Hundreds died on that plane in D.C., and hundreds more at the White House. They even killed our president!"

Kyle's scowl darkened as he slammed a hand flat against the table. "I tell you, man, if we don't find a way to track down all these freaks of nature and exterminate them, the rest of us are history."

Exterminate them? He had to be messing with me.

I searched his face.

Nope. He was serious.

And everyone else at our table was nodding right along with him.

CHAPTER 3

Tuesday, December 1st
Hayden

As expected, my family's first Thanksgiving holiday without Damon was grim, in spite of how hard Mom and Dad worked to keep things upbeat with all their forced smiles and too cheerful chatting about nothing of any importance. I still hadn't gotten used to Mom's continued habit of setting a place at the dining table in memory of Damon, and it was all I could do to choke down even her excellent cooking while staring at that empty plate and chair. Watching the annual football game between Texas A&M's Aggies and the University of Texas Longhorns with Dad was worse. I kept expecting Damon to stroll into the entertainment room with the usual bowl of seven layer dip and platter of little smokies on toothpicks that we'd always end up fighting over till Mom made more.

By the end of the break, I was all too ready to return to school where I figured things would be a little more chilled out and back to normal.

I was wrong.

I had hoped all the talk about the Clann and freakish abilities would die out over the break. But then on Tuesday I discovered Tarah and a group of her weird friends gathered near my locker. In her hot pink sweater over a bright blue tank top and blue jeans, Tarah stuck out like a neon light in contrast with all the black the others wore as she leaned against the wall of red lockers.

Yet again, I had to wonder why she wanted to hang out with them. Clearly she didn't fit in, and not just because she liked to wear a little color now and then. The girl I'd once known was always happy, upbeat, nothing like the emo crowd she now called her friends.

Usually the closest I ever managed to get to Tarah was in World History class. But not today. Her back was so close to my locker that when I opened the door, my hand brushed her thick ponytail. She glanced at me over her shoulder, her ponytail swishing over my fingers again. Then she went back to comforting some girl who was crying. The girl was really laying into it too, the black rings around her eyes melting into dark rivers down her cheeks.

"Hey. What's up with her?" I asked Tarah, leaning in towards my locker so I wouldn't have to yell over the noise of the crowded hall.

After a long pause, Tarah answered me with a sigh. "Aimee's cousin, aunt and uncle are all missing."

"They're not missing, they were taken!" Aimee wailed through her hands. "You heard the phone message."

"Phone message?" I kept my voice lower this time so only Tarah could hear, trying not to set off Aimee again. With a wail like that, she must have descended from banshees.

"It did sound kind of...suspicious," Tarah murmured. "Aimee's cousin was in the middle of leaving a message. Then she just stopped, made this weird gurgling noise, and then it sounded like she dropped the phone or something.

You can hear some people shouting in the background. Then it just ends."

I frowned. "Anyone stop by their house? Maybe they went somewhere for the holidays and got stuck there by bad weather or something."

Tarah frowned. "No, they were staying home for the holiday since Aimee's aunt had a bad cold. Aimee's mom went to their house to check on her sister and said the front door was wide open with all the lights still on in the middle of the day. Aimee's mom said she talked to the neighbors too. They claim some men in camouflage uniforms with big guns showed up, busted into the house, then took the whole family off in a military-style truck."

"When were they last seen or heard from?" I asked.

"Friday night." A hint of pink spread over Tarah's cheeks. I noticed she was careful not to turn her head towards me. If she had, our mouths would have been inches away from each other.

"Military types, huh?" My fingers itched to touch her thick hair, see how soft it was. "Was the family connected to terrorists or something?"

Tarah scowled. "According to your buddy Kyle, they are. Aimee's aunt posted a video on YouTube showing how she could...um..."

"Play with fire?" I suggested without even the slightest urge to smile.

She watched me for a few seconds, seeming to debate, before shaking her head and saying, "Before showing how she could create water out of the air without anything other than her mind."

Suddenly, Tarah's hair was the last thing on my mind. I straightened up. "You're screwing with me. Right?"

Tarah shook her head. "I warned Aimee days ago that her aunt ought to take that video off the internet."

"We shouldn't be afraid to be ourselves," Aimee sobbed.

"You heard what Simon and that Phillips brother said. We outcasts have to speak up, reach out to others like ourselves, or we'll never learn how to control what we can do!"

The short, wiry guy beside Aimee hugged her to him, his dark eyes narrowing. Over her head he told the group, "Aimee's right. Why should we be afraid to be ourselves? We need to rise up and fight back, not hide."

I swallowed down a curse, my skin tightening all over.

"Don't be stupid, Gary," Tarah said.

"Don't be a doormat, Tarah," Gary fired back before leading Aimee and the rest of their group away.

Someone bumped into me from behind. Ordinarily I would have turned to see who it was. Today I was in too much shock. At the last second I realized I was about to collide with Tarah, and my hands snapped out to catch my weight on the lockers at either side of her shoulders.

She tilted her head back, staring up at me with wide eyes, and everything inside me knotted up into an even bigger tangled mess. I froze there, our faces inches away from each other, unable to even breathe.

Was this why she'd stopped being my friend all those years ago? Because, like me, she'd felt the friendship start to change into something else?

For what had to be the millionth time, I wondered what was going on inside that head of hers. I used to know everything about her. Or at least I'd thought I did, till one day out of the blue she told Damon and me that we couldn't hang out together anymore. No eye contact, no emotion, and no explanation either while she ended what had once been the best part of my life.

I searched those eyes now for answers, but only found more questions.

"Sorry. Crowded in here today," I muttered.

"I…" She hesitated, took a deep breath. "I have to go."

She was running away again. From me? From herself?

I pushed off from the lockers, stepped back and let her go.

As she headed down the hall, she glanced back at me, her eyebrows drawn. In confusion? Or was she just annoyed?

If only I could read minds too.

Thursday, December 3rd

Two days later during lunch, things got even crazier at school.

Something had Tarah's crowd riled up more than usual in the cafeteria. Everyone at her table, including Tarah, had their heads down, hunched over their phones and tablets. I stopped in the aisle behind one of them, trying to sneak a peek over their shoulder to see what was going on.

Before I could see anything, Kyle walked over and clapped me on the shoulder hard enough to rock me. "It's finally happening!"

"What is?" I asked.

Tarah pressed a shaking hand to her mouth, then glanced up across the table and caught my stare. Her eyes were wide open, rounded as if in shock, and shiny, tears at the edges ready to fall.

I froze. Unlike most girls, Tarah never got weepy.

Once when we were kids and Tarah's family still lived beside mine, Tarah cut her hand on a rusty nail that was poking out the side of her family's back deck, which we'd been playing under and pretending was a fortress under siege from an enemy wizard. Her dad had let Damon and me go with them to the hospital so Tarah could get the cut cleaned. The nurse had also given her a tetanus shot. And throughout it all, Tarah never cried. Even Damon had said she was the toughest girl he'd ever met.

So if Tarah was upset enough today to nearly cry in front of the entire school, there had to be something seriously wrong. Had someone said or done something to hurt her?

I took an instinctive step towards her, but Kyle shifted his weight and blocked my path.

"Hey, wait, you've got to see this video! The government's cleaning up our freak problem. Check it out." He whipped out his phone, already displaying some website called The Truth Is Out There. "This Clann chick and her family were actually tagged and bagged live on internet TV."

I couldn't have cared less at that moment about anything on the internet. But Tarah was talking with her friends now, everyone huddling in close like they were a sports team coming up with a new game plan. Eyes narrowed, Tarah shook her head with a scowl, muttered something I couldn't make out, and stabbed the tip of her index finger against the table top as if to make her point. Her statement was met with a chorus of groans and mumbled curses from the rest of her table.

Somehow I doubted they would appreciate my barging into their group conversation right now. And knowing Kyle, he wouldn't get out of my face about his little video clip till I watched it. The fastest way to get rid of him was to watch the stupid thing and get it over with.

"Fine. Show me." Sighing, I rocked back on my heels and settled in for the minute long video.

He tapped the video's Play button, and the four inch wide screen filled with the image of a raccoon-eyed girl sitting at her desk in her bedroom while talking to her webcam. She looked familiar.

Wait, I knew her. It was Tarah's friend, Aimee, the Goth girl who'd been crying earlier this week in the hall about her missing cousin, aunt and uncle. I glanced again at Tarah's table. No Aimee in sight today. A chill spread down my back and arms.

The cafeteria's dull roar of too many people fighting to be heard over each other made it impossible to hear what Aimee was saying on the video. Then something appeared in the side of her neck. It looked like a short syringe.

"What the heck is that?" I jabbed a finger at the screen, accidentally pausing the video.

"Tranquilizer dart. Probably a sniper shot it through the window," Kyle didn't hesitate to answer as he pushed Play on the video again. "I asked Dad about it last night."

His father being ex-career Army, he should know.

"Keep watching." Kyle held the phone right under my nose. Out of self defense, I grabbed it from him before he could hit my face with it. He grinned and rocked back and forth on his feet.

In the video, Aimee slumped at her desk. As her head hit the keyboard, Kyle said "wham!" and snickered. My stomach knotted.

In the background, Aimee's bedroom door flew open. A man dressed in khaki slacks and a maroon and white Texas A&M University sweatshirt ran in, maybe her dad. He rushed over to Aimee and shook her.

Behind him, two soldiers dressed in camo without any patches tried to enter the room. Aimee's dad raised a hand toward them, and a blue light I recognized all too well burst out at the soldiers. Both intruders collapsed, either unconscious or dead.

Bile rose up to the back of my throat, and I had to swallow hard to force it down.

"See that? I *told* you those freaks are dangerous!" Kyle growled. "That dude probably used a killing spell or something on those soldiers."

Aimee's dad shook his daughter hard, but she wouldn't wake up. In an apparent attempt to save her, he slung the skinny girl up and over his shoulder like a fireman. He managed to stagger halfway to the door before a second dart appeared, this time in his neck.

Two more soldiers appeared in the doorway just as Aimee and her dad hit the floor. One of the soldiers pushed a black band at his neck and said something. Then the video ended.

No wonder Tarah was so upset. She must have seen this video too.

"Isn't it awesome?" Kyle hooted. "Down with the freaks! Rumor is the government's doing this all over the U.S. in a major secret cleanup mission. Though why it's gotta be a secret is beyond me. They should be proud they're actually taking action! Dad says they're probably having to create special prisons out in the middle of nowhere for the Clann. He says it'd be safer than putting them in regular prisons with normal humans they might hurt."

Because now "normal" prisoners were more valuable than people with a few extra abilities? Weren't they all still just humans?

I stared at him in disbelief, my jaw clenched, a sour taste filling my mouth. How had I ever wound up being friends with him? Just because Dad was friends with Mr. Kingsley...

"So listen, I'm putting together a group," Kyle said as he took back his phone and started fiddling with it. "TAC. Teens Against the Clann. You want in?"

At the word "Clann", Tarah's head popped up. This time when our eyes met, hers were narrowed with unmistakable fury as she watched me.

I pushed past Kyle to our table a couple of yards behind Tarah's and dropped into my usual seat. "Why would I want to get involved with anything like that?"

"Why wouldn't you?"

I could feel more than one person's stare as I cracked open the tab on my soda can. "Don't we already have enough to deal with? It's basketball season. We should stay focused on that, not be messing around with starting some club that's going to waste our time."

"TAC will be a serious group, not some kiddie club. We'll be doing something important."

"Oh yeah? Like what?" Probably just sit around in his basement listening to him talk a lot of crap about people he didn't even know.

"The government's going to need all the insider tips they can get to help track down all these freaks. And who's more in the know around here than us?" He tapped his phone's screen then put on his best evil grin.

My phone beeped in my jacket's pocket. I pulled it out to find the screen lit up with an invite to an online group called Teens Against the Clann that Kyle had just created.

"This way we can send group texts and and videos and set up private chats and stuff," Kyle explained as phones all around our table began to beep.

"Cool," Becky said with a grin as she accepted the invite on her phone.

Heads nodded all around as thumbs hurried to accept the invite. All except mine.

"Well?" Kyle asked, staring at me now. "You in?"

Feeling the back of my neck burning, I glanced behind me. Tarah was still staring at me, her seat well within hearing range. She arched an eyebrow in silent question. Or challenge.

A loud bang in the cafeteria made me jump and several people whoop out in surprise. I looked in the direction of the sound. Apparently someone hadn't shut the cafeteria doors well enough on their way through, and the wind had caught and thrown the heavy metal doors open against the brick wall outside. That same winter wind whipped through the cafeteria now, rocking my food tray. Taking a deep, slow breath, I steadied the rattling tray by casually draping a hand over one of its rounded mint green corners.

As the wind died back down and I stared at the tray, I could feel two pairs of eyes boring into me.

Tarah at my back, still eavesdropping, waiting for me to turn down the invitation to join TAC.

Kyle at my left, waiting for me to accept the group invite.

Worst of all, though, was my dad's voice inside my head, telling me over and over to fit in no matter what. *Don't make your brother's mistakes,* he always said. *Remember, image is everything. Never forget what the Shepherd name stands for.*

Dad would be seriously ticked off if I refused to join TAC. Helping the law root out dangerous rebels for the safety of the rest of society was exactly the kind of thing he'd build a political campaign platform on. In fact, if he were here, Dad would already be angry that I had hesitated this long to answer. Maybe if Tarah hadn't been listening to the whole conversation, I could have accepted the group invite without hesitation or worry. After all, how much could a bunch of high school seniors really do, especially with Kyle leading the charge? Kyle would have his harmless fun with his big ideas for a few weeks, then everyone would get bored and too busy to make the meetings, and that would be the end of it.

But Tarah was here. She was listening. And she would remember, and always hold it against me probably, if I joined.

It shouldn't matter what Tarah thought of me anymore. But it did. And even though I knew I really didn't have a choice here, I wished for her sake that I did. Because I knew exactly how she would feel about it. She probably saw this as a black or white issue with an easy answer. But then everything was easy for Tarah, especially when it came to judging others. She had no idea what it was like to be weighed down by a family legacy, to grow up under the expectations of others, to have her entire life mapped out for her even before her birth. Tarah could be and do anything she wanted. She wasn't a Shepherd.

"Well, Shepherd?" Kyle said.

I gritted my teeth and tapped my phone's screen to accept the invitation. "Yeah, I'm in."

Just as all the Shepherds before me would have expected me to say.

Friday, December 11th
Tarah

Over the next week, word spread fast about the video of Aimee's arrest. It even headlined on Yahoo as breaking news. Gary was ticked off that his girlfriend had been arrested, but he was also proud of Aimee for gaining the outcasts so much national attention. He was convinced everyone in our group must be outcasts from the Clann and their families just didn't know it or want to admit it.

Unfortunately, her arrest didn't seem to scare him at all.

There was some evidence that the U.S. government tried to step in and stop the video from going viral...YouTube's first upload of it was mysteriously "removed by user", and the new website where it appeared next was soon replaced with a generic download error message. But in our hyper connected world they couldn't move fast enough to counter technology, and by the next week, almost everyone worldwide had either seen the video, reposted it online on their blogs, social media sites, YouTube accounts, and websites, or shared it with everyone they knew by email and text message attachment.

As a last resort, the U.S. government must have felt forced to do a little spin doctoring, judging by what happened next in World History class.

That Friday, Mr. Sherman didn't say anything before starting a video on the classroom TV as soon as the late bell rang. His mysterious behavior was the only thing that helped me resist the nearly overwhelming urge to turn and glare at the traitor sitting directly behind me.

In the video, another podium, this time an old fashioned wooden one, stood before the White House seal on a dark blue curtain. This time the speaker was the former Vice President Palmer, now our new president. She cleared her throat, shuffled some papers before her, then finally looked up at the cameras through rimless rectangular glasses that made her eyes seem eerily huge.

"Ladies and gentlemen," she began in a sharp, high voice that reminded me of a parrot with a Minnesotan accent. "As you know, the NSA has been relentlessly investigating the explosions that took place here in D.C. several weeks ago. I am currently speaking from a secure location, where we are working tirelessly to bring to justice the true terrorists behind these crimes. And today I am so happy to be able to say that our investigation has made several definitive breakthroughs. We now believe the explosions, while directly set off by Eli and Caleb Phillips, were actually part of a larger plot spearheaded by an international terrorist network who refer to themselves as the Clann with cells right here in our own nation."

The Clann...an organized *terrorist group*? What the heck was she talking about?

"These so-called 'Outcasts'..." President Palmer made air quotes, her long, bony fingers and sharp-edged French manicured nails looking like claws raking the air. "...claim to be only peace-loving, innocent people who were born with some kind of magical abilities that they merely wish to learn how to control and use for good."

Now she gripped the edges of the podium like some

creepy pterodactyl roosting on a rock while scoping out the air for its prey. "But make no mistake about it, these Clann members are nothing more than your average suicide bombers, and there is nothing good about their intentions. We have discovered that they are using ordinary, magic-themed books and arcane symbols to secretly communicate their plans with each other and find new recruits, recruits whose once innocent love for fantasy is all too quickly perverted by the Clann into a desire for destruction, anarchy, and chaos. So if you or someone you know has publicly accessible books on a magic theme, please consider temporarily pulling these items from public usage for the safety of your local residents. In doing so, you will be helping us thwart these terrorists' encoded recruitment endeavors."

My jaw dropped. "Is she for real? Give me a break! Why should we get rid of our books? Harry Potter had nothing to do with—"

Several people shushed me. I grumbled but shut up again if only to hear what else the crazy lady had to say.

President Palmer took a deep breath, and her face assumed a more pleasant expression that was apparently meant to make viewers feel comforted. "While these terrorists have wounded our nation and taken out many loved ones and our former president, they can not and *will* not win this new war on terror. The fact that I am here standing before these cameras today is proof that our great nation's government will prevail. We as a people are strong as long as we stand united against terror. We can send them a bold message...that this is the United States of America, and we will not be made to cower in fear. To support that message, we at the federal level have taken careful steps to empower officials at the federal, state and local levels so we can all work together to bring these terrorists to justice for the fear and pain they have inflicted upon our country. To this end, we will be using any and all means to root out and capture these Clann members, as well as anyone else who seeks to undermine our great country's laws, which have been enacted for all of our safety."

Uh oh. That didn't sound good.

But President Palmer didn't stop there.

"But we can't just sit back and wait while the government and law enforcement do all the work," she continued. "All of us must come together and declare that we are not afraid, and we will not stand by and let a few bad apples send the rest of us into the darkness of fear. So I am also asking you and everyone you know not only to avoid reading, selling or sharing books about magic, but to go one step further, to join with us in stopping these terrorists' campaign of fear by notifying your local police if you have any knowledge of others who are distributing these books about magic in potential Clann recruitment efforts. Any and all tips will be greatly appreciated. And you never know, your tip just might be the one that helps us turn the tide in this new war on terror. Remember, we are *not* a country of individuals who stand apart weakened by our personal limitations, but rather we are a nation, one and indivisible, and together we will stand strong and brave."

Amid clapping and more than a few hoots and hollers, Mr. Sherman turned off the TV.

I nearly threw up in my mouth.

I honestly couldn't decide if our new president was misinformed, nuts or just full-on diabolically terrifying. Maybe all of the above. Regardless of why she'd come to her crazy conclusions, one thing was clear. With her holding the reins, America was now on the brink of total disaster. And judging by the response from most of this class, way too many people were actually dumb enough to support her.

Shaking my head, I looked around me at my fellow

seniors in disbelief. "Please tell me I'm not the only one here who heard what she was really saying?"

"Which would be?" Mr. Sherman encouraged.

"Gee, let's see, where do I start? Censorship of books? Or how about that she's obviously trying to turn us all into spies against each other in the biggest witch hunt ever!"

Murmuring broke out on all sides of the room.

"All right, settle down," Mr. Sherman said. "One at a time, please."

Kyle snorted. "All I heard was that these Clann members are going down exactly as they deserve. It's bad enough that they went all suicide bomber on our government and hundreds of innocents. Now they're using our own books against us to try and pull in more recruits. I say we burn every magic book out there and force them to go back into hiding like the cockroaches they are."

I smacked a palm against my forehead. Oh geez. Where did I start? "Okay, first off, Eli and Caleb Phillips, the so-called 'suicide bombers', actually didn't mean to kill anyone. If you saw their dad on TV, he explained how they just lost control of their abilities. And second, where is that woman coming up with this whole story about there being some secret Clann terrorist organization? Real descendants of the Clann don't gather to learn how to terrorize people. They gather so they can help each other learn how to control their abilities so things like the explosions in D.C. *don't* happen. Palmer didn't even give anyone any proof! She just stood there flinging completely unfounded accusations against an entire group of people, kind of like Hitler did against the Jews, to try and make everyone afraid of the possibility of real magic instead of our being amazed and in awe of it. And isn't spreading terror the definition of what makes someone a terrorist? If so, then *she's* the one who sounds like the real terrorist here."

I thought it was a pretty darn good argument, and I

looked around, expecting at least a few nods of agreement. Instead, all I found were frowns and scowls, a look of pure horror on Hayden's face, and the usual evil smirk on Kyle's.

Kyle stared at me. "All the proof you need is in the name Clann. Sounds an awful lot like the KKK to me."

"It's Gaelic Irish for—" I began.

"Yeah, yeah, whatever." Kyle snorted. "If they were smart, they would have picked a different name, Irish or not. And besides, if they're not really evil, why go with the whole magical abilities story for a cover? Everyone who's ever read the Bible knows God hates witches. These Clann members might as well just go ahead and call themselves demon worshipers while they're at it! And who would go around proudly telling the world that they worship demons? Someone who wants to make others afraid of them. In other words, a terrorist."

Oh wow. I had to blink fast a few times at that. I felt like I'd just woken up in the middle of a plague of stupidity. "You've got it all wrong. Their magic has nothing to do with religion. I'm sure quite a few of them are Christians too. It's like Simon Phillips said. They're born with these abilities, and someday science will be able to explain exactly how they work. It's a genetial gift, not terrorist activity. For all we know, they could end up changing the world for the better."

"What have you been smoking?" Kyle said. "Lay off the incense and wake up, hippie! You heard the president. The Clann isn't a bunch of peace-loving vegans dancing around a bonfire singing 'Kumbayah'. They blew up our freaking president! Who knows what they'll do next? And did you notice how nobody can explain what the bombs were made of or how the terrorists got the bombs past security onto both a plane *and* right outside the White House gates? How do we know these Clann members really *don't* have some freaky abilities the government can't explain, like that Simon Phillips guy claimed on TV, and all those other outcasts on YouTube? Abilities that probably came from...where?"

Several students murmured "from demons" and nodded.

No matter how much I yearned to, I would not jump out of my chair and try to smack some sense into them or Kyle. That would just be giving them what they wanted.

So I gripped the edges of my desk, took a deep breath, and did my best to stay calm. "How do we know our own government's not actually behind the explosions? Simon Phillips could have been wrong about his boys' causing them. He wasn't there. At the very least, the government could be making up the terrorist story to cover up the fact that they haven't got a clue *what* really happened." I sat back in my seat and tried not to notice how the plastic chair bumped against a certain someone's desk behind me. "I think the government's just using misinformation and scare tactics so they can eventually push through laws that will allow them to censor our books and internet and who knows what else. And obviously the scare tactics are already working if you're ready to start burning books now."

"I'm not scared." The muscles in Kyle's jaw knotted. "I just think everyone has the right to know who could use dangerous and weird new abilities on them at any second, especially when no metal detector or bomb squad dog can say who the threats are. We have a right to be able to protect and defend ourselves."

Murmurs of agreement hummed throughout the room, making his scowl turn into a smirk of victory.

Spurred on by the sounds of agreement around him, Kyle added, "Think about it. Anyone around us could secretly be one of these freaks, capable of blowing us up or who knows what else at any second. Why would anyone in their right minds want to have to deal with the possibility of being around someone literally going nuclear just because they missed the latest shoe sale, or some chick's PMSing, or they walk in on their husband cheating on them with some other woman? I say we get rid of the problem instead. We should do whatever it takes to make everyone else safe again. Let's go a step further. Instead of burning the magic books, let's leave them out there as bait then throw anyone who reads them into prison. Or hey, better still, let's study these Clann members, figure out a way to stop their abilities and develop a blood test or something that we can give to everyone to find out who has these abilities in the first place. Then we wouldn't even need to bait them into coming out of hiding because we could just test their blood!"

A groan escaped me, despite my best efforts to hold it in. I twisted in my seat so I could look directly at Kyle without getting a crick in my neck. "This is so ridiculous. You're saying everyone should ignore the possibilities for human evolution, even purposefully stop that evolution, just because humans can't be trusted to learn how to control themselves? That's like saying all guns should be destroyed because some idiots out there use them for bad instead of good."

Rumbles of murmurs around the room as that particular argument hit a nerve, just as I'd expected. Not too many southerners wanted to hear about gun control. They needed to understand that locking up descendants and outcasts from the Clann who might or might not be dangerous was the exact same thing.

I shook my head. "History's full of people who were afraid of new technologies or abilities they couldn't understand, so they called it dark magic and started burning people at the stake. But we should be smarter as a species by now. Why not give these outcasts the chance to learn how to develop control over their abilities and use them to improve all our lives instead?"

"Or—" Mr. Sherman began.

"Or we could just do exactly like we're already doing," Kyle said. "Get rid of the problem."

"By banning books about magic and throwing anyone who's different into *prison*?" I said, beyond all hope of keeping my voice calm at this point as the blood rushed to my head and made my eardrums feel like they were going to explode. He was talking about our fellow students, our neighbors and friends, people like *Aimee*.

How in the world could Hayden be friends with idiots like this? Kyle was beyond narrow minded, beyond anything I'd ever seen. And I'd thought my mother was inflexible. At least she wanted to help the 'delusional' Clann members and outcasts with psychotherapy, not kill them!

Mr. Sherman raised his hands palms out. "Okay, guys, let's take this down a notch. Of course we're going to be a little nervous now with all this terrorist talk. But what about the positives? I think Tarah's on to something here. What if these Clann people did have magical abilities that could be used for good, such as healing cancer, or controlling the rain to help areas hit by drought or flooding, or even the ability to freeze bank robbers in their tracks without anyone getting hurt?"

Kyle snorted. "This ain't a comic book we're talking about here. They're demon worshippers, not Superman."

Breathe, Tarah, I told myself yet again. *Just do like Mom taught you and breathe slowly and deeply.*

Mr. Sherman frowned. "All I'm saying is, even if there are many others out there with the same type of special abilities as Simon Phillips demonstrated and described, there's no reason to assume the worst would happen. We should try to see the positive potential in the situation too. Like Tarah said, just because two Clann outcasts might have caused harm doesn't mean all of them will, any more than everyone who owns a gun will use it to rob and murder. Now, I've heard that instead of being imprisoned, these descendants and outcasts are actually being sent to internment camps created specifically for this situation—"

"Yeah, that's the rumor," Kyle said. "But I think that's dumb, even dumber than sending them to a regular prison would be. Why bother locking them up at all? Then the taxpayers, the ones who followed the *law* in the first place, are stuck with the bill of feeding and housing the freaks. Better just to shoot them all and let God sort them out."

Shoot them all and let God sort them out?

I gripped my desk with both hands, afraid if I let go that I might do something stupid, as my entire body vibrated with a level of fury I'd never felt before.

Hayden

I didn't know what to flip out about first...the fact that the entire country had just gone on a witchhunt for the Clann, or that Tarah was obviously one of them.

All those years we were best friends, playing Medieval Times with Damon in the woods behind our houses and at school during recess, she'd never once given any hint that she was different. But obviously Tarah must have developed her ability to do magic of some kind. Otherwise why get so worked up about it now?

Her being a descendant or outcast would certainly explain a lot of other things too.

Was that the reason she'd stopped hanging out with Damon and me, because she'd started to develop weird abilities that made her feel like a freak and she couldn't hide them from us anymore? If so, then I clearly never knew her as well as I'd believed.

From what little I did know, it seemed like these Clann

people tended to specialize in working with only one or two of the elements...fire, water, earth, wind. What elements could Tarah work with? And how had she managed to hide what she could do while at school?

"Let's stay with the possibility of those internment camps," Mr. Sherman said. "I've heard enough rumors about them in the news to think it's probable they're actually being built. Which leads us to this week's assignment. A thousand word essay, due on Friday, comparing today's Clann internment camps to the Japanese-American internment camps that were used after Japan's attack on Pearl Harbor as well as the concentration camps where the Nazis sent the Jews during World War II."

A chorus of groans rang out as Mr. Sherman listed all the subtopics to be covered in our papers. The subpar conditions in the Jewish and Japanese-American camps, and ways that the modern internment camps might be better or worse due to the United States' Patriot Act and the unique powers Clann descendants and outcasts might have. The financial loss as a result of being imprisoned. The moral and ethical considerations of our current government's segregation of Clann people. The possible physical and psychological consequences.

But it was hard to focus on the details of the assignment. While he spoke, Mr. Sherman flipped through pictures of the Jewish and Japanese-American camps on the computerized projector. And I kept thinking about the people I knew who might already be labeled by the government as Clann terrorists. People like Aimee, who must have been sent to one of the new internment camps along with her family.

And people who were still free, but might not be for long. Like Tarah.

The bell rang, and I had to fight the urge to run to my

AP English class, eager to get my mind on something else for awhile. Something that wouldn't make my stomach roll and my gut knot up.

But then Ms. Brown announced our newest assignment, the movie *Schindler's List*, and I realized just how long a week it was going to be.

Because the movie was too graphic to be shown at school, Ms. Brown had us watch it at home that night on the school's On Demand website, then write a five hundred word essay summarizing how Oskar Schindler grew from a selfish, opportunistic entrepreneur into a selfless savior of a thousand persecuted Jews.

Mom tried to make me come down for dinner halfway through the movie. But no way could I eat. Every Jew hiding under a bed or inside a piano from the Nazis, every prisoner forced to work in their labor camps, every woman who was shoved into the gas chambers to be turned into dust and ashes, could have been Tarah being sent to her death.

Why hadn't she told Damon and me about her growing abilities? We were her best friends for years. Did she think we couldn't keep a secret, or that we'd be too afraid of her to want to still be friends? Was that why she stopped hanging out with us and started hanging out with her new friends instead, because they knew what she could do and helped her hide it?

If so, she wasn't nearly as smart as I thought. How many times had Damon and I pretended to be knights saving our Queen Tarah's life? She had to have known that wasn't only kids' games, that we really would have done anything to help her if she had only asked us to.

Instead, she had entrusted her secrets to people like that hotheaded Gary and Aimee, people who thought it was cool to make videos of themselves standing up to the government and showing off on the internet. They couldn't even keep their own secrets, much less someone else's. As soon as some FBI agent brought them in for questioning, they'd throw Tarah under the bus in a heartbeat just to save themselves.

Damon and I would have *died* to save her if necessary.

Now Damon was gone, and Tarah hadn't said more than a hundred words to me in years, and she could be thrown into one of those internment camps at any moment...

I took a deep breath, then realized I'd been too lost in thought and missed half an hour of the movie. Time for a break to refocus. Now more than ever I had to stay calm and keep it together.

I paused the video, grabbed the basketball off my bedside table, then flopped back on my bed and set the ball to spinning on my fingertips, one finger at a time. After a couple of minutes, watching the brownish orange blur helped clear my head.

I was probably worrying for nothing. Tarah had been smart enough to keep her Clann side a secret this long. If not for the openly rebellious crowd she hung out with and her slinging clearly anarchist views in World History class, I never would have guessed her for the Clann type. Maybe I could talk to her in between classes, get her to see that hanging out with her current group of friends was too dangerous for her. Unlike my dad, Tarah's parents must have never warned her that our friends in high school were like team mates in a four year long game of basketball. We didn't have to like our friends, but we did have to choose them carefully and make sure they didn't bring us down or trip us up.

Right now, Tarah's choice of friends was an added danger she couldn't afford. It was only a matter of time before her opinions and their loose lips got all of them into trouble.

Tarah had always been stubborn and opinionated, but surely she'd listen to a former friend and change up her game plan.

Especially if it meant keeping her butt out of an internment camp. Or worse.

CHAPTER 4

Saturday, December 12th
6:14 am

The nightmare that night hit me hard and fast. It was nothing I hadn't dreamed about or seen in person before...full of the smoke of burning leaves and trees and human flesh and screams, and Damon shouting my name.

But what happened when I woke up was definitely not the norm.

It took a few minutes to separate myself from the dream, to resist the urge to lash out at no one. I peeled the sweaty sheets away from me and let the air conditioner dry me off.

Then I realized I was levitating three feet above my bed's mattress.

I hissed out a curse. This could not be happening! Not now. If my parents saw this...

Calm down, Shepherd, I told myself over and over, forcing my breathing to slow down.

Slowly my body lowered back down to the mattress. But even then I couldn't fully relax. This was getting out of control again. I had to find a way to rein it in. But how? My only guide had been Damon.

Damon. He might be gone, but surely he'd left behind something that might help...a journal or notes or a spellbook maybe?

Walking as quietly as I could on bare feet, I eased down the second floor hallway, its unyielding hardwood surface cold against my clammy soles, until I reached the door that no one, not even the housekeeper, dared touch.

I hesitated there for a minute, trying to gather my courage. I hadn't been in my brother's room in months. And yet when I finally made my hand turn the doorknob and open the door, the room was exactly the same as I'd remembered it. The desk, computer monitor, nightstand and shelves full of sports trophies were all dust free too. Mom must have been in here to clean it.

Would she have thrown out any magic books Damon might have had lying around?

No. This place was like a shrine to my brother's memory. Even embarassing or potentially soon-to-be-banned books would never be thrown away. She might have hidden them somewhere out of sight, though.

I opened the window's curtains so the sunlight could come in and give me something to see better by. Then I started checking drawers and under the bed and mattress, finding a couple of dirty magazines that would have made Mom gasp, but nothing that would have tarnished Dad's ultra conservative political rep.

The closet. It was the last place left to check.

I ignored the floor's pile of cleats, muddy sneakers, baseball mitts and footballs, and went straight for the shelf that ran above the hanging rod of clothes. The shelf was full of shoeboxes with weird stuff in them...dried plants, rocks, some velvet pouches I wasn't stupid or brave enough to open.

No books or journals, though.

Then my hand dropped down to the clothes hanging below the shelf, and as if drawn like metal to a magnet, my fingertips found fabric I would never forget the feeling of till the day I died.

The robes were made out of something coarse and nubby, like some kind of old fashioned, hand woven wool. I'd never asked Damon where he and his buddies had gotten them, or what had possessed them to choose a fabric that must have been hotter than Hell itself in the East Texas summers. Not that I'd had to personally deal with that problem, considering Damon hadn't let me wear the robes because he'd claimed I was still too much of a newbie.

"You've got to earn them, jerkface," Damon had said with a laugh, taking my punch to his arm with nothing more than a cocky grin.

I'd vowed to buy my own robes if necessary. But I'd never gotten the chance.

"I thought your mother threw that out." Dad's voice inside the bedroom doorway made me nearly jump out of my skin.

It took a few seconds to catch my breath and think of a reply. "I guess not."

"She always was overly sentimental." He stayed in the doorway, as if something about the room disgusted him. "What are you doing in here?"

I shrugged, my heart racing. "Had bad dreams and was thinking about him."

Dad nodded. "I come in here too sometimes when I'm missing him more than usual. He was a great kid."

"A great brother too." My throat tightened to the point of pain.

"Too bad he had to act so stupid sometimes."

"You mean...the party?" I'd lied to my parents about it

too, never once even hinting that the real reason Damon had taken me to that secret gathering was so I could learn how to control the magic growing like a cancer inside me, waiting to lash out if I didn't put a leash on it. The training sessions had been a secret Damon had tried to pass down to me. A secret he'd ultimately died for.

"He never should have been there. Never should have gotten involved with that crowd. I warned him about having friends like that. Damon died because of them." Dad's voice was harsh, grating with barely controlled fury. "He wouldn't listen to me. He was always too good hearted, always looking to make friends with anyone at all. Always looking for the good in others, even when there wasn't any good to find. I couldn't make him see how important it was to fit in. He thought being nice made it okay to be different, that he didn't have to worry about trying to fit in. And he paid for it with his life."

So Dad had spent the last few months pounding the lesson into my head instead.

"But what happened to Damon won't happen to you because you understand, don't you?" Dad's tone and the way he was staring at me made the words sound more like a warning than a reassurance.

I felt old, weighed down by something invisible on my shoulders and back as I shut the closet door. "Yeah, Dad, I understand. No matter what, fit in."

"That's right." He reached out and ruffled my hair as I passed him on my way out of the room, even though we were both six foot two and he had to reach up to do it. Then he shut the door behind us both.

I returned to my room. But going back to sleep was out of the question. Somehow, I had to learn how to control the magic inside me. Otherwise, my secret would be blown in no time. And then I'd wind up in an internment camp too.

Okay, so Damon's room and the public libraries were out. Probably the big bookstores had already gotten rid of all their magic books too by now. But what about small bookshops? The ones in the small towns might have reacted quickly to the government's new anti-magic stance. But the ones in the big cities might not have.

I pulled up the Internet, did a quick search, and found four independent bookshops in the Dallas/Ft. Worth metro area, which was only a couple hours' drive away. Surely one of them still had something about magic.

I didn't risk looking up their book catalogs online, though. Dad had told me a long time ago how all Internet activity was rerouted through NSA servers housed in the AT&T building in San Francisco. By now, they would definitely be tagging all searches for magic-related keywords. And maybe even arresting people based on it.

I would just have to go to the bookshops in person and see what I could find.

"Hey, kiddo, where you headed to in such a rush?" Mom called out from the kitchen as I tried to jog past.

I grabbed onto the kitchen doorjamb to stop myself. My sneakers squeaked on the tile floor in protest. "Oh, just headed into town."

It wasn't a complete lie. I just wasn't saying which town.

"Okay." Mom glanced up from the blender she was filling with chopped greens, probably for yet another wedding she was catering for, and frowned. "Are you feeling all right?"

"Sure. Why?"

"Because you haven't gone out with any of your friends after school all week, and you look terrible this morning. Are you coming down with something? Maybe you should get some breakfast before heading out."

"I'm fine. I'm not hungry. I'll grab some coffee later."

"Mochas aren't breakfast. Come here."

I groaned. "Mom—"

She snapped her fingers then pointed at the floor beside her as if I were a puppy in need of obedience training.

Grumbling, I gave in and walked around the granite and oak island that took up most of the room, feeling like a kindergartner again as I stopped before her for inspection.

She slid a hand under my hair to test my forehead. "Hmm. You feel okay. But maybe you ought to drink some orange juice to boost your immune system, just in case."

"Mom, I feel fine."

Her lips pursed. "Are you sleeping well? You've got such dark circles under your eyes."

I tried not to wince. "I said I was fine."

One perfectly waxed eyebrow arched in doubt. "At least have a glass of orange juice. Or I could make you a quick smoothie if you want." She reached for the blender as if to dump out its contents into a nearby bowl. Or maybe use those green and orange contents to make me a liquid breakfast.

I darted around the island to the fridge, grabbed the orange juice from inside, and chugged down a few long gulps of acid straight from the carton, nearly wearing it when her gasp of disapproval tried to make me laugh.

I dragged my coat sleeve across my mouth and managed half a smile. "Good enough?"

"Ugh. Do you have any idea how disgusting that is? I swear, I must have raised you in a barn and didn't know it."

I shoved the juice carton back into the fridge then gave her a quick kiss on her cheek. "Later."

"Speaking of, don't be late! Remember, your curfew's midnight."

"Aw, come on, Mom!" I yelled out from the foyer, my hand on the front door's handle now. "I'm eighteen now. I'm going to college soon. You going to be there to tuck me in at midnight too? Two o'clock at the earliest."

"Keep being such a pain in my butt and you'll never live to see college. Midnight and not a minute later or I take the keys."

"Fine," I grumbled for the sake of getting out the door sometime this year.

I eased the heavy wrought iron, glass and oak front door shut behind me, then jogged across the front lawn to the circle drive where my pride and joy waited.

Even though I was in a hurry and worried about hiding the magic that now felt like a curse running through my veins, I still felt a flash of joy as I climbed into the cab of my new baby, which my parents had just given me in August for my eighteenth birthday. The gleaming white Ford F-150X Super Cab Hybrid was the single coolest personal truck I'd ever seen, complete with voice-activated heads-up display, twelve CD changer music system, a 4-wheel drive system that I had yet to manage to get stuck in the mud with, a super extended cab big enough to handle the entire Raiders basketball starting team, computerized back up and parallel parking assistance, and a towing package with a computer sensor to help overcome wind or bumpy roads while towing up to eight thousand pounds. So far, I'd only used the tow kit to help pull some of the Raiders basketball team's wimpier trucks out of the mud. But Dad had promised we'd get to try out this feature for real with the family boat next summer before I went off to Yale.

In the meantime, I was enjoying the fact that nobody else in East Texas probably had a truck like mine yet. Dad had to pull in some private favors to get one of the first hybrid personal trucks off the assembly line for my birthday last August. He liked the "green effect" it added to his political image. I just liked the freedom it gave me. Its electric/gas hybrid fuel system with increased battery storage meant I no longer had to ask the parents for gas money or explain why I'd put so many miles on it already. All I had to do was plug it in every night and it was ready to go another 100 miles the next morning without using a drop of gas.

Thankfully, it also had a GPS, making it easy for me to get directions to the bookstore.

If only girls like Tarah came with some sort of GPS to help us guys navigate their minds.

The first two bookshops were total busts. Not even a Harry Potter book in sight, so they must have already cleared their shelves of all magic related books, both fictional and nonfiction. And the third shop came with its own set of problems, namely a group of loud protestors out front that had drawn the attraction of a local news crew.

I debated skipping this shop entirely. The last thing I needed was for my face to show up on the news right now. But with only one other bookstore to check after this one and the odds so high against its having anything on magic to help me, either, I decided to risk it. If I pulled up my hoodie and kept my face turned away from the cameras, nobody should even notice me much less recognize me.

I parked around the corner from the street the shop was on, shoved my hands in my pocket, and slowly joined the edge of the group shouting and holding posters saying things like "Save Our Country!" and the words "Demon Worshippers" with a big red circle and a line through it over them. A few feet away from them, a smaller knot of people shouted back, calling them bigots. Gleefully shouting right back into their faces was some idiot with shaggy blond hair that could have been Kyle, but I couldn't be sure because all I could see from this angle was the back of his head.

Even more reason to keep my head down, avoid being recognized by anyone, and get in and out as fast as I could before this turned into a full scale street fight.

I eased around the arguing protestors, gradually getting closer and closer to the shop's front. Finally I was able to grab the door's handle.

One of the protestors, a big bear of a guy, grabbed my shoulder. "Hey, you're not going in there, are you?"

"Got to," I shouted back over the noise. "I need a book for school, and they're the only ones who've got it."

I pulled free of his grip, reached the entrance door, and managed to open it just enough to squeeze inside.

As soon as the wooden door shut behind me, all hint of the crowd outside cut off. The peace and silence within was almost shocking in its contrast. After only a minute, I could feel the knots releasing in my shoulders.

I could feel something else, too. The tiny hairs at the back of my neck and arms stood up. It was like sensing a storm coming in the distance, with that promise of energy and power.

This place didn't just hold books on magic. Someone was actually *doing* magic here.

I walked up and down the aisles, trying to figure out how everything was organized. By subject, apparently, since it obviously wasn't by author.

I checked every bookcase, every single shelf from top to bottom and end to end.

Nothing about magic.

But there had to be something. Anything. Even a beginner book on magic for kids.

I went down the stacks again, slower this time, even looking behind the books in case the magic ones were hidden.

Nothing.

"Can I help you find something?" The woman's voice was warm, the tiniest bit raspy, and with a hint of some foreign accent I didn't recognize. She had kind eyes. They reminded me of my mother for some reason.

Was she a Clann member? She wore a loose, flowery dress made out of something that flowed light as smoke every time she moved. No black clothing. No spiked jewelry. No makeup at all, much less the heavy black rings around the eyes like Tarah's friends preferred.

Then again, Tarah didn't look like a Clann member either.

Maybe I should just thank her and get the heck out of there.

And then what would I do? Keep holding the magic inside and pray it wouldn't leak out of control anymore?

Sure, because *that* had been working so well.

I straightened up, took a deep breath, and joined her at the front counter. "I feel something...special here. And I need help with something like that."

She froze and glanced down at the goose bumps on my forearms below where I'd pushed up my sleeves. After a long pause, she nodded. "I think I have what you need. Come with me."

I followed her past the counter and down a short hall towards an open doorway. She entered the room then turned to watch me.

At the threshold, energy crackled over my skin. If static electricity could form a wall, this was how it would feel. I leaned into the wall and it gave way.

Some sort of magical safeguard? But for what? The room was plain, with floor to ceiling, unfinished pine shelves on all four walls. No pentagrams, runes or otherwise witchy-looking symbols anywhere. Even the stuff on the shelves looked like boring textbooks and office supplies.

And yet...the room seemed to pulse with its own heartbeat.

"You are looking for a book to help you learn how to

control your magic?" she asked, almost snappy in her business-like attitude now.

I started to answer her, then hesitated. What if this was a trap? She seemed all right, but what if the government was using her to get to others with magical abilities?

She watched me, a knowing look in her eyes.

Then again, maybe she was wondering the same thing about me. I could just as easily be an undercover agent sent to entrap her.

"How do we know we can trust each other?" I asked.

She shrugged. "I know I can trust you. The front door has a spell on it that will not let anyone through with evil intentions against me."

But that only answered half my question. "And how do I..."

"The same way you decide to trust anyone else in life. Either you do, or you don't."

Or you can learn to trust your own instincts, her voice suddenly whispered inside my head, making me jump. She smiled.

Okay, that was more than a little creepy.

But she was also right. Either I trusted her or I didn't. If I didn't, I'd have to try to find help somewhere else.

"Okay, I guess I'll have to trust you. Now what have you got that can help me get rid of this curse?"

She frowned. "Magic is a gift, not a curse. Surely your parents explained this to you."

"My parents didn't tell me anything. I'm having to figure this all out on my own as I go."

Her eyes flared wide for a second then narrowed. "That must make you an outcast then. I am not supposed to help you."

"I'm not an outcast. I'm not anything. I just have these...things that happen sometimes that I don't know how to control. Please. I don't want to become like those

Phillips brothers." The words blurted out of me unplanned, but too true to take back. "I just need a way to fix whatever's wrong with me."

She stared at me. Finally she sighed. "There is nothing wrong with you, only different."

"I watched that Simon Phillips interview. Is it true that the magic's like a muscle that will atrophy if you don't use it?"

She nodded.

"Then why does mine seem to be getting stronger not weaker? I swear I try not to do anything, but..."

"Because right now you are still in the early years of gaining your abilities. And during those years the energy inside you is too strong still. You must first learn how to ground off all that excess energy. It is like asking a muscle in your leg to relax and get smaller while you hit it with electricity from a taser. Get rid of the energy first, then the muscle can relax enough to do as asked."

"Okay, fine. How do I do this...grounding stuff?"

She walked over to scan a row of books. "You are...in high school?"

"Yeah. A senior."

She selected one of the books and closed her eyes. Holding the book with both hands, she took a deep breath, and that electric sensation brushed over my arms and the back of my neck again. Then she sighed, opened her eyes, looked at the book's cover, and smiled.

"It is ready for you now."

"Ready for me?"

She turned it so I could see the cover. *World History: An Open View.* It looked like a regular, modern day history textbook. "A disguise spell."

A disguise. I looked around the room in sudden curiosity. "So everything in here—"

"Is disguised as well, yes."

I spotted a jar of pencils and pointed at them. "Even those?"

"Wands. In disguise."

I took a step in that direction.

"Oh no, not for you. They are strictly for twelve and thirteen-year-olds in need of help to direct their intentions. You're far too old. You would look like a grown man riding a bicycle with training wheels still attached."

An unexpected sense of disappointment shot through me. A wand would be pretty cool to wave around, especially one that was disguised.

Would I have gotten a wand as a kid if I'd grown up in a Clann family?

My gaze landed on a stack of printer paper on the shelf nearest the door. "And that? Is that like magical spell paper that you write out invisible spells on or something?"

She glanced at the paper then headed for the doorway. "No, that's printer paper."

I followed her out to the check out counter. "So how do I read this book?"

"Watch and see. But first, forty dollars please."

I gave her cash. No way was I dumb enough to use a credit card for this. As she accepted the money, I hesitated. If this was a setup, right about now was when the authorities would come busting in to arrest me.

But no one came into the store.

I let go of the two twenty dollar bills. As she put it in the cash register, her mouth twitched, as if she were trying not to laugh.

"The disguise spell only works once the book changes ownership," she explained as she reached for a plain white plastic bag from under the counter. Then she handed me the book. More static electricity arced up my arms. "The book only reveals its true self to its owner at first."

I glanced down at it and froze. "I...see what you

mean." What had once been a brightly colored, modern looking school book was now covered in aged red leather with glowing gold lettering. Inside, the seemingly new pages had turned yellow with age as well and were now filled with hand written and drawn text and sketches.

"Even if you read it in public, no one else will see its true nature until you choose for them to by saying 'revelattio,'" she said. "Say it again and it hides itself once more."

"That's a good idea."

At that, she flashed the brightest smile yet. "Thank you. I thought so too. Much better than the size changing spell others use."

At my confused look, she explained, "An old fashioned idea, so witches on the run could swallow all their books like pills before fleeing."

And then what, barf them back up later?

Disgusting.

I looked around again, wondering.

She laughed. "Don't worry, that's a new copy."

I smiled, but it was short lived. I'd lucked out big time today in finding this place. But what if I needed more help, more books and supplies eventually? Would this store even still be here? Would she?

"You know people are protesting outside your shop, right?"

"Yes. They are misguided souls, listening to the fear and negativity within them. They don't know how to be positive and follow their bliss."

I wasn't so sure. Both sides looked pretty happy to be getting in each others' faces out there. "You should be careful when you leave. Do you have a back exit you can use? Maybe some friends who can help protect you? You should call the cops too. They look like they're about to start fighting." I hesitated. "If you want to close up early, I could walk you to your car."

Her smile grew. "They will not harm me. But thank you for your offer. You have a kind soul."

Still I couldn't leave. Didn't she understand how dangerous the situation was? "Have you seen those people? They look crazy. Are you sure you'll be alright here?"

"Hayden, I will be fine. It is only you who should be concerned. You are untrained and very vulnerable to external influences, and your thoughts are allowing them to participate in your life right now. You must learn to focus your will on only what you want."

I scowled at that. I might not be out of high school yet, but I wasn't some little kid. I could handle myself out there. "Well, thanks for the book. And, uh…good luck."

"And the same to you."

I could only push the front door open a few inches and had to turn sideways to get out of the shop. The bright sunlight was a shock to my eyes as they tried to adjust after being in the dim and cozy shop's lighting. When I could see again, I thought I was hallucinating. The protestors had gotten hold of several books from a sidewalk sale rack outside the shop and dumped it over to create a pile in the middle of the street. It was a bunch of Harry Potter books, from what I could make out over the heads of the crowd. As I stared in disbelief, someone tossed a plastic lighter at the pile and set it on fire.

Holy hell, they were burning books in the street now! Where were the police, the crowd control teams? This was getting way out of hand.

"Hey, boy, whatcha got there?" Someone grabbed the book I'd just bought.

"Hey! That's mine!" I yelled, reaching for it, but people shoved in between us and I couldn't get around them.

The man opened the book, flipped through the pages.

"Aw, it's just some dumb school book," he yelled to the crowd then tossed it down on the ground dangerously close to the fire.

I ducked down, risking being stomped to death by countless feet as I retrieved the spellbook. As I straightened up, a knee caught my eyebrow and I saw stars. I stumbled, half bent over, trying to find my balance and keep a grip on the spellbook at the same time.

"Hayden, are you okay?" A familiar woman's voice shouted from somewhere towards my right.

The bookshop owner. She must have known I was in trouble. She shouldn't be out here. "Go back inside!" I yelled to her. But it was too late. She'd already fully exited the shop.

"There she is!" someone screamed. "Burn the witch!"

She tried to hold onto the door handle, but the anti-magic side of the crowd tore her away, lifting her up off her feet and over their heads like a body surfer at a rock concert.

"No!" I yelled, trying to push through the people nearest me to get to her. "Stop, put her down!"

She thrashed and yelled at the people below her, telling them to let her go. I grabbed shoulders with my free hand and yanked, using the spellbook in my other hand like a battering ram to shove through. But I wasn't fast enough. Within seconds, the protestors had passed her to the edge of the crowd at the fire.

And then they tossed her onto the flames.

"No!" I shouted, losing control, even as the anti-magic protestors roared with victory and drowned out me and the other pro-magic people.

Weren't any of the Clann people going to do something to save her?

Her scream unlocked something within me. I cursed, and heat rushed through my body from my chest outwards and down my arms like hot water from a shower racing along my skin.

A burning wind, so hot it could have come straight from the Sahara Desert, whooshed over us all, knocking down half the crowd as it raced towards the fire.

The flames went out.

I climbed over the flattened people to the smoky pile. The bookstore owner's clothes and hair were burned in places, and the skin on her hands and forearms was red. But she was still alive. She must have used a spell of some kind to keep the fire from burning her worse.

I helped her to her feet, slung one of her arms over my shoulders, and half carried her out past the shocked crowd still struggling to get up.

"Go left," the shopkeeper said near my ear, and I helped her around the corner of the building. She nodded at a small silver car parked at the curb, and we stumbled over to the driver side door. "Thank you, Hayden," she whispered as she opened the door and slid inside.

"I'm sorry—" I tried to say, though I didn't know what for, but she shook her head and started the car.

"My choice to get involved. Read that book." She jerked her chin at the book I still clutched in my free hand. "It'll save your life."

I shut her door, and she drove away.

I walked the four car lengths down the sidewalk to my truck, unlocked and opened the driver side door, and tossed into the backseat the spellbook that had got me caught up in all this mess to start with. It had better be worth it.

The sound of smashing glass at the bookstore's front entrance made me jump and look back at the protestors filling the street. At the edge of the crowd stood a girl with a familiar head of thick, wavy black hair above a hot pink quilted coat. I froze, my heart racing again. Surely not...

The girl turned on the sidewalk enough to give me a view of her profile, and I cursed. Yep, it was Tarah. What was she doing here?

I knew I should leave before anyone got a good look at me beneath my hoodie and recognized me as the one who helped the bookstore owner get away.

Instead, I gritted my teeth, ducked my head to hide my face, and walked up behind Tarah in time to hear her shout to someone in front of her, "Dad, give it up already. It's like I told you, they're outcasts, not lab rats! They'll never let you test them."

The man in front of her half turned to shout back, "Sure they will!" It was her dad. He looked a lot different than I remembered, shorter, skinnier, his hair all gray and wispy now. But he still wore those same wire rimmed glasses. "We've just got to make them understand that I can help them learn to control it."

Dr. Williams turned to shout something in a nearby stranger's ear. The other man scowled at the professor and moved away.

"Tarah!" I touched her shoulder to get her attention, unsure if she could even hear me over the crowd.

She jumped and twisted away from me, her already large dark eyes going even wider with fear. When she recognized me, her shoulders dropped several inches away from her ears. "Hayden! What are you doing here?"

Before I could answer, her upper lip curled. "Oh. TAC. Of course." She turned away from me.

I risked looking again at the anti-magic protestors, spotting Becky's familiar red bow above her plastic-stiff curly ponytail. So that blond guy I'd seen earlier was Kyle after all. She'd never be at something like this without him. Knowing Kyle, he might have even instigated the whole protest.

I opened my mouth to argue that I wasn't here with the

TAC, then gave up. She wouldn't believe me anyway. Why waste time trying? "Tarah, we've got to get out of here. It's not safe."

"I'm fine! I'm with my dad."

Oh sure, the skinny stick of a professor was going to save her. Especially since it sounded like their being here was his idea in the first place.

Suddenly, sirens began to wail in the distance, growing louder with each second. The police. Oh hell.

The crowd went nuts, shoving in all directions as protesters tried to get away but didn't know which direction to run. Several tried to run straight over Tarah, crushing us both together and towards the building in the process. Cursing, I braced both forearms against the wall at either side of Tarah's head, using my body to take the hits from the fleeing crowd. Beneath the protestors' screams, I heard Tarah screaming as well.

At the first break in the traffic, I looked around and found her dad a few feet away clinging to a desperate woman's wrist.

"Dr. Williams, we've got to get out of here," I shouted to him, figuring Tarah wouldn't leave without him.

He held up an index finger in the air in our general direction, asking us to wait a second as he tried to give the terrified protestor his card.

He was just as nuts as his daughter was.

Seeing the lost cause that he was, I focused on Tarah. I didn't care whether she liked it or not. We were getting out of here.

I started pulling her with me, but she fought me. "No! I'm not leaving my dad!"

Another protestor ran past, his shoulder ramming into mine nearly hard enough to knock the breath out of me. When I could speak again, I said, "Tarah, the cops are going to arrest everybody in sight, including you and your dad!"

"I don't care, I'm not leaving him."

Several deep "thumps" sounded several yards away. Instinctively I ducked low, pulling Tarah into a half crouch with me, as we heard what sounded like soda cans hitting the pavement around the edge of the crowd.

Someone screamed out in pain. Smoke formed in a ring around the protestors, growing fast as it rose up in the air then spread like a dancing wall of gray.

"Let's go!" I yelled to Tarah. I couldn't see her dad anymore through the sulphur-scented smoke, could barely even see her though I still held her hand.

She twisted, trying to get loose. Growling, I bent low and threw her over my shoulder, then stood up and started strong arming my way through the panicked crowd on the sidewalk as people stumbled and fell and pushed and shoved each other in mindless attempts to escape the rotten egg-smelling smoke only to get lost in the streets.

A breeze kicked up, parting the smoke slightly to my left and giving me a glimpse of my truck parked half a basketball court length away at the curb. Keeping a hand on the wall so I couldn't get lost in the smoke again, I gritted my teeth and fought to stay upright as more elbows and shoulders rammed into my other side.

Tarah wasn't helping, either, as she screamed and beat at my back, making it nearly impossible to hold onto her.

I cursed. "Tarah, stop it! We'll come back for him after the smoke clears."

She stopped fighting me, and a long minute later I finally managed to get down the sidewalk and over to my truck without dropping her.

At my truck, I quickly threw open the driver side door and set Tarah inside.

She coughed then spat out, "You arrogant son of a—"

"You can cuss me out later. Get in." I nudged her legs

over so I'd have enough room to get in behind the wheel. Apparently wanting to avoid being so close to me, she scooted over to the passenger side and reached out towards her door's handle. But I'd engaged the child safety locks on it long ago to keep Kyle from trying to do any more Chinese fire drills every time he rode with me anywhere and we stopped at a light in town. I hit the electric locks before she ever grabbed the door's handle.

She tried the handle anyway, slammed both palms on the door in frustration when it wouldn't budge, then turned to me, a dangerous light in her eyes.

"Would you settle down?" I told her. "I said we'd go back for your dad and I meant it. Just let the smoke clear out so we can see him."

Huffing out a loud sigh, she crossed her arms over her chest but thankfully sat back in her seat and waited.

Satisfied she was calming down a little, I twisted to look over my shoulder, trying to see where Dr. Williams might have run off to. My heartbeat skipped then pounded even harder than it had while I had been running with Tarah over my shoulder.

Those sirens weren't coming from police cars. They were coming from a bullhorn held by a soldier who stood by a huge, six wheeled military truck with a khaki-colored canvas roof over the back end that had pulled up at the other end of the street. Even as I watched, soldiers continued to flood out of its cab and back end. All of them were dressed in gas masks and brown camo, none with any patches, each carrying what looked like pump action shotguns that were probably filled with all kinds of anti-riot fun.

I cursed under my breath. "Tarah, get down. If those guys see us in here..."

This time she didn't argue but slid down low in her seat like I did. We both carefully peered over our seats through the back glass window, watching in silence as protester after protester was grabbed by the soldiers, thrown face down on the asphalt, and their hands zip tied together at their backs.

Then I noticed something...not a single TAC member had been caught. Because they'd somehow managed to get away in time?

Or had Kyle and his dad been the ones to use their military connections and call in the troops, allowing Kyle to give his TAC members advance warning so they could escape?

"Oh God. Dad!" she whispered then started crawling across the front seat towards me like she planned to get out through my side of the truck.

I stuck an arm out to block her then looked in the direction she was staring at. Yep, she was right. Now that the smoke was clearing, we could see the soldiers had caught her dad and were zip tying him. He tried to say something to them, and a soldier hit him in the mouth with the butt of a gun.

Tarah shrieked, forcing me to reach out and clamp a hand over her mouth. With my free hand I pulled her back down low in the seat so we wouldn't be spotted.

"Tarah, listen to me! We can't save him, and you'll only make it harder on him if they catch you too."

A pointy little elbow jabbed me hard in the ribs. "I don't care!"

"Your dad does. Do you think he'd want you to be arrested too?"

Tears began to pour down her face, every single drop of them killing me a little more.

"I'm sorry," I told her. "But we can't just go running out there to try and save him."

She stared at me with big, pleading eyes...the same look she used to give me when we were kids. She knew how hard it was for me to say no when she used that look on me.

I swore again under my breath. "Stop looking at me like that. You know I'm right."

She pushed backwards until she flopped down low in the front passenger seat again and stared out the windshield as more tears slid down her cheeks.

Unable to stand seeing her cry anymore, I turned away, watching the soldiers wrapping up their arrests as they hauled their prisoners up onto their feet then pushed them into the back end of the military truck. I noticed a soldier up in the truck bed was slapping every prisoner's neck as they were loaded in.

Ten minutes later, the truck started up and slowly pulled down the street, passing us in the process.

"Start the engine," Tarah hissed.

"What?"

"Hurry up, before they get too far ahead of us!"

I stared at her. She'd stopped crying. But now her eyes were dark and narrowed into determined slits, another look I knew far too well. I think I preferred her crying.

"We are not following them," I said.

"Yes we are."

I shook my head and started the truck's engine, planning to take her home instead.

"Hayden, either you follow that truck right now or I will find a way to make them arrest me! I have to at least know where they're taking him."

Her eyes widened, turning wild in that way they always used to when we were kids just before she went berserker crazy on her enemy, regardless of whether that enemy at the time happened to be me, my brother, or an imaginary dragon. Once her temper was up and she'd made up her mind, there was absolutely no stopping her.

Seconds ticked by as the military truck got caught by a

light one block ahead of us, giving me a little more time to decide but not much.

If I didn't help her follow that truck full of prisoners and her dad, she would do something crazy to purposely get arrested. And then I'd have no hope of helping her. At least this way I would be the one behind the wheel and able to keep her safe.

"Fine," I growled. "Put on your seatbelt."

Dad was really going to kill me if we got caught doing *this*.

We stayed several car lengths away from the truck while it was in town, the frequent stoplights and the truck's height making it easy to keep the truck in sight despite the distance and other cars between us. Then it turned onto the highway and headed west. It looked like we might have a long drive ahead of us.

I let the distance grow between us and the bigger truck.

"What are you doing? We're going to lose it," Tarah muttered.

"No we won't."

"What if it turns off—"

"Then we'll see it turn and follow," I said. "But we've got to stay back far enough so they don't notice us. If your dad is at the nearest camp, we won't be any use to him if we get caught following them and they throw us in with him."

"Oh please, like you're really worried about that. You're Senator Shepherd's son. You're not going to do time in any internment camp or prison no matter what you get caught doing."

"I wouldn't be so sure of that," I grumbled.

She glanced at me, one eyebrow raised. "What are you talking about? Your dad would bail you out in a heartbeat."

But she didn't know my dad or his idea of tough love. Dad had called in a ton of favors to get my last mess cleared up after all those deaths. If I wound up in trouble over this Clann business too, it might push him too far.

Knowing my dad, he might decide to let me spend a few weeks in an internment camp just to teach me a lesson, especially since the media would never find out about it. He could always explain away my absence, say I went on a trip abroad or was studying at some secluded private school for final college preparations. Mom would be ticked off at him, of course, and she'd probably work hard to convince him to reduce my sentence. But if a short stay in an internment camp seemed the way to finally ensure I got the message to fit in or else, he just might allow it.

Feeling Tarah's waiting stare, I glanced at her. She was frowning, confused, trying to understand. But she'd never get it. How could she? Before they'd moved away across town, I'd spent enough time as a kid at Tarah's house eating homemade cookies and snacks to know she came from a tight knit family who actually loved each other, in spite of how much they used to yell at each other. Tarah would never have to fight to earn her parents' approval, never have to doubt their love.

Growing up as one of the many generations of Shepherds destined for political greatness, and all the endless pressure of expectations and responsibilities that came with it, was an experience no outsider would ever understand. So why try to explain?

Tarah

Silence filled the cab as I waited for an explanation Hayden didn't seem to want to give.

I drummed my fingers on my thighs. He had to be joking. How could his parents really be that horrible? Sure, his parents had never been around when we were kids, leaving their boys in the care of a housekeeper while they went to charity and political events. But even busy parents still loved their kids. And no parent would ever knowingly let their kid stay in an internment camp. Right?

As the silence stretched on and on, I started to wonder. Maybe I knew even less about Hayden than I'd thought.

My parents would do anything—absolutely *anything*—to get me out of an internment camp as fast as they could. Even my mother, who never agreed with me on anything, would still fight tooth and nail to free me.

When the silence lasted longer than I could stand, I sighed and gave in to at least part of the source of my nagging guilt. "Thanks for getting me out of there back at the bookstore."

One corner of his mouth lifted then relaxed in a half smile so brief if I'd blinked I would have missed it. "Old habits are hard to break."

At first I was confused. Old habits?

Then I remembered a thousand and one playdays spent with Hayden and Damon in the woods behind our houses before my family moved closer to the university and Dad's lab: The boys dressed up in plastic armor with shields and helmets and swords left over from Halloween costumes. The feeling of dragging around that old red and gold embroidered comforter their housekeeper Hilda had given me for a robe, wearable only in the fall and winter because of the blanket's thick, hot weight. The way I'd pretended to knight the brothers with one end of a black iron curtain rod-turned-scepter, its one fleur de li-shaped finial adding to the royal illusion, and the lump I'd accidentally given Damon over his right ear from it. How many times had the boys pretended to save me from a nasty dragon or evil wizard so I could join them as a warrior queen and turn that scepter into a wand that wreaked havoc on weeds and imaginary wizards alike?

Then I realized the truth behind what he'd said. *Old habits are hard to break.* So he'd only saved me from some old childhood habit?

My throat tightened.

Blinking fast, I stared out the passenger window again. "So what were you doing at the protest? Helping out your buddy's new club?"

He hesitated, then said, "Something like that."

"What's it called again? Jerks Against Humanity?" I'd only meant to tease him, but my tone came out ruder than planned.

Before I could apologize, he frowned and said, "Not exactly."

More silence while I waited for him to explain, until it became clear that he wasn't going to. Again. Talking to him was about as enlightening as talking to a fence post.

"So why did you join TAC anyways?" I grumbled, crossing my arms over my chest to keep from fidgeting.

"I had my reasons."

"Peer pressure made you do it?"

He snorted. "You're one to talk about peer pressure. Rumor has it you're doing weird rituals with that emo crowd of yours every weekend in the woods. Since when did you get into all that crap?"

"Crap? It's not crap! And speaking of doing weird stuff in the woods, rumor has it *you're* the expert in that area."

He froze, even his chest no longer moving with his breathing. "I have no idea what you're talking about."

"That night in the woods last summer? With Damon and all those other people? Y'all were doing magic, weren't you?" I didn't bother to give him an opening to lie again. "Gary's older brother was a friend of Damon's. He was there. He died. Gary heard the doctors tell their parents that everyone who died there looked like they'd been hit by a bomb blast or something, but they couldn't tell what the bomb materials were made out of."

"That doesn't prove anything."

"Gary talks about it all the time, you know. Most people believe the only way you could have survived that night is if your spells were more powerful than everyone else's there. But there is one detail Gary and the others at school are still divided on."

"Yeah? What's that?" he said between barely moving lips.

I wasn't sure why I kept pushing the issue. To distract myself from the fear that was trying to crush my lungs every time I looked at that truck ahead of us with my dad trapped in the back? To hurt Hayden? To finally get the truth out of him about Damon's death?

Whatever the reason, something made me push on. "Well, some of them have this theory that the normals who died that night showed up in order to attack the ones who were doing a ritual or magic training, and both sides took each other out in some kind of massive blaze of glory or something. Their theory says you were the lone survivor because you were able to use a spell to protect yourself while everyone around you fell. Those are the people who believe you'll use your power to follow in Damon's footsteps someday."

"What people...Clann people? Outcasts?"

"Maybe. At least, they think they are."

Silence for several long heartbeats before he muttered, "And the others? What's their theory?"

"The others, Gary included, think you..." But the words didn't want to come out of my mouth. As irritated as I was with his insisting on lying to me, Hayden had once been my best friend. I didn't really want to hurt him. I just wanted the truth.

"Go on," he muttered.

I took a deep breath. I'd started this. I might as well finish it. "They think you were the only survivor because...because you killed everyone else in the woods that night."

More silence, in which I could both feel and hear my heartbeat racing in my chest and ears. And that's when I realized just how much learning the truth about that night mattered to me. This wasn't just some distraction. I wanted to know, *needed* to know the truth. And yet I was scared to hear the answer.

Most of me said there was no way Hayden could ever hurt, much less kill, seventeen people. At least, not on purpose. And especially not his brother, not for any reason.

But there was this tiny part of me that just wouldn't shut up about how long it had been since I'd ended our friendship. How little I knew about Hayden now. How much a person could change over time, especially once they realized the heady and sometimes addivtive power their abilities gave them. And how accidents could happen when a novice first tried to learn how to use and control their magic.

He glanced sideways at me, his eyebrows pinched together, his eyes completely unreadable. "Which side do you believe?"

I chose my words carefully. "I'd like to believe a former friend of mine could never kill a bunch of people. And especially not his brother. At least, not without one heck of a good reason to."

"Like?"

"Like maybe self defense. Or it was an accident."

As I braced for his answer, an awkward silence filled the cab. And this time, Hayden was the only one who could fix it. But his next words weren't what I'd dreaded *or* hoped to hear.

Hayden

"They're turning off." I had to work to keep the relief out of my voice. How the heck had we ended up talking about the one subject I'd sworn never to discuss with anyone ever again?

"Should we get closer?" she asked, those probing eyes of hers now thankfully locked on the military truck again.

"Not yet. It's pretty open out here." We'd driven far enough west that the rolling hills had flattened out and turned dusty with few buildings and more scrub than actual trees or bushes. We could hang back quite a ways and still not lose sight of them.

Then the truck turned off the state road into what looked like a field. I slowed our truck to a crawl and had an idea. "Hey, would you mind looking in the backseat for a set of binoculars? They'll be inside a hard case."

Tarah unbuckled her seatbelt then leaned over the seat back to dig through the piles of stuff. I tried not to get distracted by how the denim of her jeans hugged all those curves she never had when we were kids.

"You mean these?" She held up a camouflaged plastic case. I nodded, and she flipped its catches open. "These are some serious binoculars. Stalk people much?"

I fought the urge to smile and almost won. "They're for deer hunting. Dad and I plan to go this year." If he could manage to tear himself away from all those mysterious committee meetings he'd had to attend lately.

"Sure they are." She removed the binoculars, made a face as she tested their weight in one hand, then resorted to using both hands to look through them. "I see the truck. It's stopping at some kind of building."

I pulled over to the side of the road and squinted. The truck was half the size of my thumbnail at this distance. "Is it the camp?"

"I don't think so. Too small. More like a guard shack or something."

"Okay. Let's find a parallel road to follow them on."

We were lucky we were out in West Texas now with its flat, treeless desert-like geography. If we'd still been in East Texas, the rolling hills and dense pine trees would have blocked our view.

I found a long dirt road to turn onto that ran the same direction as the one the military truck had taken. Our path was probably someone's driveway running through a field half a mile away from the internment camp. If anyone showed up and asked us what we were doing on their property, we'd say we were lost.

"I see two buildings, big ones," Tarah called out a few minutes later. "They're pulling up to them. I think it's the camp. There's a smaller tent-type building too, and a huge fence around the whole place with barbed wire on top."

The problem with how open it was out here was that the visibility went both ways. Which meant if we could see the camp, then they could see us with binoculars too. We needed more cover.

I pulled over in the ditch on our right, hoping the slope of the dirt would at least partially hide our vehicle if anyone looked our way from the camp. "Come on, let's take a walk."

We crossed the road then walked hunched over in the ditch closest to the camp, our shoes fighting the sandy dirt for a few minutes, till we found a mesquite tree. The tree wasn't much, its low, zigzagging branches bare for the winter and hazardous to get under with their thousand and one thorns. But at least we wouldn't be the tallest objects out here. I checked for snakes and cacti. Then we hunkered down near the twisted tree trunk, hiding as much of ourselves from view as we could.

"They've got a lot of guards," she said, frowning as she

passed me the binoculars.

I scoped out the camp. She wasn't kidding. In addition to the barbed wire-topped fence that must have been at least twenty feet high and surrounded the entire compound, they had two lookout stands at the double gate entrance, each with a guard posted, two more guards on the ground at the inner gate, and seven more spaced out along the fence. They were armed too, every guard holding a rifle in addition to side arms strapped to their outer thighs.

Strangely, though, none of the guards were facing in towards the prisoners. It was almost as if they only worried about an outside attack on the camp and not the prisoners themselves.

And then I realized why.

CHAPTER 5

I'd expected them to keep everyone locked up inside one of the buildings. Instead, the camp looked more like an old fashioned asylum for the insane, with zombie-like "patients" shambling around or seated on the ground.

The military truck pulled into the center of the camp yard and parked. The soldiers exited first, dragging out prisoners between them. But none of the prisoners from the truck seemed able to stand, their feet dragging behind them, so it took two soldiers to unload each prisoner. They set the prisoners half upright on their knees in the dirt in two long lines as more soldiers came out of the tent building to help, followed by someone in a white coat like a doctor might wear. I zoomed in more and noticed each new prisoner now had what looked like a nicotine patch on the side of their neck. Some kind of short term tranquilizer patch for the ride over to the camp? That must be how they kept the outcasts from using their abilities to get free before reaching the camp.

They were holding each new prisoner still on the ground while the guy in the lab coat gave the prisoner an injection of something in his or her upper left shoulder.

"Tarah, I think I found your dad." Dr. Williams was on his knees on the ground and clearly struggling to talk to one of the soldiers. After a minute, the soldier pressed a black band around his neck, and another soldier came out of the tent to join them. The new guy spoke to Dr. Williams, reached into his coat, pulled out what looked like a wallet and studied something inside it.

"What's happening? Is he okay?" Tarah asked.

"Yeah, I think so. They're talking to him." I froze. "Wait, they're standing him up."

Were they about to execute her father?

I held my breath as they steadied Dr. Williams on his feet.

Then they cut his zip ties, releasing his wrists, and led him over to one of the long metal buildings, where all three disappeared inside.

I told her what I saw. Her eyes widened with renewed terror.

"Relax," I muttered, hoping I wasn't about to lie to her. "If they'd wanted to hurt him, they wouldn't have bothered to take him away first."

Still, I kept my ears trained for any gunshots in the distance. Other than the occassional howling of the wind, it was so quiet out here I was pretty sure we'd hear if a gun was fired.

I checked the gated entrance more closely. "Looks like only one way in and out, through a front double gate system." The place looked impenetrable. Even if someone managed to tunnel in through the sandy soil, guards would spot them in no time.

The last of the new prisoners had now been unloaded from the truck and dosed. Other guards checked the new prisoners' eyes after they were dosed then cut the zip ties at their wrists and let them shamble off. Whatever drug they were using must be pretty darn potent to work that quickly.

Even the biggest guys lurched and stumbled or sat on the ground in a daze.

No telling how many of these camps had been set up all across the country. The tent, rounded top buildings and fencing system could have been erected in a matter of days and just as easily moved again if needed. Now I undestood how they kept their camps' locations a mystery.

Knowing I couldn't help the prisoners, I tried not to focus on them but failed. Seeing the adults wander around lost and confused was bad enough. But the kids... There was something so wrong about them, like the scene of a car wreck I couldn't look away from. Little kids should be running around, making noise, laughing. These weren't. They simply sat on the ground, some in pairs, some alone, a few near adults. I zoomed in on them, hoping to see at least a few digging in the dirt or talking to each other.

No movement from any of them. All of them sat staring at nothing, their mouths hanging open, drool shiny on their chins.

I froze, barely breathing, trying to hold myself as still as possible while I checked for some signs of life in them.

Then I caught a blink. And another. They blinked so slowly, it was hard to actually see the movement. If I squinted just right, though, I could also barely make out the movements of their chests and stomachs as they breathed.

I started counting. Twenty. Twenty-five. Twenty-seven. No, make that twenty-nine. One sat on the ground leaning against a seated woman's leg. And in the woman's arms rested...

"What's happening now?" Beside me, Tarah sat with her hands clasped together in a fist she pressed to her lips as if in prayer. Probably praying for some miraculous way to get her father released.

"There's a baby." The baby kicked its bare arms and legs in the air, knocking loose a thin blanket that fluttered in the wind and was held only where it was caught between the baby and its mother's arm. Beside them sat a little girl with curly, tangled blonde hair.

Tarah leaned in beside me, nudging me with her shoulder till I shifted the binoculars so we could both look through them.

The sun began to set behind us, dropping the temperature a few degrees at a time, aided by a wind that blew over us again from the camp's direction. I shivered inside my hoodie.

That baby didn't have on anything except a diaper.

Tarah drew in a sharp breath. "Where are its clothes? It'll freeze out here."

The mother's button-up shirt flapped loosely in the breeze. The now loose blanket and her body heat must have kept her baby alive.

The baby opened its mouth, and seconds later the wind carried its cries over to us. No response from its mother even as the baby rooted its face around against her until it managed to nurse through her shirt.

I watched the baby's feet, kicking in the air at first, then slowing down. Was it falling asleep?

It seemed to, its tiny head rolling away from its mother after only a minute of nursing. Its eyes were closed, its arms and legs relaxing spread eagled, one hand almost touching the little girl's hair beside them.

The baby's tummy expanded and contracted with each breath. But the longer I watched, the slower those movements became. Then there was no movement at all.

I held my breath, thinking I was moving too much to see it at this distance.

As I watched, the pale pink tint slowly left the baby's skin, replaced by a mottled, bluish white color.

The binoculars slipped. Tarah grabbed them to steady them. I let her take them completely.

"Hayden, the baby...something's wrong with it," she muttered.

She rose up onto her knees, pressing the binoculars harder against her face. I should have stopped her, but I was numb with shock and hopeful that I was wrong.

She frowned. "It's not moving. Is it..." She froze. "I can't see it breathing."

I wasn't imagining it.

"Why aren't the guards coming over to help it?" she muttered. "It's like they don't even care!"

Because they didn't. I didn't have the heart to tell her that, though. So I sat there, leaning against the tree, grinding my skull against its rough bark while a sick feeling grew in my stomach.

A baby had just died, and not a single guard there cared.

"Wake up," Tarah whispered. "Come on. Wake up."

She whispered it over and over, her shoulders shaking, as if she could do a spell to will the baby to live again. Heck, maybe she could. But it seemed an awful long distance for her to use any special healing abilities over.

After a few minutes, I had to stop her. If she was able to heal others, it wasn't working right now.

"Tarah," I croaked, reaching for her hand, unsure which of us I was trying most to comfort.

She slapped it away. "No. It's going to wake up. Just wait a minute."

Was it the cold? It had happened so fast...one minute the baby had been kicking and wailing, thin but at least okay and moving and hungry. The next...

The breast milk. If its mother was being drugged, didn't the drugs get passed on through nursing?

And if the guards couldn't care enough about a Clann member's baby to ensure it had a blanket around it in November, then what would it matter to them if that baby overdosed? To them, the death of that baby must have meant nothing more than just one less prisoner for them to have to keep an eye on.

Despite all the drugs being pumped into her system, that mother had still managed to hold onto her baby. She must have loved it a lot.

I hoped she never woke up from the drugs. If she did, and found her baby dead in her arms...

Horror mixed with the fast rush of fury, making my head reel. I wanted to hit something, throw something, yell. But what good would any of that do?

I cupped Tarah's elbow, trying to lead her away. But she refused to move, still watching the camp. Then she gasped. "There's a man near the gates. He's... I think he's trying to climb them." Setting the binoculars on the ground between us, she pulled her phone out of her coat pocket, tapped its screen a few times, then held it up to the binoculars, using them like an advanced zoom for her camera.

"What are you doing?" I said.

"Recording this. People need to know what's going on at these camps. There's no way this is legal!"

I leaned over and watched the recording on her phone's screen.

A big guy, built like a bear ready for winter, had apparently not been given enough drugs for his large size. He was scrabbling at the fence gate, trying to claw his way up.

The two guards posted on stands at either side of the gate looked down at him. The two guards on the ground near the fence also turned towards the man. I figured they would move in and physically drag him away like they had with Tarah's dad.

Instead, all four guards raised their rifles.

"They're gonna tranquilize him again," Tarah muttered.

One of the soldiers who had taken Tarah's father into a building stepped out. He stood outside the building's door, watching the scene at the gate, his hands on his hips. The guards' leading officer probably.

It was like watching that video of Aimee's arrest again. I couldn't do anything to stop it, and at the same time couldn't look away. Any second now, the darts would appear in the man's neck and...

The officer in charge touched the black band at his neck, his lips moving as he apparently told his guards something.

Shots cracked through the air.

The prisoner fell from the fence. Red spots bloomed on his back then quickly puddled on the cement around him.

Live rounds. The guards were using real ammo now instead of tranq darts.

Tarah

I stopped the recording then played the video again on my phone's screen, holding it close to my face so I could see it better. "They...they shot him. They actually *shot* him!"

The guards had just murdered a prisoner. But how could they? Weren't we still in America, where there were rules about how prisoners must be treated? Just because he was a Clann descendant or outcast trying to escape...

"Come on. We've got to get out of here." Hayden spoke low and fast, taking my phone from my hands that had suddenly gone numb.

I tried but couldn't move. My body didn't seem to want to work anymore.

"Tarah, we've got to go. Now!"

Dimly I heard him, but his words were like an alien language. They didn't make any sense.

They shot that man. And that baby, dying in its mother's arms...

Something heavy wrapped around my shoulders, lifting

me up onto my feet and pressing me against Hayden's rock
hard body. It was like being trapped against a warm wall,
only to find the wall was guiding me up out of a ditch and
down into another to his truck. I couldn't find the will to
resist, though I knew there was some important reason why
I needed to stay.

At the passenger door, we stopped, and I didn't know
what I was supposed to do. My mind didn't want to work
anymore, either. Strong hands took hold of my hips then
lifted me, and I found myself on the truck seat and my legs
tucked into the passenger side floorboard before the door
swung shut.

The world tilted as Hayden drove us away. He cursed
under his breath, fighting the wheel as we nearly rolled in
the sandy, steep ditch before he got us turned around and
headed down the road again.

My father was a prisoner there too. How would I get
Dad out of that place?

"Tarah, are you okay? Talk to me."

Talking took too much effort. I bent my knees up
against my chest, tucking my arms in between my knees
and chest to try and stop my hands from shaking.

Should I call someone for help? A lawyer maybe?

Would Dad be okay there?

How could he be? They'd killed a prisoner and let
another die right in front of them! Nobody who wasn't a
guard could ever be safe in a place like that.

"Tarah?"

But how to get him out?

Out of the corner of my eye, I saw an arm reach out
towards the dashboard and turn a knob. Air rushed out of
the vents, a dull roar in the cab's silence.

It seemed only seconds later that a low buzzing sounded
from somewhere at my left. After a long moment, Hayden
picked up my phone and read the screen.

"It's a text from your mom. Do you want to reply to her, let her know you're okay?"

And then what? What could Mom possibly do to free Dad? Mom was a psychiatrist, not a Navy Seal. What would she do, *talk* them to death? Get the guards to tell her their feelings?

Maybe she could torture them all with the same psych tests she'd tortured me with. If she did, they might let Dad go free just to get rid of her.

I had to fight the insane urge to giggle at that thought.

Even if we found a way to get Dad out somehow, what about the rest of the prisoners? How would we get them out of there?

A warm hand gently touched my wrist, making me jump. Then its warmth began to seep into my skin. I stared at those long tanned fingers, fingers that were so often seen spinning basketballs on their tips for hours in the halls at school between classes like some character from a High School Musical movie. Shouldn't Hayden be at practice right now? Or a game?

What time was it anyway? It was getting darker, the sun setting behind us, taking all the light with it so we were forced to drive into the growing darkness.

It would be getting dark at the internment camp. And cold. And no one had any blankets there. Would Dad be warm enough?

My fault he was there. If I'd never opened my big mouth about the strange abilities I'd seen others do, he never would have insisted on going to that protest today to try and find willing outcasts who would let him use his biofeedback equipment to try and help them learn to control their abilities.

A low curse rumbled in the air to my left as the truck slowed and eased over to the side of the freeway then stopped completely. A loud click then a bang made me jump as a door was opened and slammed shut, then my door fell away from my side. It took me a few seconds to realize it was because Hayden had gotten out, come around to my side of the truck, and opened the door.

"Tarah, look at me," Hayden growled from the open doorway.

Something in his tone made me look at him standing there, his breaths puffing in the cold evening air, his eyes intense but unreadable beneath that mop of hair over his forehead.

Maybe he could tell me how to save my dad. "They shot that prisoner," I whispered. "And that baby..."

"I know." He rubbed my arms then the outside of my legs through my jeans for some reason, and though it was a strange gesture for him to make, the friction from the brisk contact was also comforting in a way, creating warmth that slowly spread across my skin and also seemed to thaw my mind around the edges.

"Why? Why did they do that?" I searched his eyes but didn't find any answers.

"I don't know."

"And that baby... No blanket. No clothes. No one to take care of it—" My voice broke as the cold air caught in my lungs and burned.

He slowly pulled me to him, wrapping his arms around me, his heart pounding beneath my cheek, and I had to blink faster as my eyes stung.

How would I save my dad and all those poor people in that place? I didn't know anyone in the military. Jeremy didn't count; he was just a journalist embedded thousands of miles away. He couldn't help. I would have to do something. But what?

Would my dad die in that camp too, like that baby and that man who tried to climb the fence? Would they start drugging my dad too so he wouldn't fight them?

It all seemed so incredibly hopeless, and stupid, and pointless. None of those people should be imprisoned in the first place, much less treated like mindless cattle!

Was I the only person on the planet who knew about this and cared? Why weren't the papers and the bloggers writing about this? Why weren't there petitions to stop this from happening, and court battles and people fighting D.C. to get the laws changed so this couldn't happen ever again? Why was Jeremy writing about some war overseas that nobody cared about anymore, when there was a war happening right here in our own country?

I grabbed handfuls of the soft cloth before my face, the only thing I had to hold on to, and tried to remember how to breathe as the fear and the horror of it all ripped through me again and again. And then, sweeping in on the heels of the fear and horror came anger, so hot and furious that it seemed to boil at my insides.

It had to stop. All of it…the arrests, the internment camps, the drugging, the deaths. Someone had to stop it. Now.

"I know what you're thinking," I whispered past the tightness in my throat.

"What am I thinking?" he murmured, resting his cheek against the top of my head. He was being so gentle with me, and part of me thought it was wonderful. But another part of me just wanted to punch something.

"You're thinking you should say something to make me feel better. Like 'that baby didn't feel any pain.'"

"Even if it didn't feel any pain, it's still an innocent life wasted."

His words froze me inside and out. He had seen it too. I'd forgotten that. I wasn't the only witness to today's horrors.

But we were only two people. It wasn't enough. Everyone needed to know about it, and more, to actually *care.*

I saw again that tiny arm flung wide, turning blue.

What kind of world did we live in, when a baby could die surrounded by people who didn't care?

I closed my eyes, bowed my head, and let the tears fall...for that baby, and that man shot to death at the camp's gates. For my father stuck inside that compound when he hadn't even done anything wrong to get arrested in the first place. And for who knew how many others who might have already died in other camps just like that one.

"You're right." I finally gave in to the urge to wrap my arms around his waist, using his solid strength to hold me up for just a moment. "There's nothing we can do to change what happened today. Nothing." I didn't even know why I was crying. What was the point in it? Tears wouldn't bring that baby back to life, wouldn't turn back time to save anyone. It was all a waste, just a complete waste.

His arms tightened around me. "I'm sorry, Tarah. I wish we hadn't seen it."

"What?" Shocked, I leaned back to look up at him. "Don't say that. Don't ever say that. We're the only two people on the planet who saw them die and actually care."

Taking a step back, I wiped my cheeks dry with my hands and took a deep breath to steady myself. I looked around us, seeing for the first time the cars rushing by us on the freeway, going so fast they rocked us a little with each one's passing, their drivers blissfully unaware of the people dying in the internment camp just miles from here. Before today, I had been just like them.

"You really think it's better not to know?" I asked him. "That's why crap like this is happening in the first place. Because no one knows about it. And the ones who do either don't care or are powerless to stop it."

We stared at each other in silence.

"We have to get them out of there." I didn't know I was going to say that until the words blurted out of my mouth. But as soon as I said them, I knew they were the truth. It was up to us. "All of them. Not just my dad."

Hayden's eyes widened then narrowed. "No way, Tarah. We'll find a way to get your dad out of there. I'll talk to my dad. Maybe he can pull some strings and get your dad freed. But as for the rest of them... We've got to stay out of that. It's a federal thing, it's too big for us to fight on our own. And anyone we try to talk to is going to see us as just a couple of crazy teens—"

"My friends won't. They're outcasts too. They don't know what's going on in the camps. But once they do... And don't forget, those soldiers might have guns, but our side's got a lot more than that. Think fireballs and small earthquakes, Hayden. The outcasts I know have all kinds of special abilities. Not as good as yours probably, but good enough to fight with. They'll help us."

"Forget it." He walked around to the front of the truck as if intending to get back in on the driver side.

I ran after him, grabbing his shoulder as he stepped into the headlights, determined to stop him and make him hear me out on this. "How many kids were in that camp? And none of them, adults or kids, had coats on or even blankets. Winter's here. They could freeze to death. And the guards would let them, you know they would. We have to get them out of there!"

"Did you see how many guards were there?" He whirled to face me, throwing one arm out wide, his eyes making these fast little side-to-side movements as they searched mine. "You saw what they did to that man. You want that to happen to you?"

The fear tried to come back. I swallowed hard, forcing it down. "Better that than to be locked up and helpless."

"Tarah, you don't have to worry about that. I would

never let you end up in one of those camps."

I gritted my teeth. "Of course I wouldn't end up there. They'd stick me in a regular prison maybe, but not an internment camp. Those are just for descendants and outcasts. Once they figure out Dad's not one of them, either, they'll probably transfer him out too."

"What are you talking about? They took everyone they caught today."

"No they didn't. They only took the pro-magic side protestors, and those were all Clann outcasts except for Dad. Trust me. I knew everyone there on the pro-magic side."

He grabbed my shoulders, his eyes intense as they searched mine. "Wait. Are you telling me you are *not* an outcast or descendant?"

"Of course I'm not."

"Don't lie to me, Tarah. Not me!"

The fact that he thought I could lie to him stung. I swallowed down the hurt. "I'm telling you the truth. Nobody in my family is from the Clann or has any magical abilities." Not for lack of trying, though. How many training sessions had I sat through, trying like crazy to make something—anything—happen?

Hayden froze for a long second. Then he turned towards the truck and braced a hand against the hood. "Let me get this straight. You don't have *any* special abilities. Your parents are normal too. And yet you're constantly trying to defend the Clann people in class. And now you want to break them all out of an internment camp?" His voice rose steadily with every word he spoke.

"Well, someone has to stand up for them. If not us—"

"Damn it, Tarah! Everyone thinks you're an outcast!" He whirled around to face me again, his eyes blazing as his voice hit a full pitched yell. "You could be arrested at any time for some of the stuff you've said. And now you want to stage a prison break? Don't you get it? It's not a game! You shouldn't be involved at all."

"Oh I guess I should be at home on the nice, safe couch in my nice, safe world instead. Just like my mother," I spat out. "Watching while the whole friggin' world goes to crap around us and she tells us all we're nuts and in need of therapy for even believing in magic in the first place!"

He stared at me, eyes rounded with some emotion I couldn't read. Anger was definitely still in there, but there were more emotions than that churning inside him now. Shock? Fear?

He took a slow step towards me, then another, closing the distance between us until he could reach out and tuck a strand of hair behind my ear. The unexpected sweetness of the gesture sent my fury draining right out of me. "You probably *are* nuts."

But then one corner of his mouth hitched up, and I knew he was going to do it. He was going to help.

I took a deep breath then let it out. "Yeah, well, you keep tagging along with me. Which makes you just as crazy."

"And I guess if I don't help you with this prison break idea of yours…"

"I'll do it with my friends. With or without you." I shrugged. "I have to, Hayden. Not just for my dad, but for all those people in the camp. They're humans too. I don't doubt you and your dad could get my dad released. But I couldn't live with myself if I didn't at least try to get everyone else out too."

He sighed. "Fine. I'll drive. You call your friends. Tell them to meet us in an hour in the woods behind my house, about two hundred yards in."

I saw what he was thinking. The Shepherds' backyard was huge, the woods behind them dense and on the outskirts of town but still within the city limits. That made the area off limits to hunters, even the ones who might be tempted by the current deer season to hunt illegally at night. Plus, a highway ran along the west side of the woods, making for a good side entrance and exit. Hopefully if anyone saw people going into or out of the woods, they would think hunters were camping out back there.

While he drove us back towards Tyler, I started making calls, ending the last one as Hayden parked in his driveway. Right behind Kyle's banana yellow Jeep. I shot Hayden a surprised look.

He shrugged. "Maybe he saw me at the protest."

"Didn't you go together?"

He shook his head. "I never got the group messages. Had my phone turned off."

"Then why—"

"We should go. You ready?"

"Hang on. Just gotta send one last email." Taking a deep breath, my thumb paused over the Send button. *Please let this be a good idea.* Then I tapped the button and sent the video to my entire email list, including several pro magic groups and newsletters I was a member of.

By tomorrow morning, I knew everyone on that list would pass on a copy of the internment camp video I'd recorded to everyone they knew. By the time the government realized what was in the video, thousands if not millions of people would have already seen it. No matter what happened tonight, at least the world would know the truth.

Leaving my backpack behind, I stuffed my phone into my jacket pocket then jumped out of the truck. We jogged around the house and across the backyard. Hayden held my hand along the way, probably to keep me from tripping over anything. It had been a few years since I'd last seen his backyard. They could have added all kinds of things out here to catch my feet in the dark…patio furniture, fountains, evil little ceramic garden gnomes. I told myself it was because we were moving so fast that my pulse had taken off like crazy, and not the feel of those long, strong fingers laced with mine.

At the edge of the woods, Hayden froze, and it was then that I remembered what these woods might mean to him now.

Once, they had been our playground, our private realm of innocent childish fantasy and fun. But that was a long time ago. Since then, these woods had also become a place full of dark secrets where his brother and so many others had died. There was no telling what horrible memories or ghosts these woods held for Hayden now.

I squeezed his hand, a silent reminder that I was here and he wasn't alone.

He looked down at our joined hands in silence. After a minute, he took a deep breath and we entered the woods together.

We walked as quickly as the branches and undergrowth allowed, the only sounds the crunching of our feet on dead, dried up pine needles and sticks and Hayden's fast, harsh breathing.

A few minutes later, we saw thin beams of light cutting through the darkness up ahead. The remaining Tyler outcasts had come as promised.

Unfortunately, so had Gary.

"Tarah, I don't like this location," he began. Then he spotted Hayden at my side. "What the—"

"He's on our side," I said, my heart racing faster. *Please don't let Gary be his usual pain in the butt self. Not this time. We don't have time for this!*

"He's a member of TAC," Gary said. "Everyone knows that. Not to mention his best friend is its leader."

Several people in the gathering grumbled.

Oh crap. I hadn't considered how word about this

meeting might spread through the entire local magic community beyond just the ones I knew, and who else might show up here as a result. At our usual weekly meetings, only teens came. But tonight's gathering included probable Clann outcasts of all ages. No doubt at least some of them had either known or been related to the group of outcasts who had died along with Hayden's brother last summer. And by the sound of their muttering, quite a few of them here seemed convinced Hayden had either killed or helped kill that night's victims.

Hayden took another deep breath, held out his free hand, and a blue orb of energy glowed into life on his palm. "If this is a gathering of magic users, then I belong here. Just like the rest of you." His grip on my hand tightened.

Staring at that beautiful blue orb, I bit my lower lip as pride surged through me. He was taking a huge risk, revealing his secret like this. Especially with this group, many of whom thought they might have good reason to hate and fear him.

And yet he'd done it to help me. He was here at my side, facing down my friends and even people I didn't know, trusting me and giving them more than enough ammunition to land his butt in an internment camp right along with them. And all because I'd asked for his help.

If we hadn't had an audience, I could have risen up on my tiptoes and kissed him. I settled for squeezing his hand instead.

"You're nothing like us, rich boy," Gary sneered. "How do we know this isn't just a trap?"

The muscles in Hayden's jaw knotted as he shrugged, closing his hand to snuff out the orb. "You don't, I guess. You just have to trust me."

"He's legit, Gary," I said. "I swear it. He helped me find the nearest internment camp today. Not to mention he saved me from being arrested at the protest this morning."

The group fell silent.

"Is that right?" Gary crossed his arms over his chest, probably in an effort to make himself look bigger and badder.

It didn't seem to phase Hayden. He used his feet to clear away matted pine needles and cones from a section of dirt, then squatted down and grabbed a stick, which he used to draw the outline of the camp. "The camp's heavily guarded. Twenty foot high chain link fence topped with barbed wire around the entire compound. Double gate, single entrance and exit point here on the west end with two guards posted on lookout stands. Six more guards posted along the perimeter inside the fence. If they work in twelve hour shifts, double that number. Or triple it for three shifts. Plus the officer in charge. And they're all armed with live rounds."

"Which they didn't hesitate to use on a man tonight," I added, working hard to keep my voice from shaking at the memory. "They're keeping everyone drugged. Even the little kids. And they're using what looks like tranquilizer patches on anyone they arrest as soon as they grab you, so don't count on using your magic to get free during transport."

Several people hissed or murmured in alarm.

For once, Gary kept his cool. "Any buildings?"

"Yeah," Hayden said. "Two long metal buildings here and here. This one on the east end's got two guards posted at the door, so it's probably where they house the prisoners while they're sleeping. There's also a tent building here towards the west, maybe the officers' tent or mess hall, maybe a communications center or where they keep the drugs and medical stuff."

Gary leaned in, checking out the sketch. "What about inside the buildings? Any idea of the layouts?"

I shook my head. "We only saw the camp from a

distance. But listen, we've got to move on it soon. The conditions there are bad. I counted twenty-eight kids there, none with coats or blankets. We saw a baby die in its mother's arms tonight, and nobody even cared. And then they shot another man to death in the back just for trying to escape." Remembering my phone, I dug it out of my coat pocket, found the internment camp video I'd recorded, and showed it to them. Everyone gathered in small huddles to take turns watching it. A few gasped, some murmured too quietly for me to fully make out. Most, however, were shocked into frozen silence.

"I sent that out tonight," I added. "By tomorrow morning, it'll be everywhere. When the government sees it, they might try to relocate the camp. Which is another reason why, if we're going to do something, we'd better do it quick. Plus..." My voice started to shake. I paused and tried again. "...they've got my dad too."

"We'll go tonight," Gary said. He turned to Hayden. "Can you get us some directions to get us there?"

"Sure." Hayden pulled his phone out of his coat pocket and mapped out the camp's location and how to get there.

Gary checked the screen. "Seems easy enough to find it. Okay, who's in?"

Roughly half the group raised their hands. I counted twenty-seven volunteers.

Gary nodded again. "Good. Here's how we'll go in." Using Hayden's dirt sketch, Gary squatted down and started pointing. "We'll fan out and approach in three teams from the north, east and south sides. We might have to come up with something to distract the guards, maybe on the north and south sides, so the east side team can get in through the fence closest to the prisoner building unnoticed. Unless anyone here knows how to do some kind of cloaking spell?"

"I can." Mike, a short sophomore at our school, had to

rise up on tiptoes while speaking in order to be seen and heard from within the crowd of taller people surrounding him. They shifted so everyone could get a clear view of the new speaker. When he realized everyone was looking at him in surprise, he grinned. "What can I say? I grew up on Harry Potter and wanted an invisibility cloak of my own. Never managed to make the actual cloak, but I can make myself invisible at least."

"Good," Gary said. "Does it only work on you?"

Mike shook his head. "I can make it work on others too. But I can only extend it onto anyone within about ten feet of me. And anyone within that zone will still be able to see me unless I reduce the reach."

Gary frowned and stared down at the dirt sketch of the camp for a minute. "Okay, change of plans then. We'll send in one team at a time through the east side only with Mike as the escort each time. Then we'll get the prisoners out the same way, one small group at a time. The problem will be getting through the fence. Is it electrified?" Again Gary turned to Hayden and me.

"Not that we could tell," Hayden answered for the both of us.

"Okay. No need for magic for this one. We can just use some bolt or wire cutters for the chain link. Now who's comfortable with throwing energy orbs and fireballs?"

A few hands rose.

"Then I want you guys to make sure you're divided up among the teams. And I want everyone else to work on learning how to do basic healing spells tonight. We'll need to detox as many of the adults as fast as possible tomorrow so they can help us take out the guards."

"And one more thing." Gary's small eyes turned beady. "There will be zero mercy for those guards. Is that understood? They let a baby die right in front of them and murdered another outcast, and who knows how many more too. They're scum, and I don't want to see a single hesitation about permanently taking them out. If they see us and you've got a clear shot, you take it."

Hayden's hand tightened on mine. "That might not be a good idea."

Gary turned to him with a scowl. "Why not? You said it yourself. They've got live ammo, and obviously they're willing to kill us. Why not return the favor?"

"Because we should show we're better than them. Use nonlethal spells instead. It gets the job done without adding to their case against us."

Gary glared at me. "I thought you said he was on our side."

"He is," I hissed. Why did Gary have to be such a monumental pain? Couldn't he see this wasn't about anyone's ego here tonight? Just because Hayden had one opinion different from Gary's...

A twig snapped somewhere in the distance.

The hairs rose on the back of my neck. We were being watched.

Hayden took a step backwards, pulling me with him.

Then the darts started flying.

CHAPTER 6

Hayden

Gary glared at me. "It's a trap! Everyone take cover now!"

It was like the protest all over again, but with the added obstacles of tree trunks and branches and roots and bushes everywhere. Chaos broke out as people ducked and tried to run but were unsure of where to go. We were surrounded, tranq darts zipping past, lodging themselves in tree trunks and the ground.

"This way!" I yelled, knowing these woods as well as my backyard. How many times had Damon and I come here to play as kids and later hang out as teens?

Tarah and I ran in a crouch in the direction of my house. I couldn't see its lights yet, but we couldn't be far.

Then Tarah was gone. I heard her scream out my name, turned toward the sound.

"I've got one, guys!" Kyle had both arms wrapped around her waist and was dragging her in the opposite direction. And immediately I knew how the soldiers had found us. While inside my house sucking up to my dad, Kyle must have seen Tarah and me arrive and slip around back. He'd probably followed us out here then called in the soldiers.

"Kyle!" Cursing him at the top of my lungs, I ran after him and Tarah even as more darts zinged past my head. "Let her go!"

He ignored me, and now I could see what he was headed for. Soldiers with rifles had circled in on our group's meeting area, pinning down Gary and three others. Several more soldiers were already carrying off unconscious prisoners.

"Guys! Look—" Kyle's shout broke off as the soldiers turned toward him. "Hey, not me! I'm the one who called you in."

Darts flew, one lodging in Tarah's upper arm.

An animal-like roar erupted out of me as I closed the distance at a dead run, ignoring the now stunned Kyle and catching Tarah just as her knees began to buckle. I carried Tarah out of there, dropping us down behind the thick, close set trees where Gary and the others were pinned.

Gary started cursing me right away. "I knew you were a traitor!"

More pops of rifle fire. I glanced up in time to see Kyle hit his knees. "I'm not one of them," he slurred out just before collapsing on his face.

"That's what they all say," one soldier said with a sneer as he and another ran out to retrieve Kyle's unconscious body under heavy cover fire.

As if any of us would fight for that piece of crap.

"Detox her. Hurry up!" I told Gary. Tarah slumped against me.

Gary grabbed her wrist, muttered something. She came around, but her eyes were still glazed.

"I can't detox her all the way, not right now," Gary panted. "Gotta save some energy for the fight out of here."

"Then you guys finish it." I turned to the others.

One made a move as if to help. Gary grabbed his shoulder. "No, we can't waste the energy. We need everyone's help to get out of here."

"Tarah—" I started to argue.

"Tarah never should have brought a TAC member here."

I could kill Gary right now. "You heard Kyle. He must have followed me. I swear on my brother's grave I didn't do this."

Gary shrugged. "Maybe you didn't mean to. But you still caused this. Besides, Tarah knew the risks involved—"

"She's not even Clann, and she's still risking her life for you." I grabbed Gary, wanting to snap him like a twig for being so selfish and uncaring.

He jerked his arm free of my grasp, leaned around the tree, and threw a fireball at one of the soldiers. The man went up in flames, forcing two soldiers on either side of him to drop their rifles and try to beat out the fire.

"What are you doing! You idiot! If you use lethal force on them—" I began.

Gary threw another fireball, taking out a second soldier. "They started it at that camp. I'm just evening things up."

I couldn't save someone who was determined to die.

I had to get Tarah out of here.

I stood up then scooped Tarah up into my arms, her head lolling backwards on my arm then sideways against my chest as I turned one way then another and tried to reorient myself. But with the smoke rising from the two men still on fire, everything was getting confusing fast.

The smoke. We could use it.

I reached for the energy, ever present inside me, twisted my hand under Tarah's knees so my palm faced outward, and mentally called to the wind. It immediately answered me, gathering the smoke to us, condensing it into a thick, short cloud with a small opening at its center so we wouldn't choke to death.

Silence fell along with the visibility.

"We move as a group," I whispered to the others. "Stay quiet and low, go slow towards my left. I'll keep the smoke between us and them—"

"For how long? You can't hide us forever," Gary hissed.

"Keep the smoke there. I'll take them out."

"No, you can't see—" But I was too late.

Gary was already on his feet and in the smoke, throwing fireball after fireball. If not for the situation, I could have appreciated his skills. The fire he threw was like nothing I'd ever seen, immediately extinguishing itself if it didn't make human contact.

But Gary was firing blind. And the light of the fireballs gave the soldiers a target to aim at.

When they fired, the sound was louder, sharper this time. Deadly.

Gary went down, a replay of the man killed at the camp today.

How many more would I see killed before the night ended?

I should leave him out there.

Growling, I moved five feet to the left then bent over and set Tarah against a tree. "Stay here," I whispered near her ear. "I've got to go get Gary."

She reached out, grabbed my wrist, tried to say something despite the drugs still clogging her system.

"I'll come right back for you, Tarah. I swear it."

Then I forced my hands to let go of her and I took off running, hunching over to keep me just below the smoke. The smell clawed at me, raking up nightmares from the past, all but demanding I run away.

When I got to Gary, he was still breathing, but every breath came out choked with blood as it poured from his mouth. I grabbed one of his arms, slung it around my neck, and dragged him partially to his feet. Then I turned and half carried him as fast as I could back to his friends.

Behind the grouping of close-growing trees, I eased him down with their help. "You two get him out of here. I'll get Tarah."

Movement at my left in the dark. Tarah trying to get up?

Gary grabbed the collar of my shirt, pulling me to him. "Fix...this." The words gurgled out of him.

I didn't know how to heal. "I can't heal—"

"Not...me. Fix...this..." He flung a skinny arm out. It flopped to the ground. His eyes rolled wildly, as if he wanted to explain more but couldn't.

He wanted me to find a way to fix the situation.

More noises from Tarah's direction, a whimper, scuffling.

"Tarah, stay down," I hissed over my shoulder at her. Hardheaded woman. Even drugged, she would have to try to be independent.

I looked back at Gary. He stared blankly ahead, his eyes different now. Flatter somehow, dull.

I checked his pulse at his neck and swore. No heartbeat, at least not that I could find.

"Can you get him out of here?" I asked the others. Maybe there was still time. There had to be.

"Yeah," one replied. Mike, or Matt, the Raiders High sophomore who'd volunteered to create the cloaking effect for the prison break teams.

"How fast can you make that cloaking effect work?" I asked him.

Understanding lit up his face. "As fast as we need it."

"Then get it ready while I grab Tarah and we'll all go together." I didn't wait for his reply before running back to Tarah.

Or at least where I'd left her.

She was gone.

I opened my mouth to call out her name then saw the drag marks in the dirt.

Instinct made me hit the deck just before a bullet exploded the tree trunk where my head had been a second ago.

The orb formed in my hand then flew out and knocked the two soldiers off their feet without my ever making a decision to use my abilities. I didn't check to see if they were alive. I just ran back to the remaining outcasts. "They've got her." Saying the words made it real and drove home the panic.

My worst nightmare had just come true. They'd taken her, and because nobody could tell who was using special skills here tonight, they would assume she was an outcast too. They would throw her into the internment camp with everyone else, drug her till she was a zombie, then leave her to freeze to death.

"Gary's dead, man," Mike said, his voice flat, maybe in shock.

His words jarred me back to life. I cursed under my breath. "Take him to a hospital anyway. They might be able to bring him back." Twigs snapped, signaling the soldiers were trying to close in on our location. "Do it now, get yourselves out of here."

"What about y—"

"Don't worry about me."

They looked at each other, then looked back at me. "We can't just duck and run like cowards. Gary would have—"

"He'll get what he really wanted. We're still going to the camp tonight. Drop him off at the ER, then meet me at Bergfeld Park by the slides in an hour. Gary's right. We have to fix this. But we can't do that if we're captured too."

They looked doubtful. Doubting me? Wondering if it was another trap?

Bushes rustled behind us. The soldiers had slipped

around us while we were talking, tightening their circle. It was now or never.

"Trust me!" I hissed.

I waited precious seconds till they nodded. Then I took off, whipping the wind so the smoke choked the soldiers long enough for all of us to gain some distance as we ran in different directions.

I took a wide circular route, heading for the side of the woods opposite the highway first to hopefully throw the soldiers off my trail, then cutting back into my own backyard.

But even after I made it inside the house, I wasn't home free yet.

"Hayden?" Dad called out from his study.

Silently cursing, I debated ignoring him. I was covered in dirt, Gary's blood all over my hands and jeans. The stench of smoke poured off me. And no way could I even hope to act like everything was normal tonight.

They've got Tarah, my mind whispered.

I promised her she'd never end up in the internment camps. Promised her I'd come back for her in the woods.

"Where have you been?" Dad said, standing in the study doorway. He took one look at me and his voice dropped an octave, becoming an order. "Come talk to me."

He didn't wait for me to follow him into the study as he turned and headed for the mini bar opposite the blazing fireplace.

"Dad…" Where did I begin? "I saw an internment camp today."

He scowled. "Why would you go looking for one of those? Jesus, Hayden, you could have been shot!"

"One man was. I saw it. The guards shot him in the back while he was trying to escape the camp. I saw a baby overdose on tranquilizers there too. They're treating them like animals. You've got to put a stop to—"

"There's no stopping this train, Hayden. It's what the public wants. It's what the government wants."

"You mean it's what *you* want."

He didn't answer, didn't even have the decency to look away or pretend to be ashamed as he took a slow sip of his scotch. "So, you want to tell me what else you've been up to tonight?"

"A bunch of Clann outcasts and I just got into a fight with some soldiers in the woods out back."

Dad slammed his glass down onto his desk, splashing scotch all over the once perfect oak. "You've been hanging out with outcasts? How many times have I told you to stay away from those types, to fit in with the right crowd? You could ruin everything we've worked so hard to build here!" He shoved a hand through his hair.

"What we're *building* here is a pile of dead bodies!" I held out my red stained hands as evidence. "Those soldiers shot a kid in the woods tonight. With real bullets, not tranquilizers. He died, Dad, right in my hands. Just because of some abilities he was born with."

His mouth twisted. "That is a tragedy. It really is. But I'm sure it never would have happened if he'd just come quietly." He turned to face the fireplace. "Why can't they see that the government's just trying to—"

"Trying to what? Exterminate them?"

His face darkened. "No, of course not! We've got the best scientists available working round the clock, trying to find ways to suppress their abilities."

"Why do they have to be suppressed? And how do you know they even can be?"

"Of course they have to be suppressed. They're dangerous genetical defects!"

"Am I a dangerous defect, Dad? Are you afraid of me too?" The words came out quietly, unplanned. Necessary. A secret kept far too long. "Because I'm starting to think

I'm one of them."

I threw a ball of fire at the fireplace. The flames became a bonfire barely contained behind the heavily carved oak mantel.

"Jesus, Hayden, you're going to set the house on fire!" Dad reached out towards the fireplace. And the fire went out, snuffed as completely as if it had never been there at all.

I couldn't speak, could barely breathe. Could hardly think at all.

I'd assumed, if I were a Clann outcast, that it must have been through Mom's side of the family. Maybe she'd turned her back on her abilities, or maybe her ancestors further back had been the ones who had left the Clann and left us all in the dark in the process.

I'd never once considered the possibility that my ultra conservative father could be the one to have passed on these abilities. Much less that he had some abilities of his own.

Long seconds passed, maybe minutes, and still I couldn't think of a single thing to say. All this time, all these months since Damon's death, I'd hidden what I was, what I could do. And Dad had known all along.

He sighed. "Yes, I already knew about your abilities. Your mother and I have always known, ever since before your birth. How could you not have them? You're a Shepherd, and Shepherds are one of the founding Clann families. Founding family descendants are all but guaranteed to have powers."

I had to fight to get the words out past the tightness in my chest. "Who kicked us out?"

"We weren't kicked out," Dad sneered. "I left. I did what was right for this entire family. I tried to take us away from that unnatural world, tried to give us a decent, normal life. And what did you and your brother do? You nearly screwed it all up!"

So that explained where the memory had come from of him telling me not to talk about the Clann. I must have heard him discussing it with Mom.

"The Clann and its descendants are evil, Hayden. They're like a poisonous vine that strangles everything within their reach. They've been using their spells and their money and power to wheedle into government positions of control to help keep the Clann a secret from the world. My brother, your Uncle Jim, tried to change them from the inside. He had all these foolishly naive ideas that he would reveal the truth about the Clann to the world, and the world would accept the descendants and maybe even revere them as demi gods. And what did the Clann do? They killed him for it."

Dad knocked back half his drink. "But I got my revenge. I had to wait years for a chance, but that Simon Phillips and his loose cannon boys finally gave me the perfect opening. Before, the Clann was much too powerful to take head on. But now the Clann has fallen. It's only a matter of time before every single descendant and outcast has been accounted for. And once we have the cure perfected, the treatments will begin, and everything will be safe again."

He actually smiled at me, as if I should feel comforted now.

All I felt was sick.

Now I understood why Dad never let Damon and me spend any time alone with my cousin Dylan or Uncle Jim. He must have worried that they would tell us all about the Clann that our father had cast our family out of, and then shown us what we could do with our growing abilities.

I also understood now why we never went to Uncle Jim's funeral, and why Dad would never talk about his brother's death. Because then he would have had to tell us about the Clann and its role in Uncle Jim's death.

Then I realized...if Dad had only told us the truth years ago, Damon and I never would have been practicing magic with others in the woods the night of Damon's death. And he would probably still be alive right now. "You should have told us the truth."

"I was trying to protect you, to keep you safe from that world."

"Yeah, well, that plan sure backfired, didn't it?"

He turned to me with a stony expression. "What are you talking about?"

"Damon would still be alive if you'd just told us who and what we are."

"Don't you try and lay the blame for his death on me. I was trying to save you two idiots! How was I supposed to know you'd go out into those woods and blow yourselves up!"

He would never see the part he'd played in Damon's death. But surely he could be made to see how wrong he was now about the outcasts. "Dad, listen to me. You might not want your Clann abilities. But you can't go around trying to strip the abilities from the others. It's their choice to make, not yours."

His jaw hardened. "Don't you tell me what I can and can't do. I'm trying to save this country, this entire world, from the evil that the Clann's lines keep spitting out into it. Those Phillips boys are a prime example!"

"No, they're proof of what happens when you try to keep people in the dark. Educate the outcasts, but let them decide for themselves whether to keep their abilities or let them fade away."

"It's a curse, Hayden. A curse that they've got to be saved from!"

"You have no right!" Somehow we were inches away from each other, all but screaming into each other's faces. I didn't even know how or when I'd crossed the room over to him.

Breathing fast, I looked down and realized I'd grabbed fistfuls of his shirt. I forced my hands to drop down to my sides again as I took a step back.

"I'm doing this for you!" he cried out. "Can't you see that? This world's not safe with those abilities loose on it. They have to be destroyed."

I didn't want to do it, but I also made myself look my father in the eye again. And in his eyes I no longer saw the man I had once yearned to grow up to be like. All I saw was a man who was filled with fear and self loathing. "Just because you hate yourself doesn't mean every other descendant or outcast does. Some of them even manage to like who and what they are. You think you're curing them. But all you're doing is killing them."

His eyes turned desperate and pleading, an expression I'd never seen on my father's face before. "Hayden, please. Just give us more time. We'll fix this, all of it. We'll fix you too."

I turned and headed for the foyer, unable to stand looking at or listening to him anymore.

"Hayden, wait! You can't leave! You don't know what's out there, why it's so important for us to become normal! There are enemies of the Clann that prey upon the power within us. But if we get rid of that power, we'll finally be truly safe!"

I continued on across the foyer and up the stairs.

"Hayden!" Dad shouted from the doorway of his study.

But I was done listening to him. I'd spent my whole life trusting him, believing in him, trying my hardest to make him proud of me, to earn his approval and love. To earn his forgiveness for Damon's death.

I was an idiot.

I went to my room, grabbed a duffel bag from my closet. I wouldn't be taking much, just some extra clothes, my MP3 player and laptop and their chargers.

I was leaving everything else behind. Maybe Mom could turn my room into another shrine like they had with Damon's. A shrine to help excuse my father's bigotry and torture and murder of hundreds of thousands of innocents all over this country.

I froze, staggering under the weight of the knowledge that I was the son of the new Hitler.

Footsteps in the hall paused at my doorway. Thinking it was Dad come up to stop me, I spun around, raising a hand, the energy orb already forming.

The door eased open, and Mom poked her head in. I fisted my hand to contain the orb just in time.

Like Dad, she wasn't surprised by the evidence of my abilities. "I take it your talk with your father didn't go too well. Did he tell you about the Clann and your uncle?"

I nodded and took a deep breath. "Our own people are dying out there because of him. And he thinks he's actually helping them."

She sighed, her teeth worrying her lower lip. I hadn't seen her do that in years. "So you're leaving."

I nodded and went back to packing.

"To find others from the Clann? Because you won't be able to. They're either in hiding or in prison. None of them will risk revealing themselves now. Not to us."

"Gee, I wonder why?" Instantly I felt a pain of guilt for the sarcasm. None of this was her fault, at least not directly.

"When will you be back?"

Never, I almost said. But when I looked at her, I noticed her eyes shown with tears. My throat choked up. "I don't know, Mom. Maybe I'll get a chance to come see you when this whole situation blows over."

Unless I got arrested. Then I'd probably never see her again for sure. Something told me internment camps didn't allow their prisoners to have visitors and Dad wouldn't be too quick to save me after that little father/son chat we'd just had.

I zipped the now bulging duffel bag shut and slung its canvas mesh strap over my shoulder. All packed up, time to go. At the doorway, I cleared my throat to get rid of the knot in it and tried to think of what Damon would say if he were me right now.

As usual, I had nothing.

She reached out for me, pulling me into a fierce hug I didn't even know her thin arms were capable of. "Promise me you'll take care of yourself," she whispered, leaning back to search my face.

I nodded, unable to speak as my throat tightened up again.

"Here." She pressed something stiff and sharp-edged into my hand. A credit card wrapped in paper with writing on it. "The card's in my catering business's name, not mine. He never sees the bills, and it's got a $10,000 limit on it."

Whoa. What was she doing with a card with that kind of limit?

It was a nice gesture, but I still wouldn't be able to use it. If Dad decided to track me down someday, the first thing he'd do was look for a credit card trail, including from her cards. "Mom, I can't—"

"Take it. You'll need it." It was both an order and a plea. "And that's the address of your Grandma Letty."

"Dad's mother?"

She nodded, her face solemn as tears slid down her cheeks. "She's a descendant, and she'd love to help you any way she can. She'll get you out of the country. Promise me you'll go to her. She'll let me know you're safe."

How could any grandma help like that, even one still active in the Clann? I couldn't even remember the last time we'd seen her.

"Promise, Hayden!" She gripped my shoulders.

"Okay. I promise." A lie, but if it made her feel better...
She hugged me again.

I wished I didn't have to make my mother cry, or could at least take the time to make this goodbye easier on her somehow. But Tarah, and all those descendants and outcasts at the camp, needed me. And Mike and his friend were probably waiting for me at the park by now too. I had to hurry.

As gently as I could, I eased her away from me. "I'm sorry, Ma. But I've—"

"I know, I know." She wiped her cheeks with both hands, her lips turned up in an embarrassed smile. "I love you."

"I love you too."

I headed for the stairs. But at the top of them, I had to stop and look back. "Why do you stay with him?"

She shook her head, smiling sadly. "Oh, son. Your father doesn't want to be a bad man. He's just trying to save the world, in his own way."

And instead, he was wrecking it all to Hell and back.

I turned, walked down the stairs, and left my home for the last time.

CHAPTER 7

I made a quick stop at a home improvement store for three flashlights, batteries, and bolt cutters. My first and last planned purchase on Mom's card. Then I headed for the park.

The trees were sparsely positioned at Bergfeld Park, letting in enough moonlight on the grounds to let me see that the park was empty.

Only Mike and his friend, who introduced himself as John, waited under the slide as we'd agreed.

"Gary didn't make it," Mike said, keeping his voice low.

While I hadn't known Gary, I had respected his intentions. He had been willing to risk his life to save others, even if it had probably been for the glory more than anything else. "I'm sorry to hear that."

Mike nodded. John scuffed the toe of his sneakers in the dirt for a few seconds in silence.

Feeling like they were waiting for me to say something motivational, I muttered, "Let's make sure he didn't die for nothing."

Mike and John nodded quickly, and then we started laying out a new plan.

"We'll ride separately to the camp." I didn't bother to make another sketch in the dirt. We'd all seen the last one in the woods. And with just the three of us, getting to the camp's perimeter was going to be a lot simpler now. "We'll need the vehicles to transport prisoners out of there. There's a dirt road with deep ditches on either side of it to the camp's south where we can park out of sight. Then we'll circle around on foot and enter the compound together on the east side near the prisoners' building. Mike, you're going to have to make sure we're completely invisible as soon as we start approaching the camp on foot. Think you can keep it up for about an hour or so?"

"No problem. But we're going to have to be real quiet. I can only hide our appearances, not sounds."

"Good to know," I said. "Once we get through the gate with bolt cutters, we'll have to find a way to get past the guards at the prisoner building's door."

"I could throw a rock or something to distract them," John offered.

I nodded. "Yeah, that could work. Nothing too major, just enough to get them both to move a few steps away while we duck inside. Once we're in, we'll have to start detoxing people. I've never tried to heal anyone, though. Have you?" I looked at them.

They both nodded.

"My mom was a healer," Mike said. "I picked up a few things from her that we've been practicing with. But we should probably detox the known healers first so we'll have some help. I don't know how much energy we'll have to work with. Healing saps it out of you quick."

"Okay." I paused, debated, then made the decision to go ahead and say it. "I guess Gary's proof that I wasn't exaggerating earlier about the live ammo. Tonight, what we're planning here, is going to be as dangerous as it gets. But if you can use non-lethal stuff on the guards, do it."

"Gary—" Mike began.

"I know what he said," I replied. "But you saw what happened to him. He used lethal force, and all it did was make them determined to kill us."

"Okay," Mike said after a few seconds. "We'll try not to kill anyone. Or get anyone killed. If we can."

John nodded as well.

"Right," I said. "Then let's get out of here."

I led the way to the internment camp in my truck, with Mike and John riding together in Mike's little black Saturn. As I drove, I tried not to think about the "leading" part of what I was doing. Every time I did, my hands started shaking on the steering wheel.

What was I doing?

I wasn't Damon. Just because I was a Shepherd didn't mean I was born knowing the first thing about leading others, no matter what my parents claimed. And Damon had never just led. He'd inspired. He'd made people want to do amazing things and believe that they could.

And now here I was trying to follow in his footsteps. But I had no clue how a prison break should be done. We probably had way too few people to even consider trying this. We were going up against anywhere from seventeen to twenty-five armed guards, with flashlights and bold cutters as our only physical tools and zero protective armor.

This was crazy.

Tarah would be proud. Maybe Damon would be too.

I just hoped I didn't wind up getting anyone else killed tonight until the more experienced Clann people at the camp could take over.

We cut our headlights as we turned off the main road onto the same side road Tarah and I had used only hours earlier. Mike parked behind me while I shucked off my bulky coat so I would be able to move around easier. My hoodie would have to be enough to keep me warm for awhile.

Then we gathered in the ditch.

"Everyone ready?" I whispered.

They nodded.

We crossed the field that separated our road from the side of the camp, circling wide along the way then cutting back to the east side. We had to move slowly, using the moonlight to help us avoid cactus, rocks and prickly mesquite trees until we reached the east fence between two guards.

The night was too still, amplifying every little crunch of rock and dirt our footsteps made. I was worried Mike's visual cloaking spell might not be as good as he'd claimed back in the relative safety of the park. Especially when we were so close to the guards that I could make out their eye color beneath the stadium lights flooding the entire camp. With all the prisoners apparently locked up for the night, there was nothing to distract the soldiers from any noise or movement they might pick up. But Gary was as good as promised. The guards never even looked our way.

It took about ten minutes for me to carefully, slowly cut the chain link with the bolt cutters so they wouldn't make noise. We probably could have used a spell for this too, if any of us had known how to use magic to cut through metal. Which we didn't.

Finally, the opening in the fence was big enough for us to slip through. Before we did, John chucked a small rock past the guard on the left, which made both guards look in opposite directions away from us. We used that fifteen second distraction to slip through the fence then creep across the twenty open yards to the nearest building where we hoped the prisoners were being kept.

John tossed a second rock he'd stowed in his pocket.

"What was that?" one of the door guards muttered.

"Dunno, but I heard it too," the other guard said,

looking around. They took a couple of steps away from the door, splitting up to look around the sides of the building.

I ran across the rocky, hard packed dirt to the door, grateful my shoes had quiet, flexible soles. As I reached for the doorknob, I held my breath. I had no clue how to pick a lock. Thankfully the guards seemed to have put all their faith in the drugs and their guns to keep the prisoners contained inside, because the door was unlocked. We slipped inside then spread out.

The long metal building's curved roof and walls had no windows and only the one door we'd entered through, so we could safely turn on the flashlights for the first time. The small beams cut through the pitch black to reveal how the building was filled with row after row of cots, each one holding a comatose patient covered in a single thin blanket. We shone the lights on the prisoners' faces in order to find some of the healers who had volunteered their skills in the woods tonight before being caught by the soldiers.

While Mike and John started detoxing a few of those healers, I searched cot after cot. But so far Tarah was nowhere in sight.

Was I wrong about the soldiers assuming she was a witch? Had they taken her somewhere else instead?

Muttering a curse, I found Mike and John as they worked separately on detoxing adult healers.

"Is it working?" I whispered to Mike.

"Yeah, but it takes awhile," Mike said, even as the man whose wrist he held started to wake up.

"Have you seen Tarah anywhere?"

Mike shook his head.

When I asked John, he gave the same answer.

While Mike moved on to detox another healer to add to our ranks, I filled in the still drowsy man on what was going on. The longer I talked, the more alert the man became. After a minute or two, he scrubbed his hands over his face, dragged himself to his feet, then lumbered over to join the detoxing efforts.

I told everyone not to detox the younger kids. The drugs would keep them in their beds, quiet and safely out of the way, while we took care of the rest of the grownup prisoners and eventually the guards. Some of the parents didn't like it, but at least they seemed to understand.

As we neared the farthest end of the building, I spotted the mother, still holding her dead baby even in her sleep, a crowd of healers forming around her cot. One of them reached down for her wrist.

"No, don't. She shouldn't have to see..." I couldn't say the rest.

Thankfully they understood. A woman who looked like she could be the mother's sister reached out, tears on her cheeks winking from the indirect flashlight beams, and gently eased the baby from the mother's arms. She wrapped the body in a sheet stolen from an empty bed, then tucked the bundle back into the mother's arms.

I could hear faint crying in the crowd, someone sniffling, men clearing their throats. But I couldn't look away from that tiny bundle.

"Hayden," Mike whispered at my shoulder. "We found Tarah."

The only words that could move me at that moment.

"Is she okay?" My gaze snapped to his face. I was half afraid of what expression I might find there.

He nodded, a tired half smile twisting his face.

I followed him to the back of the building.

She looked like an angel in her sleep, her ponytail loose so her thick dark hair made a tangled cloud against her cheeks. Mike picked up her limp wrist, and my gut knotted. I'd never wished for a special ability more than I did in that moment as I had to wait for someone else to fix her. I should be the one who was healing her. I'd promised to protect her and failed.

Her eyelids fluttered open. Mike was closer to her head, but somehow she looked right at me instead.

My breath caught in my lungs. "Hello, Sleeping Beauty."

She rolled her eyes but smiled anyway.

Mike moved on to the next prisoner.

Tarah struggled to sit up. I slid an arm around her shoulders and helped her, then ended up hugging her in relief, burying my face and a shaking hand in her hair. "Told you I'd come back for you."

"What took you so long?" she whispered in my ear.

"Oh, you know how bad traffic on the interstate gets," I joked. "That and facing down my father about being an outcast."

She leaned back to search my face with wide eyes. "You, or him?"

"Both, actually."

Her eyebrows shot up. "And how'd it go?"

I scowled. "Not great. Turns out he's a total hypocrite. The jackass actually thinks he's helping everyone by trying to find a way to permanently suppress our magic and make us 'normal' again. And remind me to tell you about the Clann sometime later."

"Okay." She shook her head. "That sucks about his lying to you all this time." She sighed. "Well, at least I'm not the only one around here with delusional parents. Speaking of…did you find my dad yet?"

"Not yet, but we're not done either."

"Hayden!" John hissed from three cots over. "This guy's not drugged, but he's not waking up. What do we do?"

"Is it my dad?" Tarah asked me, her eyes wide with a combination of hope and fear.

Tarah

I tried to stand up too fast and nearly fell back on the cot again as the blood rushed from my head. The drugs they dished out around here were some seriously potent stuff. Hayden helped steady me, then tucked one of my hands through the bend of his elbow so I could hold onto him for balance.

A thin blonde woman overheard us and stumbled over, wobbly from either just waking up or maybe too much healing tonight. "I'm a healer. Let me check him." I didn't recognize her. She must not have been part of the Tyler outcasts' community.

I tried to move faster, but the numbness in my feet had turned into a pins and needles sensation, making every step excruciating as the blood flow returned to my lower limbs. By the time Hayden and I got to the man's cot and could tell that it was definitely my dad, the woman had already knelt on the floor beside him and pressed both her hands on his temples.

After a minute of frowning with her eyes closed, she said, "He's got a bad concussion."

The breath caught in my lungs. Someone had hit him?

I sank down onto an empty cot beside Dad. Would he be okay? Would he suffer any long term damage? Dad had always been the smartest person I'd ever known. The thought of him losing any of that brilliant intelligence made my eyes sting.

"Can you help him?" I asked.

"Give me a minute. Maybe I can reduce the swelling," the woman muttered, her eyes still closed.

I felt every second tick by, could hear my every breath along with Hayden's and the woman's and my dad's.

Finally, after what felt like an hour, the healer opened her eyes and smiled. "There. All patched up. He should come around in a few seconds."

We waited, watching Dad's face in the beam of Hayden's flashlight. When Dad's eyelids began to flutter, I reached across the aisle and grabbed his suddenly too frail hand to let him know I was here.

Jumping at my gentle squeeze of his hand, Dad opened his eyes and looked around. "Where—"

"Shh, Dad," I whispered. "We have to stay quiet. We're in the prisoners' building at the internment camp. Hayden's breaking us out of here."

Dad grimaced and rolled up onto an elbow, using his free hand to check the back of his head. "Oh boy, that hurts. That's what I get for refusing to join the mad doctor here. Feels like I cracked my brain pan."

"You did," the healer murmured with a small smile. "You might have headaches for awhile as your skull finishes healing. Take it easy moving around, okay?" She slowly stood up. "I'd better go help the others."

"Thank you..."

"Pamela," she said, holding out a hand for me to shake.

"Thank you, Pamela."

Dad smiled his thanks at her as she got up to go help someone else. Then he looked at me, blinked fast a couple of times and frowned. "Tarah, what are you doing here?"

"Rescuing you, of course." Well, minus the small hiccup of getting myself arrested and rescued first.

Dad sighed. "Your mother's going to kill me."

I winced, realizing I'd forgotten to call her earlier and let her know where I was and that I was okay. "Not if she kills me first."

"You feel up to getting out of here, Dr. Williams?" Hayden asked, offering my dad a strong hand.

"I was ready to blow this joint the second I arrived," Dad muttered. He let Hayden pull him upright.

The three of us were pretty slow in joining the group of

detoxed adults at the dark end of the building farthest from the door. Dad's knees kept popping so loudly I worried the guards outside would hear them.

"You've got a plan for how to get everyone out of here, right?" Mike whispered to me once we'd joined the others. "This whole prison break was your idea, after all."

I winced. "Yeah, well, I was kind of hoping you guys would fill in the details."

Hayden crossed his arms over his chest and frowned at Mike. "Can't we just use your cloaking spell again to get them out a handful at a time the same way we came in?"

Mike cringed. "Sorry, but no. We're going to need a plan B. All this detoxing's tapped me out. I've got five, maybe ten minutes of cloaking left in me tops."

That wouldn't be nearly enough time to get all these people out.

"Can anyone else do a cloaking spell to get us out of here?" Hayden asked the group.

The answer was a whole lot of head shaking.

Oh crap. I shared a worried look with Hayden.

Trying not to panic, I said, "Come on, everyone. We need ideas here."

Silence as everyone looked to everybody else in the dimly lit circle.

Finally a short guy at the back stepped forward. "Uh, what about a freezing spell on the guards?"

"You can freeze someone?" I hadn't even known that kind of spell existed in real life.

The man nodded. "The body's ninety percent water. I just concentrate on that while using a basic freezing effect, and it locks them right up like a cryofreeze. Used to do it on my kid brother all the time when he was acting like a punk."

A few men chuckled quietly and were quickly hushed by the rest of the group.

"Is your brother still alive?" Hayden asked, eyebrows raised. "We're aiming for nonlethal stuff here."

The man grinned. "Yeah, he lived through it. Can't promise he didn't lose a few brain cells, though. I 'might' have forgotten to unfreeze him for a half hour or so once or twice."

One corner of Hayden's mouth twitched. "Good enough...uh, what's your name?"

"Harvey. Harvey Lansing."

"Good to meet you, Harvey. Mike, can you cover him while he freezes all the guards?"

Mike nodded and walked with Harvey towards the building's door at the other end. When they were about ten feet away from us, they simply faded out of sight. A few minutes later, the building's door eased open several inches, paused, then closed shut again without a sound.

"Stay quiet and wait for the signal," Hayden told the rest of the prisoners. Then he and I carefully picked our way through the rows of cots to the door, pressed close to the cold metal and listened.

We couldn't hear a thing out there.

After a couple of minutes of waiting in dead silence, Hayden turned off his flashlight and risked cracking the door open a centimeter. After several long seconds, he pointed to the left then the right and gave me a thumbs up, which I took to mean the guards at the door were frozen now.

Curious to know just what a frozen person looked like, I slipped in between him and the door and peeked out through the tiny sliver of an opening. The guards at either side of the doorway weren't moving. They weren't breathing either, but were still standing at attention, which seemed a good sign. From what I could see of the nearest perimeter guards, nobody else had noticed yet.

I couldn't see the freeze team. They must have moved

away so we weren't included in Mike's cloaking sphere. At
first, I couldn't even tell which perimeter guards they'd
frozen so far. The guards didn't move that much anyways.
But after a few minutes, I could detect one difference.
Unfrozen guards turned their heads an inch or two from
side to side as they scanned the perimeter beyond the
fence.

Three minutes passed. Then five. Then seven. How
much longer could Mike keep up the cloaking spell?

The flap on the tent building rustled. The wind, or an
outcast?

The crowd at the far end of the building began to get
antsy. Someone whispered "did it work?" too loudly and
was hushed by several others.

The guard building's door opened a few inches and
stayed open. Two more minutes passed. I glanced at
Hayden in time to see a bead of sweat slide down his
temple despite the cold before he reached up and dragged
his hoodie's sleeve across his forehead.

Suddenly, our building's door moved out of Hayden's
hand. At the same time, Mike and Harvey reappeared
before us.

Mike grinned, his eyes tired but relieved. "Done."

I blew out a long breath. "Good job, guys." Maybe we'd
actually get out of this place alive after all.

Hayden turned towards the rest of the group and gave
the thumbs up.

Muffled whoops and whispering broke out as parents
rushed to find their children and remove the drugs from
their systems. I hurried to the back end to find my dad
intently watching Pamela, the female healer who had fixed
his concussion, as she bent over a tiny blonde version of
herself. When the little girl woke up and said "Mommy!",
Pamela's teary smile brought tears to my own eyes. Dad
grinned too, but his eyes still looked worried.

Pamela wasn't the only happy parent as more kids were detoxed. But the relieved parents' smiles didn't last long.

"What's the matter with Mommy?" one little girl asked as she joined the group.

She was the kid who had been leaning against her mother while her baby brother or sister died.

Pamela, who held her hand now, froze then crouched down beside her. "She's still asleep, honey." Then she looked to Hayden, her eyebrows raised.

Wanting him to decide whether to wake up the girl's mother into a living nightmare.

The hint of Adam's apple in his throat worked as he swallowed hard, and my chest ached. No one should be forced to make this decision. Who would want that woman to ever wake up and have to deal with such a loss?

"Detox her only enough for her to be able to walk," Hayden said, his voice gruff. Then he glanced down at me and caught me staring. "It'll be safer and easier on everyone if the mother doesn't have to be carried out completely. And this little girl needs her mother at least semi-awake too."

But there was a haunting tightness around his eyes. Was he worried that he was making a mistake?

I slipped my hand into his. He stared at me for several long seconds, then squeezed my hand.

Pamela touched her sister's wrist. After a couple of minutes, two men helped her sister to her feet. She was obviously woozy, her eyelids only half raised, her eyes unfocused. And yet she still never let go of the bundle in her arms, even as she reached out to take hold of her daughter's hand.

Hayden's jaw muscles clenched and unclenched as he took a few deep breaths and seemed to assess our group. "Everyone ready to get out of here?"

Nods all around as families joined hands with their

loved ones, all of them looking to Hayden to lead the way out.

"Then let's get out of here." He opened the door wide and stepped out into the lights that flooded the camp like a football stadium, blinding me and forcing me to raise my free hand to shield my eyes until they could adjust to the radical change in light. He continued to hold my hand, guiding me while I couldn't see. My dad shuffled behind me, the heel of his left shoe squeaking with each step in a reassuringly familiar way.

After a lot of blinking, my eyes finally started to adjust. As we walked across the rocky, hard ground towards the gates, I looked back over my shoulder at the massive exodus of people following us to freedom. There must have been at least a hundred people in our group, maybe more, and every single one of their faces was so eager and hopeful. And all because of Hayden. In that moment, I had never felt so much pride for someone as I did for Hayden.

Again he caught me looking. One corner of his mouth hitched up as his eyebrows rose in question.

"You did it," I told him, wondering if he had any idea just how huge his actions tonight were, what they meant for all these people here.

One corner of his mouth tightened in a half grin. "Nah. It was really Mike and John who got us in here. And then all the healers helped out once they were awake. Not to mention how that guy Harvey really saved our butts with the freezing spell. All I did was buy a few flashlights and some bolt cutters."

I shook my head. He was just being modest. If not for him, I knew without a shadow of a doubt that we would all still be drugged out of our minds in that building, prisoners here until either the government changed its collectively crazy mind about descendants and outcasts or found a way to stop their magic. Or maybe killed all the outcasts instead.

Hayden had saved us. And I had a hunch I wasn't the only one here who would never forget it.

He reached for the gates' control box and hit the green buttons. Both gates started to slide open with a loud clatter of metal. This was it. We were free and taking everyone with us!

Jeremy would be so jealous. He was always talking about how much luck and determination it took to be in the position of having a firsthand account of an event like this. I glanced around me, wanting to remember every single detail so I could describe what this moment was like to him. He'd be able to write one heck of a story about it.

"Hey!" a man shouted from the opposite end of the compound.

Hayden dropped my hand as we both spun around to find a perimeter guard running around the buildings towards us.

Then the two at the prisoner building entrance stumbled back to life.

A fourth emerged from the guards' building, sleepily rubbing his eyes.

Either the freeze team had missed a few guards, or the freeze spell wasn't lasting nearly as long as our guy had expected. Whatever the reason, we were all totally screwed.

"Stop or we'll shoot!" one of the guards yelled.

Three of the guards raised their rifles. The fourth froze then took off for the officer tent. Probably to call for backup.

Hayden burst into a sprint towards the tail end of our group, yelling, "Everyone run! Get out of here now!"

Then he started throwing energy orbs from both his hands at the remaining three guards.

I wanted to run, knew Hayden was right and I should turn and lead everyone through the gates as fast as we could go. But I was paralyzed. I couldn't look away from

Hayden, his face set with determination and complete focus as he fought the guards single handedly with his magic.

His energy orbs started hitting his targets. One guard went down. Then another.

A sharp crack rang out, and that's when I saw the gun raised in the third guard's hands. Oh God. They were shooting at Hayden!

Hayden turned and threw two orbs at the shooter, one from each hand, driving the soldier to the ground unconscious.

Hayden lowered his hands, watching the downed guards, probably to make sure they didn't get back up again. Then he turned towards the tent and tried to raise his hands as if to hit it with energy orbs or another of his spells. But his hands were only halfway up before he groaned and fell to his knees, his right hand darting up to clutch at his left shoulder. Eyebrows pinched, he looked down at his hand as it came away covered in blood.

"Hayden!" I screamed, finally able to move.

I ran around the stunned group of prisoners to Hayden, noticing two of our men also take off running towards the tent, hopefully to finish what Hayden had started. My pulse boomed in my ears like a car stereo system's subwoofer turned up too high as I reached Hayden's side a second before he began to topple over sideways. It took all my strength to hold his weight and ease him the rest of the way to the ground.

I knelt beside him, brushing aside his hand so I could see his shoulder. Red bloomed through the cotton hoodie, rapidly spreading down the sleeve. "Oh God. Hayden, your arm."

"The tent—" he groaned, his eyes rolling wildly.

"They're taking care of it."

I unzipped his hoodie, peeled back the now soaked

layers of his jacket and shirt, and the blood bubbled up to the surface like a natural spring, robbing me of the ability to breathe.

"We've gotta go," Hayden choked out. "Are there any military trucks?"

"What?" Was he insane? He was hurt! How could he still be worrying about getting us out of here?

Dad joined us, crouching at my side to rest a hand on my shoulder. But he wouldn't be any help. He was a scientist. Hayden needed a real doctor right now.

The prisoners had also figured out Hayden was hurt. They gathered around us, muttering. Then Pamela pushed through the crowd and knelt at Hayden's other side. Immediately she called for someone to find a first aid kit, sending more men scattering.

"Trucks." Hayden tried to sit up. I pushed him back down, scared for him to even move until we got the bleeding to stop. "We gotta get these people out of here."

"I'm on it," a man said from somewhere towards my right. He took two guys with him at a jog.

"Uniforms. For the men," Hayden muttered as Pamela ripped the bottom two inches off her sweatshirt, using part of the strip as a compress against his wound. She wrapped the rest of the strip around his shoulder to hold the wad of fabric in place.

"And those...those walkie talkie things. On the necks..." Hayden added.

Two more people, overhearing their new leader's probably insane ramblings, took it as an order and ran towards the guard building.

I shook my head in disbelief. He was badly wounded, slurring every word, barely able to talk from either shock or the pain, and *still* trying to boss people around. Yep, he was definitely a Shepherd.

"And food...and water..." Hayden said, his voice

growing fainter now.

"Okay, Hayden," I said. "Relax now. Everyone's working on it."

He squinted at the sky and said something that sounded like "'S it gonna rain?"

"Rain?" At first, I thought he was delusional. Then I realized what he meant when I heard the thunder-like rumble too. "Oh. No, that's the trucks." The men were driving two military trucks around from behind the guards' building where the vehicles must have been parked out of sight.

Pamela partially lifted Hayden, checked the back of his shoulder and grumbled. "The bullet went straight through."

"Is that good?" I asked, thinking, *Please let it be a good thing.*

"Yes and no. There's no bullet to dig out, and it missed all his organs. But it means twice the holes to lose blood from."

Hayden tried again to sit up but was so weak I was able to hold him down with a single hand on his good shoulder.

"I found some uniforms and those communication thingies," someone reported in.

Hayden tried to look in that direction. "Get everyone...on the..."

"Hayden, I said we've got it!" I honestly didn't know whether to laugh or cry. He seemed determined to die a true Shepherd, still mumbling out orders like a general on the battlefield. Couldn't he just rest and let us figure out what to do?

"Don't forget food. And water." His eyelids began to droop.

"Hayden, shut up already!" I finally had to say, exasperated beyond measure. "You've been shot, you idiot!"

He made a face that would have been comical if not for

the fact that he could be dying from blood loss. "Well, that sucks."

And then his eyelids drifted closed and stayed that way.

"Hayden?" I tapped his cheek, getting no response. "Hayden!"

CHAPTER 8

"Hayden's right, we've got to go," Pamela muttered even as she pressed her hands to the front and back of Hayden's wounded shoulder and closed her eyes.

"We can't move him while he's pouring out blood." Why did I feel like I was the only sane one around here all of a sudden? Couldn't this woman see how hurt Hayden was?

"I've slowed the bleeding already. I can heal him more in the back of a truck while we're putting some miles between us and this place."

Dad pressed a heavy hand on my shoulder. "She's right, Tarah. I'm pretty sure that guard had time to send out a request for backup. This place is going to be crawling with a fresh wave of soldiers soon."

I blew out a long breath through puckered lips then nodded. "Fine. Let's go."

I supported the heavy weight of Hayden's head while Dad, Pamela, and two men carried the rest of his weight over to one of the two trucks they had parked close to us. Getting him up into the high back end was another matter, though, requiring Pamela and me to climb in first and both hold the tent-like flaps open as well as guide Hayden's head and shoulders in while several men lifted his body from below. I was scared so much movement was going to reopen his wounds, but Pamela didn't seem concerned at all. Maybe she knew she could reheal him if necessary. Or maybe she didn't know him, didn't really care whether he lived or died, and just worried about getting herself and her family out of here.

All I could think about was making sure Hayden was going to be okay. Thankfully the others had heard Hayden's orders and were following them, grabbing all the water, meals-ready-to-eat, and blankets in the camp. Four men dressed themselves in soldier uniforms and took over the driving. Mike made a big sacrifice, leaving behind his car he claimed he'd never liked anyway and driving Hayden's truck instead behind the bigger khaki colored military trucks. I had no clue why Hayden would care about his truck, but Mike insisted he would when he recovered. Maybe it was a guy thing. Or maybe Mike just wanted a chance to drive Hayden's hot off the line hybrid truck.

I couldn't care less about the stupid truck. All I cared about was seeing Hayden wake up.

Except he didn't.

At first, all the rest of the group cared about was getting as far away from the camp as fast as possible. But once Pamela stabilized Hayden, I was able to calm down enough to start thinking more clearly about a long term solution for our group.

We stopped after an hour at a bus station, where roughly half the outcasts left us. Apparently they had their own plans for where to hide. But the rest of them didn't have the money to escape, or else they had nowhere safe to go. Even those who had contacts didn't want to risk endangering those relatives or friends by asking for their help.

They might be free, but for so many of our group, these prisoners were still just as trapped by the situation as they had been before escaping the internment camp. They were lost refugees with no one else to turn to for help or hope. And for some strange reason, they seemed to believe that Hayden had some sort of plan to get them to safety, judging by how they kept whispering and staring at him with a combination of gratitude and desperation. Maybe it was because he'd gotten them out of the internment camp. I was guessing it was because of who his dad was, though. They probably thought he could pull some strings with Senator Shepherd to get all their names cleared.

Considering all that they had been through already, I didn't have the heart to tell them the truth, that Hayden was just as lost and on his own as they were. He was the only hope they had left. How could I take that away from them?

So I made the difficult decision to tell everyone the tiniest of lies.

"Uh, to be honest, I don't know if Hayden's going to be able to get his dad to clear our records," I said, wincing as fear returned to make their already pale faces even paler. Several women hugged their children closer, pressing kisses to the little ones' heads or turning their faces into their husbands' shoulders.

"But, um, I'm sure Hayden does have a place for us to go where we can figure it all out," I stammered, praying I wasn't getting us in too deep here. "I'm just...not sure where it is."

"He had to have written down the address somewhere," someone cried out.

"Uh, right," I said, mentally scrambling now. This was why I always tried not to tell lies. It was too hard to cover my tracks. The truth was so much easier. "Can someone radio Mike and ask him to check Hayden's truck? Maybe we can find something there." He had to have a phone with a list of friends and relatives or something.

"What about this?" Pamela held out a thin black leather wallet. "One of the guys said it fell out of Hayden's back pocket while we were loading him."

Holding my breath, I sent a silent apology to Hayden for violating his privacy then dug through the wallet, nearly weeping when I found a credit card wrapped in a piece of paper with the name "Grandma Letty" on it plus an address and phone number. It was worth a shot at least.

"Anybody got a phone?" I asked.

Dad surprised me by holding up a hot pink phone that looked suspiciously familiar. "Apparently the soldiers had a huge pile of all our personal belongings stashed in their building. Including your phone. We left the others, assuming they would be traceable by now. But since they just nabbed you tonight..."

I hesitated, weighing the odds and the risk. But we had to have a place to go to, and no way was I going to tell the drivers to take us across multiple states without first making sure we would be welcome.

Taking a deep breath, I made the call.

A few minutes later, I could breathe a little easier. Smiling, I tapped the screen to end the call and said, "Tell Mike to plot us out a new course. Looks like we're headed north."

Our truck full of weary passengars erupted in cheering.

Having heard my entire side of the conversation with Grandma Letty, Dad didn't need any filling in. While Pamela used the walkie-talkie neck band things to relay the address to our caravan's lead driver, Dad cleared his throat and leaned in closer at my other side.

"You have noticed there's still approximately fifty, or more, people in this group, right?"

I nodded, focusing on making sure the blanket rolled up

beneath Hayden's head by my hip was still in place to protect him from the hard, cold metal truck bed.

"Just where do you think his grandma's going to put all of them?"

"You mean us." I hadn't realized I was going to say that until I actually did.

Dad's eyes blinked behind his glasses like an owl's in the flashlight's indirect beam for at least twenty seconds. "No. You are not going with them. And neither am I. As soon as we have them headed in a new direction, you and I are getting on a bus and heading straight back home before your mother goes nuclear." At my raised eyebrows, he added, "I read her text messages that you missed. She's worried sick about the both of us now."

"We can't go home, Dad. Homeland Security and all those other agencies will be looking for us. But you could arrange to meet her somewhere. You guys are going to have to go into hiding for awhile, unless you want to be dragged right back to that internment camp to start drugging the next batch of lab rats they haul in."

He grumbled under his breath. "Fine, I see your point. But you're coming with us."

"No, I'm not." I took a deep breath. "I'm staying with this group until they're safe."

"Tarah, these are not our people!" he hissed, his words lost to the rest of our truck's passengers thanks to the roar of the road noise the huge wheels made on the asphalt.

I winced. Like I needed a reminder of how very unspecial I was. Still, I got the point he was trying to make. Logically, I wasn't from the Clann and I had no special abilities whatsoever, so this wasn't really my fight.

Except in my heart I knew this wasn't about logic or facts. It was about doing what was right, not what was easy. And I knew if I ran away and abandoned these people now, I would never be able to live with myself. I had to see this through, wherever that path led me.

Maybe Mom was right. Maybe I was crazy after all.

"You could die," Dad said. "You understand that, don't you? You could have died last night. We all could have."

I nodded. "If not for Hayden."

Dad groaned. "Please tell me you're not doing this for that boy."

"I'm not." At least, not entirely. Hayden was only part of it. Even if he woke up in an hour and drove away from this group in his truck, I would stay with these people.

"Then tell me *why*."

Pressing my hands against my temples, I struggled to explain my decision to myself as much as my dad. "I..I need to know, okay? I need to know what happens to these people. And not through some news article or book someone else writes years from now. I need to see it with my own eyes, to be a part of it. To..."

"Is this some late blooming teenage need to fit in somewhere?" Dad's face scrunched up, as if channeling even a few seconds of Mom's therapist line of thinking hurt his brain.

I swallowed a laugh. "No. I've known for awhile now that I'm not an outcast and will never truly fit in with them, at least not in that way. It's more about..." I tried again to understand, to put it into words. "Jeremy sees it all, you know? He sees the true world around us, not just the sanitized or safe parts, and not the lies told by the governments. He's right there in the middle of it all, doing something important just by being there, by witnessing it and then writing it down as best he can so others can experience it too. He makes his readers see it and feel it and smell it just like he did just by reading one of his articles. He gives a voice to people who have none."

"And he could get seriously hurt or die in the process. Is that what you want? Are you jealous that his life is more exciting than yours?"

I did laugh at that. "Dad, there is no way his life is more exciting than mine right now." I shook my head. "This isn't some thrill ride for me. I think..." I remembered how I felt every weekend, watching Gary and Aimee and the others as they experimented with their growing powers, how it had felt to see that process taking shape right before me even when my own attempts to do magic failed. "I think maybe this is what I was always destined to do. I want to be a part of the real world, not just watch it safely from my couch at home. And I want..."

I hesitated then finally said out loud the words I'd hardly even dared to think to myself in secret. "I want to live it, and then I want to write about it so others can live it too. I want to be a voice for people who have none. Like Jeremy."

Dad groaned. "That's what this is about? You want to be a journalist like your big brother?"

I smiled tiredly, my free hand absently stroking the side of Hayden's forehead where my fingertips found his reassuringly steady heartbeat pulsing just beneath the skin at his temple. "I don't know if I want to write for a newspaper or magazine, or if I just want to write a book someday. I guess I haven't quite got it all figured out yet. But I'm working on it. Promise I'll let you know when I know?"

"And just how long do you plan on...embedding yourself with these people before you've seen enough to write your story?"

I shrugged one shoulder. "No idea. I guess I'll know the ending to their story when I see it."

Dad sighed and shook his head. "Even if you do get the story written and out there someday, just how long do you think you'll be able to hide before the government comes after you for writing it? You're going to be in enough trouble as it is just for breaking out of an internment camp. The government's sure to believe you're from the Clann now. If you write a story revealing what's really going on, and they find you—"

"*If* they find me."

"*When* they find you, they're not going to let you escape again. They'll throw you right back into another internment camp. How am I and your mother and brother supposed to save you then? Especially if we don't even know where you are?"

Again he had a good point. "Maybe I'm turning into a rebel, but Jeremy's not. You know he's smart enough to always dance on the right side of the law. So we'll just use him as our go between. When I change locations, I'll post a message on this forum he likes to use all the time to find new sources. I'll use that nickname he always used to call me by."

"Worm?" Dad said with a half smile.

I nodded, remembering how Jeremy used to love to sneak up behind me, grab my ankles, and yank me into the air upside down while saying "look, Ma, I hooked a worm!" So stupid of him, and yet now I'd give anything for him to do it again. But it had been years since I was small enough for him to pick me up. And now there was no telling when I'd even see my big brother again.

I sighed.

Dad shook his head, his eyes turning sad. "Do you honestly expect me to let my little girl just go running off with a bunch of strangers for who knows how long on some crazy mission to become a Pulitzer prize winning writer?"

"You let Jeremy."

"He's—"

"Do *not* say it's because he's a boy," I warned.

"I was going to say he's older," Dad muttered. "Not to

mention he at least went to college first. And he's being as safe as he can. He's with the military everywhere he goes, in armored vehicles, wearing protective gear. And on the right side of the law, as you just pointed out."

"But he's still in war-torn areas risking getting blown up by some road side bomb or a missile toting terrorist at any second. And if he gets caught by the other side, his being a legally embedded American journalist will only make things worse for him."

Dad grunted his reluctant agreement with those points, and with that single sound, I was taken right back to the countless family debates I'd managed to survive sitting through all my life.

Family debates I might never be a part of again.

I cleared my throat as it tried to tighten. "And besides, what does going to college have to do with it? I don't have to go to college to become a journalist."

"Maybe not, but at least your brother's college years gave your mother and I more time to try and talk him out of his crazy plan. We were supposed to have at least four more years to coerce you into a career of our choosing. You're barely eighteen!"

I couldn't help but smile and lean my cheek against my dad's shoulder. We both knew my parents never would have tried to push me into a career of their choosing. They were too proud of how independent they were raising both of their kids. "Well, think of it this way. You'll be saving gobs of money on student loans for me."

"Like I care. I'd pay it all three times over just to know you were safe."

"I know, Dad. But sooner or later you have to let me go out into the world on my own."

He went silent for a long moment. Finally he muttered, "What am I supposed to tell your mother?"

I cringed. Now that was one scene I was glad I wouldn't

be around to have to witness.

Sunday, December 13th
Hayden

Quiet. Warmth. Soft hands stroking my right hand.

I peeled open my eyelids, then wished I hadn't as a thin line of daylight stabbed at my eyeballs. I groaned.

"Shh," Tarah whispered against my ear. "Don't talk now."

I took a few seconds to open my eyes, letting them adjust to the light. Finally, I could see a little.

Metal floor beneath us. Dark greenish brown canvas roof and walls. We must be in the back of one of the camp's military trucks. Which meant at least a few of us had made it out after all.

I used my stomach muscles to help me sit up. The movement made the several layers of scratchy wool blankets fall away from my chest and my left shoulder twinge in protest. I remembered Tarah's voice at the camp telling me I'd been shot. My shoulder continued to burn and throb with a low pulse of pain in rhythm with my heartbeat. But for a bullet wound, it didn't hurt nearly as much as I'd always imagined one would. I wanted to see what it looked like, but my entire left shoulder had been wrapped in gauze under the white T-shirt I wore now. The shirt fit looser than normal. Probably swiped from the camp's guard building by someone to replace my other shirt and hoodie. If not for the blankets, I would have been freezing.

Then the blood rushed away from my head. My upper body swayed out of my control, and nausea hit me so hard and fast I feared I would puke right then and there. While I saw dots and little squiggly lines dancing over a dark and blurry field of vision, Tarah helped me scoot backwards till

I could rest upright against the metal side of the truck. I closed my eyes and clamped my teeth shut till both the sensations passed.

Her shoulder brushed my good one, tempting me to open my eyes again and watch her as she twisted to peek outside the truck through a tear in the canvas.

After a minute, I heard a car start up a few feet from us and drive away.

Tarah sighed. "Okay, now we can talk. How do you feel?"

I grunted.

Whispers and rustling as bodies shifted all around us, and for the first time I noticed we weren't alone. The truck bed was full of outcasts I recognized from the internment camp. And all of them were watching us.

"How many made it out?" I muttered to Tarah and braced myself for her answer, knowing whatever she said, ultimately it would be my fault and everyone in this truck would blame me for it.

She grinned. "Everyone."

What? What about the fight at the end? "How many were wounded?"

"Just one. You. And Pamela said you should be pretty close to healed by now. The healers are really good. They took turns fixing you up. Though they said you might still end up with a scar. The bullet went right through your shoulder. You might also feel a little woozy for a while since you lost a lot of blood."

I blinked, unsure how to react. On the one hand, I hadn't gotten anyone killed or seriously hurt, other than myself.

On the other hand, I was the only one who'd gotten hurt at all. Now that was just plain embarrassing. "Guess I should've ducked, huh?"

Tarah stared at me without a hint of a smile now. "You

saved everyone's lives, Hayden. Because of you, no one else was hurt, and everyone's free of that place."

"Yeah, well, still, no one else ended up being carried out of there. I bet they had a good laugh about it."

"Uh, no one's laughing about it. In fact..." She leaned in closer and whispered, "I think you're developing quite a fan club. You're a real life hero."

She made a point of raising her eyebrows and looking around.

That's why everyone was staring at us? I thought they were blaming me for not getting everyone out of the camp.

I looked again at all the faces surrounding us, this time daring to make eye contact. While I didn't see any glares of hatred and blame as expected, what I did find made me almost as uncomfortable. Their eyes shone with something like gratitude mixed with hope and a whole lot of questions I couldn't answer for them.

I cleared my throat then whispered, "How many's in the group? And where are we headed now?"

"Well, some of the families already had their own plans for what to do next. So we dropped them off at a bus station along the way. Including my dad." Tightness crept into her voice on that last part, and I looked at her. Her chin rose a bit as she continued. "The rest of us decided to stick together. Now we've stopped for gas. I think we're somewhere in Oklahoma?"

She still hadn't told me where we were headed.

"Where are we going?" I leaned over to peek out through the tear in the canvas at what looked like a dusty gas station.

"I...um, found that name and address in your pocket. I called her, and she said she's your grandma? She said we should bring everyone to her house, and we could figure out the rest from there."

I froze, hoping I'd heard her wrong. "We're all going to

my grandma's? In South Dakota? Tarah, that's over a thousand miles from the camp."

She rolled her lips in and pressed them together then shrugged. "It's a safe haven. Besides, you weren't exactly available for consultation. But if you want to change your mind about South Dakota and take us all somewhere better, no one's gonna argue with you."

This felt like a really bad idea. "Why is everyone sticking together anyway? Don't they realize they can hide better if all these families split off on their own? A group this big is too noticeable. We're going to attract too much attention."

Tarah stared at me, her expression unreadable. "I don't think they know what to do. And most of them weren't carrying much cash on them when the soldiers dragged them off to the camp, and of course now the government's frozen all their accounts so they can't get to whatever funds they did have in their banks. So there's no way they can afford to go off on their own anyway. At least together they can pool what they have for enough gas to get us all to South Dakota."

"I've got a credit card I can use." Unless Dad had heard about my small part in the prison break. Then I would be just as screwed as everyone else, depending of course on whether he chose to cover my tracks in order to keep his own name clean or else use all of his political resources to hunt me down. I thought about Mom's business card. It might still be safe. Maybe. "Look, why don't I just give them some money and—"

"And then what? They're all probably wanted by the FBI by now. If they try to leave the country or cross any of the borders, they'd get caught and thrown into another internment camp. And either they have no family and friends who can hide them, or they don't want to endanger them. Plus, I think they kind of feel safer together as a group. Even if we are more noticeable this way."

I groaned under my breath, using my good hand to scrub my face. This was nuts. What were we supposed to do with them once we got to my grandma's house, stick them all in the basement for who knew how long till the government changed the laws again? That could take months, or even years.

A car engine grew louder as it pulled into the gas station and stopped. What few whispered conversations had broken out in the truck cut off as a car door clicked open then slammed shut just a few feet away. Adults grabbed their younger children and clamped hands over their mouths to keep them quiet. The children didn't resist, their faces extra pale beneath the streaks of dirt.

Even the youngest of these outcasts had learned the importance of hiding.

Carefully I peeked out through the tear in the canvas then silently swore. A local police car had pulled up across from us at the gas pumps.

I turned to the group and mouthed "cop".

Tarah blindly grabbed my good hand, her nails digging into my skin as she clamped down.

Two men in badly fitted military uniforms exited the gas station. The police officer nodded in greeting at them. One driver nodded back. The other soldier pretended not to notice.

I silently swore again. I'd seen enough photos at Kyle's house of his dad and Mr. Kingsley's military buddies to know that no way did these fake soldiers look the part. One outcast had obviously thrown his uniform on in too much of a hurry, missing a button near the top. His jacket gaped to reveal a gold chain necklace over a blue t-shirt. The other pseudo soldier's uniform was about two sizes too small, stretched to near bursting around his gut, several inches of his wrists exposed below the sleeves.

Not to mention, both wore sneakers.

Keep walking, I prayed as the police officer headed for the gas station.

He went inside the building. The fake soldiers parted ways, each climbing behind the wheel of a separate truck.

Then the police officer came back, walking faster this time, heading straight for my truck driver's door. His two hard slaps on the metal exterior echoed throughout the covered bed, making several kids jump.

Everyone's eyes either rounded with fear or clamped shut in terror as we all fought not to panic. A couple of the older kids not held down by their parents twitched. I held a finger to my mouth, and they froze again.

The truck door hinges screeched as our driver opened it and stepped out.

"Yes sir?" the driver drawled.

"Where you coming from?" the police officer asked.

Despite the lack of heat in the truck bed area, sweat beaded and slid down the center of my back. I resisted the urge to throw off the blankets from my legs, worried any small movement would still make enough of a sound for the cop to hear through the canvas.

The driver's reply was a murmur too low to make out. And definitely not the snappy answer Kyle's dad would ever give anyone. If Mr. Kingsley was anything to judge the typical soldier by, we had yet another mark against us.

Apparently the police officer thought so too. "I'm going to need to see the contents of your truck." He didn't wait for a response, striding straight towards the back end of our truck bed.

Our driver's hands shot out, and two blue lights flashed. The police officer's body made a smacking thud as he hit the pavement face first.

I froze in disbelief for a few seconds, staring.

He didn't get up.

The gas station door squeaked open as the attendant

gave in to his curiosity and stepped outside.

I saw my truck's driver turn towards him. But the gas station employee was just a kid, maybe my age or younger. Way too young to die just for being in the wrong place at the wrong time.

"No!" The roar erupted out of me unplanned as I shoved aside the wool blanket covering my lap then stumbled up to my feet and through the people packed inside our truck. My hurt shoulder burned in protest as I climbed over the tailgate then leaped down to the ground.

The drivers and gas station attendant all spun towards me.

"What are you doing?" I yelled at the drivers.

"You saw what he was going to do," my truck driver answered, his expression hard.

I crouched beside the police officer, trying to find a pulse in his neck.

Nothing. Not even a hint of a heartbeat.

"Hayden?" Tarah held up one of the two flaps covering the back end of our truck.

"We need some healers," I told her as I began CPR on the man, fighting to keep my own energy under control even as a breeze kicked up and swirled dirt around the gas station.

Out of the corner of my eye, I saw the tear in the side of the canvas bulge out, like someone was trying to peek outside through it. A kid or an adult? If any kids got curious…

I yelled, "Tarah, the kids. Don't let them see."

Whispers from the truck bed behind me. The torn bit of canvas closed again.

Two women crawled out of the nearest truck, jogging over to join me.

"Pamela—" The same truck driver who had hit the police officer with the energy orbs called out to one of the healers now.

"Shut up, Steve," she replied, not bothering to look at him as she hastily pushed her chin length blonde hair behind her ear. I recognized her then as the same woman who had healed Tarah's dad at the camp. The other healer looked like a real dragon lady, big hands proudly resting on her big hips like she not only enjoyed her size but also was used to throwing her weight around a lot to get what she wanted.

"Can you fix him?" I asked Pamela, standing up and getting out of the healers' way.

"We can try," Pamela muttered as she and the older woman laid their hands on the police officer, one pair of hands at his head, another pair on his chest, and closed their eyes.

After a minute, Pamela then the other healer opened their eyes and shook their heads.

"His heart's too damaged," Pamela said. "He's gone."

I stared at the man dead at my feet, and acid rose up to burn the back of my throat. A dead cop. At my feet. Murdered right in front of me by people I had helped free.

Tarah joined me. "Is he...?"

I nodded.

She drew in a long, deep breath. "I...I don't think any of the kids saw."

We needed to get out of here. Fast, before anyone else saw what had happened. I turned to the two drivers with the gas station attendant. "You two let him go and come help me pick up this cop."

"What?" Steve asked. "We can't let this kid go. The second we do, he'll call the cops on us."

"No I won't," the gas station attendant stammered. "I'm like you guys. Here, look." He turned his hand up at the wrist where Steve held it. A tiny flame flickered to life on his palm. "See? I'm an outcast too. I mean, that is what you guys are, right? That's how you hit him with those blue lights, isn't it?"

"Like I said, let him go," I repeated.

The other driver started to release the attendant. But when Steve didn't budge, the other driver froze in place, his eyes shifting from me to Steve and back again.

Gritting my teeth, I crossed the oil-stained stretch of cement until only a foot separated the trio from me. I wanted to physically shove Steve away from the attendant, but he might retaliate with energy orbs or something.

So instead I stepped closer to the attendant, locking eyes with him. "These guys want to kill you for what you just saw. And they have ways to know if you ever tell." That last part was probably a lie, but then again, who knew what kinds of spells they knew? Maybe it was the truth.

The attendant nodded fast, his eyes even rounder. "I won't tell. I swear it."

I searched his freckle covered face, weighing the odds though I knew I didn't really have a choice here. I'd made a lot of crappy mistakes this year. No way was I going to add to that list by letting them kill someone else. "You heard him, Steve. Now let him go."

"No," Steve said. "He's a witness. He's seen our faces, our license plates. He'll turn us all in before we can get five miles down the road."

"No he won't," I said.

"How can you be so sure?" Steve's eyes narrowed.

I thought fast then yelled over my shoulder, "Tarah, have we got any phones?"

Tarah hurried over and held out a pink phone that looked a lot like the one she used to have.

"Can you shoot a quick video of this guy creating fire in his bare hand?" I nodded at the attendant.

"Sure."

Steve hesitated then let go of the attendant's arm so he

could raise his hand. The attendant took a deep breath, stared at his hand, and the tiny flame reappeared on his palm.

Tarah held up her phone and hit a button on the keyboard to start the recording, making sure to get the attendant's entire upper body and face along with the evidence of his abilities.

"Okay. Here's the deal," I said to the attendant when she was done. "You don't turn us in, and we won't turn you in. Got it?"

The attendant nodded fast again. "I swear, I won't tell anyone. That cop was a jerk anyways, always demanding free donuts and coffee like I owed him, just because he caught me smoking outside once when I should have been behind the counter. I ended up having to pay for all his freebie snacks out of my own paycheck every week when we came up short!"

So the police officer wasn't a saint. That still didn't make his death right.

And then I remembered fighting the guards at the internment camp, hitting them with energy orbs, uncaring how hard I hit them or where as long as they went down and stayed that way...and that night in the woods when Damon and sixteen others had died because of me...

I was the last person to judge Steve.

But I still couldn't let him kill the gas station attendant.

Silence as Steve debated and I wondered what this situation might come down to. Would I have to fight, maybe even hurt or kill, Steve just to save the attendant? Would I have to fight the other driver too? Would the others in the trucks and maybe even Pamela, who seemed to know Steve, jump into the fight as well?

This could end in a bloodbath if Steve didn't make the right decision.

Finally, after what felt like half an hour, Steve scowled

but stepped away from the attendant. The other driver took a hint and also stepped back. Letting out a huge sigh of relief, the attendant immediately dug in the pockets of his slacks, found his pack of cigarettes, and lit up, his hand shaking as he took a long drag.

"Great. Now we've just got to move the cop," I muttered, my stomach rolling and knotting like a tangle of snakes fighting to get free.

"What for?" Steve demanded.

"We're going to put him back in his car and hope his death looks like a heart attack."

I didn't want to be here, didn't want to be saying any of this, and sure as heck didn't want to have to cover up a police officer's death. But we had to at least try to cover this up. We were already criminals on the run from the government. If we stayed under the radar, we had a sliver of a chance of making it to safety. But if we became labeled as cop killers, there wouldn't be a single police officer, sheriff, deputy or prosecutor in the country who wouldn't want to see us all dead.

CHAPTER 9

Grunting a bit, we moved the dead man into the car, arranging the body so it slumped back against the seat. A heaviness grew inside me, like my body was slowly turning into stone from the inside out.

"Let's go," I managed to mutter, turning away from a scene I knew without a doubt would haunt me for the rest of my life.

What would Damon think of me now if he were alive?

I walked without seeing, heading by instinct for the back end of the nearest military truck.

"Hayden?" Tarah called out from a few yards away.

I stopped and blinked in confusion. She was behind the wheel of my own personal truck now, leaning out the open window, her elbow draped over its gleaming white side. I hadn't expected to ever see my truck again. Someone must have been driving it for me at the front of the caravan.

Later I might be mad about some stranger driving my baby. Right now, it was like discovering my favorite floatie while I was drowning in an ocean.

I changed direction, heading straight for the driver side door. "Scoot over."

I expected Tarah to argue about my hurt shoulder and how I shouldn't be driving yet. Instead, she silently slid across the seat so I could get in.

I slammed the door too hard, rocking the truck as I started it. The familiar curve of the gear shift in my hand as I shoved it into drive was like coming home. But even that couldn't remove the crushing weight on my back and chest. After everything that had happened over the last few hours, being back in my own truck's familiar surroundings with the GPS's calm voice calling out directions felt unreal, like I was still asleep in the military truck and dreaming all of this. But then two louder engines roared to life as the military trucks fell into line at our rear, reminding me that this was anything but a dream. It was real.

Lost in thought, I tried to steer with my left hand, and my shoulder zinged me a little reminder that I was still recovering from being shot.

I'd been *shot*.

I'd broken over a hundred prisoners out of an internment camp.

I'd just helped cover up the murder of a cop.

Muttering a curse under my breath, I switched back to driving with my right hand, ducking my head so I could gingerly scrub my gritty face with my left hand instead.

What was I doing?

I checked the GPS screen. Ten hours to go. All we had to do was get to South Dakota without getting caught. Then everyone would be safe and could figure out where they wanted to go next. We could do this.

The silence stretched out, filling the cab like a thick but invisible fog that ate up all the oxygen in the air between Tarah and me. It was probably better this way, though. If we started talking, then I'd start thinking. And thinking wasn't a good idea right now, not after everything that had just happened. Better just to stay quiet, stick with the plan, don't overthink it, maybe listen to some tunes to kill the awkward silence.

I reached for the radio.

Tarah sighed. "Want to talk about it?" Her voice sounded shaky and tight.

"Not really."

"A cop's dead back there. You must have some feelings about that."

"Let me guess, you were going to become a psychiatrist just like your mom."

"Uh, no, more like a journalist like my brother."

"How is Jeremy? I heard he's overseas covering the war?"

"He is. And quit trying to change the subject, because you suck at it." She stared at me with those big, dark, all seeing eyes. "Come on, Hayden. I know you're sick about what just happened too."

"I thought you said I'm just a cold blooded serial killer. After all, I killed seventeen people, including my own brother. And no telling how many guards at the camp. What's a dead cop to me?" That weight I couldn't seem to shake was growing on my shoulders and chest.

"I did not say I agreed with that theory about all those deaths last summer. And all those guards were still breathing just fine when we left the camp last night."

The weight eased up a bit. I glanced at her. "They were? You're sure?"

"Yes. Pamela checked on them to be sure they wouldn't need any life saving healing. She didn't want their deaths on her conscience, either."

I cleared my throat. "Good. That's good."

She continued to stare at me. After another minute of silence, she said, "Hayden, just stop with the macho act already, okay? I know you care. And I know you didn't kill all those people last summer either."

"Actually I did."

Her mouth dropped open, closed, opened again as she struggled for a response. "You...you did?"

I nodded once, shifting as the invisible weight grew by a couple more pounds on my shoulders.

"What happened?"

"Does it matter? I was there. People died because of me. End of story."

"Of course it matters. Accidents happen a lot when outcasts are first learning to work with magic. If you—"

"It wasn't an accident, Tarah. I meant to use my abilities that night."

Her mouth snapped closed. Then her chin jutted out. "I know you, Hayden. You might have intended to use your abilities that night when the anti-magic guys showed up and started a fight, but you never meant to kill anyone. You were probably just trying to help protect your brother and his friends and lost control. It happens."

Her blind faith stunned me, actually rocked me back against the seat. I looked at her. She meant what she'd said.

I didn't know what blew me away more—that she was so determined to believe in my innocence, even when I'd just told her I was the bad guy—or that her guesses about what really happened that night were so dead on. How could she still know me so well even after all these years?

But in the end, it didn't matter what she thought of me. I would never be able to escape the fact that even accidentally killing a whole bunch of people didn't make them any less dead. And their deaths would always be on me.

My throat got so tight it felt like invisible hands were choking me. "Thanks for the faith, but I don't deserve it. I'm not the white knight you're making me out to be."

"Yes you are. Look at what you did last night! You just marched right into that camp and saved all those people—"

"No, I saved *you*. All the rest of them were just an accidental part of the process."

She snorted and rolled her eyes. "You are so full of crap. Why don't you want to tell me the truth about that night?"

"Because I don't want to talk about it at all."

It hadn't been long enough, and even thinking about it still sucker punched me in the gut. Remembering that night made me feel like I didn't deserve to be alive. Damon was the one who should have survived, not me. His destiny was to lead others. Mine was to always come in second best at everything except maybe basketball.

But mostly, I didn't want to talk about it because I just wanted to forget it ever happened.

"Well, I want to talk about it."

"God, you're a spoiled brat. You always think you should get what you want in life? News flash. Most people don't."

Her eyes narrowed. With a huff, she crossed her arms and sat back in the corner.

This time, the silence felt even worse. I lasted all of five minutes till I had to break it. "Look—"

"No, no, it's fine. Obviously you don't want to talk about it. Especially with me."

"You know, you like dishing out the questions about the past, but I don't see *you* answering any."

She scowled and stared out her window, her stubborn silence proof that she understood exactly what I wanted to know.

My fingers drummed on the steering wheel. "Well? How about it, Tarah? Are you ever going to explain why you stopped hanging out with Damon and me? What was the deal? Were we too boring for you all of a sudden? Not cool enough? Did we wear too many colors and not enough leather and spikes and black nail polish for your taste?"

She rolled her eyes. "That's such crap and you know it."

"Then why'd you turn your back on us like we were nothing? You never even bothered to try and give us a reason. One day we were all best friends, the next it's 'I'm sorry, I can't hang out with you guys anymore.'" I shot her a quick, furious glance. "We were best friends for years, Tarah. Didn't we deserve at least an explanation?"

She made a disgusted sound. "Gee, Hayden, I never realized you cared so much. Especially when the very next day you had zero trouble replacing me with Kyle the Vile for your new BFF."

"I did care. A lot. And Kyle was my dad's idea, not mine."

She frowned at me for awhile, blinking fast, thinking so loudly I could almost hear it. One corner of her mouth tightened. "I'm sorry. I really am. I...didn't handle the whole thing very well." She shrugged one shoulder. "What can I say? I wasn't the most mature fifth grader, I guess. I saw you do something you shouldn't have been able to do one day, and me and my big mouth blabbed about it to my dad. He got all excited, started doing research on human evolution developing extraordinary abilities, told my mother where he got the idea from, and she freaked out. She thought I was either lying or confusing fantasy with reality, and that playing all those medieval knights games with you guys was retarding my developing maturity or something. Next thing you know, we're all doing family therapy sessions and I was forbidden from ever hanging out with you guys again."

I glanced sideways at her. "What exactly did you see me doing?"

She shrugged. "Floating in your sleep. You fell asleep in the woods one day while we were waiting for Damon to go and bring back some snacks back to our hiding place. We were doing a dragon recon mission, I think." One corner of her mouth twitched. "She was probably right. It was time for all of us to grow up. I just wish I could have handled it all better."

"And then the next year your family moved closer to the university," I muttered.

"Right. Dad was teaching, doing lab research, and working on getting yet another Masters degree. Mom figured if we lived closer to the campus and he had a shorter commute, we might get to see him more."

So that was it, the answer to the big mystery of why I'd lost my best friend. Because Tarah had seen my Clann abilities starting to develop and had talked about it with her dad.

"And then you became friends with the outcasts."

"Sure, why not? Back then, they were just regular kids like me, and unlike all the other kids in my class, they never teased me about running off into the woods with the Shepherd boys. And becoming friends with a bunch of people got my mom off my back."

"I guess she never thought you'd end up getting arrested because of them, huh?"

"It's actually the other way around, Hayden. My friends got arrested because of *me*. If I'd never seen you levitating, I wouldn't have gotten so obsessed with magic, we never would have ended up having all those weekly meetings in the woods to try and develop our own abilities, and maybe they wouldn't have learned how to throw fireballs and energy orbs and make it rain on command and stuff. But they did. They discovered their Clann abilities because of me. And even if they hadn't gotten arrested, they still would be in constant danger because of me. There were so many times that we nearly blew ourselves up while they tried to learn how to control their magic."

She looked at me then, her eyes big and soft. "That's why I'm telling you I know how out of control these abilities can get, and how easily accidents can happen with

them, and how guilty you can feel afterwards about it.
Because I've been there. I've seen it happen. And if anyone
in our group had ever gotten hurt, in the end it would have
been *my* fault. We were being really stupid messing around
with stuff we had no understanding of."

She was tempting me to open up about what happened
to Damon and the others. And part of me wanted to give
in. I was tired of having secrets between us.

Except every time I looked at her, I remembered the
way she'd smiled at me when first waking up at the
internment camp. That dazzled look in her eyes, that smile,
had made me feel like I was her hero.

It was easy for her to claim to be understanding now
while the past was just a bunch of crazy rumors for her.
But once I told her everything, how could she not look at
me differently? I wouldn't be Hayden the savior of an
entire internment camp to her anymore. I would become
Hayden the Screwup.

I knew it was selfish. But for just a few more hours, I
wanted her to keep looking at me like I was special for a
good reason for a change.

When I didn't speak, she continued, the corners of her
mouth turned down slightly. "Anyways, experimenting with
the outcasts in the woods might not have helped me find
any special abilities of my own like you guys have, but it did
help me in a lot of other ways."

"Like how?"

"Well, just how many journalists out there can say they
helped found a new outcast group and got to be a part of it
for years way before the internment camps were ever even
created? Or got to help break out an entire prison camp full
of Clann people? I've even got video evidence of what we
saw in that camp. This is history in the making, Hayden.
And we didn't just get front row seats for it. We're actually
right up on stage with everybody else."

Yeah, getting thrown into prison and now running from the law just like everybody else. I shook my head in disbelief. "Tarah, your entire life has been wrecked because of all of this."

"No, I found my future because of it. Thanks to all of this, I finally figured out that I want to become a journalist like Jeremy. If not for going through all of this, I might never have realized that, or maybe I would have, but I never would have found the courage to actually go for it. Now? This story is practically writing itself for me. All I have to do is see it through to the end."

She was delusional.

My hand and forearm were getting tired holding the wheel. Forgetting about my hurt shoulder, I tried to switch hands on the steering wheel and cursed under my breath from the resulting pain.

"Shoulder hurting?" she asked.

I nodded. "Too bad I can't just hit it with a spell to heal it up fully or something."

"Do you know how to heal like Pamela?"

I shook my head. "To be honest, I never really got to train with my abilities much. Damon and I had just started before he died."

"Hmm. You'd think the Clann would have some spellbooks or something. I wonder how the descendants still in the Clann train their kids when their abilities start showing up?"

"Actually, they do have spellbooks." I told her about the bookstore where her father had gotten arrested.

Her eyes grew wider and rounder the more I told her about the magical items hidden in the back storage room. "Is it dorky of me that I really wish I had one of those wands now?" she asked.

I grinned. "Well if it is, then you can call me a dork too. I was actually kinda jealous of the descendant kids when I heard about them. The store owner said we're too old for wands, though. Apparently only twelve and thirteen year olds get to use them."

"So did you get to buy anything?"

"Yeah. I got a spellbook. It's in the backseat." Which reminded me... "Hey, do you want to check it for a healing—"

But she was already diving over the backseat. "What does it look like?"

"Uh, like a history book."

Papers rustled as she dug through the crap in the backseat. "Got it!" She sat back in her seat with a huff, pulled her seatbelt back on, then flipped through the book with a frown. "Hayden, you got robbed. It really is a history book."

"No it's not. Hold it closer to me." When she did, I murmured, "Revelattio."

The book's cover and contents changed, making Tarah gasp, "Holy crap."

"Yeah, that's about what I said the first time too."

She started flipping through the pages. "Whoa. This has some seriously deep stuff!"

"Anything on healing?"

"Um..." She quickly flipped through the pages, the sound of the paper pages crackling in the quiet cab. "Yep, here's a whole section on it."

"Want to read it to me?"

"Right now?"

"Why not?"

"But you said you just got this book, and Damon and you didn't get a chance to train together long, either. Which makes you pretty much a beginner, I'm guessing." She flipped through the spells again, her frown deepening.

"Yeah, so what's your point?"

"My point is I'm pretty sure you're supposed to learn

these kinds of lessons in order so each lesson can build on the one before it."

"Tarah, what part of this little road trip we're on says I'm a huge fan of following the rules right now?"

One corner of her mouth kicked up into a reluctant smile. "Point taken."

While she read the directions, I gingerly switched to steering with my bad arm, freeing my good hand to apply the spell on my wounded shoulder.

Nothing happened.

"Did you read it right?" I asked.

She rolled her eyes. "Yes, I read every word in this section. But you obviously weren't listening. You can't heal yourself, dummie."

"Why not?" Seriously, what was the point of being a descendant from the Clann if I couldn't even fix myself?

"Because it doesn't work like that. It says when you heal someone, you take a little of their pain into yourself, and you give them a lot of your energy in return. If you try to do it on yourself, there's nowhere for the pain to go and no fresh energy coming in to heal you."

I scowled at the road ahead of us. "Huh. Well, what else has it got?"

"Nope. I'm not reading anything else from this book unless you agree to do the lessons in order."

"But—"

"Nu uh. I'm serious here, Hayden. You can't mess around with magic. If you do, bad things can happen. It's like playing scientist with acid and other dangerous chemicals and having no clue what you're doing or how to stay safe."

"Oh come on. I don't need to know the whole book. Let's just pick out a few spells—"

"No. I am not letting you blow us up or turn us into chickens or something! Either do it right or not at all."

"Chickens?" I snorted.

I glanced at her to see if she was serious. Yep, she was serious, judging by the mulish set of that chin and lower lip.

That lower lip that I really wanted to kiss right now.

I sighed. "Fine. Start at the beginning, I guess."

Smirking in victory, she flipped to the first chapter then started reading.

CHAPTER 10

The girl should've considered a career in the military, because she drilled me harder on those spell basics than any drill seargeant ever could have. My hands began to ache as I practiced making various spells' gestures over and over until she was satisfied they matched the book's illustrations. Only then would she teach me the words to think or say that would complete each spell.

I didn't feel like I was learning all that much. But then I discovered I didn't really care as long as she kept reading to me. Her voice had changed since we were kids. Even back then, her voice had never been very high or squeaky. But now it had a husky yet honey smooth richness to it. I liked hearing it enough that she could have been reading a cookbook to me for all I probably would have cared.

It wasn't until she shivered two hours later that I noticed how much time had passed and that the sun had dropped to just above the treetops. As the sun set and we continued straight north, the temperature both outside and inside the truck's cab had also begun to drop.

I switched to driving with my left hand, bracing it against my thigh for support, so I could turn on the heater with my right. And then I froze.

"Hayden? Are you okay?"

I barely heard her, my mind racing. If it was getting cold inside my enclosed truck, what did it feel like under those canvas top trucks behind us? They'd grabbed wool blankets from the camp for everyone to share. But it still couldn't be comfortable for them. Most of them didn't even have on coats because they'd been grabbed from their homes and taken straight to the camp. The only ones with coats were the few who had been taken as they'd arrived home from work and school, or the outcasts who had been grabbed from the woods behind my house along with Tarah. Not to mention, they would all need food and water and bathroom breaks.

I checked the GPS. Still eight hours to go till we reached the safety of Sioux Falls and Grandma Letty's, and it was only going to get colder as night fell and we traveled farther north. I swore under my breath.

"What's wrong?" she asked.

"It's getting cold. They've got blankets, but they'll need more. Not to mention more food and water and bathroom breaks. And those trucks have to be missed by now. We've got to stop somewhere, get some supplies and different transportation."

She reached for the GPS unit and started tapping at its screen. "If you take the next exit, they've got a Wal-Mart and a bookstore with free WiFi."

"Okay." I threw an early blinker in warning before taking the exit. The military trucks followed. At the stop sign, Tarah told me to turn left.

Two miles down the road as promised, we crested a hill and discovered the town below with a Wal-mart and a bookstore in front of it. Once we were parked, I grabbed my laptop from the backseat and flipped it open.

"What are you doing?" she asked, staring at the laptop

with wide eyes. "Can't they track us through that thing if you turn it on?"

"Probably. But they also could have tracked us through that GPS unit if they'd wanted to."

Her eyes widened even more. "Then why haven't they found us already? Isn't your dad looking for you?"

I didn't hesitate before shaking my head. "If that internment camp does have any proof that I was involved in the prison break, he's already pulled strings to get my name cleared of it. The last thing he'll ever allow is for his name to be linked to something like that." I started booting up the computer then handed it to her. "Would you mind looking up a local place to rent a bus of some kind? One that's big enough for everybody to ride in together?"

She gave me a strange look I couldn't read, but her fingers began to fly across the keys without any further argument. "Sure. You want a school bus or a charter bus? A charter would have a bathroom on board so we wouldn't have to stop as much."

"Good thinking. Okay, let's try for a charter if we can find one. Don't worry about the cost." When her gaze darted over to me, her eyebrows sky high, I smiled. "We're packing Mom's business plastic. No daily spending limits, and only Mom sees the bills."

She frowned, opened her mouth as if to argue, then ducked her head and focused on the laptop's screen instead. Her fingers began to fly across the keys. "I should have something for us in a few minutes. In the meantime, what will you be doing?"

"Shopping. I'll be back in a few." Her head popped up in surprise as I shut the driver side door.

I stopped by each of the trucks to explain the new plan. The kids all grinned with relief and excitement; the parents looked cautious, as if afraid to even hope. I knew how they felt. I also suggested they split up into small groups of two or three at a time to go to the nearby gas stations' bathrooms so they wouldn't be as noticeable. We could only hope no one would pay as much attention in the growing darkness to a few people climbing out of two military trucks behind a huge bookstore.

But in case anyone did, I got the shopping done as fast as the superstore's size and my list would allow. By the time I made it out of Wal-Mart, my cart was loaded down. But I was worried pushing the cart all the way to my truck at the farthest edge of the parking lot might attract the attention of security watching on the store's cameras. So I looped my hands through the huge haul of plastic handles, left the buggy at the nearest cart collection area, and hoofed it like an overloaded mule back to the trucks.

When I passed everything out to the group, though, it was worth it. Everyone acted like it was Christmas, their faces lighting up at the sight of the cases of bottled water, bags of apples and oranges, PB&J supplies, and coloring books and crayons for the kids.

Tarah joined me just as I got to the last items in the pile...unscented boxes of baby wipes.

Her raised eyebrows prompted me to explain. "My mother always carries these in her purse. I figured they could use them too. You know, to clean up with after they eat the fruit or PB&J or whatever." Embarrassed, I ducked my head and focused on passing the plastic boxes to the mothers in the group.

When I snuck a glance at Tarah a few minutes later, she was staring at me with a strange smile.

Once everyone was busy with their new stuff, I handed Tarah one of the two disposable phones I'd picked up at the store to replace our old ones in case hers was being tracked.

Then I leaned in close and quietly asked her, "Any luck with the buses? Or should I go buy more blankets now?"

"I found a place one town over that rents charter buses
and is open on Sundays. Their buses aren't fancy, no DVD
players or high tech stuff on board, but they come with
bathrooms and plenty of seating for everyone. They're
open till eight tonight."

I glanced at my watch. Six-thirty. "Okay, I'd better head
over there now."

She held out a slip of paper between two fingers. "I
wrote down the address."

"Thanks." I shoved it into my front pocket, then
hesitated. "I guess you'd better wait here with them till I get
back. You know, in case your face is on a government most
wanted list or something." I tried to make a joke out of it to
lighten the mood, but my stomach was knotting up. I didn't
like leaving her here. But the Most Wanted list was a real
possibility. "Maybe you should come with me anyway. You
could always lie down out of sight in the backseat while I'm
inside renting the bus."

She smiled. "Yeah, I could if you didn't keep so much
crap back there."

"I could move some stuff around to make room for
you." I acted like I was offering to do her a huge favor,
knowing it would make her keep smiling.

She did one better and actually laughed. "Gee, thanks.
But I think I'd better stay. You never know, they might
need someone to keep them calm or something while
you're gone. Plus I should charge up and activate our new
phones."

Everyone had looked pretty tense, though the supplies
had at least given them something to do and a way to get
some decent food in their stomachs. And Tarah was right.
Maybe with her here to keep everyone calm, we wouldn't
have a repeat of the gas station incident in Oklahoma.

Wishing I hadn't remembered that, I hesitated, staring at
the khaki colored trucks. Would Steve be able to keep cool

for an hour or two? If he didn't, would Tarah be able to stop him from doing something else stupid?

"Quit worrying," she murmured. "We'll be fine."

"Who said I was worried?" I'd forgotten how easily she used to be able to read me. Apparently she hadn't lost the ability despite the long break in our friendship.

"Hey, did I hear you're going to rent a bus now?"

Steve had gotten out of the cab of one of the trucks and was headed our way. At the sound of his voice, the healer Pamela poked her head through the truck's flap. Below her, a miniature version of her also looked out past the flap, the little girl's matching blonde hair a tangled mess of curls. Her dad reached up to ruffle her hair, making the girl's solemn face break into the briefest of smiles.

"Yeah," I answered Steve, cautious now. "Tarah found a rental place one town over. I should be back in about an hour with a charter bus."

Steve frowned. "Not without a legal driver, you won't. You're what…seventeen?"

My shoulders stiffened. "Eighteen."

"Yeah? Well, you've gotta be at least twenty-five to rent even a regular car. I'm sure the same applies for renting a bus."

Tarah and I shared a look. Great. I wasn't old enough, and everyone else was on the run from the law. The whole group probably was on the FBI's Most Wanted list by now. If the bus owner ran any of their IDs, we would all be toast.

"Anyone any good at making fake IDs and a good disguise to age me up some?" I was only half joking.

Pamela nodded. "Steve could pull off some spells like that."

After a long pause, he nodded. "Not for long, though. And I'd have to go with you or else they would wear off."

"Let's try it," Tarah said.

I didn't like any plan that involved Steve and his anger management issues. But what else could we do? I nodded.

Pamela reached down to squeeze Steve's shoulder. He climbed up on the end of the truck to give her a quick kiss. Then he turned to his daughter. "Daddy's gotta go rent us a bus, sugarplum. I'll be back in a little bit, though. Okay?"

The girl's lower lip and chin trembled.

Jumping back down from the truck's bumper, Steve peeled off the badly fitting military shirt and matching stolen pants from over his regular t-shirt and jeans.

"I've got a spare jacket in my truck," I offered. I would have already given it to Tarah instead, but she still had her thick, quilted coat that she'd been wearing during the meeting in the woods.

"Thanks," Steve said, his tone clipped.

I turned back to Tarah. "See you in a few. If police show up, or anybody else who's acting suspicious of you…"

"I'll get us out of here," she said.

I found myself wishing I'd gotten the courage to kiss her goodbye as Steve and I got into my truck. When I looked back, I caught one last glimpse of Tarah as she climbed into the back end of one of the military trucks.

Too late now.

I punched in the bus rental place's address into the GPS, ready to get this over with as fast as we could. We were so close to reaching South Dakota. If we could just get there, Grandma Letty could probably help these people find somewhere more long term to hide out. And Tarah and I…well, we'd figure it all out then too. Maybe she and I could go to the west coast. I'd always wanted to see California's beaches, maybe learn to do a little surfing in the sun. And Tarah in a bikini would be a sight worth seeing several times over.

As I drove, my right hand began to ache. I switched hands on the wheel, flexing my cramped fingers.

"Nervous?" Steve suddenly asked.

I started to shake my head then shrugged instead. "Yeah, I guess so. A lot of people need this to work."

"I'm glad you realize that. Leading a big group of families like this would be a tough responsibility even for an adult under normal circumstances." He leaned back in the corner against the door and stared at me.

What was with the "even for an adult" crap? I was eighteen, not eight.

"Yeah, well, I'm not really leading anybody here. Y'all are just following me to my grandma's."

"That's not the impression everyone else has. They all seem to think you're some big shot master wizard here to save the day."

How was I supposed to control what others thought? "I never made anyone any promises."

"Your girlfriend did, though."

"Tarah's—" I started to say she wasn't my girlfriend then gave up explaining. "I don't know exactly what she told you. All I know is Tarah and I are headed to South Dakota, you guys are following us, and we need a rental bus to get everyone there safely without getting caught. You know, I don't want to go to prison any more than you do."

"You mean back to prison," he said.

"Right."

"Except *you've* never actually been in prison. You would never end up in a place like that, 'cause your daddy wouldn't allow it, would he?"

What was with this guy? Was he determined to tick me off or what? Just because it was along the same lines as what I'd told Tarah didn't mean I liked how it sounded coming out of this guy's mouth.

My silence only seemed to goad him on. "I guess this all seems like a big adventure to you, don't it, rich boy?"

I worked on breathing deep through my nose and

resisting the urge to lean across the seat to punch him.

"Fact is, if you got caught right now, all they'd do is ship you back home to your mansion on a hill. While the rest of us would get thrown right back into another interment camp and doped up out of our minds again. Or shot."

Finally I'd had enough. "What is your problem? I'm trying to help you and your family and everyone else's. You're right, I don't have to be here, and I don't have to try to help. But I am. So why are you giving me grief about it? You should be thanking me."

"Because I don't like you and I don't trust you. I don't like what you stand for, what your whole family stands for, getting rich off the imprisonment and mistreatment of others who don't have your connections or money. And most of all, I don't want your help."

"Then why'd you come? You didn't have to come with me to get the bus. You volunteered, remember?"

"I'm only doing this to ensure you don't screw this up. Believe me, if I could afford to rent the bus on my own, I would. The only reason you're here and I'm not doing this on my own is 'cause of your money."

"I don't have money. My mother does. There's a difference. Maybe I should just give you some. Then you can get your family some bus tickets—"

"So then you can make me look even worse in front of my wife and kid? I don't think so."

I took another deep breath, but it burned in my chest. "What do you want from me?"

"I want you to stop being a kid, to realize what you're doing here. For you to take responsibility for your decisions and your actions. I want you to grow up and see that you're holding a whole lot of lives in your hands right now."

I snorted. "You think I need you to point that out to me? I already know if I don't help you guys, you're going to screw this up just like you almost screwed up everything with your stupid decisions at the gas station. What were you thinking, killing that cop? And then you wanted to kill the gas station attendant too? He was just some kid working the wrong shift on the wrong day. But you wouldn't have any problem killing him anyway, would you?"

"Not if it meant protecting my family. I'd kill a thousand cops and gas station workers if it meant keeping Pamela and Cassie safe," he muttered, staring out the passenger side window. "Including anyone who gets in our way of renting this bus."

"You're not going to kill anyone else on this trip, Steve. Not if you want to keep tagging along with our group. Every person you kill just brings more heat on the rest of us. We've got hours to go till we get to Sioux Falls. We don't need even more people trying to hunt us down along the way."

"Oh yeah? And if I do take out someone else, what you are going to do about it? You going to try and take me down like you did those guards at that camp last night? Or how about all those people you killed last summer?" His face twisted into a sneer. "You think it's fine for you to judge me, but you're not so spotless yourself, are you? Or did you think only your town's outcasts had heard about that?"

My throat knotted, forcing me to swallow hard.

Again I heard the shouting from that night, saw the blue and red flashes lighting up the woods, heard Damon yelling out my name for help followed by his last words. *Run, Hayden!*

And then I'd lost control, my fear twisting my willpower as it exploded out of my control, killing him and everyone else and nearly myself too, the whole world turning into shades of gray and navy and black. And then it seemed like only seconds later I was waking up in the hospital...

"You and I aren't so different," Steve went on, his words yanking me back to the present. "We do whatever it takes to survive. And that's exactly what we're going to do now. I'll try to keep things cool as long as I can. But if it comes down to using force in order to get a bus, then that's what I'm going to do. And I hope you'll be smart enough to either help or stay out of my way. Understood?"

Oh yeah, I heard him loud and clear.

But I still wasn't going to let him kill anyone else on this trip, no matter what it took. I had enough names and faces on my conscience to deal with when I looked in a mirror as it was. No way was I going to let him add another death onto the list.

The GPS broke that train of thought, the female voice directing me to turn off the interstate at the next exit. I took the turn a little too fast and had to force my foot to ease up on the gas pedal. Having a wreck was the last thing we needed.

We headed down the town's main street in silence, the GPS's instructions the only sound now as we took the last two turns then pulled into the bus rental company's pitted gravel and dirt parking lot. Only one beat up old truck sat at the front of the small main building. But at least four or five buses of different types formed a hulking row behind the building under a tall, open ended metal shed, and the main building's lights were still on.

"All right, give me your ID," Steve muttered after we parked near the building's front door.

Adrenaline pumping, I dug out my wallet from my back pocket and gave him my driver's license. He stared at it for a moment, tilting it so the parking lot light shown down on it through the windshield. He pressed it between his hands, closed his eyes, and began to mumble something I couldn't quite make out.

I waited for some sort of sensation to hit me. But I

didn't feel anything at all. After a moment, he handed me the ID.

Before I could look at it, he raised a flat hand in front of my face, his jaw set with determination, and started mumbling again. I braced myself for pain, but again I felt nothing. Was he even applying the effect yet?

"How long till—"

"It's done."

I looked in the mirror and swore. I looked like my dad minus the gray hair and crows feet. Steve was a borderline sociopath, but I had to admit at least to myself that the guy had skills. "Can you do this to anyone?"

"Anyone who lets me. Or has a weak will to start with." He opened his door and got out. "Now hurry up and let's get this done before it wears off."

Yeah, that made me feel real confident.

CHAPTER 11

A bell dinged over the door as we entered the office. The man behind the counter looked up, his eyes squinting. The fluorescent lighting was just bright enough to show white sprinkled throughout his whiskers and the few hairs combed over his head. A maze of wrinkles cut through his still partly tanned face. He looked like he should be wearing overalls and riding a tractor under a hot sun instead of working at a bus rental.

He nodded hello, then asked, "What can I do for you?"

I started to open my mouth, but Steve cut me off, stepping around me and up to the counter with a swagger I hadn't noticed before. When he spoke, his strangely heavy new drawl nearly made me stare at him.

"Well, now, we heard you maybe had a bus we could rent. It's for our church group. We figured, seeing as how it's nearly Christmas, we'd all get together and take a little trip up north."

We should have worked out our story together ahead of time. I worked to keep my face still.

"Is that right?" He stared at Steve, then me, then Steve again, squinting so hard I couldn't see his eyes beneath the bunched up skin anymore. "You say you're headed up north? Whereabouts?"

"South Dakota. We've got a sister church up there we're wanting to visit."

I worked not to flinch. Steve was taking a risk telling this guy even that much. What if the feds somehow traced our path to this man and asked him what we'd said?

"Huh." He rubbed a gnarled and weathered hand over his gut in thought. "You need a school bus or a charter?"

"Charter if you've got one available." Steve never missed a beat with his answers. I had to give it to him, he was good. "We've got a few little ones wanting to come along. So we're hoping to keep things as comfortable for them as we can."

The man nodded slowly. "Yeah, I might have a charter available. When'd you need it?"

Here was the only time Steve paused. He gave a sheepish smile and rubbed a hand over one cheek. "Well, to be real honest, we're kind of in a bind here. See, we're actually from out of town. We were already headed on our trip, and our church bus broke down. So we're needing some new transportation real quick if we can find some."

At this, the old man frowned. "You've got little ones stranded out in this?" He jerked a thumb at the windows, as if a blizzard were raging outside.

"Yes sir," Steve replied. "So you see why we're kind of in a hurry. I mean, I suppose we could just send everyone home and try again in a few weeks when our bus is repaired. But everyone was sure looking forward to this trip…"

Oh man, Steve was good. Even my own mother, the queen of guilt trips, couldn't have pulled one off as well as this.

Just how much did Steve practice lying to people?

The proprietor grunted. Then he looked at me again.

"And who might you be?"

"Church treasurer." The words just rolled out of my mouth. Maybe Steve was contagious.

"I've got a charter we can set you up with." He reached under the counter and brought out a clipboard. "Treasurer, if you're the one with the money then you've got to fill out this form. How long are y'all going to need it for?" He looked to Steve again for the answer while I tried to confidently step up to the counter and start filling out the form.

"Oh, maybe a week or two? We've got some pretty chatty ladies in our bunch that are going to want plenty of time for visiting and picture taking and all that."

The old man nodded. "Yeah, I've got a sister-in-law the same way. Always talking and taking endless pictures for that scrapbooking stuff. Got herself a whole club of women who get together for it. Drives my brother crazy."

Steve grinned. "Yeah, our church ladies got a scrapbooking club of their own. Meets every Tuesday night like clockwork."

"Hey, you're at least twenty-five, right?"

It took me a second to realize the old man was talking to me. I looked up. "Yes sir."

"I'm going to need to make a copy of your ID for insurance purposes," he said.

Dutifully I pulled out my wallet, praying my hand wouldn't shake as I handed over the hopefully still altered license.

He held it up to the light and squinted at it for a long minute. Then he reached into his shirt pocket and pulled out some bifocals. Without putting them on or unfolding them, he held the glasses near his face and peered through them at the ID. My heart raced faster with every passing second.

Finally, he shuffled over to an antique looking copier

machine and made a copy.

I let the air out of my lungs slow and easy through my nose and finished filling out the forms.

He handed me back my ID, looked over the form, then said, "Now who's your driver going to be?"

"Uh…" I hesitated.

"I've got to put down their name for the insurance," he added. "And they'll have to come in and we'll need a copy of their CDL. It's federal law."

I glanced at Steve, wondering how he planned to solve this one. Another driver's license makeover spell? And if it worked, then what? Could Steve even drive a bus?

Before Steve could answer, I jumped in. "Well, Steve here has a CDL. But it's a pretty long drive, and it'd be nice if we could find someone else to drive us instead. You know, so Steve could relax and see the sights with everyone else. You know any qualified drivers we could maybe hire?"

The old man's bushy eyebrows shot up. "Well, my brother John could. But he's an idiot, and I'm not too keen on trusting him with one of my charters that far away. Especially for a couple of weeks."

"I'm sure I can handle—" Steve said.

"What about yourself?" I said to the bus owner, ignoring the quick glare Steve shot me. His look seemed to ask whether I knew what I was doing here. Unfortunately the answer to that was no, I had no clue. I should have shut up and let him continue with the lies. But for some reason I was acting on a hunch. Tarah would probably be proud, what with all her beliefs in listening to emotions and instincts.

Both men stared at me.

"I was just thinking if you drove us, you could personally ensure your bus was safe at all times."

Silence. I could hear each of our breaths, mine a little too quick but hopefully too quiet for elderly ears to hear,

Steve's slower, more deliberate, the old man's shallow with just a hint of a wheeze at the end.

The bus owner rocked back on his heels and rubbed his gut beneath the silver snap buttons of his white and brown plaid shirt. "Well, now, that's an intriguing idea. John could watch the shop, it's the dead season anyways, ain't nobody renting right now. And I would like to do some traveling and sight seeing."

"Aw, I don't know if it'd be right, taking you away from your family right before Christmas," Steve said, his words nice and slow. But a certain tightness around his eyes gave him away at least to me. He didn't want a normal, as Tarah called them, joining our outcast group.

But he could get over it. We needed someone who could actually get everyone to South Dakota safely. And legally.

The old man's shoulders lifted and fell. "Only folks I see Christmas Day are John and his wife. And frankly getting out and about on a working vacation would be a real treat." He hooked his thumbs in the front pockets of his stained, worn out jeans. "After working out in the fields most of the year, spending winter all cooped up in this place gets to choking on you after awhile."

"Well, alright then," I said with a smile of relief. "You mind adding on your driver's fee to whatever we owe you, and putting it on this?" I held out Mom's card.

He took the card but didn't look at it. "I haven't said what that fee would be yet."

"I know. But I've got a good feeling about you. You seem the type of man who'll do right by us. So you go on and put what you feel is fair for a charter with a restroom on it and your time. And of course we'll cover your food and hotel expenses on the trip too."

I must have surprised him, because his eyebrows shot up. "Well, that's real good of you, boy. My name's Bud

Preston, by the way." He held out his hand.

My insides tried to catch a little as I told him my real name. Would he recognize the connection to my father? But he didn't hesitate as he shook my hand. I'd learned lately that Dad had been wrong about a lot of things over the years. But right then I hoped he had at least one thing right, that you really could judge a man by the way he shook your hand. If so, then my instincts about this guy were also correct. Bud's grip was firm despite his years, with none of those power plays of using his free hand to cage mine or grip my arm or shoulder like my father did to voters around election time. Bud's handshake said he was a simple, honest, strong man, the calluses promising he was also a hard worker.

We'd all have to hope his handshake didn't lie.

"Well, let's get this show on the road then!" Bud said, cracking his first smile yet. It transformed him, lighting up his eyes.

Tarah would probably like him a lot.

"What do you say we meet up over in Clemens?" I suggested, naming the neighboring town our group was waiting in. "Our group's in the Wal-mart parking lot behind the bookstore, if you know where it is?"

He nodded. "Yeah, that sounds real good. Give me, say, forty-five minutes. I'll get the ole girl warmed up and gassed up, give her a good check up and all that. Maybe run by my house, call my brother and grab some clothes and a razor."

"If you need longer—" I started to say, sweat sliding down my back at the thought that he might agree.

He waved me off. "Naw, old man like me, I don't need much for a trip. Besides, we got to get those young ones warm and back on the road."

"Alright, see you there." Still smiling, I headed out the building, jumping into the truck with more hope than I'd felt in a long time. Maybe Tarah was right about this positive thinking stuff after all.

Steve wasn't quite as optimistic, judging by the way he slammed the truck door shut after climbing inside.

As we headed back to our group in the festering silence, I wondered if Steve would continue to hold his tongue or let it all out. Minutes later, I had my answer.

"I guess it was just too much of me to ask you not to make any stupid mistakes back there, huh?"

I counted to five before replying nice and slow. "Something on your mind?"

"Yeah. Your stupidity. Do you want to get us all killed?"

"We need to get there safely. Or do you really have a CDL and know how to drive a bus after all?"

"I could've figured it out." His tone was sullen.

"Before or after causing a wreck? Besides, why break the law if we don't have to?"

"How do you know he won't learn the truth and run off to the authorities the first chance he gets?"

"Like I said, it's a necessary risk. We need him to get us there safely and legally. I'll make sure to pay him more than enough to keep him quiet."

Silence.

As we turned off the interstate and headed back into town, he muttered, "Just so you know, if that bus driver finds out the truth and turns us all in, I'll be holding you one hundred percent responsible."

"Yeah, you and everybody else," I muttered.

I eased the truck into the bookstore parking lot and around the building to the back. And got another sucker punch to the gut that robbed me of the ability to breathe.

The military trucks were gone.

Steve cursed loudly.

"Don't panic," I said, more to myself than him. "Maybe they had to move the trucks somewhere out of sight nearby."

We cruised around the store, even checking the nearby Wal-Mart parking area and the neighboring gas stations. No military trucks anywhere.

"Do you think..." His voice trailed off, like he couldn't stand to even finish the idea. My mind finished it for him, dark possibilities instantly exploding into life fueled by what I'd seen with my own eyes in the last two days. What if they were hauled off by the police? What if...

No. They had to be around here somewhere, or at least had left behind some kind of clue or something to let me know what had happened to them. Tarah would have made sure of it. She would have trusted that I would try to find her.

I turned around in the Wal-Mart parking lot and headed back towards the bookstore again.

"What are you doing? They're not here!" Steve was definitely panicking now, both hands buried in his hair as he bent over and braced his elbows on his knees.

I didn't say anything as I slowed the truck to a crawl.

Suddenly, it was as if an invisibility curtain parted behind the bookstore, revealing Tarah's disembodied head then her floating hand as she cheerfully waved to us from several feet up in the air. What the...?

Steve seemed to understand, though, tearing out of the truck before I even had it fully stopped. I followed a few seconds later as soon as I had the truck parked.

"Pamela?" Steve called out.

Pamela's head appeared beside Tarah's.

Steve reached up and hugged his wife as best he could without the ability to see a bumper to climb onto. "God, you scared me!"

Well, at least we could agree on one thing.

Tarah bit her lower lip. "Sorry. There was a sheriff's car that kept passing by out on the street. So we got Mike to do his cloaking spell on the trucks. Pretty good, huh?"

I choked down the insane urge to laugh. "That's an understatement. We thought..." I cleared the knot from my throat. "Never mind." I told her about the latest developments with the bus driver. "I know it's a risk hiring him, but it seemed like a good idea at the time."

Her smile flashed bright, lighting up her eyes. "You followed your instincts?"

"Yeah."

"Then you did the right thing. We'd better warn everyone about keeping our new cover story, though. Especially the kids."

I nodded. "I'm going to move my truck so it doesn't draw attention before Bud gets here." I hadn't even left it in a parking space. It was still in the way of other drivers.

"What's he like?" she asked before I could turn away. "Bud, I mean."

I paused, trying to think of how to describe him. A farmer. An old man. Weathered, lonely and bored. A man I sure hoped I was right about hiring. "I think you'll like him." I turned away, then had to pause again. "We're going to have to ditch these trucks somewhere after we get everyone loaded onto the bus. When you were looking up local bus rentals, did you happen to see—"

She held out a slip of paper with a cheeky grin. "GPS coordinates for the nearest lake. It's supposed to be a deep one too."

I had to smile at that. "You are a mastermind's dream."

"I know. And speaking of which, I had another idea..."

Tarah had suggested we get walkie talkies so I could keep in contact with the bus for the rest of the trip. She also thought at least one of the outcasts would be able to jam Bud's cell phone signal if he tried to call his family and tell them our destination. So while she plotted with her truck's half of the group, I ran back inside the superstore to do a little final shopping, returning with walkie talkies and batteries only minutes before Bud was supposed to arrive.

And that's when I realized just how good Mike's abilities were. Even knowing their approximate location and slowly walking all the way around them, I still couldn't see a single hint of the stolen vehicles. Now that I was on the receiving end of the illusion, I was blown away by the spell's complexity. This had to be way harder than simply gathering your energy into an orb to throw at something or directing the wind or even creating fire on the palm of your hand. What Mike was doing with his mind was directly messing with other minds, making our own eyes lie to us.

"Tarah," I whispered, stopping a couple of feet short so I wouldn't run into the invisible trucks face first and make a fool out of myself.

Her head popped into view. "Is it time?"

I nodded.

She whispered something over her shoulder to her group then climbed down. We worked together with the tailgate till we managed to find and release the catches to lower it. Then we started the process of guiding everyone out of the truck.

"Steve," I hissed in the general direction of the other truck. "Time to get moving."

He peeked out at us, then climbed down and dropped his truck's tailgate. I noticed he only helped his own family down from the cargo area, ignoring the others as they struggled to exit as well. Most of the adult passengers didn't have too much trouble jumping down or else stepping onto the flat metal bumper and then hopping the rest of the way to the ground. But the younger kids and the elderly found the distance to the ground to be too much to manage on their own. Muttering a few choice names for Steve under my breath, I left Tarah and Mike to help their group while I went to assist Steve's.

Once they were outside the trucks, everyone began to shiver as the wind cut through their thin wool blankets and their breath made puffs of fog in the air. Thankfully Bud showed up right on time, so our group didn't have to stand around in the cold for long. As soon as the charter bus pulled into the parking lot and stopped, Steve hurried his family over to it. The rest of the group trailed more slowly after them, with Mike and the trucks' drivers hanging back to maintain the cloaking spell on the trucks till the last possible moment.

The bus's door opened with a hydraulic whoosh, then Bud eased down the stairs. "Ladies and gentlemen, your chariot awaits."

Smiling so the wrinkles in his face turned into folds, he grandly swept out an arm, indicating the group should climb aboard. Steve and his family eagerly took the first seats.

Tarah took a dazed elderly woman's elbow and slowly helped her up onto the bus. As they passed Bud, Tarah paused to tell him, "Thank you so much for helping us out on such short notice."

Bud's leathery cheeks turned pink. "Well, that's alright, little lady." He must have been a John Wayne fan. He sounded just like The Duke.

Tarah and I worked as a team, me on the outside guiding the shell-shocked group onto the bus, while Tarah helped everyone find a seat inside. Most had no trouble getting settled in. However, the mother and child who brought up the last of the group didn't seem so eager to board. It was the catatonic woman, the one who had lost her baby, and her little girl. The child clung to her mother's seemingly unfeeling hand as they stood there, the child's eyes darting from side to side in fear, the mother's eyes open and unseeing.

I bit back a curse. I'd thought for sure the mother would have come around by now and started taking care of her surviving child. From the look in the little girl's eyes, I had to wonder if anyone had even explained to her what was going on.

I squatted down in front of the kid. "Hey, sweetheart. I'm Hayden. What's your name?"

"Kristina." She had a strong lisp. It came out as "Kwithina."

"Nice to meet you, Kristina. Listen, we're all going to go on this bus together because it's nice and warm and comfy. Doesn't that sound much better than riding in the cold?"

Her big brown eyes blinked at me. She didn't respond.

Great. She'd probably been told not to speak to strangers, and her mom wasn't making any move to get on the bus on her own. I could just lead the mother on board and the kid would probably follow. But what if Kristina freaked out from confusion or fear at some point when her mother didn't reassure her? I didn't know much about people in shock, and there was no telling how long it might be before the mother came around. In the meantime, her daughter at least deserved to know she could rely on others in the group to help keep her safe.

"What's your mommy's name?" I asked her.

One tiny shoulder lifted and fell. "Mommy. She doesn't talk anymore. Can she hear me?" Her voice was so quiet I had to strain to hear it under the wind as it whipped around us.

"Yeah, kiddo, she still hears you. She's just kinda sad and doesn't really feel like talking much right now. But if you keep talking to her, I bet that will make her feel better soon." Please, God, make it true.

Kristina nodded solemnly. Straightening her shoulders, she took her mother's hand in both of hers and tugged the woman towards the bus. "Come on, Mommy. Let's get on the warm bus."

Her mother shuffled along behind her, Kristina's blanket dragging up the stairs after them. I followed them onto the bus, picking up the tail end of the grungy fabric and handing it to Tarah at the top of the stairs so the mother wouldn't trip over it. Tarah and I shared a look as the little girl led her mother to a pair of seats near the end of the bus.

"Pamela and some of the other women are taking turns looking out for them," Tarah murmured. "They're making sure they both eat and drink and stay warm."

"Where's the baby?" I'd noticed the woman wasn't carrying the sheet-wrapped bundle anymore.

"The others buried it outside the camp before we left."

I took a deep breath, letting it out slowly. Kristina couldn't be more than four or five. She'd lost her baby brother or sister. And now she was surrounded by strangers and trying to take care of her mother.

Shaking my head, I exited the bus again, feeling the hours of stress starting to pile up on me.

Then I caught Bud still standing on the ground by the open door and frowning after the pair too, the questions clear on his face in the light spilling out from the bus's interior. "They gonna be alright? They sure look shaken up for just a broken down bus."

"She lost a baby recently," I murmured. "I'm hoping being with our group will help bring her out of it."

He sighed and slowly shook his head. "That's a shame. Sure hope the momma pulls out of it. Little girls need their mommas."

"Yeah, I hope so too." I took a deep breath. "Well, that should take care of most of the group. But I've still got a couple of guys who needed to get a few things for the road. They took off a while ago; I've got to go get them and bring them here. Shouldn't take more than a half hour or so to round them up. Will everyone be okay on the bus in the meantime?"

Bud waved a hand. "She's got plenty of gas. We'll just let her idle so they can stay warm while they wait. I just wish I'd gotten those newfangled DVD players installed like John's been suggesting."

I smiled and patted his shoulder. "You're already doing more for them than you realize. And the kids have coloring books to keep them busy for a while. Mostly they'll probably just sleep, though. It's been a rough trip so far." I went to rest my hands on my hips and bumped into something. "Oh yeah, nearly forgot. We've got walkie talkies we can use to communicate. I thought they'd be easier to manage instead of trying to dial buttons on a phone while we drive." I unclipped one from my waistband where I'd attached it earlier while waiting for Bud to show up. "I already put in fresh batteries, so you're good to go for awhile."

He took it with a slow nod. "Good thinking."

I turned towards my truck.

"You're not riding with the others?" Bud asked me.

I silently muttered a curse. Bud's likeability made it way too easy to relax around him and forget the charade we were supposed to be maintaining here. It didn't help that my liking this man also made me hate lying to him.

Tarah saved me as she came down the steps. "Hayden joined us after we'd already gotten started on the trip. The goofball overslept and had to catch up in his own truck. He's been tagging along ever since."

Of course her story would involve my looking like an idiot. I smiled my thanks at her. "All right, I'm off to get the guys. We'll be back in a few." I gave Tarah's ponytail a tug, earning a quick flash of a grin from her in return. "Call me if you need me."

I got back into my truck, waiting until Tarah and Bud were on the bus with the others before I slowly cruised back to the where the truck drivers were waiting. Following the plan, Mike dropped the cloaking spell, leaving the trucks in full view. I was tempted to ask him to put it back on. Driving the trucks to the local lake would be a lot safer if no one could see them. But then I remembered how both Mike and Steve had said their abilities had limited range. Mike probably couldn't even hide both trucks at the same time while we drove them down the road. Better just to get rid of the trucks as quickly as we could versus their suddenly popping into view in front of other drivers and really drawing attention. Or worse, causing a wreck when someone ran into the invisible vehicles.

Also according to plan, we got another guy to replace Steve behind the wheel of one of the trucks. Without Steve's volatile temper around, things went a lot more smoothly. Tarah's researched coordinates and my truck's GPS also made reaching the lake pretty easy. Unfortunately, finding a way through the trees to the water wasn't so simple. Other than driveways to people's lakehouses, the shoreline was surrounded by an unbroken forest that even a golf cart would have had a hard time squeezing through. We had to drive along a dirt road that skirted the lake for ten minutes until we found a break in the trees wide enough for the trucks. Then there was the small matter of how to get the trucks into the water without any of us having to go in with them. None of us knew any spells that would help. Thankfully the trees themselves gave me the idea of wedging branches between the seats and the gas pedals, a crude but effective method.

The other driver was still in his borrowed guard uniform. He shucked off the camo, revealing a blue t-shirt and jeans underneath, and stuffed both his and Steve's uniforms under the trucks' front seats. Then we lined up the stolen vehicles, braced the branches in place, and the drivers jumped out. I had worried that the weight of the trucks would cause them to get stuck in the dirt along the shoreline. But here the winter season proved a benefit for once...the cold and the lack of rain had dried out the bank, turning what would have been a sloppy mud pit into a rock hard path of doom. Their engines roaring, our group's twin monsters of transportation slid right down the short bank and into the water, quickly sinking beneath the black surface. By the time anyone found them, if they ever did, we would be long gone.

We all exchanged a few high fives and fist bumps then jumped into my truck and headed back into town one more time.

While Mike and the drivers joined the others on the bus, I took my time checking the rest of the route to South Dakota on the GPS, making the simple process take longer than it should have. I was stalling, waiting for Tarah. Except I'd never asked her if she wanted to keep riding with me or with the others.

Was she settled into a bus seat, comfortable and ready for the rest of the trip to get underway? I could imagine her all too happy to ride with a whole bunch of outcasts, pelting them with a million questions about spellwork for hours on end. Should I just get going without her?

I waited half a minute, then a full minute, the silence of my truck's now empty cab expanding and pressing down on me so the drumming of my fingers on the steering wheel seemed as loud as a rock band gearing up for a concert. I turned on the radio, tried to find a station I liked, then turned it off again.

She wasn't coming. I'd be finishing the trip alone.

I reached for the gear shift.

Tarah came flying out of the bus and around to my window.

"Hey," she said after I rolled down the window. "Sorry, I was helping Kristina learn how to use the bus's restroom." She looked down at my hand on the gear shift. "Were you going to leave without me?"

I shrugged. "I thought maybe you'd prefer to ride with the others. Learn all their secret Clann ways, or whatever."

"Um, yeah, eventually I'd like to. But I figure there's plenty of time for that in South Dakota. Once we get there, though, we might not get another chance for just you and me to hang out together." She hesitated. "I mean, if you *want* to hang out, that is. If you'd rather be alone, I totally understand."

I jerked my head towards the passenger door, the combination of my relief and her cute awkwardness making it impossible not to smile. "Get in."

She flashed a grin at me then ran around the front of my truck. While she hopped in on the passenger side and buckled her seatbelt, I let Bud know we were ready on the walkie talkie. Then we took off, back on the road to South Dakota with only a few more hours to go till we reached the safety of Sioux Falls. And for the first time, I felt really hopeful that maybe, just maybe, this crazy, unplanned journey might not end in disaster.

The next hour was the best I'd known in too long.

Tarah had a way of making me forget the world racing by outside the few feet of space inside my truck. I'd always loved this truck. But Tarah made me love it even more with the way she stretched her legs out across the seat or propped her ankles up on the dash. She made me laugh at the way she liked to play with the CD changer, making her nosy and opinionated way through my eclectic music collection. She made me smile at how she insisted on reading more spells to me from my new magic book, but only in the right order, using a penlight she found in the backseat.

It had been so long since I'd really laughed or even wanted to. But Tarah made it feel easy and natural again.

And then, with one push of a button, that too short moment of peace was shattered.

CHAPTER 12

Tarah

"Hayden, we've got to pull over," Bud barked through the walkie talkie, making me flinch. "That little girl you were talking to earlier...something's wrong with her. I'm trying to call 911, but my phone's got no signal."

Kristina.

"Pulling over now," Hayden replied in the walkie talkie as he slowed down and pulled to the side of the road. Thankfully the traffic wasn't too bad here.

Hayden and I both dove out of the truck the moment it was parked and ran to the bus. Bud immediately opened the door.

Hayden vaulted up the steps and down the aisle, joining the crowd that had gathered towards the back. Being tall had its advantages, letting him peer over heads and shoulders, while I had to crane my head and peer through an opening between shoulders to see several hands trying to hold down Kristina's body as she thrashed like a wild animal. Her fluttering eyelids revealed eyes that rolled in every direction.

Then the energy in the air ramped up as the healers closed their eyes and focused.

Under the dim overhead lighting, the bus was dead silent.

"What's wrong with her?" I whispered to Mike at my left.

"I don't know. Nothing happened that I could see," he whispered back, his eyes wide and staring at the little girl. "Everyone was sleeping. Next thing we know, she just started flopping around like that."

"I think she's having a seizure," Pamela muttered without opening her eyes or letting go of Kristina's head. "Give us a minute."

"Hey, anybody got a phone with a signal?" Bud called out as he slowly made his way down the aisle to join us.

"Shh," Pamela hissed.

"They wouldn't get here in time," Hayden told Bud, reaching for a plausible excuse as to why we couldn't call an ambulance.

Grumbling, Bud tried punching buttons on his phone again anyways.

In those long, surreal minutes, I looked around me, remembering what Jeremy always said. *It's the details, Tarah,* he said over and over. *They're the only way to keep yourself grounded. When everything around you goes insane and you can't get your bearings, open your eyes and ears and look for the details. They'll help you know the moment is real, that what you are seeing, smelling, feeling, hearing, living is real. And then, only then, will you be able to catch your breath and think again and remember that it's just a moment in time and someday you'll write about it and that moment will become a story the entire world can share.*

The bus smelled of peanuts and strawberry jelly, dirt and unwashed bodies, the subtler scent of the baby wipes the outcasts had tried to clean up with, and the stronger, sharper assault of disinfecting wipes Bud must have used to wipe down the seats before our group boarded his bus. The bus seemed so quiet at first till the pounding of my own heartbeat faded from my ears and I could hear everything else again...Kristina's whimpers and grunts and the rustling of her clothes and the thuds of her sneakers as she thrashed and occasionally made contact with a seat.

Hands reached out to try and hold Kristina's limbs still.

"No, don't hold her down," Pamela said. "You'll hurt her."

It seemed way too warm in here, the air stifling to breathe. Should we open some windows to help Kristina breathe easier?

I looked around for the nearest window to see if they could even be opened and found Hayden standing there, and I couldn't look away from him. He was staring at the little girl and the group of healers around her, his eyebrows drawn, fists clenched at his side, his entire body rigid. Watching so intently, like all the others. But not like the others.

Some of the men's faces were resigned, waiting for more death and destruction to come into their world. Only a few of them held any hope still. They had learned the hard way that keeping bad things from their loved ones was no longer within their control.

The women's and children's expressions were more openly afraid.

But none of them, including Hayden, feared themselves. Not this time.

They cared about Kristina. And so did Hayden, but in a different way.

Unlike the others, he wasn't just watching. He was assessing the situation, his body weight balanced on the balls of his feet as if ready to spring into action and only waiting for his mind to make a decision on what to do. His hands were still clenched into unyielding fists, his jaw muscles knotting and relaxing, knotting and relaxing. He was upset, almost as if he wasn't just wanting to fix this newest problem but *needed* to because…

Because…

Because he felt *responsible* for these people.

And then I understood. I understood why he'd never wanted to do the prison break in the first place, and why he didn't want to talk about what happened with Damon, why he'd seemed not just freaked out but guilty too after the police officer's death at the gas station, and why he'd decided to rent this bus and buy all those things for these people.

It was because he was a Shepherd. Because Shepherds always became leaders. It wasn't just in their history. It was trained into them from birth. He'd known that once he helped free these people, they would become his responsibility, his to lead and take care of, regardless of what other plans he might have once had for himself.

The air caught and held in my lungs, and I raised a hand to my mouth as my eyes stung.

What had I done?

Suddenly, Kristina grew still, and I watched her as everyone else did, forgetting to breathe, waiting for some movement, some sound that would tell us she was still alive. Some sign that everything could still be okay.

Long seconds ticked by. Then a minute.

"Pamela?" I murmured, not wanting to distract her or the other healers who had laid their hands on Kristina's limbs and temples.

Pamela didn't move, her eyes still closed, a slight frown of concentration telling us nothing as she slowly slid her palms from the sides of Kristina's head to the back of the little girl's skull. Kristina's eyes rolled in their sockets, unseeing, each blink too slow in coming.

Finally Pamela opened her eyes. "She's going to be okay.

She's just epileptic."

A collective sigh whispered through the bus.

"I know what you're doing here," Bud said.

Beside me, Hayden jerked once then froze, his gaze dropping down and to the side in Bud's direction. He winced, and I knew instinctively what he must be thinking. He was hoping Bud wouldn't say anything else, that Bud wouldn't become a problem. That Hayden wouldn't have to do something about that problem. Because, like me, Hayden liked this old man. It was why he'd risked hiring him to be our driver in the first place. He wanted to trust that there were others like me in the world, normals who wouldn't join the rest of the world in turning against him and his kind.

But these people on this bus had become his, for better or worse. And if necessary, he would do what he must to protect them.

"Why don't we move closer to the door?" Hayden said, keeping his voice low as he led them both up the aisle towards the front of the bus as if to avoid disturbing the recovering child.

I half turned towards them so I could listen and watch them out of the corner of my eye. And pray with every ounce of willpower within me that Bud would say and do the right thing.

Please. Please don't make Hayden do something he doesn't want to do here.

At the steps, Hayden stopped and turned to face Bud, his neck and shoulders stiff.

"That was a prayer circle, wasn't it?" Bud blurted out, and I nearly dropped to my knees with relief.

Hayden's eyebrows shot up as his eyes darted from side to side, studying Bud for understanding.

"I've seen them before," Bud continued. "Some call it laying hands on a person, healing hands, healing circles.

Things like that."

"Yeah, I guess that's what you'd call it," Hayden said, his tone neutral. "Is that a problem?"

"Oh, don't you worry," Bud said with a firm nod. "I understand completely. Churches don't do them too often nowadays, what with all this anti-Clann craziness going on. Gives some people the wrong idea." He crossed his arms over his chest and leaned against the side of the driver's seat. "I can keep my mouth shut about it."

"I appreciate that, Bud." Relief added the tiniest hint of a sigh to Hayden's voice. "These are good people here. They were just trying to save a little girl's life."

I heard Pamela murmur to the others and risked joining Bud and Hayden. "Um, Hayden?"

"It's all right." Hayden's smile was sincere, warming his eyes though it couldn't erase the tiredness from around them. "Bud knows all about prayer circles. And he's promised not to mention anything about it to anyone. You know, so no one gets the wrong idea about us."

I turned to smile at Bud. "Thank you. Pamela says Kristina's going to be okay. She just needs some rest and quiet."

"Why don't Pamela and Kristina ride with us?" Hayden suggested. "That way Kristina could stretch out in the backseat. We could keep things a lot quieter for her there. And Pamela could be there in case she has another seizure."

"That's a good idea. I'll ask Pamela." I turned and made my way down the aisle, having to wait a few times for the others to get back in their seats and clear the path. Behind me, I sensed Hayden following.

Kristina now lay half draped across Pamela's lap and the neighboring seat, which was too short, forcing Kristina's legs to hang over the edge. Her little body was twisted awkwardly.

Pamela immediately agreed to the idea. But her husband wasn't happy about it.

"What about our little girl?" Steve hissed. "Cassie needs her mother too."

Pamela's eyes widened then narrowed. "She'll be with her father, of course. And it's only for a few hours."

Hayden surprised me, ignoring the little marital tiff completely as he eased past me and bent down to carefully gather Kristina into his arms. Pamela gave her daughter a quick kiss on the top of her sleepy head, then followed us out of the bus and into the truck. We got Kristina settled in the backseat and were still trying to decide where Pamela should sit when Hayden took off without a word back towards the bus.

Pamela looked at me with eyebrows raised. I shrugged. I might know Hayden well enough to read his body behavior and facial expressions in general. But I wasn't a mind reader.

"Maybe I should sit with Kristina," Pamela muttered, rubbing her upper arms through the sleeves of her sweatshirt as she studied the sleeping child. "She's going to be out of it for hours. She might need someone to keep her from rolling off the seat."

"I could move some stuff out of the way for your feet." We'd already pushed the pile of books and hoodies, CDs and laptop and duffle bag onto the floor. But I thought I might be able to condense it all into a pile at one end of the floorboard with a few good shoves.

I was just finishing exactly that while marveling at how messy some guys could be, when Pamela tapped my shoulder. "Um, Tarah? Hayden's coming."

I straightened up, turned my head to look, and my jaw dropped. Hayden was helping Kristina's mother off the bus.

Again, I felt my eyes burn and fill with tears as the two

slowly made their way over to the truck, Hayden guiding her by her elbow but letting her move as slowly as she needed to despite the group's need to get to South Dakota. Again and again, he continued to amaze me. How had he known Kristina should have her mother with her? Most guys would never even think of this, much less go to such effort to see the right thing done.

Pamela and I stood there in teary silence until they reached us. Then we jumped into action again, Pamela helping the mother into the backseat while I leaned over the seat and held up Kristina's head for her mother to get settled in beneath. Once Kristina's head rested in her mother's lap, Hayden unfolded one of three blankets he'd also brought from the bus and covered Kristina with it. The second blanket he draped over the mother, repositioning Kristina's head on top of it. The third blanket he rolled up and used as extra padding between the mother's head and neck and the unyielding head rest.

"I think I'd better ride in front with you guys," Pamela murmured as we watched Hayden ease the back door shut beside the mother. "If they need me, I'll just lean over the seat to help them."

I nodded, and we both walked quickly around the truck. Pamela waited for me to get in first, and it was only as I climbed in that I realized I would be sitting right beside Hayden now. I tried not to react but could feel my cheeks growing warm as I put on my seatbelt. Then Hayden got in, his thigh brushing my hand on the seat. I jumped, mumbled an apology and clasped my hands out of the way in my lap, looking everywhere but at him.

What was wrong with me? Just because Hayden had grown up and become a total hottie didn't change who he was. This was my long time best friend here. Just because I'd always secretly imagined us becoming more didn't mean Hayden thought of me as anything other than a friend. And besides, how could I possibly still be wishing for more when we'd only just repaired our friendship?

Thankfully he didn't seem to notice my awkwardness as he checked that Pamela and I were both ready before he started the engine. A quick confirmation on the walkie talkie with Bud to be sure the bus was ready to get going again, and then we were on our way once more.

Only this time I couldn't seem to relax no matter how much I told my muscles to. Every cell in my body kept alternating between a crazy, wild joy at our physical closeness, followed immediately by a terrible longing for more. My left hand itched to slide over from my lap onto his thigh so I could feel the muscles bunching and relaxing beneath that worn denim as the traffic forced him to ignore the cruise control button and manually speed up then slow down. Every bump in the road that caused my shoulder to nudge against his made me yearn to nestle more fully against his side and rest my head on that shoulder's hard muscles, muscles I had watched in action from a distance way too many times at countless basketball games over the years.

Being this close to him was both wonderful and torture all at the same time.

But at least some of the truck's passengers had no problem with the new arrangement. Some combination of stress and maybe the act of healing too had worn Pamela out. She started softly snoring in seconds. I couldn't see Kristina's mother to see if she was sleeping too.

"If you get sleepy, feel free to take a nap if you want," Hayden murmured suddenly, making me jump.

But there was no headrest for the center of the seat. My only pillow would have to be the top of the seat itself, and resting my head on it would only result in a bad crick in my neck. "It's okay. I'll just wait till we get to your grandma's."

One thick eyebrow rose. "If you need a headrest, my

right shoulder's not hurt, you know."

"Oh. Right. Thanks." I swallowed hard.

"You okay?" He glancing at me with a frown.

"Uh, sure, why wouldn't I be?" My smile felt stupid and overly bright even to me. I was acting like an idiot.

It's just Hayden, I reminded myself.

To prove to myself that everything was normal between us, I tilted my head to the left, resting it against the hard curve of his shoulder. A sigh slipped out through my nose, and my face burned again.

"Tired?" he asked.

I nodded, not trusting how my voice might sound if I tried to speak right now.

"Then sleep, Tarah." He sounded like he was trying not to laugh. "I promise I'll wake you up if anything worth reporting happens."

I smiled. "Okay." I hesitated, my smile fading, then had to say it. "Hayden, for what it's worth…I'm sorry I got you involved in all of this."

Silence for a long minute. "Don't worry about it. It was worth it."

I closed my eyes, and the need for sleep won.

When I woke up some time later, I could practically hear Hayden's thoughts churning.

"What are you thinking about?" I mumbled, comfy and warm, unwilling to move yet wanting to hear his reassuring voice for awhile.

He hesitated before replying, "When did you wake up?"

"Just now. You didn't answer my question."

He hesitated again, and the fog of sleep slipped further away from the edges of my mind. Now I really wanted to know what was going on inside that head of his.

"You. I was thinking about you." His voice sounded

gruff. Embarrassed?

"Oh?" I smiled, glad he probably couldn't see my face right now since I was still leaning against his shoulder.

"Yeah, I was just wondering if..."

"Mmm?"

"If you...still sleep with stuffed animals. You know, since you're using me like a giant teddy bear here." Definite humor in his voice now.

I glanced down and realized I'd wrapped my right arm across his waist at some point in my sleep.

I sat up straight. "Sorry!"

He chuckled. "It's all right. Actually, it was kind of nice. Made me feel all soft and squishy, and a little furry too..."

I lightly swatted his arm, grinning in embarrassment. "Yeah, yeah, enough with the Teddy jokes. I haven't slept with him in years." This was what I got for oversharing with Hayden when we were kids. He would never let me live it down now.

"Well, since you're up now, Sleeping Beauty, why don't you take a look outside?"

The weather must have gotten even colder the further north we'd traveled, because white flakes began to fall. Growing up in East Texas, we saw snow maybe once or twice a year at best.

"It's snowing!" It was hard to keep my voice down, especially with the way the flakes were pelting the windshield as we drove straight into the wind. "Oh wow, that is beautiful. Look how huge those flakes are. They look like chicken feathers."

Hayden's left hand jerked on the wheel, and I felt the back end of the truck get squirrelly. His whole body tensed up as he grabbed the wheel with both hands and hissed out a curse. The truck righted itself as he let off of the gas a little.

"Sorry. Road's getting slick," he muttered. "Better warn

Bud. We'll have to slow down till the roads clear up."

If they cleared up. After all, we were headed almost straight north in December. The weather and the roads might both get worse from here on out.

I grabbed the walkie talkie and warned Bud.

"Can you also check to be sure they're all belted in back there?" he asked, nodding towards the backseat.

"Sure." Twisting, I leaned over the seat to help get Kristina and her mother belted in.

Beside me, Pamela stirred, yawned then frowned. "What's going on? Is Kristina okay?"

"She's fine," I told her over my shoulder. "Just belting them in since the roads are getting bad."

"Thanks," Hayden told me when I was done. "Don't forget to put your belt back on too."

Twisting back around to face the front again, I followed orders then gave him a snarky salute with a grin to try and keep the tension in the cab down. "Aye aye captain. Copilot secured."

"Are you sassing me?" he said, trying to joke but completely failing to hide the tightness in his tone as the wheel jerked beneath his hands again. He let our speed drop to ten miles under the limit.

The back end of the truck slid sideways again. Hayden whispered another curse then winced as we heard a small voice cry out from the back seat, "Mommy?"

"Shh, honey, it's okay," Pamela murmured, turning to look over the seat at her patient.

But Kristina wasn't soothed. She wanted her mother and fought to sit up despite Pamela's murmured pleas for her to stay down.

"Mommy, I'm scared," Kristina whimpered, wrapping her arms around her mother.

One of her mother's hands drifted up to stroke her daughter's arm. Then the woman began to hum something.

It took me a half minute to recognize the song as "*Somewhere Over the Rainbow*". Kristina must have heard it a lot; she managed to stop crying and stumbled through singing along with her mother.

Hayden glanced at me, his eyes wide as he realized Kristina's mother was finally starting to come out of her zombie-like state. Then he had to refocus on the road as the gathering ice pellets turned the interstate into an endless hockey rink with our too light ended truck trying its hardest to be the puck.

By the time we had to merge onto I-229, Hayden's knuckles had turned white and his jaw muscles had knotted.

Then we spotted the cop cars blocking the road up ahead, their lights flashing.

I swallowed hard, praying Hayden was right about his father not turning him in and tracking us down. If he was wrong and Senator Shepherd had called in the locals to help intercept us...

But before we reached the cops, other lights brightened the night...large, electronic road signs warning that I-229 was closed due to icy conditions and all traffic was to detour onto Minnesota Ave. I sighed in relief as Hayden took the exit I could now see the cops directing everyone towards.

"Can you reroute the GPS and find us a new way to Grandma Letty's?" he said.

I fiddled with the GPS for a minute. "Okay, it looks like we can take 14th Street to Phillips, and then to 10th Street and cut across that way."

But 10th Street was where it got confusing. Just as Hayden was about to take a right onto it, I shrieked, "Stop, it's a one way!"

Hayden hit the brakes, muttering a curse.

From the backseat, we heard, "Ooo, Mommy, he said a

bad word!"

I pressed my lips together to keep from laughing at him.

"Keep going straight," I said.

When the light turned green, Hayden headed straight. "Okay, now what?"

I zoomed out on the map. "Um, just keep going straight. I'm trying to find a place for us to turn around."

So we kept going straight as building after building of rose-colored stone passed by. White Christmas lights wrapped around old fashioned street lamps would have made the drive a nice one, if we weren't lost and tired and hiding from the law. Not to mention the ice pellets still pelting the windshield and making it tough to read the street signs.

"Tarah? Got a new route yet?" Hayden grumbled.

"Working on it," I snapped. "Just keep going straight. There's a place to turn around up ahead."

The buildings ended, and we drove beneath a metal arch. I could barely make out the words "Sioux Falls Park."

The ice pellets stopped falling just as we headed underneath a metal railroad bridge. As the road curved sharply to the left, the view ahead burst into life with countless numbers of Christmas lights.

"Turn right here," I whispered.

We'd reached the waterfalls for which the city had been named.

As we viewed the area, lit up by display after display of animated lights in white and gold and green and red, I suddenly realized. It was almost Christmas.

"Look, Momma," Kristina whispered in the backseat.

I didn't trust myself to speak, afraid my voice would come out all choked up. After everything our group had gone through, the combined sight of the snow-covered grounds all lit up like a winter wonderland, falling away into the icy waterfalls, was almost too much to believe. It was like waking from a too long nightmare into a fantasy fairytale.

"Good detour?" I asked.

"Yeah. Good detour." Hayden returned my smile with one of his own.

Behind us, the bus rocked a little, probably from everyone rushing over to look out the right side windows at the falls.

"Hey, Hayden, everything all right up there?" Bud asked through the walkie talkie.

"Yeah," Hayden said, clearing his throat as his voice came out in a croak. "Don't let anyone out. We won't be here long enough for that. We're just turning around. But let's give them a couple more minutes."

Hayden reclipped the walkie talkie onto his belt then leaned back, staring out the windows at the sight before us. Without looking at me, his hand slid over to hold mine. Surprised at the gesture and a little confused by it too, I wanted to look down at our hands laced together on my thigh but was afraid doing so might break the moment. So I simply squeezed his hand and kept staring at the color changing lights that turned the ice draped waterfalls red then green then blue, grateful to be here in this moment with him.

Something tightened so hard in my chest that it was almost a struggle to breathe. I wanted to memorize every detail of this moment so I would never forget it. I tried to remember what Jeremy had said about using all five senses so I could be a good reporter. But all I could see was the surreal beauty of the winter wonderland, and all I could feel was that strong hand, so large compared to my own, heating up my skin everywhere we made contact.

After another few minutes, Hayden sighed, eased his hand from mine and reached for the walkie talkie again. "Okay, Bud, let's get going."

CHAPTER 13

Hayden

Twenty minutes later, we pulled into Grandma Letty's driveway. Her house, a huge Victorian situated on a hilltop at the end of a winding dirt and gravel road, was a welcome sight. The driveway ended in a cement pad in front of a three car garage, giving Bud plenty of room to park the bus beside my truck. Slowly, with stiff movements of obvious soreness or fear or both, everyone got off the bus and gathered on the wraparound porch.

I rang the doorbell with no idea what to expect. The last time I'd seen my father's mother was at Damon's funeral, and even then she hadn't stayed long. Since he had become a senator, my father apparently hadn't wanted anyone to know about his witch of a mother, though I used to think it was because she was a little too blunt to be politically correct. Contact with her had consisted of only a few cards each year on the holidays.

The door opened to reveal a stooped over old woman in brown slacks and a pink and brown polka dotted blouse with a floppy bow at the neck. Her body seemed frail, but her gaze was still as sharp as I'd remembered it beneath that same perfectly poufed salt and pepper helmet hair.

"Hi, Grandma," I said. "Uh, I hope you were telling Tarah the truth about having room for about fifty people 'cause...here we are."

Her papery cheeks bunched into a big smile as she stepped forward to grab my shoulder. "Hayden Shepherd. My lord, you've grown tall! Come here and give your grandma a hug." She tugged me down to her height with a grip that was none too shabby. I awkwardly patted her back, afraid I'd break her bones if I patted too hard.

"Is this Tarah?" she said, turning to her. "Yep, just as pretty as I pictured you from your voice on the phone. But my lord it's cold out here! Come inside, please, everyone come on in."

She led us all inside, where the group sort of spilled across the adjoining living and dining rooms, growing noisy as Grandma Letty insisted on make refreshments in the kitchen and Pamela, Tarah and a few other weary women helped her. I joined them, needing to warn my grandmother about the bus driver and our church group cover story. I spoke to her in as low a voice as I could, praying she wasn't deaf since the living room, only yards away from the open kitchen area, was closed off by only an L-shaped wall with large arched doorways leading to the kitchen and dining rooms.

"I've got just the thing for him." With a wink, she grabbed a tiny bottle from a nearby cabinet, poured a healthy dose of it into one of the hot chocolates the ladies were fixing trays of, and told Pamela to be sure the bus driver got *that* drink. Nodding, Pamela took the tray of drinks into the living room.

"Grandma, we don't want to kill—" I started to say, but she shushed me.

"A potion of sleepy time herbs, completely harmless.

From the looks of this group you've brought me, a few more could do with a dose of it too." Her thin lips pressed themselves temporarily out of existence.

"They've been through a lot," I agreed, the memory of the dying cop flashing through my mind. "Right now, they probably just want somewhere safe to stretch out and sleep for a while."

"Let's get them squared away then," she suggested. "You can fill me in on it all later."

I followed her to the living room, where Bud was already asleep sitting upright in a green wingback chair by the crackling fireplace, despite the noise of the exhausted adults trying to corral their equally fussy kids. The adults who weren't busy trying to calm down kids were nodding off where they sat or stood leaning against door jambs wherever they could. It was a lot of people to cram into this house, but Grandma Letty managed them like a general, working with the few remaining conscious parents to get whole families set up in the rooms upstairs or on pallets in the living and dining rooms.

Forty-five minutes later, the house was quiet and dim except for the occasional opening and closing of a bathroom door. Tarah had shyly asked if she could take a shower, and Grandma Letty had sent her off to the master suite upstairs before nudging me over to a barstool at the kitchen island. Grandma Letty took a stool opposite me, and I finally had time to look around. Her kitchen wasn't as big as Mom's, the appliances regular sized instead of the industrial versions Mom preferred, the cabinets older, more traditional and less contemporary. Cozier. I could feel myself sort of melting into the barstool and had to fight the temptation to use the island as a pillow for my head.

"Fifty people tucked in in under an hour," I said, forcing a tired smile. "Even for a grandma, that's got to be some kind of record."

"This was nothing. I had practice. Getting you and your brother to go to sleep when you were little was much harder."

I had a brief memory of her hollering at us to settle down, back when we lived in our old house. I'd forgotten she'd come to stay with us a few times when I was a kid.

"You've sure gotten yourself into it this time," she murmured before taking a sip of chamomile tea. "This is a lot of lives to take responsibility for, Hayden. I mean, I've heard of people creating their own careers, but this isn't a career you're building here, hon. It's a life calling."

Life calling. The words sent actual chill bumps racing down my spine.

I gulped. "This isn't a career *or* a life calling. I just promised I'd get them here safely so they could figure out what to do next."

One gray eyebrow arched. "I see. So your grand plan was to get them through the woods to Grandma's house and then dump them off for me to deal with?"

I scrubbed my hands over my gritty face. "I didn't say I was going to abandon them. I'll help them out if they need it."

I didn't like the way her eyes narrowed at that.

She took a slow sip of tea. "What about that cute girl you were standing so close to on my front porch? Does she have somewhere to go from here?"

I thought about my answer to that one. "Tarah's not really a witch. She can't do magic, though she claims different. So she might be able to go back home with the right help from a lawyer to clear her name. She's only guilty by association."

Both her eyebrows rose. "I see. So she's just tagging along for the fun of it then?"

"Well, it started with her trying to free her dad. He's a scientist who got arrested at a protest while trying to

convince some outcasts to let him test their powers. He got
thrown into an internment camp out in west Texas. But
then she ended up being caught in the wrong place at the
wrong time and got thrown into the camp too, along with
everyone else here."

"Ah, now I understand. She's why you broke everyone
out of that camp, isn't she?"

I nodded then told her about getting shot, waking up to
see one of the prisoners kill a cop at the gas station in
Oklahoma, and having to work with that same outcast in
order to secure the charter bus. As I summed up the mess
of events, the house shifted and creaked from the
temperatures dropping still further outside.

"So you did it all because of her," she whispered, her
eyes widening beneath their saggy hoods of loose skin. She
was silent for a few seconds before shaking her head and
sighing. "Such is the power of love."

Love. The word did weird things to my stomach and
chest. A random memory flashed through my mind of
Tarah's lips softly curving into a smile...

In a firmer voice Grandma Letty asked, "What about
Tarah's father? You didn't say what happened to him. Were
you able to free him from the camp too?"

"Yeah. He went back home to get Tarah's mother and
take her into hiding somewhere. Tarah should have gone
with them, but she's sticking with this group for the story.
She wants to be a journalist like her older brother. Probably
thinks she'll get the Pulitzer for it." I stared down into my
mug.

"Is this the same Tarah you and Damon used to play
with every day?"

"Yeah. How'd you know about that?"

"Your momma and I have always kept in touch. By the
way, you and Tarah should probably bunk in my room
since it's just about the only space we've got left by now.

She's short enough that she should be able to fit on the loveseat in there without much trouble. You okay with a pallet on the floor beside her?"

I nodded, turning my mug around and around in silence, the sleeping arrangements the last thing on my mind at this point.

"Okay, so you saved the girl, you saved her dad, you saved a whole bunch of others, and you got 'em all here in one piece. You ought to be grinning like the Cheshire Cat right about now. So what's with the long face?"

I sighed. "This situation's no good for Tarah, but I don't know what to do or even if I can do anything. She needs to be with her family. I'd try to change her mind about staying with this group if I thought she'd listen. But she's way too hardheaded. She thinks she's lucky to have been mistaken for an outcast and thrown into the internment camp and forced to go on the run with them. Like it's some big career making opportunity for her or something."

I looked up at her, expecting to see some sympathy on her face. Instead she was scowling at me.

"You make having a little ambition sound like a sin," she said.

"Well, it's certainly nothing worth risking your life over."

"Sometimes a little ambition can be just what you need to drive you to do the great things in life. You think I would have ever hooked up with your grandpa if not for my wanting to help lead the way towards a better world for all of us?"

I remembered the crazy story of how they met, my grandfather a legal aide in the district attorney's office rushing up the courthouse steps late for a trial and bumping into my rabble rowsing grandmother as she led a protest for women's rights.

"Things are different now, Grandma," I muttered. "You can't just go out and protest and make a difference anymore."

"Don't I know it. Your grandpa's probably rolling in his grave over what we've done with our country's so-called democracy lately."

"What I don't get is why people aren't trying to do something to stop the government." I settled back in my stool, crossing my arms over my chest.

"But you did. You freed an entire camp of Clann people." She beamed at me like I was two years old and had just learned how to walk right before her very eyes.

"That was one camp. There's probably hundreds of them all over the country. I can't free them all. We need a change in how the masses think about the Clann in order to force the politicians to change. Why isn't the media covering these camps and showing everyone what's really going on inside them?"

"You said Tarah wants to be a journalist. There's your first inroad with the media."

I glared at her. "I meant someone other than her."

"Because she's not good enough?"

My scowl deepened. "Because it's not safe for her."

She snorted. "Sounds like she begs to differ."

Since glaring at my grandma wasn't changing anything, I stared gloomily down at my mug instead.

She let out a heavy sigh. "As for stopping the government, well, normally I'd be the first one to advocate that we get a team of lawyers and take this all the way to the Supreme Court if we had to. But the world's gone mad, Hayden. Things are crazier than I've ever seen them, and that's really saying something. I imagine you haven't seen the news in a while?"

I shook my head. We hadn't even listened to the radio, sticking with CDs or an oddly comfortable silence instead.

"People are dying out there now," she said. "Right there in America's streets, trying to fight our government over this Clann crackdown. But it's like trying to stop a tsunami. The more the Clann people fight back for freedom, the more the government and the media portray us as a danger to everyone else's safety. Now the whole world's split right down the middle, and either you're with the government or you're a threat that has to be locked up and hidden away as soon as possible."

Her mug shook as she lifted it for a slow sip of tea. She had to use both hands to set it down on the counter again. The dull thud was loud in the kitchen, which was silent except for the ticking of the grandfather clock in the dining room. "No one's listening to reason out there anymore. All they know is fear and hate."

A too familiar anger warmed back to life in the pit of my stomach. "What happened to the Bill of Rights and all that? I mean, Tarah and her dad weren't even given a chance to call a lawyer or anything when they got arrested. The soldiers just assumed she and her dad were Clann too, pumped them full of drugs and locked them up with the rest of them."

"That's because the police and the military don't have to worry about first amendment rights anymore. The Patriot Act lets them arrest anyone even remotely suspicious, and if you side with the Clann, that definitely makes you suspicious. No such thing as freedom of speech, freedom of the press, or freedom of religion now when it comes to protecting the U.S. government. To them, talking about using magic is the same as if you were talking about assassinating the president herself. There's no guaranteed phone call, no promise of legal representation. Heck, if someone even demonstrates an ability to use Clann abilities in public, that's seen as equal to trying to set off a nuclear weapon. You can be shot on sight now for that. The Supreme Court can't rule fast enough to overturn even a hundredth of what our government's pulling every single second of the day. Your grandpa would have worked himself into another heart attack over this mess if he hadn't already passed away."

We stared at each other as I tried to take in this crazy new world she said we lived in now. But I couldn't. I'd grown up like every other kid in America with my hand proudly over my heart every morning in elementary school as I practiced saying the Pledge of Allegiance. For years, I'd been taught all about America's history...how we were a country made up of religious and cultural misfits who'd come to these shores to escape the tyranny of other countries' restrictions. How the Bill of Rights was sacred, how the government's system of checks and balances ensured that we'd never be in the kind of situation we were now in, because if the president and Congress went out of whack, the Supreme Court would set them straight again. What happened to "give us your tired, your poor, your huddled masses yearning to breathe free"? They might as well tear down the Statue of Liberty at the rate our fear-crazed government was headed.

Grandma Letty patted my forearm, making me notice how tightly my muscles had cramped up. "Don't lose hope yet. America's been through a whole lot of crap, as you younger generations like to say, and she's pulled through it all before. We made it through McCarthyism, didn't we? With enough people like Tarah out there, we'll make it through this phase too. Or as your Grandpa Mathew used to be fond of saying, 'this too shall pass.'"

I remembered how Tarah had argued so hotly in World History class with Kyle, despite how it made her look like a Clann member. "You don't understand. Tarah doesn't have much of an off switch on her mouth. What she believes, she preaches everywhere to everyone within hearing distance. Even if we got a lawyer to clear her of the existing charges, she'd probably find a way to rile somebody else up. She'll wind up right back in jail again." Or worse.

"Then maybe it's a good thing you saved her when you did. Maybe being with this group is exactly where she needs to be for awhile until things simmer down out there."

"But I don't want her with this group!"

It was insanely dangerous for her to be here. She could be arrested anytime, anywhere as soon as she was recognized. What was I supposed to do, keep her hidden away like some caged animal for her own protection? Like Tarah would even let me do that in the first place. Besides, spells and disguises failed, and criminals got caught after decades of being in hiding for making mistakes as simple as driving with a headlight out. And even if Tarah did keep quiet about her beliefs and we got her name cleared, she'd never be truly happy like that. She'd feel driven to stand up for the innocents being imprisoned and slaughtered all around her. It was part of who she was.

How could I keep Tarah safe for long in a world as far gone as my grandma described?

A sane person would cut his losses. He'd see how useless this was. He'd walk away and let Tarah find her own path through life.

But I admired Tarah for her beliefs and the way she stood up for them. She was only telling the world what a lot of the rest of us wished we were brave enough to say. She acted when everyone else was too scared to. She shouted back when everyone else was hunkered down hiding out in the corner.

She was a lot like Damon.

The problem was Damon had died for his beliefs. And Tarah could end up the same way.

"I'll have to find some way to change her mind, make her see reason and help find her parents for her to hide with instead." At least if she hid with them, she might be motivated to stay out of trouble for their sakes.

A creak on the stairs had me twisting to look over my shoulder, but nothing was there. I turned back and scrubbed both hands over my tired, gritty eyes.

"You look awfully miserable every time you talk about sending her away," Grandma said.

I leaned heavily on my forearms against the countertop, using the polished granite to hold me upright. It felt like the entire house was pressing down on me. "Because I don't really want her to go. At least when she's where I can see her with my own two eyes, I know for sure she's alright. But sending her back to her parents is what's safest for her. Right?"

"Hmm."

I looked at her in silent question.

"You know, I might just have a solution to help both Tarah and the rest of your group. But it needs refining."

That didn't sound good. "What are you—"

"Nope." She gave a single, firm shake of her head. "Don't even try to pry it out of me tonight. I'll tell you all about it once I've worked out the kinks, maybe tomorrow sometime. Until then, why don't you just go get yourself a shower and some sleep because frankly, my dear, you smell and look awful. We'll talk more tomorrow. Now scoot." She made shooing motions with her hands, and warily I gave in. There was nothing more dangerous than a plotting Shepherd, especially one with as long a history of activism as my grandma. Unfortunately, there was also nothing harder to crack. She'd tell me when she was good and ready to, and not a second before.

I waved goodnight then pulled myself up the stairs and down the hall past five doors that couldn't quite hold in the sounds of exhausted snoring. The sixth door was slightly open, spilling out a narrow beam of light. I pushed it open and found an angel in a flowing white gown busy spreading a sheet over a loveseat.

Tarah

I stuffed the sheet in around the edges of the loveseat's flower print cushions in Grandma Letty's huge bedroom, my back teeth clenched so hard the sides of my face hurt.

I couldn't believe Hayden had just said all that stuff about me. And worse, he'd said it to his *grandma*.

After finishing my shower, I had headed down the stairs, intending to join them in the kitchen. Halfway down the staircase, I'd heard them say my name. So I had stayed on the stairs and listened for awhile instead.

I should have gone right back upstairs.

The loveseat finished, I moved on to making a pallet on the floor in front of it. As I turned around to grab the stack of sheets and blankets I'd found in the hallway's linen closet, movement in the bedroom's open doorway made me glance that way and freeze. Hayden was standing there staring at me with a weird expression on his face, as if he'd never seen me before or something.

"What?" I asked.

He looked from me to the pile of linens at my feet and back again with a frown. "How did you know Grandma Letty wanted us to bunk in here with her?"

"After my shower, I was going to join you guys in the kitchen. But then I heard what y'all were saying and decided I didn't want to butt in after all."

"Okay." He said it slowly, still frowning. After another minute of silence, he said, "I guess I'll grab a shower then."

"Great. Enjoy." I flopped back onto the loveseat and jerked my comforter into place over me.

A few seconds later I heard the bathroom door shut and the shower turn on, leaving me with only the moonlight from the window behind the sofa to light the room. In the darkness, I replayed what I'd overheard, wondering if I'd misunderstood. But the words only stung me all over again.

No, I hadn't misunderstood anything. I'd heard him loud and clear.

Obviously I had completely misread Hayden. I thought he was happy to have me around, or at least glad that we'd repaired our friendship and were working together to help a huge group of outcasts to freedom.

Apparently I was wrong.

His grandmother thought I could make a difference for the Clann's cause as a journalist. But according to Hayden, I was just some hardheaded crazy chick. Oh and let's not forget my inability to...how had he put it? Switch off my mouth for my own safety?

The shower shut off. Cabinet doors squeaked open in the bathroom then thudded shut again.

I kicked my legs free of his grandma's old fashioned and annoyingly long nightgown. Then I jumped to my feet, too restless to even hope for sleep. I paced around the bed, trying and failing to understand Hayden, trying and failing to forget the feel of his hand around mine as we'd run together across his backyard into the woods, and again in his truck as we'd viewed the icy waterfalls here in town.

How could he go from the one person on this earth whom I felt the closest to, to someone so completely unfathomable in the space of an hour?

I sat on the edge of the bed facing the bathroom door and waited, holding onto handfuls of the comforter at either side of me.

Finally the bathroom door opened. He froze there, dressed in his jeans and shirt, a towel hanging from one hand. Backlit from the bathroom's light, his expression was unreadable in the shadows.

After a minute of silence, he finally cleared his throat. "Hey. You okay?"

His voice was even deeper than usual, gruff with some emotion I couldn't label. Whatever it was, it worked across my nerve endings like a hand caressing my hair, trying to take away my anger.

"Did you mean it, what you just said to your grandma?" Though I was mad enough to want to shout the words at him, I fought to keep my voice low so I wouldn't wake up anyone in the neighboring rooms.

He slowly scrubbed his wet hair with a towel, and my stomach knotted still further. "Uh, which part?"

"About how I should go home."

"Yeah, I meant it. You should go home."

So it was true. He did want to get rid of me. "Well, I'm not going to."

"I know. Which is why I never tried to convince you to."

"Oh, but you could tell your grandma how desperate you are to get rid of me." I was shaking, I was so mad. But worse was how my eyes had begun to sting and my vision blur. Oh no, I *refused* to cry. Not now, not in front of him. He did not get to see how much his words hurt.

"That's not what I meant. Obviously you left before hearing the end of the conversation or else you'd know that. I told her I don't *want* to get rid of you. I just want you to be safe. But I can't protect you as long as you're with this group."

My hands ached from clenching the comforter. I forced the muscles in my fingers to relax so I could drag my hands into my lap instead. "It's sweet of you to want to protect me, but I'm not a little kid anymore, Hayden. It's my decision to be here. It's not your job to keep me safe. And just because you helped us out of that camp doesn't mean you're responsible for protecting these people, either. I respect your grandmother for taking us all in, but she's got some seriously warped expectations of you."

Silence as he stood there for a long moment then turned away to hang up his damp towel in the bathroom. When he returned, he stopped so close before me that his legs almost touched my knees. "She has a point, though. When you save someone, a certain amount of responsibility does come with the territory—"

"That's crap and you know it. You think firefighters and cops spend the rest of their lives taking care of every person they rescue on the job? You're still free, Hayden, no matter what she says. These people will be just fine on their own now. You got them here and that's enough. Grandma Letty can keep them safe while she helps them figure out a new game plan that has nothing to do with you. If she's so proud of that Shepherd legacy of leadership, then let *her* fulfill it. You can leave here tomorrow and go anywhere and do anything you want."

Frowning, he crossed his arms over his chest and rocked back on his heels, staring down at me, his gaze slowly moving over my face. "What about you? Are you really going to stick around and see what happens next?"

I nodded. "I need to know the ending to their story before I can write it."

"And then what? Once they've all moved on, what will you do then?"

"I don't know. Find my parents, I guess." My stomach knotted at the thought. "Or maybe see if I can join Jeremy overseas." But the knot remained in my stomach. "Or maybe I'll follow one of the outcast families and see what the life of a Clann family in hiding is like. Could be a good follow up story. What *I* do next isn't the point, though, so quit worrying about it. The point of this conversation is you and helping you see that you're not tied down to anyone else's plans for you."

"You're one to talk. Who was it that ended our friendship because your mother demanded it?"

"Exactly! I learned this lesson the hard way. I gave up everything that mattered the most to me because of what somebody else wanted. I don't want to see you make the same mistake. That's why you've got to learn that it's okay for you to be selfish now and think about what you want, not what your dad or mom or even your grandma wants. Live *your* life, not the one they want for you, so you don't have to look back at your life with regret."

One corner of his mouth tightened. "What if I want some of that responsibility? What if I want to be tied down to someone?"

He called me stubborn, when he was the one holding on to some stupid family legacy of leadership? "Then I guess that's your choice, isn't it?"

"Not just mine."

Unbelievable. I turned my head, so frustrated I couldn't even look at him.

Blowing out a noisy sigh, he walked away. I glanced in his direction in time to see him drop down onto his knees before the loveseat and begin to make his pallet on the floor from the stack of blankets and sheets I'd left for him.

Slowly I stood up, watching the movements of his broad shoulders and back as he spread out a comforter for a makeshift mattress, then added a second layer of blankets for warmth. I wished I could reach out to him, physically or with the right words, and somehow make him see.

"Why is it so hard for you to say what you want, Hayden?"

He stopped moving, staring at something I couldn't see. "I...don't know. I guess because it's never been about what I want. It's always been about sticking to their plans for me."

He sat back on his heels and looked at me, and the vulnerability on his face seemed to reach out and steal the air from my lungs.

I walked over to him, stopping before him, hesitating. He was so tall that even on his knees his face was level with my stomach. "I'm sorry I got you involved in all of this. I never should have made you follow that truck of prisoners to the camp. And I definitely shouldn't have asked for your help with the prison break. I should've found another way to pull it off—"

"Then I would have ended up going to some college my father picked out and eventually becoming a politician just like him. I still would have ended up leading people, but I never would have learned the truth. My grandma's right. I'm a Shepherd. It's pretty damn clear I can't escape that destiny no matter what I do."

"I don't believe in destiny. We choose our own futures. The families we're born into are nothing more than an accident. Their choices have nothing to do with ours unless we let them."

His eyebrows pinched together. "How do you know that? How do you know I'm not supposed to lead others, when that's exactly what I've been trained all my life to do and it's all fate seems to keep pushing me towards?"

"Does leading others make you happy?"

He shrugged. "What does that have to do with it?"

"It's everything. If it doesn't make you happy, then it's what someone else wants instead of what you really want. And as for fate, *fate's* not pushing you into it anymore. *You* are. I needed to rescue my dad and these people, and I'm grateful you helped them when I failed. And I know I sort of used their hero worship of you to get us all this far. But I didn't mean to create a monster or make you feel responsible for everyone. What happens next to us all isn't on your shoulders anymore. You've got to let everyone handle their own problems now."

"When I do that, people die, Tarah. Look at what happened to that cop in Oklahoma! If I'd been awake and telling others how to deal with the situation, he wouldn't have figured out something was wrong, and Steve wouldn't have overreacted and killed him."

"You don't know that for sure. And besides, what about when you got shot and we had to figure out what to do next? You were unconscious. But we managed on our own, didn't we? We worked as a group and figured out what to do, even if our decisions weren't perfect. And we'll do the same thing tomorrow morning when we all sit down and figure out where to go from here. Without you."

He froze then slowly looked up at me. "Sounds like you're trying awful hard to get rid of me now."

"No, I'm setting you free of any responsibility."

His jaw clenched. "What do you want from me here, Tarah? Seriously. You keep pushing me to tell you what I want. How about you tell me what *you* want. You want me to go away? Then say the words."

I growled in frustration. "That's not what I'm saying at all. I'm just saying..."

I looked around the unfamiliar room, trying to sort through my exhaustion to find the right words. Why was it always so much easier to write down what I meant in my journals versus saying it out loud?

I sighed. "I'm saying I chose this path. You just got dragged into it. But you don't have to be a part of it anymore. You're free to make your own decisions from now on. And that's what I want you to do."

Most of all, I wanted to see his eyes shine again and his shoulders free of all the weight he had put on there and allowed others to add to. Including me.

Finally I gave in to the urge I had been feeling for days and brushed his shaggy, wet hair out of his eyes. "So yet again I ask what do *you* want?"

I started to let my hand fall away from his face, but he caught and held it. It became hard to breathe as he studied my hand as if trying to read my future in the lines on my palm.

"Do you remember when we used to play Medieval Times," he murmured, "And Damon and I were the knights, and you were our queen?"

I blinked at the strange subject change. Was he trying to distract me and make me forget my arguments? "Um, yes. Why?"

"That was the last time I can remember doing anything I wanted to do. Well, that and play basketball. And even the basketball's kind of turned into another way to keep my dad happy. He thinks sports help me learn leadership skills."

So the only purely fun thing he'd done was play in the backyard with his brother and me. That had been years ago.

The ache in my throat and chest intensified. I wanted to shake every member of his family until their teeth rattled for brainwashing him into thinking his dreams had no value whatsoever if they didn't mesh with what his family wanted.

"Sometimes I still dream about it," he said. "I can still see you in that blanket you always wore like a robe with that old curtain rod for your scepter, standing on the steps of your back deck like it was your castle."

My mouth twitched with the sudden urge to smile. "I was such a goof."

"You were beautiful. You still are. I always thought you should have a crown too, but even without it, you looked...right. Like you really should be a queen."

I pressed my lips together, remembering the pure joy and exhilaration of those times when life had been so much easier. When I read motivational books about finding your dreams and following your bliss, those were the times I thought about. Talk about following our bliss. Back then, that was all we ever did. But then somehow along the way we let others' beliefs and demands intrude, and ever since then no matter how hard I tried, I hadn't found a way to feel such pure joy like that again.

Then Hayden did something that made me forget all about the memories and regrets. He reached up, cupped my cheek and the side of my neck, and slowly pulled me down to him for a kiss.

I don't remember consciously telling my eyes to close, and yet they did, shutting off my sight so every other sense became heightened and filled with him and only him. The smell of Irish Spring soap on his skin, the taste of him on my lips, the feeling of his nose against the side of mine and his mouth moving over mine and my head tilting on its own in an instinctive search for the perfect angle for our mouths to meet. My heartbeat thundered in my ears, robbing me of all sound except a single moan, his or mine I couldn't tell. Then his hands were on me, cupping my shoulders, sliding along my arms and around to my back, tugging me down to my knees and against him.

I held onto his shoulders, afraid otherwise I would fall, and then uncaring if I did, I wrapped my arms around the back of his neck so the short hairs there tickled my palms and the pads of my fingers.

How long had I wished for this, dreamed about this moment, yearned to feel exactly these sensations? And yet I couldn't have ever possibly imagined just how intense it would feel to kiss Hayden. My first best friend. My partner in crime in leading this tiny, dangerous yet thrilling revolution.

The only boy I had ever loved, secretly or otherwise.

"How's that for going after what I want?" His whisper was harsh against my cheek and ear as he held me so close against him that I could feel his heart pounding in his chest. His fingers were spread wide across my back as if trying to cover as much territory over me as he could.

I blinked fast, struggling to regain the ability to breathe and think straight. "Are you sure that wasn't just some really creative way to win an argument?"

He laughed, and the husky sound of it sent a ripple like an aftershock over my nerve endings. "Maybe it was a little of that. But it was also something I've wanted to do for a really long time now. When I said maybe I want some responsibility and to be tied down to someone, I was talking about *you*. I want to help you, not just protect you." He leaned back, his smile fading. "So now it's my turn. What do you want?"

"Right now?" I bit my lower lip as it stretched into a wide smile. "For you to do that again."

Grinning, he leaned in close again and ducked his head for another kiss.

But eventually the exhaustion won and we had to give in to the greater need for sleep instead of kisses. So we pulled the comforter down from the loveseat to cover us then laid on the pallet together, my head on his shoulder, his arms around me, my hand resting on his chest so I could feel his racing heartbeat gradually calm and slow.

Part of me wanted to relax into the moment, soak it all up like a sponge and hopefully remember every detail of it for the rest of my life. Another part of me wanted to analyze it, to question what this meant and when his feelings for me had changed and where we would go from here. I had to keep reminding myself to let the questions go and simply enjoy the moment for however long it lasted.

I fell asleep still smiling.

CHAPTER 14

Monday, December 14th
Hayden

I woke up alone. Worried, I turned and found Tarah watching me from the couch, her hair a sexy tangle over one shoulder.

"Hey, what are you doing up there?" I must have been pretty out of it. I never felt her leave my side.

"I had to move. You snore."

I made a face.

She laughed. "Just kidding. Actually, I heard your grandma coming to bed, and I didn't think she'd like me sleeping down there with you. So I moved up here."

"Sounds like everyone's up already." And all downstairs, judging by the muffled quality of the noise. Smells of bacon and eggs wafted in, making my stomach grumble. "Man, I'm starving."

"Me too." She jumped up from the couch and tried to step over me.

I grabbed her ankles and tugged until she fell laughing on top of me.

"Hayden, I've got morning breath," she squealed, trying to lean away.

"So? Can't be worse than mine." I cupped her face with one hand, staring up into her eyes as light from the windows above the couch made her irises sparkle. "You're so beautiful."

"Come here, cactus face," she murmured with a smile, leaning down to kiss me.

It was the only way I ever wanted to wake up again, with her soft lips on mine, the tip of her nose brushing mine, her wild and crazy hair falling around both our faces like a dark cloud. Perfection.

Perfection soon shattered by a giggling, curly haired girl who burst into the room shouting, "Breakfast!" Pamela and Steve's kid, Cassie.

Tarah burst into embarrassed laughter, which she tried to muffle by burying her face against the side of my neck. "Come on." She rolled up to her feet then pulled me up after her.

She grabbed her clothes and ducked into the bathroom to get dressed, then reemerged with a sheepish smile. "My ponytail holder broke. And I feel weird about using your grandma's makeup..." Which she'd obviously opted not to do, considering her face was still bare.

"Nope, give it up, gorgeous. You're still beautiful." I pulled her to me for one more quick kiss before we headed downstairs.

I should have made my move with her years ago. Why had I waited so long?

Everyone seemed to be up and roaming around, obviously enjoying their newfound freedom outside a cramped vehicle. I snagged the only seat left, a barstool beside Steve at the kitchen island. We exchanged cool nods of greeting before ignoring each other again. News on the small kitchen TV competed with cartoons blaring from the living room. In the dining room behind me, people both sat at the table and stood around it eating as mothers tried to get their hyper kids to sit still in their laps and eat.

The kitchen was even more chaotic, filled with women and men trying to cook, clean plates at the sink and load the dishwasher, or dart in for a refill from the coffeemaker. I was half worried Grandma Letty would already be frazzled and ready to kick us all out. But she didn't look it as she stood at the counter flipping pancakes on an electric griddle with one hand, pouring a glass of grape juice for Cassie with the other hand, and laughing at something Pamela said as the younger woman cooked bacon and eggs beside her on the stove.

It was hard to believe all these people weren't related. If not for the worry lines still etched into every adult face, their shoulders slumped and rolled forward with some combination of despair and resignation, this gathering could almost be mistaken for one big family gathering for some holiday.

Steve snagged his daughter's shoulder as she tried to run past us with her juice. "Walk, Cassie."

Cassie took off at a slightly slower pace, a ring of purple lining her upper lip.

Steve was still smiling as he raised his head and caught me watching them. His smile disappeared.

Tarah joined us, leaning her forearms on the end of the island countertop. Keeping her voice low, she added, "Have you see the news this morning?"

In this noise? Who could hear it? "No, what did I miss?"

She swiveled the small flatscreen toward us and cranked up the volume enough for us to hear. It was already on a CNN show featuring international news. The clips of violence in streets all over the world made me nauseous. In the last clip, leader after country leader ceremoniously signed something while seated before their countries' seals and flags.

"The United Nations has banned Clann activities and abilities worldwide," Tarah said, her voice hoarse. "And all the countries are agreeing to support it."

"They can't all be anti-Clann," Steve protested, his voice too loud. The lower floor of the house became quiet. So much for the holiday family fantasy.

He didn't seem to notice or care as he continued, "What about the smaller countries? The ones who always stay neutral?"

Tarah shook her head carefully. "No one wants to go against the U.N. Not on this. They're all afraid of what would happen if they get flooded with the Clann refugees no one else wants."

What she meant was that none of the other countries wanted to get blown up by angry, displaced outcasts like the previous U.S. president had.

"Well, great. Now what?" Steve spat out.

Good question. Because that sort of killed all my ideas for Tarah and me too.

"I might have an answer for that," Grandma Letty said, her confident voice breaking the tense silence. She flipped the pancakes onto plates and brought them over to the island, sliding a plate before Tarah and myself. But the smell didn't interest me at all now as my stomach rolled and churned with acid.

Pamela turned the stove off with a loud snick, her half turned body and frequent glances our way showing she too was listening in. At the dining table behind us, several chairs squeaked as people turned to listen.

"I think we should create a safe haven for Clann descendants and outcasts right here in the U.S.," Grandma Letty announced.

Someone in the dining room snorted.

"And how would that work?" I asked. "We'd need a

huge tract of land. Not to mention a long list of resources just to get started."

"Well, I just happen to have a huge tract of land over in the Spearfish area," Grandma Letty said. "Your Grandpa Mathew always wanted to build a retirement home on it but died before he could get around to it. It's got a small river running through it with a stone bridge already in place and well maintained, and it's deep in the middle of a narrow valley full of trees nestled between several small mountains. Do a little clearing and you've got the perfect place to hide a small and possibly self-sustainable village."

"A secret magical village," I said, trying but failing to keep the disbelief out of my voice. I knew she needed my support right now in front of all these people, but really? A secret village? *That* was her grand proposal? "Even buried in the woods, people would find it. Planes and helicopters flying overhead would spot it in a second. Not to mention satellites and hunters—"

"No hunting's been allowed on it for years. And you told me last night you've got an outcast who can do a cloaking spell, which I'm sure could be used to shield it from view."

"Mike's cloaking spell only reaches so far," I said. "No way it'll cover an entire village."

"I could probably teach others how to do it," Mike mumbled around a mouthful of omelet from the dining room table. "Working together, we might be able to cover a small village."

Steve leaned back in his stool with his arms crossed, ignoring his breakfast. "You can't be serious. How do you expect anyone to survive in this village? Think about it. Food, water, clothing, shelter. It would take countless amounts of money just to get set up, and even more to keep it going."

"I can certainly help you get set up for awhile,"

Grandma Letty offered.

"Don't you need to save your millions for your Clann hating son's next political campaign?" Steve sneered.

I jerked towards him, but Grandma Letty answered him before I could. "My misguided son makes his own way in life, as he always has."

Pamela scowled. Leaning a hip against the island, she crossed her arms over her chest and turned toward the rest of the group. "We could learn to be self-sufficient, Steve. Use solar, water and wind power. Grow our own food. Use the river for water. Make what we need. We can do our own healing, home school our children the way we want to. We'd be our own little town. Our kids could grow up surrounded by magic and people just like them. We could finally be ourselves and be *proud* of it."

Steve looked around him, prompting me to do the same. What I found was amazing. People who had been afraid and angry, their faces dark with despair and resignation, were completely transformed, their shoulders back, standing straight, their faces alive with...hope.

"You're all crazy," Steve said. "You'll get yourselves killed. There's no way to keep a group this size a secret for long, especially if they try to stay in one place together."

Pamela stared at him in silent argument until he stood up and stomped out of the kitchen.

After his footsteps faded up the staircase, Pamela said, "We *could* do it. How many of you would go?"

I swiveled my barstool's seat so I could see the group behind me better. The adults had all trickled in from the living room at some point, crowding into the kitchen and dining room.

Several people nodded or murmured their agreement. A few even raised their hands shoulder high to signal their vote.

Everyone wanted in. Including Tarah, judging by the

way her eyes were all lit up with excitement. When our eyes met, she bit her lower lip and looked away.

I turned back to Grandma Letty. She gave me a challenging half smile, one eyebrow arched, and said, "Well, how about it? Are you in, or are you out?"

Last night Tarah had told me to forget the Shepherd family legacy of leadership and go my own way, to do what I wanted from now on. I looked at her again, openly staring, but she still refused to meet my eyes. She was trying to keep her face blank, probably so she wouldn't influence my decision.

"You know the logistics of pulling this off is going to be a nightmare," I muttered, looking around me at all the hopeful faces. "We're going to need immediate temporary housing, at least till spring, before we can build more permanent shelters. We'll also need water treatment systems, septic systems, green power of several kinds like Pamela said—"

"So that's a yes?" Grandma Letty prompted.

I turned to her, Tarah's words from last night running through my mind on a loop. *What do you want?*

I wasn't sure I wanted to make this my life calling. But at least for awhile, it seemed a good route to take. "Yeah, that's a yes."

Excited conversation broke out all around us, allowing Tarah to edge closer to me without an audience and whisper, "Are you *sure*? You know you don't have to do this."

"I know. And yeah, I'm sure. I want to do this."

Finally she met my eyes, searching them to make sure I wasn't lying just to make everyone else here happy. After she found whatever reassurance she needed, she smiled and took my hand in hers. "Okay, then. If this is what you want to do, then we'll do it."

It *was* what I wanted to do. I just hoped it wasn't a huge

mistake. For all of us.

The next few days flew by in a storm of activity as we tried to get it all pulled together. Bud was kept knocked out except for brief semi-conscious bathroom breaks or to eat groggily. Pamela and some of the guys shopped together online for solar, wind and water energy and treatment systems, while the other ladies kept the kids busy in the basement, which turned out to be a crafter's mecca. There was a reason Grandma Letty hadn't set up any sleeping pallets down there...you could hardly walk between the towering shelves and tables full of craft supplies. This at least gave the kids plenty to do as they made little gifts for everyone for Hanukkah and Christmas. Also sharing basement space was the laundry room, which was kept going full tilt twenty-four hours a day as my grandma nearly bought out the local Goodwill and consignment shops for clothing for everyone, and the ladies tried to keep us all in clean clothes.

When we weren't shopping at Wal-Mart, we were shopping online or with Grandma Letty at local mobile home centers. The shout of "mail!" became like a fire drill bell, signaling for everyone to either run upstairs or down to the basement to hide as Grandma Letty and I accepted countless deliveries of power systems, seeds, and books on everything from farming, weaving and soap making to raising sheep, cows, chickens and goats. We had so many books we could start our own library. It was probably the first town building we'd have to build in the spring, just to have somewhere to house them all.

Unfortunately, not everything went so smoothly. The last day we went to look at mobile homes, Grandma Letty and I got into an argument.

"Be reasonable, Hayden. You and Tarah need a place of

your own so you can have your own bedrooms. Right now, we've only got enough bedrooms for the families, and even they are going to have to sleep in bunk beds in order to fit. We need at least one more small house."

"For just Tarah and me? No way. That's a waste of money and land."

"Then exactly where do you think you two will sleep? In your truck?"

"You're getting huge sectional couches for each house, right? So Tarah and I can sleep on them instead."

"In one of the living rooms? Oh please. Be serious. You've never even had to share a bedroom with your brother. All your life you've lived in a huge house. And don't forget, you're not in East Texas anymore. Winters are long and miserable up here, and everyone's going to be cooped up indoors for months. Just where do you think they'll be spendng all their waking hours other than the living rooms? You'll have zero space of your own to get away to, and neither will Tarah. At least let me get you a camper to tow behind that truck of yours for you and her."

"Thanks for the offer, but I can't take it. Spring will come soon enough. When it does, everyone's going to start building their own homes and free up the bedrooms in the starter houses. Until then, sleeping on a couch will be fine for us."

She spent another ten minutes trying to convince me, but there was no way she was going to change my mind on this. Tarah would never agree to having a whole room of her own. And if I took an entire room for myself while asking each family of three or four to share a bedroom and bunkbeds, that would only cement everyone's idea of me as a spoiled rich kid. While I wasn't sure how long I'd be staying in the village past spring, I definitely knew even a few months of winter would be far too long if everyone treated me like a spoiled brat.

Finally Grandma Letty gave up. Or so I thought.

She still got her way in the end. She just had to be a little devious about it. Just like a Shepherd.

Saturday, December 19th

On the day before the advance logging team was scheduled to leave, a honk outside had me yelling out, "FedEx." While everyone scrambled to hide, I looked out the window. It was a delivery truck, all right. But it wasn't FedEx, unless they'd switched to hauling strange, plastic-wrapped pallets on flatbed trailers behind big red trucks.

Grandma Letty took off outside without a coat, a bad habit of hers when she got excited. I grabbed her coat from the entrance closet while pulling mine on, then followed her outside.

She clapped her hands together like a little kid on Christmas morning, ignoring me as I draped her coat over her shoulders. "Oh, it's here! I was so worried it wouldn't get here in time. You have no idea how much extra I had to pay to bribe them to even get it here today. Normally they take weeks to put together, but we were in luck. They just happened to have this model in storage. Apparently somebody ordered it for Christmas then changed their minds."

I studied the giant plastic wrapped cube on a trailer. "What is it?"

"Your future new home, of course!"

I groaned. "Grandma, we talked about this."

"You said I couldn't get you a trailer or an RV. This is neither. Technically it's a house *kit*. You did not say I couldn't get a house kit for you."

"That pile of stuff is supposed to become a house?" Hands on my hips, I walked around the cube in disbelief. Not a window or door in sight. Maybe she was pulling a prank here. Shepherds could be weird like that. It was the reason my father had always claimed it was safer to avoid family reunions. Of course, now I knew he was mostly just ashamed of all the Clann descendants in his family tree.

"It's a prefabricated tiny home. It includes a RV septic system, a toilet and shower, a ten gallon water tank with a Y shaped feeder system, an on-demand water heater, and detailed instructions. It's prebuilt then taken down again for shipping, so it's supposed to take only a hammer, a drill and a few days to put together."

"What's the point of prebuilding it then taking it down again for shipping?"

"So you can have the fun of putting it back together again, of course." She grinned at me.

She had lost her mind.

"It's going to be perfect for you and Tarah. It's got loft beds at either end, one over the kitchen and one over the porch area, so you can both have your own little spaces to get away from everyone else as well as each other. And it's got beautiful arched windows to let in lots of sunlight and a little wood burning stove for plenty of heat. The stove works for cooking too, though I also bought you an energy efficient griddle to run off the solar power system."

I could tell she might go on for hours. Taking her short pause for an opening, I jumped in with, "Thanks, Grandma. I appreciate this. I mean, I've got no idea how I'll put the da—I mean, darn thing together. But it was very...creative of you to think of this."

Actually, the longer I thought about it, the more creative a solution it seemed. It wasn't even a fourth of the size of the mobile homes we'd bought for everyone else. And unlike an RV, it was going to take a heck of a lot of work on my part to get it put back together somehow, which should make everyone else feel a little better about Tarah and me having our own house. I could also imagine Tarah loving having her own tiny house to fix up. She'd always whined as a kid about not having her own playhouse in her backyard. Now she'd have one that went anywhere we did.

The delivery guy hopped out of his truck and held a clipboard for my grandmother to sign. While she did, I studied the trailer and frowned.

Then again, would Tarah even want to share a house with me? Grandma Letty was assuming a lot there. Whatever this thing was between Tarah and me was still new. We hadn't even had a real date yet, and here my grandmother was trying to get us to shack up together. Tarah might freak out about that.

Well, maybe we could include a third bed in the living room area and Mike could live with us too. That might make it more a group thing with less relationship pressure on Tarah. And she could always get a place of her own built in the spring if she wanted.

A loud clanging rang out as the delivery guy unhitched the trailer from his truck then left.

And then I saw the full ingenuity of my grandmother's plan. She was giving me my freedom, ensuring I'd always be able to move on if I wanted and still have a home I could take with me anywhere I wanted to go. But the complication of having to build it would force me to stay put at least long enough to give the village time to get off the ground.

Strategic planning for the long term, with plenty of manipulative incentives thrown in for good measure. Yep, Grandma Letty was definitely a Shepherd at heart.

CHAPTER 15

Sunday, December 20th

And then it was time for the logging party to leave. I was
going to take three men with logging experience to make a
clearing for the houses that were due to be delivered to the
village's site in three days. Three days wasn't a heck of a lot
of time for us to make the size of clearing we'd need for
four mobile homes. But we needed to get our group out of
Grandma Letty's house as quickly as we could before her
neighbors started to ask questions about all her visitors. We
couldn't go on hiding the bus and keeping Bud drugged
and away from his family forever.

Tarah looked worried as we said goodbye early that
morning.

"Hey, it'll only be for a few days," I said, rubbing a
thumb across her lips, which were currently set in a dark
scowl the likes of which I hadn't seen since we were kids
and she had to get that tetanus shot after getting hurt on a
rusty nail.

"Yeah, I know." She sighed.

Smiling, I pulled her in for a hug and a kiss on her

forehead. It was nice to know she'd miss me while I was gone. "We'll be fine. Just make sure this group doesn't get too rowdy while I'm gone."

She laughed. "Yeah, right. Like your grandma would let us get away with much anyways."

We kissed goodbye, then the guys and I left.

It was an eight hour drive to Spearfish, South Dakota, made even longer when we had to drive slower due to icy roads. Just to be on the safe side, I'd gotten rid of the GPS unit, so we followed a paper map instead.

But when we got there and then found our way onto the Scenic Byway in the Black Hills National Forest, oh man, was it amazing, with steep, snowy limestone mountains towering at least a couple thousand feet above us on either side and the narrow Little Spearfish Creek winding alongside the road. Cabins dotted the mountains' charcoal gray and tan sides here and there, easier to see now that all the icy hardwood trees were stripped of their leaves. In the spring and summer, those houses were probably hidden fairly well. But in the winter...

We'd have to be careful and try to leave as many evergreens around our village as we could for more year round coverage.

We followed the directions Grandma Letty had written out for us, passing a turnout area for tourists to view the Bridal Veil Falls and later a red brick building on the left side of the road with a large sign labeling it as the Homestead Mining Company's Hydro Electric Plant built in 1917. Along the peaks' ridgeline at our left, a row of electric lines on wooden poles indicated a public source of electricity to homeowners even here in the mountains, though I had a hunch maintaining those lines was probably a big enough pain to drive electricity prices sky high for anyone requiring the service. Thankfully we would be completely off the grid and able to avoid that ongoing cost for our village.

About thirteen miles along the bypass, we reached the Roughlock Falls Road, a lightly graveled and recently plowed sandy road that Grandma Letty's map said we needed to take. The road went on forever and at first seemed way too public and popular, with the large Spearfish Canyon Lodge at the road's beginning complete with a big, well maintained parking lot and another parking area for tourists to view the Roughlock Falls and the long metal bridge spanning it. But the farther we went along the winding single lane road, the more civilization seemed to fall away.

Even with the map, we still had a rough time finding the property. The clue to its location was the wide stone and cement bridge spanning the creek, which at this point was only five or six feet wide and looked to be about two or three feet deep at most. Then the logging started. When Grandma Letty said the area was untouched beyond the bridge, she'd meant it. So we had to start by cutting a road wide enough to let houses through. I really wasn't happy about this part; the stone bridge plus a road would invite curious drivers down it, even with a No Trespassing sign posted. We'd have to think up a solution for it later, maybe replant some trees and teach several people how to do Mike's cloaking spell so they could work as a group to hide both the entrance and the houses. Thankfully the snow was hard and crunchy, compacting down under my truck's tires like a dirt road as we worked, so we didn't have to fight getting stuck as much as I'd expected.

For all Dad's faults, at least I could thank him for dragging Damon and me out to join loggers in the woods a couple of times a few years back. He'd intended the logging lessons to serve as nothing more than a photo op and a commercial shoot to prove he and his boys were real East Texas men in order to gain votes from the local logging industry. But the brief experience had also taught me enough to know how to handle a gas powered chainsaw safely.

And the work felt pretty good after doing nothing but riding around in a truck and planning for days. The job itself seemed pretty simple...cut a tree, then use chains and the truck to haul the tree off to the side out of the way, and repeat. The cold was crazy, though, burning my nose and throat and every inch of exposed skin until I worked hard enough to get warm. Then I started sweating inside my coat and snow pants and gloves. Still, the frigid air helped me stay sharp and alert. And it was great to be actively doing something useful for a change instead of sitting around talking. I wished we could have used some spells to get it done a lot faster. But all we could think of to use was fire, and the resulting smoke volume would have been way too much for even Mike to hide.

As I worked, I tried to imagine what the village would eventually look like. Of course, eventually spells of all kinds would probably end up getting used to design the village in the spring, either in the architectural designs of the eventual permanent buildings or in the landscaping or something. Did we have any outcasts who specialized in guiding the growth of plants? Maybe they could get creative, really help make this village look like a proper town for magic users. And did outcasts have to follow regular growing seasons like everyone else, or could we get started right away?

Revved up by the possibilities, I made a mental note to ask our group all these questions and more. The sooner we could work as a team to design our village, the better. It would give us all something to do while we waited out the long winter.

As my arms fell into a rhythm of planned destruction, I kept my mind busy by imagining ways we could use spells to grow it all back even better. My favorite movies, which

I'd never told anyone about except Damon because he was a LOTR nut too, was the Lord of the Rings trilogy and its prequel The Hobbit trilogy. In my opinion, the best parts were where they showed Lothlorien, the elven village that was magically erected along the steep sides of mountains. All the buildings in the movie featured these crazy, highly detailed, symmetrical Celtic-style weavings of tree branches that looked as if they'd been grown that way. Maybe something like that would look good here too.

We worked past dark, using the truck's headlights to light our path. I think we all would have stopped by about one or two in the morning for sleep if we'd been working as individuals. But something about working as a team helped us push on past the exhaustion. Or maybe it was the thought of all those people counting on us that kept us going. We'd brought bottles of soda, six five-gallon gas cans, oil and sharpening tools for the saws, which also helped.

Around sunrise, we got our second or third wind, the growing daylight shining through the forest spurring us on. It was a beautiful area, and exciting to think that soon it would be our new home.

But by nine a.m., we were running out of gas and energy, even as determined as we were.

"Hey, guys," I yelled over the whining of the saws.

One by one, they shut off the machines.

"How about we stop for awhile, grab a meal and some more gas and oil?"

Wearily, they brought the chainsaws back to the truck and I unhooked the chain from the back hitch. I tried not to cringe as we piled into the cab, our heavy boots knocking off clumps of muddy snow into the floorboards. Mentally I promised my truck a full bath inside and out someday soon as I drove us back into Spearfish.

We opted to eat at the local Perkins restaurant, where

we plowed through what my mother would have called an unholy amount of cholesterol and pork fat with good sized dollops of ketchup and Tabasco sauce on the side. Then we had to chug more than a few pots of coffee to counter the food as all the blood rushed to our guts and turned our visions blurry.

To say we were pretty dang tired was an understatement.

The guys were all for taking a few packs of beer back with us to ease the pain of our overworked muscles. But I'd met some loggers with missing toes and fingers as a result of combining high speed cutting tools and alcohol. Not a good combination. Besides, buying alcohol might require one of us to show an ID. Also not a good idea for people on the run from the law. So we settled for ibuprofen, packs of cola and bags of gas station sandwiches for later. Then we headed back to the woods.

Our woods.

By that night, I was referring to them as "that God-awful group of trees," with more than a few curse words thrown in there. My arms ached from lugging around a sixty-pound chainsaw and fighting tree after tree. My back ached like an old man's, popping and creaking every time I moved, especially when I had to bend over to deal with the chains to drag the felled trees out of the way.

Finally, I'd had enough, and a glance around told me the others had too. I let out a loud whistle and made a slashing motion at my neck to signal it was break time. Then we all trudged back to the truck.

We sat on the tailgate, cooling off while we ate in silence and chugged down the caffeine as quickly as we could. But my body didn't care how much caffeine I drank. I'd hit the point where it had no effect on me whatsoever.

I swore, scrubbing at my eyes. "All right. I know we all want to get this done. And I know a whole lot of people are counting on us. But if we don't snag a few Z's, somebody's gonna end up cutting off something vital. And that ain't gonna help anybody." Geez, I was so tired I sounded drunk. I was actually slurring my words.

"I can keep—" One of the men began.

"Shut up, Harvey," someone else said. "The kid's right. Let's rest a few hours."

Harvey grumbled but climbed into the truck with the rest of us. I cranked the engine, set the timer on my watch for four hours from now, and we all promptly commenced to sawing a different kind of log.

Beeping, high pitched, quick, and extremely annoying, dragged me out of a deep and dreamless sleep. I reached out for my bedside alarm but found nothing but air. Somebody must have moved my clock. Probably Mom in an attempt to help me be on time for school for a change.

"Aw, come on, Ma. Ten more minutes," I begged, reaching for my pillow so I could use it to drown out the noise.

No pillow, no Mom arguing back. Only male laughter. What the...?

I cracked one eye open then sat bolt upright as I realized I was in my truck a few thousand miles away from my old bedroom. With a bunch of older men who were snickering at me.

Scowling, I shut off the alarm on my watch, opened the driver side door and had to roll out of the cab. Holy crap, my whole dang body hurt!

Apparently I wasn't the only one in pain as the other three doors opened and more groans and cussing filled the air.

"Aw, just ten more minutes, Mom," Harvey whined then snickered again.

"Yeah, yeah," I said with a grin then called him a name

my mother would have smacked me on the back of my head for saying. My hands hurt too much to flip him off instead.

Laughing, Harvey and the others walked around to the front end of the truck to survey the woods ahead.

"How much further, Dad?" one of the others joked in a whiny, little kid voice.

Smiling, the oldest of our group scanned the area then said, "Probably another six or eight hours. If we work fast. And we'll still have to squeeze the houses in pretty tight."

"That could be a good thing," I said, trying to picture four mobile homes packed into this area. "We can face their entrances in towards each other. It'll add more shelter from the wind if we keep the outer perimeter of trees fairly close to the houses. And it'll mean less area to have to hide with a cloaking effect, too."

Grunts, either of agreement or disagreement, I couldn't tell which and was frankly too tired to care either way.

"All right, let's get her done," I sighed, reaching for the chainsaw I'd recently come to view more as a torture device.

We had to stop again a few hours later for more gas and oil and to resharpen the saws. None of us was very hungry; all we really wanted was sleep. So we settled for more gas station sandwiches with a healthy side of ibuprofen and sodas. Then we were back at it. I had a feeling if the group had arrived right then, we might have all looked crazy to them, covered in sweat, sawdust, oil and gas fumes, our hair standing on end, noses steadily dripping from the cold, our eyes gritty and too round as we pushed ourselves way past our bodies' natural limits.

We were on a mission. And that was all that kept us going.

The sound of big engines drawing closer pulled me from the circling fog of my thoughts sometime later. I turned off my chainsaw, nearly cutting off my own leg when I set it down before the chain had fully stopped cycling.

Ready or not, the houses were here.

I looked around me and sighed with relief. Yeah, we should have enough room to position the houses. But it would be tight, and the drivers would have to be careful not to puncture their tires driving over the stumps we'd left everywhere.

We had to help the drivers position rubber mats along the makeshift road into the clearing to give their tires enough traction. Then we had to prune back a lot of branches along the perimeter to keep them from busting out the windows of the houses as they were arranged.

While the drivers finished arranging and leveling the houses with cement blocks, the logging team and I leaned against the hood of my truck, half asleep on our feet.

And then everything became a series of minute long moments separated by long, slow blinks.

Long blink.

"Sign here, and here, and here, and here," someone said, thrusting clipboards in front of me that I clumsily forced my gloved fingers to scrawl some attempt at a signature on.

Long blink.

The tail lights of the last delivery truck turned at the end of our newly created road and faded. I hoped Grandma Letty remembered to do something about the paperwork trail for the houses. She probably would. She was one smart old lady.

Long blink.

My chin bounced off my chest and I stumbled sideways. "I've got an idea," I muttered, scrubbing my face. "Let's cut up one of these trees, stick the logs in one of those houses' fireplaces, and see how soft the living room carpeting is."

Somebody laughed, which was kind of annoying because I was totally serious.

"Yeah, sure. You volunteering to chop the firewood?" Harvey said.

I scowled. "On second thought, my truck sounds better."

Grunts of agreement were all the votes I needed. We pulled ourselves into the truck, and this time I didn't care at all about the snow we tracked in on the floorboards. I had just enough energy to crank the engine, turn on the heat, and call my grandma. No one answered, so I left a message to confirm the houses were in place. Then I conked out.

Wednesday, December 23rd

Tapping sounded against something hard near my left ear. I jerked awake to find the sweetest smile on earth on the other side of the glass.

"Hey, guys, they're here!" I cut off the truck's engine and tried to casually unfold my stiff body out of the truck. A series of pops from my joints gave me away.

"Oh my lord, Hayden, are you okay?" Tarah gasped as I hugged her with one aching arm I nearly couldn't move.

"Nothing a bottle of aspirin won't fix," I joked, drawing in a deep breath of shampoo from her hair.

She shook her head and looked up at me with a smile. "Did you have much time to miss me?"

I knew she was teasing me. So I didn't tell her the truth, that thoughts of her were just about all that had kept me going the last few hours. She probably wouldn't have believed me anyways.

So all I ended up saying was, "Yeah."

"Everyone's checking out the houses and putting together the bunk beds. Should we help assign families to each room, or...?"

"Nah, let them sort it out." Slinging an arm around her shoulders, I grandly swung an arm out towards the grouping of houses, intending to say, "So what do you think?" But before I could speak, I got a good look at the place in the daylight, and my free arm dropped to my side, screaming muscles already forgotten.

Cut trees formed haphazard piles all around the perimeter like forgotten Jenga pieces some giant had thrown down and forgotten to put away. Despite the use of the rubber mats, the delivery trucks had still managed to plow deep ruts into the snow in places. And though we'd tried to cut the trees as close to the ground as we could, there were still stumps left visible everywhere.

And then there were the mobile homes themselves. Grandma Letty and I had picked out a design that had a short, narrow porch on the front and a peaked roof with green shingles. So they didn't exactly look like metal cans on wheels. But...

I walked over to the nearest cement steps leading up to one of the house's porch. I must have dozed off when the delivery drivers had set up the steps for each house.

"What's wrong?" Tarah asked.

I didn't know how to answer her. I looked around us, at the four matching white houses resting several feet above the ground, their wheels exposed below. Then I flopped down onto the nearby steps.

Tarah sat beside me with a frown, waiting.

"Well, this sucks." I was too tired to be mad. All I felt was beat up and defeated.

CHAPTER 16

"What sucks?" Tarah looked around us, clearly lost.

"This!" I threw my hands out at all the houses, the clearing, the stumps like huge zits making the whole area ugly. "This is supposed to be a village for people with powers so dangerous the government's afraid of us?"

"What's wrong with it?"

I growled in frustration, trying to sort out my groggy thoughts enough to put them into words. "It's...not right. It's just a bunch of ordinary houses in the middle of nowhere. Where's the fantasy that says 'secret Clann village?'"

She burst into laughter. "Hayden, what exactly did you expect, Disneyworld?"

I lunged off the steps, giving in to the urge to pace though my sore leg muscles protested loudly. "Not a trailer park in the woods, that's for sure. Look around you. Does this look like Hogsmeade or Lothlorien to you?"

She snickered. "Okay, first off, you're talking about made up places. And secondly, this is just temporary until spring. The fantasy village will come. We just got here." She stood up, walked over to me, and wrapped her arms around my waist. "Give it time while everyone settles in and gets used to their new home. Come summer time, I bet you'll get your Lothlorien." She rose up on tiptoe and nuzzled her nose against mine. "And your elven ears, too, if you want them."

I tried not to smile, but it was a useless fight. "And one of those clingy elven dresses for you?"

Laughing, she kissed me, and I let it ease away the frustration of the moment a little.

But the disappointment wasn't completely gone, because I wasn't sure I would still be here by summer time.

Still, I tried to forget about it. Why should I care what this place looked like? These people didn't care, that was for sure. All they wanted was some place safe where they could be themselves. My ideas for a cool looking village for magic users had no meaning or purpose to people who were more concerned with just surviving right now.

So I focused on what was important instead, helping set up the solar panels and wind power systems so we could start generating electricity. The water proved to be tougher. The ground was hard and cold, requiring the use of spell fire to first melt the snow and then warm the earth enough so we could dig trench lines from the houses to the water system, and from the water system to the creek. Even with the help of magic, it would still probably take the digging team a week to get it all completed. Until then, people from each house would have to haul water from the creek.

And then there was the bus driver, Bud Preston, to deal with. Grandma Letty had woken him up enough to safely drive the group here. But she'd also sent her homemade sleepy time potion with Pamela so we could knock him out again and keep him that way overnight. Tomorrow, however, we'd need to wake him up and send him on his way back home.

As I took a turn fetching water from the creek, I

worried about what using sedatives for so long on a man Bud's age might do to his health. Grandma Letty claimed the homemade herbal mix was harmless, but had she ever used so much of it for so long on someone Bud's age before? I doubted it. And it wasn't like the FDA had done tests on the stuff either.

While returning to my assigned house after fifteen long minutes spent breaking up ice at the edge of the creek, two loud voices behind one of the houses brought me up short. Water from the plastic bucket sloshed out onto my jeans, forcing me to bite back a curse.

I recognized those voices. Steve and Pamela. What the heck had they felt the need to discuss out in fifteen degree Fahrenheit weather in the woods at night?

I edged closer until I could make out their individual words.

"What is your *problem*?" Pamela said.

"Seriously? You have to ask? We can't stay here!" Steve all but shouted.

"Why not?" she said.

"Four people packed into every room? No running water, and twelve people sharing just two bathrooms in every house *and* I have to pour my own toilet water every time I flush? That idiot kid and his grandma have got us packed in like frigging sardines here! Is this what you really want for our family, for Cassie?"

"It's just for a few months, Steve. Then spring will come, we'll build our own house exactly the way we want it, and everything will be fine. And besides, you should be grateful. These four houses alone probably cost Grandma Letty a quarter of a million dollars."

Actually, it had been closer to half a million once you threw in the furniture and dishes and stuff. I'd seen the paperwork when Grandma Letty had bought them.

"Besides," Pamela continued. "We have a shot at a real

life here. No more hiding—"

"But we *are* hiding! We're in the freaking woods—"

"But we don't have to hide our abilities within these woods," Pamela said. "Cassie won't have to feel like a freak anymore."

"No, just grow up in some backwoods hillbilly commune with second rate education and no health care."

"Which is a lot better than no education at all and drugged out of her mind in an internment camp! Or have you already forgotten that place? And while you're struggling with that memory of yours, why don't you also try remembering that you're talking to one of the resident health care providers around here, you insensitive jackass! Second rate health care? I can heal us just *fine!*"

Pamela was nearly shrieking at this point. I was surprised the rest of the group hadn't come outside to see what was going on. She took in a long, noisy breath, then let it out slowly. "Look, I'm not discussing this with you any more. Cassie and I are staying here where we're safe and accepted. If you want to go brave that crazy world out there on the run, you do what you have to."

I took that as my cue to leave in the other direction. I wasn't sure why I'd even listened in as long as I had. All I'd really wanted to know was if Steve's pissy mood was based on something I did, or if the whole situation ticked him off in general. Obviously it was the latter. And definitely none of my business.

Though I sure wouldn't have been sad to see Steve go, if that was his decision. The guy was an idiot to think he could possibly keep his family safe somewhere else. With the way the international politics were shaping up, there weren't too many safer places on the *planet* right now.

But Steve struck me as the hardheaded loner type. Maybe he figured he could put a disguise spell on his family's faces for the rest of their lives and keep them safe that way. Whatever he was thinking, I doubted it included giving up on his family this easily. I'd have to keep an eye on Pamela and Cassie for the next few days just in case Steve tried to force them to leave with him against their will, or something crazy like that.

After seeing him kill that cop back at the gas station with zero hesitation, I had no doubt Steve was fully capable of anything in the name of protecting his family.

Once I finished delivering the water to the ladies giving sponge baths to toddlers and washing dishes in the kitchen, as well as refilling the toilet tanks in the house where Tarah and I would be staying for awhile, I joined Tarah in the living room.

She was playing Monopoly with Cassie and Mike. Grandma Letty had suggested a huge stockpile of board and card games for each house since we couldn't safely have cable or satellite TV. I had a feeling we'd all be getting tired of the games before winter ended, as they would be our only entertainment for months.

"Mikey, you're cheating again," Cassie cried out, her wild head of white-blonde curls bouncing as she whapped Mike on the arm.

"Cassie, play nicely," Pamela called out from the kitchen where she was drying dinner plates. To her credit, she gave no sign of her recent argument with her husband. Maybe they argued all the time and it was no big deal to her.

"Oh please. How can you tell?" Mike said to Cassie, his eyes gleaming with mischief. "All I did was roll the dice."

"And then used mag—" Cassie hesitated, her hand flying to her mouth as her eyes widened. She turned to her mother in fear.

"It's okay, honey." Pamela smiled, but sadness kept it from reaching her eyes. "But only talk about it here with our friends."

What had our country's latest civil war done to kids like

Cassie? How long would it take before they learned to feel safe again? Months? Years?

"Anyways, you can't tell I used magic just now," Mike teased the little girl. "Everyone's using magic around here."

"So? I can tell it was you who did it just now," Cassie insisted. "I can smell it." She tapped her tiny button nose.

I burst out laughing. "Mike, she says your magic stinks!"

"Shut up," he muttered, punching my shoulder. He turned back to the little girl. "Oh yeah? What does it smell like?"

"Oranges and sunshine," she chirped with a giggle.

Mike grinned. "Ha! See? She says my magic smells good."

Tarah rolled the dice then asked, "And what does Hayden's magic smell like?"

Cassie frowned. "Hmm. Do something, Hay-Hay."

"Hay-Hay!" Mike fell over sideways laughing.

Hay-Hay? Couldn't Cassie pick a different nickname for me?

I tried to forget about my new nickname and focus on doing something magical on a small scale. But what?

Then I had it. I held out a finger a few inches from Tarah's neck and blew softly, pushing a tiny bit of my will into the breath of air. The breeze lifted a strand of Tarah's hair and coaxed it to wrap around my finger several times. As Tarah's cheeks turned a light shade of pink, Cassie giggled and clapped her hands.

"Blankets!" she cried out. "It smells like the blankets after Mommy washes them."

"I think she means the fresh breeze scented laundry detergent we used to use," Pamela explained with a grin.

My magic smelled like laundry soap. Great.

Steve walked into the room, joining us from the master suite his family had claimed, his face clouded. He added a log to the fireplace, jabbing it way harder than needed with the poker before jerking the metal safety chain curtain back across the opening. Muttering about how we'd all die of the cold, he stomped back to his family's bedroom. Either they had taken the master suite, or everyone else had assigned it to them so we wouldn't have to see Steve every time he needed to visit a bathroom. But apparently the compromise was that his end of the house wasn't getting much heat from the fireplace. Probably because he insisted on keeping their bedroom door shut.

That reminded me. "Hey, Tarah, want to help me bring in more firewood?"

"Sure."

As we pulled on our coats and boots at the door, Mike waggled his eyebrows suggestively. "Keep her out there a while, would you? I need to get past her Boardwalk and Park Place in a few turns, and I'm running short on cash."

"Cassie, you keep an eye and a nose on him for me, okay?" Tarah said, tapping the side of her nose. "Play my turns for me till I get back. And don't let him cheat anymore."

Cassie nodded solemnly.

As I held the glass and metal storm door open for Tarah, I heard Cassie howl, "Mikey, you heard Tarah. Quit cheating!"

Chuckling, I followed Tarah down the steps, pulling her in against my side as we strolled along the houses. We'd chopped up and piled firewood behind every house earlier so no one had to go too far, and taking a shortcut in between the houses would have been quicker. But I wanted time alone to talk with her, so we walked past the shortcut and took the long way around instead.

As we crunched along on the snow, carefully avoiding the tree stumps everywhere, I told her about the argument I'd overheard between Pamela and Steve. "So we might want to keep an eye on at least Cassie when we can."

"You don't think Steve would really try to take her away, do you?"

"He killed that cop in Oklahoma without even blinking an eye. I don't think there's anything he wouldn't do for his family."

"Well, what if he uses magic on them to make them agree to go with him? How would we know if they'd really changed their minds or not?"

Good point. I sighed. "I guess we'll have to deal with that possibility if it comes up. Maybe some of the others have a way to break another's spell?"

Tarah shrugged. "I know as much as you do about what Clann people can and can't do."

A breeze stirred through the pines, making them sigh and sway. As the breeze passed us, it brought with it the scent of the freshly cut firewood and pine sap.

Tarah shivered. I threw an arm around her shoulders and grinned. "You're getting cold. Let's grab some firewood and get back inside before you turn into a human popsicle. I don't want a girlfriend with ugly, frostbitten toes."

She gasped and whapped my shoulder. "You'd just have to learn to like me anyway. 'Cause I don't want a boyfriend who's too shallow to like a girl with frostbitten toes."

"I would not like you with frostbitten toes." At the firewood stack now, I loaded her arms with a small pile of wood then filled mine with chopped logs up to my chin.

"You really wouldn't?" Her eyebrows drew together.

"Nope." Leading the way back towards our house, I added in a murmur, "I'd *love* you. Even with fugly toes."

Grinning, she pushed me away with her shoulder. "You'd better."

"Think we'll ever get everyone out of the living room so we can get some sleep tonight?" she whispered as we awkwardly navigated our house's stairs and storm door.

The scent of pine from the fresh cut logs inches from our faces was nearly overwhelming now.

I managed a shrug without dropping any of the firewood. "Eventually."

Once inside, we toed off our snow boots then dumped the logs by the fireplace and shucked our coats.

Cassie sniffed the air. "Mmm, pine trees! Smells like Christmas."

Which had been a touchy group subject at Grandma Letty's. Our group's religious preferences were too diverse for it to be a good idea to have Christmas trees in the main areas of any of the temporary homes, even though Christmas was just two days away now. But each family was welcome to decorate their bedrooms if they wanted to. I'd spotted a couple of fathers cutting baby pine trees earlier this evening. The sight of those puny trees had reminded me of the Charlie Brown Christmas movie Damon used to insist we watch on DVD every Christmas Eve.

But Tarah and I didn't even have a room of our own to decorate. I was starting to see the point in Grandma Letty's argument for private rooms for us now. Did Tarah miss having a tree to decorate with presents underneath it?

I turned to ask her about it but got distracted in the process. Bud, who we'd almost forgotten about in the recliner a few feet away, moaned in his sleep, his head turning to one side then the other.

Nightmares?

I watched him for a few seconds, then looked at Pamela in the kitchen area. "Is it time for another dose?"

"No, he shouldn't wake up for at least another couple of hours," she replied with a frown. She dried her hands on a dish towel then took the three steps over to Bud's chair. "He looks a little flushed." She touched his forehead and hummed. "He's running a fever. Let me get my kit."

She was gone in her family's bedroom for a few

minutes, returning with what looked like an ordinary women's shoulder bag. From it she took out an electronic thermometer, the kind with a short wand on one end topped by a white plastic ball. She slowly ran it across Bud's forehead then froze.

I didn't like her body language. I walked over to see the reading for myself then silently swore. Bud's temperature was a hundred and two degrees Fahrenheit. I didn't have to be a doctor to figure out that wasn't good.

CHAPTER 17

"A problem with the sedatives maybe?" I murmured, my mind racing. This was not a complication we needed right now. We needed to be able to send him home tomorrow with no memories of this place so we could focus on getting our new community through the winter.

"Maybe a reaction to them? He's been on them off and on all week. Maybe his body's signaling he's had enough?" Pamela said.

Sweat beaded on Bud's forehead and upper lip, trickling down the gullies of his weathered face. He moaned again through lips that looked dry enough to crack soon.

"What should we do?" I asked.

Pamela shook her head. "If his fever was a little lower, I'd say just cover him up, monitor his temp and let the fever break on its own. But a hundred and two is pretty high. We need to cool him off. A lukewarm bath might help, and I've got some acetaminophen we can give him. If that doesn't work, we'll have to try more aggressive methods."

"Master bath, or the other?" Every house had the same layout with two full baths at either end. The master bathrooms had larger garden tubs.

"Master bath," she said. "I'll set up a pallet in the bedroom too. We can keep Bud there for the night so I can monitor him without having to wake everyone else. Plus, it's flu season. If that's what this is, things could get messy soon."

Meaning Bud might start vomiting. Great. And the flu was pretty darn contagious too.

"Maybe Cassie should bunk with Tarah and me in here tonight?" Tarah and I only took up two of the U-shaped couch's sections, so Cassie could have a whole section to herself.

Pamela nodded, her face grim. "Let's hope it isn't the flu, though. If it is, it'll spread fast and we'll have a rough few days till I can catch up to it and get everyone healed. Normally the flu only takes me about an hour or two to detox out of a person's system, but since it's so contagious and with the housing situation being what it currently is…"

I looked around us, trying to see the situation through Pamela's point of view. She was right. The central air and heat might not be working, but everyone's bedroom doors were open to allow the heat from the fireplace to warm them. Making this house one big box of communal germs. If Bud was contagious, every person in this house had already been exposed.

"I'll tell everyone to stay in the house away from the others tonight just in case," I said. "At least that will contain it to just this house. We'll know more tomorrow whether he's contagious, right?"

She nodded.

"Alright. If he is, we'll do an official quarantine then."

"Sounds good." Pamela bent down and lifted Bud's arm as if she planned to haul him off to the bathtub herself.

"Mike and I've got this." I took Bud's arm from her then called out for Mike. He hopped up from the living room floor by the coffee table to join us. "Bud's sick," I explained. "We need to get him into the master tub to cool him down."

Mike grabbed Bud's other arm, and between the two of us, we managed to haul the unconscious man up out of the chair, through the kitchen, through the master bedroom past two metal frame bunk beds and a startled Steve who was reading in bed, and into the master bath. We set Bud on the linoleum covered steps that edged the garden tub. Mike held him upright while I got Bud shucked down to his underwear. Pamela brought a few buckets of room temperature water plus one pot of warmed water to fill the tub a few inches. Once she gave the go-ahead, Mike and I managed to lift Bud over the lip of the tub and into the lukewarm water.

I tried not to think about how similar this was to arranging that dead cop's body behind the steering wheel of his car.

As soon as he was in the water, Bud began to shake. And yet he still didn't open his eyes.

"What the heck are you doing?" Steve asked from the doorway behind us.

"The bus driver's sick," Pamela said. "We've got to get his fever down. He'll be sleeping in our room tonight." She wasn't asking his permission and clearly didn't care about her husband's opinion on the subject.

I kept my back turned toward Steve to hide my grin. Pamela was a lot stronger than her tiny frame looked.

"What about Cassie? I don't want her to get—" Steve began.

"She'll be sleeping in the living room tonight," Pamela said, leaning over to dip a washcloth in the water so she could cool off Bud's face and neck.

"I want her out of this house. Now," Steve said.

"There's no telling how long this man has been running

a fever," Pamela said. "If he's contagious, she's already been exposed, along with you and me and everyone else in this house. We need to try and keep this contained if we can. We don't even know what it is yet."

Steve cursed loudly. "I told you this might happen. If Cassie gets sick—"

"Then I'll heal her, just like I always do every year during flu season." Pamela's voice was still firm but turning tense at the edges. "Let's just see what this is first before we start panicking, okay?"

Growling, Steve turned and stomped off.

Pamela sighed. "Hayden, can you call your grandma and see if this could be a reaction to the sedatives? We won't give him any more just in case, but there might also be something we can give him to counter the reaction, if that's what this is."

"Yep, I'm on it." I'd left my phone in my truck, so I headed through the house towards the front door now. But what I found in the living room made me instantly change direction.

"Steve, stop," Tarah said, keeping her voice low as she stood behind Cassie, holding onto the little girl's shoulders. "You know her mother doesn't want her to go."

"What do you know about my family's business?" Steve snarled. "And she's *my* kid. I'll take her wherever I want! Now let her go." He wasn't dumb enough to touch Tarah yet, settling for tugging at one of his daughter's hands.

"Pamela," I called out, crossing over to stand at Tarah's side and add my hand to Cassie's other shoulder so we both had a hold on her. The kid was shaking, but she made no attempt to be free. Instead, she'd actually grabbed Tarah's shirt tail with her free hand and was leaning back against us as if for support or comfort.

"Steve, what do you think you're doing?" Pamela cried out as she entered the living room.

"I've got to get her out of here," Steve said. "Can't you see how dangerous this place is for her? Don't you want her to be safe?"

"She is safe, Steve," Pamela said, moving to stand in front of her daughter. She reached out, and I thought she was going to try and tear Cassie's hand free from Steve's grasp. But Pamela simply laid her hand on top of theirs. "Please calm down and think about this logically."

Several people poked their heads out through their doorways, then came all the way out into the hallway to watch. Part of me worried that our new audience would cause more trouble. The other part of me hoped they might serve as backup if Steve resorted to Clann abilities I might have never seen before.

"Logic? There's nothing illogical about my thinking here," Steve said. "That man is sick in there, and now you want all of us to get sick too."

"It's probably just the sedatives," I said, working to keep my voice calm and reasonable when all I really wanted to do was punch the crap out of this man then kick him out of the village before he started a group wide panic.

"Exactly," Pamela said. "Too much sedatives, and he just needs to sleep them off. Worst case scenario, it's the flu, and he'll be sick for a few days then right as rain afterward, and I can detox anyone else who gets it in a matter of hours. There's no more danger to any of us here than if we were back home and one of Cassie's classmates or our coworkers came down with it."

"The flu?" someone murmured in the hallway.

"Yeah, the flu," I barked, fast losing my patience. "Everyone gets it every year. You feel like crap for a few hours while Pamela detoxes you, then you're back to normal. It wouldn't be the end of the world here, people." Geez, they acted like we had no healers and were incapable of reaching the town a few miles away if necessary.

"But the flu's really contagious," someone else said. "And people die from it every year."

"If they're already weak and don't get help," Pamela countered. "I'm not the only healer in this group, and the city's got a good hospital just a few miles away if needed. I've treated the flu in my family every year. There's really no need to panic. Steve, you know I can handle healing someone with the flu. How many times have I taken care of you when you came down with it?"

Steve shook his head. "But that was when we lived in town—"

That was it. I'd had enough. "Steve, cut the crap. You know this is really just about you wanting to take your family away from here. Tell the truth and quit trying to scare everyone."

Silence in the hallway as the attention shifted back to Steve.

His eyes narrowed as his scowl deepened. "Yeah, I want my family out of here. Why wouldn't I? You think I should be happy having to share a house with other families? And now we're probably going to be quarantined in here too."

"That's true about the quarantine," I said, figuring we might as well get this issue out in the open as a household now. "That's just to keep the flu, if it's even that, from spreading to the other houses. Why risk getting other people sick if we can avoid it? It'd be no different than if each of us was back home and someone in our family got sick. Except here our family's a little bigger, right?" I looked at the people in the hallway, deliberately making eye contact with everyone. Debate class was finally starting to prove useful after all.

I saw the few worried faces in the hall relax and a couple of heads nod. They were starting to see reason again instead of panicking.

Taking a deep breath, I turned back to Steve. "Now as

for taking your family away, I think it's obvious that your wife wants to stay. Cassie, what do you want to do?" I knew I was putting the kid in an awful position, but I wanted everyone in this house to be real clear on what could seem a muddy issue of parental rights.

"Daddy, please can we stay?" Cassie's voice was shaky with tears. "I like it here. And in the spring you can build us our own house with a yard and flowers and everything."

I saw Steve flinch, his eyebrows drawing together.

"How about it, Steve?" I murmured. "She's right about building your own house. These mobile homes are just temporary. Come spring time, everybody's going to be free to build their own homes here. Heck, you can get started right now if you want to brave the cold and deal with the snow and frozen ground."

"Can we stay, Daddy? Please?" Cassie whispered, pulling away from Tarah and me so she could grab her father's hand with both of hers.

Steve crouched down in front of her. "But sweetie, don't you miss your school and your friends?"

"Nope," Cassie didn't even hesitate to answer. "I've got better ones here. Even if they do cheat at Monopoly."

Mike snickered in the kitchen. He tried to turn it into a cough.

After a long minute, Steve sighed. "Fine. I guess we'll stay. For a few months, at least. But Pamela, you've got to promise, if this flu thing gets out of control..."

Pamela nodded.

Feeling the tension in the air fade, I stepped around Steve and Cassie so I could talk to the other families. "So listen, like Pamela said, we need to be safe and quarantine the house till we know for sure what's going on with the bus driver. But that doesn't mean you're stuck inside the house. If you get restless and want to go outside, feel free. Just make sure you don't go visiting the other houses, don't let them come into this house, don't trade stuff with them, and if you talk to them outside, avoid touching them or standing too close while you talk so you don't spread any possible germs."

"When will we know for sure what it is?" One of the men asked, and I realized I didn't even know the names of all my housemates yet.

"Pamela says we should know by tomorrow."

Nodding, they drifted back to their rooms.

Satisfied the general panic was over, I turned to find Tarah standing behind me.

"I've got to go grab my phone from the truck," I told her, reaching for my coat and boots. "Want to go with me?"

She nodded, and once she was ready, we went outside, walking fast, the snow crunching loudly beneath our feet.

We wove our way through the tree stump obstacle course to my truck. I found myself wishing I'd started building that tiny house back at my grandma's. Then maybe Tarah would have had a house of her own now away from all the drama and possible virus infection.

At my truck, I quickly grabbed the disposable phone from under the driver's side of the front seat and called Grandma Letty. Unfortunately the news wasn't good.

"What'd she say?" Tarah asked after I hung up.

"There's no way it's the sedatives. She says Pam's probably right and it's the flu." I hid the phone again, this time wedging it under the backseat on the seat frame. We got out of the truck and started to return to the houses. Then, on second thought, I turned back and, as quietly as I could, popped my truck's hood.

"What are you doing?" she whispered, though no one was outside to hear us.

"Getting more car insurance," I muttered as I removed one of the spark plugs from the engine. Steve seemed okay for now, but who knew if he might change his mind and try to make a fast escape with Cassie in the future? If he did, he'd have to do it without transportation. I added a spark plug from the bus's engine with my truck's plug in my coat pocket. Then we headed back to our house.

At the porch, I was reluctant to go inside. It was freezing out here, but it was also peaceful.

I took a deep breath of sharp, cold air, then another. "Cassie's right. It does smell like Christmas here." The crisp, pine-filled air cleared out my lungs, taking the last of the tension with it. Inside the house, it was too easy to forget where we were. Out here, I could think clearer, breathe easier.

"Yeah. It makes me miss Christmas back home a little."

I glanced sideways at her. "Missing your family?"

She shrugged. "Yeah, but we were already sort of prepping for the separation for when I went off to college."

"You could still go, you know. If we got your name cleared..."

"I know. But to be honest, college was really their dream, not mine. You don't have to have a degree to be a journalist."

"True. But still, they've got to be worried about you."

She looked down at her feet. "Yeah, um, about that...at your grandma's I might have posted a message under an alias in a forum my brother visits online a lot. The alias was a nickname he gave me when I was little, so he'll recognize it."

At my widening eyes, she hastily added, "Don't worry, I didn't give any hints about our new location. I just told him in a roundabout way that I was out of state and starting a new life and that I'm safe. I disguised it to look like someone vaguely talking about shopping for a vacation home, but he'll get what I really meant and tell our parents."

I thought it over, then realized I'd just have to trust her. I let out a long, slow breath. "Okay."

Tarah leaned against my side at the porch railing and tilted her head back. "Wow. Have you ever seen so many stars?"

Despite seeing through her attempt to distract me from worrying, I still looked up and was stunned. Back home, even outside of town the nearby city lights made it hard to see the night sky, so only the brightest stars showed up. Here, the mountains helped block the lights from the nearest town, allowing the full moon to light the world around us. As a result, not only was every star easy to see above us, but I could even make out the Milky Way.

And then there were those amazing peaks all around us. Back home, East Texas wasn't flat. It had rolling hills everywhere. But we didn't have anything like the Black Hills mountains. The steep peaks here rose on all sides, with our settlement nestled perfectly in the middle. The effect should have been imposing. Instead, it was...comforting.

I understood then why Grandma Letty had suggested this place for our village. It wasn't just that she already owned the property. If she'd liked another area better, she would have raised Hell itself to buy the right land instead.

It was because everything about this area promised safety. The shelter of the surrounding peaks, the camouflage of the thick pines and cypresses and the hardwoods that would eventually add their own color and beauty in the summer and fall. The stillness of the place, so quiet we could hear the gurgling creek where it still ran free in the unfrozen middle of its course.

I could see how this place might look in a few months, maybe a year or two. It really could be stunning in every way, from its gifted people that it kept safely hidden, to the eventual town those people would build with their own sweat and imagination. That is, if they could find the courage to make it happen. Right now they seemed broken and shaky. But this place could fix that, could heal them and build them back up again.

This village didn't have to be some sad place for society's rejected and unwanted, where they simply hid away and tried to survive.

They could all be *strong* here.

"What are you thinking about?" Tarah murmured.

I smiled down at her. "Possibilities."

She smiled back, slow and sweet, and her smile was a thing of beauty all on its own, a piece of her heart and soul shining through for only me to see.

I kissed her, just a short kiss, but it was like sipping from the fountain of strength itself. She grounded me, reminded me with her every look and smile and touch that she believed in me.

"Come on, let's go see if Pamela needs help with Bud," I said then led the way back inside the house.

Thursday, December 24th

It was a long night. Even after the lukewarm bath and acetaminophen, Bud's fever refused to come down. Pamela, Tarah and I took turns switching out wet washcloths on Bud's forehead after we got him set up on the bottom bunk of one of the master bedroom's beds. Pamela insisted Tarah and I stick to the original plan and sleep on the living room couches, where Steve had also set up a pallet on the floor by the coffee table. Apparently he didn't want to risk sleeping with his wife in the same room as someone who was sick. And he wanted nothing to do with the germ-ridden recliner, either.

What a wimp.

At least this way I could keep an eye on him easier.

The next day, Pamela looked tired and frustrated. "I don't know what it is," she murmured as we stood watching her patient toss his head from side to side in his sleep. "It's not the flu, that much I'm sure of. When I look inside his body, the sickness is everywhere and nowhere at once. It's not located in just one place, making it more like a virus. But I can't get a feel for what it is. It's like trying to grab onto water with a single finger. It just keeps escaping me."

My chest grew tight, and I realized then that I'd believed Pamela would be able to heal Bud no matter what. Her confusion chipped away at that confidence. "Should we take him somewhere?"

It was like she didn't even hear me. "It has the symptoms of flu. It almost feels like it too, but..."

I touched her shoulder to get her to focus. "Pamela, should we take him somewhere?"

Her chin rose. "No, not yet. Let me try a few more things first. It could just be a different strain of flu. As long as we keep him hydrated, and the fever doesn't get any higher, he should be okay."

I was tempted to point out that Bud was old. But Pamela already knew that, and as a healer for our group, she needed us to trust and support her. Just like Tarah trusted and supported me.

"Okay, it's your call," I told her, working hard to keep the doubt out of my voice. "But if he needs to go to the hospital, you let me know, all right?"

Pamela nodded, her frown fixed like it might become her new default expression. "I'm going to need some supplies soon. More acetaminophen and ibuprofen. A few herbs."

"Make me a list and I'll take care of it," I promised.

"Thanks, Hayden." She patted my shoulder, her attention still on her patient. The absentminded gesture reminded me so strongly of my mother that I had to clear my throat and duck out of the room.

In the living room, everyone had gathered for a Monopoly tournament, apparently tired of being cooped up in their rooms. Tarah was in the kitchen washing the breakfast dishes, with Mike at her side drying them using a combination of a towel and a spell. With each flick of his wrist, a plate rose into the air and was dried by a towel without his ever touching them. Tarah stared at the display of abilities in obvious amazement, both her eyes and her smile huge. Laughing, she waved a hand around the floating plate and towel like a magician's assistant, proving to the imaginary audience that there were no strings attached anywhere.

For a split second, jealousy shot through me, and I wondered if Mike was interested in Tarah. But when they both looked up me and smiled, I didn't get even a hint of a weird vibe from either of them. So I brushed off the stupid worries I couldn't do anything about right now and focused on the all too real problems at hand.

"Hey, I've got to run into town and pick up a few things for Pamela," I said. "Can you two keep an eye on things here?" I wanted to invite Tarah to come with me, but that would require asking Steve to do his face altering spell on her. And since he was currently content playing Monopoly with Cassie and the others, I didn't want to risk setting him off again before I had to leave.

Plus, I wanted to get something for Tarah for Christmas.

"Yeah, sure," Mike said.

"You might want to check and see if anyone else needs anything," Tarah suggested. "And at the other houses too."

Oh. Right. It was too easy to forget about the three other houses full of people here when I spent so much time in just this one. "Okay, I'll ask around. Tarah, do you mind getting a list for this house while I'm at the others?"

"Sure."

I headed out to the other houses, careful to keep my distance from each door while I warned them about the quarantine at my house. Everyone put together their lists, which I was worried would be a mile long and full of items like flat screen TVs and cable. Surprisingly the requests were more for things like crochet needles and yarn, more board games, and after hearing we might have a flu outbreak, lots of requests for antibacterial wipes and hand soap.

Pamela's list was the longest, including disinfecting supplies plus several herbs I doubted I'd find anywhere but at a health food store. At least the neighboring town of Spearfish was a decent sized one and should have everything we needed.

Tarah

While Hayden went into town to pick up a few things, I did the best I could to help the healers in any way possible...at least for someone who had zero Clann abilities. I fetched and heated water, switched out hot washcloths for cool ones, tried to keep Cassie occupied with board and card games. But not having any healing abilities to help out with made the situation frustrating.

When Hayden returned, I helped him deliver all the requested items to each house. Then with a big grin, he led me to his truck where I found the strangest surprise waiting for me in the front seat.

"Merry Christmas," he said as we climbed into either side of the front seat.

My mouth dropped open. It looked like a two foot tall Christmas tree complete with a skirt around the base. The entire decoration was positioned in the center of the front seat, so we had to lean forward in order to see each other around it.

"I thought about cutting down a real baby tree," he mumbled with suspiciously pink cheeks. Was he *blushing*? "But then we'd have to water it, the water would freeze in here, and the tree wouldn't get any fresh air. And then they were all sold out of mini trees and ornaments—"

"Is this the top of a regular sized artificial tree?" I blurted out, stunned by his creative thinking.

"Uh, yeah. It wouldn't stay upright, so I used this box for the base and poked a hole in the top." He lifted the full sized tree skirt he'd tied around the wire base of the tree top to reveal how the tree was duck taped to the box. "And I was thinking, since all the mini ornaments were sold out, we could, I don't know, make our own?" He lifted the tree and the lid it was attached to, revealing how the box was full of scissors and glue sticks and packs of Christmas cards and gift wrap.

How had he known how much I was missing getting to decorate the tree with my family? It was one of the best parts of the holiday. I bit my lower lip as my eyes stung.

"It was a stupid idea, I know," he said. "I wanted you to have a tree, but—"

"No, I love it," I said, daring to look at him though my eyes still threatened to overflow. "It's brilliant really. Way better than any tree I could have come up with. It's the sweetest thing anyone's ever done for me."

"Aw crap, don't cry," he muttered then leaned around the tree to give me a quick kiss. "It's not that great. It doesn't even have any lights or decorations yet."

"We'll make it beautiful."

The next twenty minutes felt like being back in kindergarten as we cut strips of paper and glued them into a tiny chain that we draped around our tree. I couldn't help but laugh a little as I caught Hayden struggling to fit his big hands into a tiny pair of children's scissors. He was trying so hard. It was incredibly cute.

Unfortunately the time flew by far too fast and eventually we had to stop. Figuring we would be missed, we packed up all the craft supplies in the tree's box base again, then headed back to the house.

It was the last bit of real happiness we'd have for a long time.

Two hours later, one of the parents in our house got sick, followed by one of the older kids.

The house smelled like a display for Lysol. And it was quiet, unnaturally so considering the number of people packed inside its walls. Mike and Hayden tried to keep the kids happy with card games when they weren't fetching more buckets of water. I spent all my time helping Pamela, grinding herbs for potions in the kitchen, switching out cooling washcloths on the patients' foreheads, making teas and terrible smelling pastes until we had to crack open one of the living room windows just to get some fresh air.

But nothing seemed to work.

Then came the knock at our door, and a message from one of the other houses. Despite all our precautions, the sickness had spread. Hayden sent around a message calling for all the healers and sick people to gather at our house. Clearly this was a tougher strain of flu than Pamela had experienced before. We needed to stop the virus in its tracks. Now.

Worried, I stood with Hayden in the master bedroom doorway as two new healers gathered with Pamela around Bud, who was still the most dangerously ill of all the patients. We set up the three new patients in here with him to make it easier to treat everyone.

After several long minutes of silence, one of the new healers, a lady in her fifties or so, growled in frustration. "It's like chasing after a mouse."

"Exactly!" Pamela muttered. "Every time I get close, it races off somewhere else. I can't get it pinned down long enough to get rid of it, or even to figure out what it *is*."

The other healers hummed in agreement. Then they noticed us watching.

"What can I do to help?" I said.

Pamela shook her head, her jaw clenched. "Nothing right now. We've just got to keep battling this thing till we find a way to beat it. Why don't you two go grab some fresh air for a few hours? We've got others coming to take a shift. I don't want you two getting too tired and lowering your immunity to whatever this virus is."

Frustrated, I went outside, making a beeline for the truck. I needed something manual to do, something that would take my mind off my lack of ability to help the situation in any real and meaningful way.

Hayden followed at a slower pace, hanging back probably because my frustration wasn't too subtle right now. He hesitated a few yards away from the truck after I got in, then he turned towards the flatbed trailer, which he'd unhitched and left a few yards behind his truck. A few minutes later I heard him tear into the tiny house kit. A smart choice since I didn't want to take my anger out on him but couldn't figure out how to stop being angry in the first place. Hearing him working on his own thing outside while I had some alone time to cool off and reset my thoughts was soothing on its own. The mindless task of cutting out Christmas card designs to hang as ornaments on our tree took care of the rest.

An hour later, I felt like an idiot for getting so angry in the first place. After stowing all the craft supplies again, I climbed out of the truck and joined him by the flatbed trailer, which had been transformed from an orderly, plastic-wrapped cube into a huge mess across the snow. It looked like a home improvement store had exploded.

"Want some help?" I said.

"Does Pamela need us yet?"

I shook my head. "If she had needed us, she would have sent one of the kids for us. She's probably busy working with real healers now." Even to my own ears, I could tell I'd failed to keep the bite out of my tone.

One corner of Hayden's mouth twitched, but wisely he didn't laugh at me. Instead he offered me the kit's instruction booklet. "I can't find part A, B or C. Everything's got a sticker on it, but there's a million pieces to wade through first just to find what we need to get going."

We didn't make a lot of headway that afternoon. Our bulky gloves made it hard to pick up the smaller stuff, but taking them off was pure agony in the cold. We did get everything more organized and a couple of sections of subflooring down, though, which was a start.

"I think Grandma Letty just gave me that kit to tick me off," he joked as we headed back to our house to warm up.

"No, it just requires patience."

He gave me a pointed look.

I laughed and was immediately grateful I still remembered how to. "I know, I know. I'm being a huge hypocrite, preaching about having patience when even I can't hold onto my own patience lately. But I never said I was perfect. I'm human. Which makes me a work in progress."

He grinned. "A work in progress. I like that."

Still smiling, I grabbed his hand and tugged him after me up the cement steps of our house and through the front doorway into the living room.

Where we found absolute chaos.

CHAPTER 18

Hayden

"What's going on?" I asked as Mike hurried by with a stack of washcloths.

"Four more sick from the other houses," he muttered, his steps never slowing.

Cursing, I told Tarah, "That's it. The quarantine's not working. Get everyone but the patients and the healers out of here. They'll have to bunk on the couches or floors or something in the other houses. And spread the word...anyone who even starts to feel like they're sick needs to be sent here immediately."

Wide eyed, Tarah darted down the hall to tell the families the new game plan, while I went to the master bedroom.

"Hayden, thank God," Pamela said. "We need more room. The quarantine's—"

"Not working. Yeah, I know. Tarah's sending our healthy families to stay at the other houses. We're setting this house up as the infirmary. What do you need?"

"More washcloths. Whatever fever reducers and flu

meds anyone's got. And anyone else with even basic healing abilities should come help too."

I nodded. "Mike helped flush the drugs out of people at the internment camp. You might see what he can do."

Pamela nodded.

I ran off to check the other houses for more supplies and to make sure the displaced families had what they needed. Some of the others acted like everyone from our house were walking talking germ pools. They'd have to get over it.

After I spoke with all the houses and delivered the requested supplies to the growing number of healers in the infirmary, I stopped outside, needing a moment to breathe and refocus. Except I was at the end of my game plan. I had no idea what to do next.

So I went out to my truck for somewhere quiet to think. I had to smile a little as I saw the latest additions to the tree. Tarah had cut out Christmas card designs and hung them like ornaments using paper clips. Which reminded me.... I dug under the backseat for the box containing Tarah's gifts. Then I pulled out the gift wrap supplies from the tree box stand, careful not to destroy its fragile new decorations.

While I wrapped her presents, I tried to work on a solution for the village's crisis. But I couldn't come up with anything. The problem was I didn't understand the first thing about healing and had to rely on whatever the healers told me. Maybe if I could learn how to heal, I could understand the situation a little better and help find a way to stop the illness from spreading any further. The adult healers were way too busy to interrupt for tutoring, though. Then I remembered a teen who did know how to heal and might not mind taking a few minutes to teach me.

With Tarah's presents now wrapped, labeled and under the tree, I headed off to find Mike.

"Has anyone told you lately that you're kind of an idiot?" Mike said an hour later as we froze our butts off down by the creek.

"Did anyone ever tell you *you're* a crappy teacher?" I barked back. "Geez, between you and this stupid spell book, y'all make healing sound so mystical or something. Can't you just tell me how to do it step-by-step? You know, like we're back in school and it's a lab project for science class?" I had to force myself not to chuck the useless book into the snow.

Mike shook his head. "Healing doesn't work like that. It sounds mystical because it *is*. You're basically astral projecting here. You're sending your spirit, or soul, or essence, or whatever you want to call it, out of your own body and into the patient's so you can then detect the source of disruption in their body. Then you work with their spirit in a partnership to take out that disruptive vibration. But in order to do that, first you have to let go of what you want. Let go of yourself, of who you are, and let your consciousness just float into the patient's body until—"

"Until the illness or wound draws me to it. Yeah, I heard you the first twenty times. And I'm really trying here, man—"

"And yet my hand still has a cut on it." He held up the palm with his tiny, self-inflicted test wound like an accusation.

I was feeling drawn, all right...drawn to punch a tree.

I shook my head. This healing business was way harder than I'd expected. No wonder not everyone in the camp could do it. "Look, just forget I asked, okay? I've already taken up too much of your time, and they're going to need you back in there."

After another minute of silence, Mike sighed. "Don't give up on it. It takes a while. But if you really want it, you'll figure it out."

Before or after everyone in the settlement was dead?

The crunch of his footsteps faded in the distance, leaving me alone in the cold darkness.

I came to this village for a reason, to help make a difference for these people. Now they were all getting sick, and I was powerless to help. I couldn't even heal a simple cut! I was completely useless here.

But the healers weren't having much success either. They said they couldn't even figure out what the virus was. Maybe that was the real problem. If we at least knew what the disease was, then the healers could know how to go after it. Unfortunately none of the outcasts here wanted to resort to seeing a regular doctor in town for fear of being turned in to the government. They'd all rather take their chances with our own healers.

But Bud wasn't Clann...

I jogged back to the infirmary, up the steps and inside past the pallets of patients that now filled the living room, till I found Pamela. I was surprised to also find Steve helping his wife change the sweat-soaked sheets beneath one of the patients.

"I want to take Bud to the local hospital," I told them. "He's not wanted by the feds, and neither am I." At least, that I knew of. "The doctors there can diagnose him, and then that should help you figure out what this virus is so you can treat everyone else. Right?"

Pamela rubbed her forehead, her movements slow and weary. "I guess so. But what about you? Even if no one knows you led the prison break in Texas, they still might recognize you because of who your dad is. What if he's searching for you?"

"Grandma Letty would have warned me if he was." No doubt dear old Dad was trying to keep my disappearance quiet to avoid the media coverage and what the reporters might dig up about our family.

"They'll want ID for Bud," Pamela said.

I searched for Bud's clothes, finding them in a pile in the bathroom. His wallet was still in his jeans' back pocket.

Steve helped me get Bud dressed and haul him out to my truck. Pamela followed with a blanket.

I stashed the miniature Christmas tree and Tarah's presents on the backseat so we could set Bud in the front. It would be too hard for me to get him out of the backseat later by myself. But I should be able to roll him out from the front seat.

"Let Tarah know where I'm headed?" I asked Pamela. In the rush to get Bud ready for transport, I hadn't seen Tarah. She must have been in one of the back bedrooms helping the other healers.

Pamela nodded as she started to close the passenger side door.

Steve's hand shot out to stop her. "Wait. What if he tells someone about this place?"

Pamela looked at the elderly man for a long minute then shook her head. "He probably doesn't have enough time to tell anyone anything. And even if he did, they would just think he was delirious from the fever."

After another hesitation, Steve let her shut the door and I started the engine.

I drove into town as fast as I could on the icy, dark roads, using the paper map of Spearfish the logging team had used to find the village site in the first place.

At the hospital's ER entrance, I parked, then ran around to the passenger side and opened the door.

Bud was awake.

"Uh, hi. Remember me?" I said, unsure what the heck I should say to him.

He frowned and mumbled, "Where are we?"

"Hospital. You're sick. But we're going to get you some

really good help." I slung his right arm over my shoulder and pulled him out of the truck and onto his feet.

He tried to walk, but I still had to carry most of his weight into the ER. Once inside, a nurse saw us and brought a wheelchair to take Bud off in. Another nurse handed me a clipboard and asked me to fill it out in the waiting area, but I didn't know any of the answers she wanted. I explained that he was just our bus driver, not a relative. Immediately her face became closed off, and I knew she was going to tell me that I was no longer allowed to know anything that was going on.

"Look, I know you're supposed to kick me out since I'm not his family. But there's another kid who's sick on our bus, and I need to know what Bud's got in case the kid has it too."

"You should bring the—"

"The mother won't let me. She's from another country and suspicious of our doctors here." I faked a smile that hopefully said "I know, crazy, right?"

Her eyebrows shot up. "I'll let the doctor know. If the patient gives her permission, then she'll be able to tell you the diagnosis."

"Thanks." I found a chair in the waiting room and sank down into it. Opposite me, my normal reflection stared back from the window's undivided glass pane.

Minutes passed, then hours. I watched the Late Night show on a TV mounted high in the corner with the sound turned off, closed captioning filling me in on what I wasn't allowed to hear. Then the news came on. The world seemed like one big endless war zone out there, the news filled with so much civil war and anti-Clann rioting that they didn't have time enough to cover it all, much less anything else.

After awhile, I couldn't watch it anymore. I tried to see the mountains in the distance through the window, but it was too dark outside. All I could see was my reflection staring back at me.

My hair was getting too long again. Mom would be nagging me to get a hair cut if she could see me now. I'd managed to at least shave this morning, but I looked scruffy again. It had been a long day.

And it just kept getting longer.

"Sir?" A sharp female voice jerked me out of my thoughts.

I stood up and turned toward the voice. A short brunette in scrubs and a long white coat stood waiting for me at the swinging double doors.

"You came in with Bud Preston?" she asked.

I nodded.

"He's asked to see you and given me permission to discuss his condition with you as well."

I tried to hide my surprise on both counts as we headed down a corridor that could have come straight out of a movie, except the paintings and photographs on the taupe walls here were mostly of the Black Hills mountains.

She stopped outside a room. The door was shut, and she made no move to open it yet.

She hugged her plastic clipboard to her chest, oddly reminding me of Tarah back in school, though she had to be in her thirties or forties.

"To be honest," she began. "We don't know what's wrong with Mr. Preston. We've managed to stabilize him for now, and of course we're still running tests, so we may know more in a few days. But as ill as Mr. Preston is, I would really like to send him to a larger hospital. Unfortunately, he refuses to let me transfer him out of here without speaking to you first."

"Are you saying he could die?"

"Of course we're doing everything we can to prevent that. But if we can't figure out how to treat him and he continues to refuse to be transferred to another hospital, then yes, that is a possibility."

Bud could die from whatever this was. Which meant everyone else in the village could too. I swallowed hard. "Is it something...exotic, or abnormal or something?"

"It appears to be the flu. At least, he has every symptom of your garden variety, everyday type of flu. But we can't seem to catch any of it in his blood work in order to verify that. We've notified the CDC who are sending someone to examine him in case this is something new we're dealing with. Now you said—"

I didn't need to hear anything more. All she was saying was exactly what Pamela and the other village healers had said, with one difference...the virus was possibly lethal and could kill its victims in a matter of days. Which meant I had no time.

And yet there was one more thing I needed to do before I left here. "You said he asked to see me?"

"Uh, well, yes, but first—"

"You also said he may not have much time?" Without waiting for a reply, I opened the door.

Bud looked even worse under the fluorescent lighting, his cheeks sunken in beneath the long folds of wrinkles that lined the sides of his nose and mouth. His thin gray hair looked even thinner now that it lay matted and limp over his head.

From a strong and fairly sharp and spry old man to this—wasted and dying—in just a few days. From an illness that neither doctors nor witches with healing abilities could name, much less cure.

And others could be dying of it too, right this very minute, in the very place where I had promised them only safety and protection and shelter.

If we didn't find a cure, how many more might die? Bringing them here to the hospital obviously wasn't the answer. For all their high tech equipment and education, these doctors seemed just as confused as the healers back at the village.

But as the doctor closed the door behind me, putting aside her professional curiosity in order to give Bud and me some privacy, I understood one thing at least. In this moment, the people at the village weren't who I needed to focus on.

Just for one moment, it was Bud who deserved time and attention. And more apologies than I could ever say.

I stepped closer to the bed. The hospital staff had left the plastic covered rails up, as if afraid Bud would roll off the bed. But he looked way too weak to sit up, much less roll around.

His breathing had grown harsher, each breath a small battle all its own for life. And an accusation. I couldn't shake the feeling that I had caused this. If I had never asked him to drive our group...

I leaned in close and murmured, "Bud...I'm sorry."

His eyelids eased open. "Hayden."

He remembered me. "Yes sir."

"I keep getting older, and you..." He struggled to swallow. "You keep getting younger."

For a few seconds I was confused. Then I remembered. The last time he'd seen me in bright lighting, I'd been disguised by Steve's face aging spell. All the other times we'd spoken to each other had been under the dim lighting of the bus interior lights or parking lot lamps. "It's the lighting."

"It's sorcery." His eyes searched mine with a cloudy desperation. As if begging me to tell the truth at last.

I nodded.

One corner of his mouth trembled upward, the ghost of a smile. "I knew it. Witches."

I nodded. He wouldn't be able to lead anyone back to

our village, and if he died, at least he would die knowing the truth as he deserved. "They're good people, despite what the news and government say. I was trying to get them to safety."

"Did we make it?"

"Mostly. But a few of them are sick now. Like you. So we're not really safe yet."

"Your healers...they working on them?"

"Yes. They tried to help you too. But they haven't found a cure yet."

"They will. Pamela...she's a good one." He stopped for breath and a long, slow blink.

I should let him sleep. I started to move away, but his eyes opened again. Wheezing, he grabbed my wrist.

"Tell 'em...tell 'em don't be afraid. Tell 'em sorcery...ain't the enemy. *Fear's* the enemy. I wish they could feel it." He sighed, letting go of my wrist as he smiled at the ceiling. "If they could know...the lives they could save..." His eyes closed. "Keep 'em safe, Hayden. Until they see..."

Then the alarms went off, all the machines Bud was hooked up to refusing to let his exit from earth go unnoticed by the strangers who worked here, even as his family back in Oklahoma had no idea he was even in danger of dying.

In the chaos of the nurses and doctors rushing in, I slipped out, numb, empty but a million times heavier, and more confused than I'd ever been before.

CHAPTER 19

Friday, December 25

I didn't turn on the radio on the way back to the village. No music would make sense of the thoughts inside my head right now.

I knew what Tarah would say, could hear her voice now, quietly telling me that Bud's death wasn't my fault, that sometimes it was no one's fault at all, and trying to blame someone or something would just be my way of trying to make some sense out of it.

But it *didn't* make sense. Why would Bud and the others get sick now? No matter what set of rules I tried to apply to the situation, none of them made sense. Why wouldn't they have gotten sick when they were stuffed together in Grandma Letty's house? Or in those cold military trucks for hours, or at the internment camp?

Age wasn't a factor either. The ages of everyone who'd gotten sick were all over the scale from young to middle aged to old. And none of them had seemed weaker than everyone else before they got sick.

And though I felt guilty about the sedatives we'd given

Bud all week, I also had to face the fact that he was the only one who'd received Grandma Letty's potion, and yet others had gotten sick too. So the potion hadn't caused it either.

By the time I pulled up the long road into the village's clearing and parked, I was no closer to an explanation. But I was close to hitting some kind of internal breaking point I was afraid to reach.

I turned off the headlights and caught a glimpse of my watch. One a.m. I tried to remember what day of the week it was, then froze.

It was Christmas day.

I reached over the seat, found the sad little tree and its box base, and eased it up and over to its original resting spot in the front seat. Tarah's presents. I'd wrapped them up together earlier. Where had I put them? I looked in the back. The single, lumpy package had slid across the backseat at some point.

A corner of the gift's wrapping was torn open. Carefully I eased the paper edges back together, trying to use a little glue to fix the tear. But the wrapping was too tight around its contents. There wasn't enough overlap at the tear to allow the paper to stay stuck together.

I could start all over.

But I didn't want to. That would mean admitting that I couldn't fix this.

I could fix this. I just needed the right tools. I dug through the tree box base, found a roll of clear masking tape. I used a piece of it, carefully lining up the edges of the torn paper before sticking the tape over it.

And it held.

I rearranged the sad little tree skirt back over the box of decoration supplies to hide it, then set the present under the tree. There, everything was ready for Christmas morning.

But when I reached for my door handle, I just couldn't make myself open the door to get out. Everyone would want to know what had happened at the hospital.

I'd been so sure the doctors would have a diagnosis. I'd promised Pamela and Steve that I would come back with answers that could help everyone. I'd thought I could finally be a real hero, and this time it would be because *I* wanted it, not because my family expected it of me.

Instead, I had returned with nothing but failure and the promise of death for everyone who was sick.

My hands ached on the steering wheel. I hadn't even been aware of grabbing it. Gritting my teeth, I tore my hands loose then pushed my muscles to carry me out of the truck.

But I still couldn't go inside my house.

Going inside meant seeing the hope in Tarah's eyes die.

I needed to do something, though. Something that would keep my hands busy and my mind empty for awhile. Back home when I felt like this, I used to shoot hoops in the backyard. But there was no hoop and no basketball here. Just the surrounding mountains' false promise of security even as we slowly died, hidden away from a world that hated and feared us.

The tiny house. That would keep me busy for awhile till I could find a way to break the bad news to everyone.

I reached for the kit's instruction booklet like a drowning man grabbing for a life raft.

I worked in the dark with a flashlight at first, focusing on being patient and going slowly. And it was slow going. But eventually I had the beam section for an exterior wall up. And then another. And then another, until the ghostly outline of a house began to take shape.

At some point, it grew light enough that I no longer

needed the flashlight to see the instructions. Still I kept
working. The others would wake up soon and come
seeking answers from me. Until they did, I would focus on
connecting bolt sixteen to beam F.

Too bad leading an outlawed group of dying Clann
outcasts didn't come with such clear cut instructions.

"Hey," Tarah murmured behind me, her voice the first
sound to break the perfect stillness of the morning.

I looked over my shoulder at her standing there in the
dim predawn light, her feet together, her hands primly
clasped in front of her. And once again, the way she stood
there with that perfect posture of hers reminded me of the
days when she had pretended to be the queen of Damon's
and my imaginary realm.

And now that queen had come to demand news of her
knight's latest quest.

I looked away, my mouth twisting. Did queens in the
medieval days ever fire knights who proved too lousy to do
the job? Or did they just behead them for their failure?

Of course, Tarah wouldn't have to go nearly that far to
punish me. All she'd have to do was look at me while her
face filled with disappointment and sadness and fear. That
would be punishment enough.

Might as well get it over with.

"Bud died." The words slipped out, harsh, with no
warning. "The doctors couldn't explain what was wrong
with him either."

There. Now she knew.

I heard her swallow hard, take a crunching step closer
across the snow. Then her hand was over mine, and my
face was buried in her neck and it was all wrong because I
was supposed to be the strong one here. But it was she
who did the holding, and me who was held, wrapping my
arms tight around her so she wouldn't see the fear I could
feel twisting my face now.

We weren't little kids anymore. This was no child's game of pretend, I was no knight in shining armor, and Tarah wasn't a real queen. But she was still mine to save.

But *how?*

There was only one way to keep her safe. "You need to go be with your parents."

She froze, but she didn't let go of me. "No."

"You have to. Otherwise you could get sick. You still could, even then. But maybe not. It doesn't seem to be everywhere right now, just here in our village. At least the odds would be better for you away from here."

"No."

"Then go to my grandma's. She'll be happy to hide you again as long as needed. She'll even get you a lawyer to help clear yours and your dad's names. I can take you to a bus station and get you a ticket—"

"I'm not leaving."

Desperate, I leaned back, searching her face. Her expression was unreadable. "Tarah, your family wouldn't want you to be here. Even Jeremy would want you to go somewhere else, somewhere safe." They wouldn't want Tarah to get sick and die in the cold woods, cut off from the rest of the world where they couldn't even say goodbye to her.

"I belong here."

"I can't protect you here! Don't you get it? I can't save you from whatever the hell this disease is."

Her chin and lower lip jutted out a bit. "I can't leave yet. I need to know how their story ends first."

"You'd really risk your life for a stupid story?"

"It's not just a stupid story. It's life or death for them. If I leave now, I can't finish their story. If I can't finish their story, I can't tell it to begin with. And if I don't tell their story, who will? I'm the only voice they've got." She stepped closer to me and whispered, "If I don't tell the world the truth about them, who will, Hayden?"

Growling in frustration, I turned away. "You are the stubbornest, most hardheaded person I've ever met!"

"So are you."

After a minute, I turned back to face her. "How can you not be afraid?"

"Who says I'm not?"

I stepped closer to her, searched her eyes, and found the glimmer of fear hidden in their depths. "Then why stay?"

"Because the world out there giving in to its fear is what got these people in this situation in the first place. It's okay to be afraid. But you can't make good choices based on it. Fear is the real enemy, not the Clann, and not the outcasts. We're all going to die someday. The real challenge is to learn how to live."

Her words reminded me of Bud's last words. *Fear is the enemy.*

I scrubbed both hands over my cold, tired face. "What do we do then? We're not healers. How do we stop this village from dying?" How did you fight a dragon that had no name and couldn't be seen?

She sighed. "Well, you could start by wishing me a Merry Christmas."

I scowled. Having a happy holiday was the absolute last thing on my mind. "I meant something to fight the virus. Do the healers need anything? Maybe some new herb I could get for them? Something they haven't tried yet?"

"They said they have everything they need for now. And we have plenty of others helping bring firewood and water."

"Then what can I—"

She tugged me toward the truck then opened the driver side door. Did she want me to take her somewhere? Slowly I climbed in, watching as she circled around to the passenger side to join me.

Once our doors had shut out the world beyond the truck's cab, she reached across the seat for my hand. "Merry Christmas, Hayden."

I stared at her, wondering if maybe she was insane after all and I should just kidnap her out of here. She could thank me later. Maybe years later, knowing Tarah's temper when it finally got riled up high enough. Dragging her away from here like some kind of caveman would definitely tick her off. But if she'd temporarily lost her mind because of the stressful situation or whatever, then taking her out of here could only do her good. Someday she'd see reason.

A long sigh slipped out from her. "Now it's your turn to say it back," she added as if she were talking to a three year old.

I gritted my teeth, calculating if I could get the truck moving fast enough to prevent her from jumping out. No, that would never work unless she was tied to the seat. The snow would slow us down long enough for her to realize what I was doing and dive out the door.

"What good is it to celebrate Christmas?" I muttered. "Do you think those sick people in there care that it's Christmas while they're dying?" I jerked a thumb over my shoulder at the infirmary.

"They need the rest of us to be strong and brave for them, Hayden."

But even in the fantasy, the hero always had to actually do battle with the dragon. Simply being brave and wishing it away never worked.

"You know, my parents are Methodists," she continued, each word slow and measured. "But they didn't force me to share their beliefs. They let me check out other religions on my own. So I got to research and try out several, and I learned some pretty interesting things along the way. For instance, did you know Christmas Day isn't just a Christian holiday? Before the development of Christianity, Christmas

Day was celebrated on the winter solstice by pagans as the time of year when the long, dark nights would begin to grow shorter and the light would return."

She lifted my hand to her cheek, closed her eyes, and kissed my knuckles. And in that act, I finally saw the smallest hint of desperation hidden within her. "Fear comes with the dark. But the dark always ends eventually. We just have to hold out and stay strong until it does."

I stared at her for a long time. Finally I managed to choke out, "Merry Christmas, Tarah."

She smiled and whispered, "Thank you."

Wordlessly I handed her present to her.

Catching her lower lip between her teeth, she eased the paper off, her eyes widening. Then she sighed, her hands caressing the red leather covered journals for a moment before she lifted the lid off the small box on top of the stack. The early morning light, just peeking over the tops of the treeline, caught the rhinestones embedded in the sides of the short pink pen as she lifted it out, making it sparkle brilliantly.

"My very own wand," she sighed, and if I hadn't been so terrified of losing her, I might have still known how to smile. "So now I can weave a spell with words." She gave it a silly little swish in the air.

"Thank you, Hayden." She leaned around the Christmas tree, and I kissed her. But it was a different kind of kiss this time. I had to hold myself still, my whole body shaking with the effort not to grab her and beg her to leave this place for her own safety, to see reason.

I could only hope that eventually she'd change her mind, before it was too late.

So I stayed quiet, letting her have her peace and happiness while she could. After awhile, she opened one of the journals, her fingertips tracing over the empty lines waiting to be filled, the rasp of that dry caress filling the silent cab with a wordless plea to be left alone so she could start writing.

"Have fun," I murmured, forcing a smile for her sake. "Come join me later if you want to."

I got out of the truck, pausing for a minute, letting the cold slap the frustration away and kick start my mind again. Insane or not, this was where Tarah was determined to stay. Before we'd come here, back when I had first tried to describe Tarah to my grandmother, I had admired Tarah's unbreakable will. Since then, it had become my biggest enemy.

I only had two choices now. I could try to break the very part of Tarah that I had once admired the most and take her out of here, probably kicking and screaming at the top of her lungs, so that she could hate me for weeks, months, maybe years to come. And in the process risk killing whatever this fragile thing was between us.

Or I could let her stay here while I did whatever I could to keep her as safe as possible and hope, as she wanted me to, that eventually the virus would run its course and die out or be cured somehow.

I walked over to the tiny house's trailer with its promise of a home outlined in posts and beams and subflooring. How long might it take to finish if I focused on it more, worked faster, slept a little less each night?

For now at least, I couldn't do much to help the other members of this village. But I could try to do something to protect Tarah, even if I couldn't take her away from here completely.

And so I went back to work on the tiny house. Maybe if I could get it finished in time, it would give us both somewhere separate to eat and sleep away from the others, reducing our risk of getting sick. It was my only hope of protecting Tarah now.

CHAPTER 20

Tarah got out of the truck a while later to help me work on the tiny house kit. She stopped again a few hours later for a late lunch, but I wasn't hungry, so she went inside one of the other houses alone to eat.

She must have told everyone about Bud's death, because no one ever came to ask me about it. She did come back later with a sandwich and a mug of coffee, which she left on top of the trailer's wheel well for me. But instead of staying, she hurried back to the infirmary to see if she could help the healers.

I doubted I would be much fun to hang out with for awhile anyways.

Later that evening, she came back with another sandwich and a cup of tea. I still wasn't hungry, worry churning in my stomach and making me nauseous. But she wouldn't leave till I ate. Silently I stuffed down the food in the biggest bites and gulps I could manage.

"Thanks," I told her after I was done, thinking she would leave again.

"Are you going to quit soon? You've been at it all day, and it's getting dark." Her voice was quiet and a little uncertain.

"Maybe later. I've got a flashlight. I'll be fine," I muttered, turning back to the work. I had too much left to do before I could quit today. I'd managed to get all the outer and inner wall supports up. But I still needed to get a roof on it to help protect all the exposed wood from the weather.

After awhile, she went back inside. I ignored the ache in my chest and kept working until it was time to start on the roof. Which was when I realized I needed a ladder, and we didn't have one anywhere in the village.

I thought about going into town for one. But most of the building supply places would probably be closed for Christmas. So I gave up for the day and crept into the new house where Tarah and I had been reassigned to sleep.

The house was dark and silent. Everyone had already gone to bed, many of them on pallets on the living room floor, turning the place into an obstacle course. I barely managed not to step on anyone on the way over to the couch, where I found a section set up for me near Tarah's head.

I took off my coat and boots but left everything else on as I eased down onto the couch.

As soon as I laid down with my head near Tarah's and got comfortable, a soft, familiar hand slipped over onto my shoulder.

I fell asleep holding Tarah's hand.

The nightmares hit me hard and fast and didn't take a genius for me to interpret. Everyone in the village had turned into zombies, their skin rotting off them in contagious pieces I couldn't stand to look at. In my dream I tried to drag Tarah away to safety.

"I can't leave them," she whispered.

In the dream, I looked down at her and realized she'd already turned into a zombie too, her once beautiful skin, pale as a moonbeam, now turned a mottled gray with death and decay.

And even then I was tempted to let her touch me, to bite me and turn me into a zombie like her, just so I could stay with her.

Saturday, December 26
Tarah

Hayden woke up with a shout. But I and several others in the house had been awake and watching him long before the noise.

Because he was floating, his body hovering several inches above the couch in the early morning shadows just like that day in the woods when we were kids and I'd learned for the first time that magic was real.

Hayden looked around him then down at himself. I tensed up, worried he would freak out. But he only closed his eyes, took a few deep breaths, and his body slowly lowered to the couch. As soon as his body made contact with the upholstery, he sat up, swung his legs over the side to the floor, and buried his face in his hands.

I reached for one of those newly blistered hands, wanting to remind him without words that he wasn't alone. But he pretended not to see the attempt, reaching down to pull on his boots instead. He was probably embarrassed that he had been seen hovering in his sleep.

I touched his shoulder. He slid out from beneath my touch, grabbing his coat on the way out the front door.

I worked to breathe through the pain of the rejection. He wasn't trying to hurt me. This was about him and his fears, not me.

Then I heard his truck start up a few minutes later, the engine's rumbling quickly fading as he drove away from the village. An icy sensation rushed over my skin, which I slowly tried to rub away on my arms.

He probably just had to run to town for another tool or something. He would never leave the village permanently without at least saying goodbye to me.

I tried to get on with my day at the infirmary, focusing on one step at a time, never thinking beyond that. But my ears kept listening for the return of that rumbling engine.

The minutes ticked by. An hour passed. Then an hour and a half. Then two.

It was a long and winding drive on the scenic byway back into Spearfish. He must have had to drive extra slow due to the ice and snow on the roads. Maybe there had even been an avalanche or a fallen tree across the road to cause further delays. Maybe he got caught behind a snow plow or something too.

Had he slid off the road? The byway didn't have a shoulder in most places. If his truck slid, he would either hit the sharply rising mountain face on one side or go down the occasionally steep bank into the river on the other side.

No, don't think that way, Tarah, I told myself, taking out my anger at myself on the washcloths I was wringing out in the kitchen's sink instead.

He was fine. He probably just stopped for breakfast in town.

I delivered clean washcloths to the healers, brought each of them fresh mugs of coffee, then took a mug of hot chocolate for myself out onto the steps. It was freezing outside and the cement steps chilled me right through my jeans. But the cold air felt good on my face and in my lungs, clean and pure, a badly needed slap to wake me up and pull me out of the fog of my thoughts.

And then Hayden's truck came bouncing back up the village road, parking in its usual spot beside his work in progress on the flatbed trailer.

I wanted so badly to get up and go over to him,

especially when those long legs unfolded out of the driver side doorway and he looked over at me. He hesitated, staring at me from across the many yards separating us. My leg muscles tensed, eager and ready to take me over to him.

But I stayed where I was. There was nothing I could say to him to change his feelings, and I refused to nag him about it. When he was ready to talk, he would come over.

He turned away, reaching into the back of the truck to pull out a metal ladder, which he set up on the trailer near what looked like the beginnings of wall frames. Then he went back to the truck's cab to get a plastic bag of stuff I couldn't make out from this distance. He took what looked like a pocket knife out of his pocket, unfolded it, and began to saw into the packaging of whatever he'd bought this morning.

He never looked my way again, not even when I got up and went back inside the infirmary.

Hayden

At noon, she showed up with two sandwiches and two cans of soda. I didn't know which I needed more...the food, the caffeine or her company. We ate inside the truck, which I started both to warm us up and to keep the cordless drill's recharger from draining the truck's battery.

She was quiet today, fiddling with the stereo till she found a CD she liked from my limited collection. After we finished eating, she surprised me by moving the Christmas tree to the passenger side floorboard, then scooting over to lean back against me.

I closed my eyes and clenched my teeth as the emotions and the sensation of her closeness tried their best to overwhelm me. My hands shook as I stroked her hair and her upper arms hidden beneath the bulk of her thick coat. I tried to memorize the silky feel of her hair against my face, afraid the memory would disappear like a popped soap bubble if I didn't make a point of memorizing every detail.

I wished I could tell her how I felt, how much she meant to me. I wished I could promise her that everything would be all right. That was how it was supposed to work, right? Once you found someone you loved who loved you back, everything else was supposed to fall into place.

Instead, everything around us was falling apart. And loving her made it all the harder to endure.

"One of our patients died."

Her words didn't mean anything to me at first. She spoke so calmly she could have been commenting on the weather, for all my brain registered it.

Then I understood, and my truck's heater suddenly couldn't keep up with the inner chill that spread goosebumps racing over my skin.

Death had found our secret village at last.

"Are you ready to leave now?" The words blurted out of me.

She froze, and I knew it was the wrong thing to say.

"We already talked about this." Her voice was a warning, low, controlled.

But I could be stubborn too. "That was before two people died."

"It doesn't change anything."

I waited a beat, trying not to react, but I cared too much not to.

Cursing, I got out of the truck, slamming the door after me, and headed for the edge of the woods, needing some distance from her before I could lose control and start yelling at her.

A few seconds later, she caught up with me. "Hayden, wait. Where are you going?"

Nowhere. There was nowhere to go to escape my feelings for her and this situation.

"You have to stop being afraid and running away," she said.

I froze, closing my eyes, my control slipping away. "You tell me someone else has died, but I have to stop being afraid." Could she even hear herself?

She didn't hesitate to reply, "Yes, that's exactly what I'm saying! Can't you have some faith, even just a tiny bit, that the healers will figure this out?"

"When, Tarah? When will they figure it out? Before everyone else gets sick too? Before you do?" Bile rose to burn the back of my throat, and I had to shut up or else throw up.

That was it. Her crazy ambition was going to get her killed. And letting her do it was just as bad as helping her kill herself.

She made a loud gasping oompf as I turned, grabbed her around the waist and tossed her over my shoulder.

"Hayden, what are you doing?" she shrieked, slapping my back as I headed for the truck.

"The only thing that makes sense...getting you out of here whether you like it or not." We were nearly to the truck.

"Oh, so you're going to just haul me off against my will? Just like Steve would do?"

I stopped, still several feet from the truck. She did not just compare me to that guy. "I'm not like Steve."

"Oh really?"

I stood there, hating her words, hating the truth behind them. I realized what we must look like to anyone watching. My grandmother and mother would have killed me if they could see me now.

Growling, I set her on her feet again, but I held on to her shoulders, forcing her to stay and talk to me. "Can't you get it through your head? You're not a witch! You don't have any powers. These people are not *your* people.

You don't owe them any loyalty at all. And you damn sure don't owe them your life."

"I know that. But I owe it to myself to see this through. If I leave now, how will I end their story?"

Their story. All of this was about telling some stupid story! Could she even hear herself anymore? "And just when and how do you think you're going to get that story out if you die? And even if you don't, what publisher would risk even publishing it now that the whole world's turning against us?"

She sighed, her shoulders slumping. "I have no idea when I'll be able to share their story. Maybe it'll be months or even years. But when the time is finally right for us to change public opinion about the Clann, I'm going to be ready to tell their story exactly the way it needs to be told. And once that story is out there for everyone to read, every member of this village will become heroes and martyrs for the cause, and the government will eventually be forced to stop what they're doing. Don't you see? It's the only hope we have to end this war! If people out there really knew what was going on, what it was like for the outcasts, sooner or later they would demand justice and equality for the Clann community. It's history repeating itself, over and over. The Nazis and the Jews, blacks versus whites, equal rights for women, safer working conditions in American factories...change only came when someone was brave enough to write the truth and share it with others."

I scrubbed a hand down my face. "So you'll risk it all for the Pulitzer and the fame."

"It's not about getting some award or being famous. It's about making all this matter and their struggles and sacrifices and deaths make a difference for others in this stupid world. If we leave, if I don't tell their story, the whole story, it'll be like it never even happened."

I stared off in the distance, feeling the crushing weight

of defeat. There was no getting through to her.

"You can't leave these people any more than I can," she said, her voice softer now. "They're not just nameless, faceless refugees. I know their names and the dreams they were forced to leave behind and the dreams they can hardly dare to dream now. I could never turn my back on them and walk away any more than you could." She swept an arm out wide to encompass the entire village. "If even one person in this village survives, then this place will be a success, because that's one life lived in freedom that otherwise would have been wasted in prison. Don't you want to stay and be a part of that?"

Her words were stirring something dangerous deep inside me, something that wasn't safe for me to think about. So I pushed those chaotic feelings away. "You're talking about staying here for years if necessary. You're really prepared to stay here that long until the world is ready to hear about some backwoods trailer park in the middle of nowhere?"

Her lips pressed tight together as she took a deep breath in through her nose, then let it out. "Actually, I'm not sure I was ever planning on leaving here. This place isn't something that will happen overnight. It may take decades for this village to grow into what it can become, and somebody's got to be here to chronicle it every step of the way so others can follow in our footsteps and start their own havens. You and I both know what it has the potential to be. You described it yourself when we first got here, so don't lie to me and say you can't see it too."

I didn't answer her because she was right. If these people could survive the disease and the rest of the winter months, this village could be amazing. But the odds were just too high against that ever happening now.

"But it means living the rest of your life here, Tarah. With no internet, no mall, no going to college. What if you can never see your brother or your parents again? Is it really worth devoting your whole life to?"

Her chin rose another inch. "I can't imagine a more worthy cause."

And that's when I knew...I was *never* going to convince her to leave. This place had become some kind of Holy Grail crusade for her. And even if I dragged her away from this place, the minute she got free she would come running right back.

CHAPTER 21

Monday, December 28th

We didn't speak to each other for the next few days. Not even after glaring at each other from opposite sides of the village's first grave as the makeshift coffin was lowered into its cold resting place in the harder than cement earth. The entire settlement, at least the ones who weren't sick yet, had argued for hours about whether they should burn the body. I'd told them to bury it; everyone was already exposed to the virus, and burning the body would only send up a huge smoke cloud that would forced the already exhausted Mike to do a spell to hide it. It was already a full time job for witches with wind control abilities to keep a breeze blowing over our chimneys strong enough to disperse our small fireplaces' smoke.

But I hadn't stuck around for their final vote. I'd only known what everyone had decided to do with the body when two guys had shown up to borrow some power tools to make the coffin with.

No one had said much at the funeral. Probably too afraid or in shock.

I watched Tarah watching me across that hole that had taken several men hours and a lot of spells to chip out, and I wondered what she was thinking. Did she understand that this was only the first of who knew how many deaths to come? Did she care that helping the healers in the infirmary every day only increased her chances of being buried somewhere near this gravesite?

How many graves would it take to convince her to leave?

I wanted to say all of these things to Tarah. But I didn't. What would be the point? If looking right at the evidence of how dangerous this situation was didn't scare or convince her, nothing I could say would either.

Thursday, December 31st

In the days after the funeral, we kept to our corners, she at the infirmary, me at the tiny house, which was finally starting to look like a real house. I'd bought LED lanterns so I could work in the dark and gotten the roof on and the exterior siding up. But with every day that passed, I became more aware of how my time was running out to find one last way to protect her. I had no idea how long I had before Tarah's immune system failed us both. How long could she go on risking the odds with constant, daily exposure to the virus before she was exposed one too many times, breathed in one too many breaths of infected air, handled one too many germ-infected washcloths?

I limited myself to a single meal a day, my dinners dropped off by Tarah in silence and received with only a brief thanks from me. She never stayed to talk or help with the house anymore, leaving me to eat alone in the cold. And yet, every night, whether she realized it or not, her hand continued to slip over and hold mine when I finally gave in to exhaustion and crashed on the couch near her.

That one bit of daily contact with her was enough to keep me hoping that somehow we'd make it through this together.

I took to reading the kit's instruction manual while I ate, counting the steps left to be completed like a general plotting his next battle strategies for his army. Except there was no army helping me out. Everyone who wasn't at the infirmary had banded together to use various spells to laboriously chip out holes for septic system tanks and field lines in the hopes that a proper indoor water system would improve the general hygiene and wipe out the disease. Which left me on my own with my limited tools and even more limited knowledge and time.

As the final days of December passed, I grew ever more desperate. I skipped steps, reasoning that I couldn't glue down the shower stall or flooring in the rest of the house due to the cold preventing the adhesives from holding and drying properly. I couldn't glue together the plumbing either for the same reason. So I just set everything in place for now.

I built the porch and loft spaces, put in windows and doors, stuffed in rolls of insulation everywhere. It was while I was running the wiring on New Year's Eve that I heard the shouting.

I opened my house's new front door, stood on my newly created porch at the end of the trailer furthest from the hitch, and looked outside. It was Steve and Pamela again. Turning around, I went back inside, shut the door and found myself silently wishing Steve good luck with his arguments. I sure as heck couldn't begrudge the guy for trying to do the exact same thing I wished I could do and get the woman I loved out of here to safety. Maybe I'd even put the spark plug back into the bus for him. The only reason I hadn't used the bus myself as a temporary home for Tarah and me was because running its engine to keep it warm enough would quickly use up its fuel tanks, and I was pretty sure the gas stations in town would notice if I kept bringing in the same bus to refuel.

Though I tried to ignore their argument, I still couldn't help but sneak a peek out through the living room window at Pamela. Maybe she and the other healers were finally making some progress in fighting the virus, and she had reason to want to stay?

The slump of her shoulders and dark circles beneath her eyes, visible even from a distance, killed that brief bit of hope.

How could Tarah expect me to be hopeful when even the healers looked defeated and ready to give up?

That evening, I had just squatted down in the living room area, getting ready to tackle the wood burning stove's installation, when someone knocked on my door.

I looked up, expecting to see Tarah.

It was Mike.

I turned up the light on the lantern and waved him in.

He entered, looking up and around him for a few seconds. "You've gotten a lot done in here." His tone sounded as dead as I felt.

Sighing, I rubbed the back of my neck where the muscles constantly burned now. "Yeah, I guess so." But was it fast enough? Something inside me kept telling me to keep working, to move faster, to skip anything not immediately needed to make the place livable for Tarah. "I don't guess you'd happen to know how to put together a wood burning stove, would you?"

Mike glanced at the cast iron contraption in front of me. "Uh, not really. Listen, I came to tell you, we had another death."

I stared at the stove. "I was afraid that was going to happen. Anyone I know?"

"Harvey Lansing. I think he was—"

"One of the loggers I worked with." Yeah, I remembered him and how he'd liked to kid around, no matter how tired he was. In fact, it had seemed like the more tired Harvey had gotten, the more he'd needed to tell a joke.

"And Pamela's sick now too," Mike added.

My insides knotted up. If the healers were getting sick now, maybe it was time to rethink that idea of tying Tarah up and dragging her out of here against her will. Grandma Letty might even approve of keeping Tarah a captive for her own good. When the whole village got sick and died, she wouldn't have much of a story to write about anymore anyways. Then she'd understand.

With the healers going down for the count, how much faster might the virus spread?

Mike shuffled his feet a bit. I glanced up at him.

At my questioning look, he quit fidgeting and murmured, "Tarah's sick too."

It felt like I was paralyzed while the entire world fell out from underneath me. "Tarah's sick?"

He nodded, staring at me. Waiting for my reaction.

My time was up.

I grabbed the lantern and thrust it at Mike. "Here, hold this up so I can see better."

He took the lantern out of instinct, his mouth opening like he wanted to say something else.

"How long?" I asked as I grabbed the instruction booklet.

"Huh?"

"How long as she been sick?"

"Pamela or—"

"Tarah! How long?" I pawed through the stove's sections and pieces on the floor.

"An hour, maybe two, but that's just a guess. You know Tarah. She was probably running a fever for awhile and just didn't say anything. One of the healers noticed she was sweating real bad and made her lie down."

I started connecting the chimney pipe sections. "Hand me that wrench over there."

Silence.

I held out a hand. "Mike!"

I looked up at him. He was standing there staring at me like an idiot. Growling, I reached past him for the wrench.

"Aren't you even going to go see her?" he asked, his voice cracking.

"I've got to get this done first." My wrist popped in protest as I screwed the connector cuff's bolt into place on the chimney pipe.

"Everyone's right. You have gone nuts." Muttering a curse, Mike set the lantern on the floor then barreled out of the house, slamming the door so hard behind him that its window pane cracked.

I worked as quickly as I could to get the stove set up. But it still took too long before I could get a fire going in it and check to make sure it was safe. Then I had to go to one of the houses for sleeping bags, sheets, a pillow, an iron pot, and a bucket. It took several trips to get everything I needed into my house, and too long to get it all set up even though I pushed my exhausted body to run every step I took.

No time, no time, my heart beat out with each pulse.

Then I ran for the infirmary, finally allowing my feet to carry me to the one place I'd wanted to go right from the start.

"Hayden," Tarah whispered as I knelt beside her pallet in what used to be the house's living room area. Her hair, once so beautiful and wild, the black curls shiny and bouncy with life, now clung to her forehead and the sides of her sunburn red cheeks in sweat-soaked clumps.

Nearby, Steve sat beside his wife. We shared a brief

look, his eyes haunted and bleak.

I peeled the damp covers off of Tarah.

"What are you doing?" Mike cried out as he returned from the master bedroom. He grabbed my shoulder.

But I'd forgotten how to be human or polite. Some part of me, the logical, sane side, watched as if from a distance while I growled at him and jerked my shoulder free. "Back off."

I slipped my arms under Tarah's wet back and bare knees. They'd stripped her down to just an oversized t-shirt and her underwear. As soon as I lifted her up, I could feel her whole body shivering.

She was too light in my arms, impossibly fragile. How could this small body house a spirit as big as Tarah's?

"Open the door," I told Mike, who continued to stare at me in shock. "Now, dammit!"

When he still refused to move, I was forced to use the hand under Tarah's back to awkwardly turn the handle on the storm door enough to get it unlatched. Then I kicked it the rest of the way open.

Tarah whimpered as the cold air hit us.

"I know, honey," I muttered, only half aware of what I was even saying as I eased us down the cement steps. "Almost there. Hang on."

By the time we reached the tiny house, her teeth were chattering so hard I was worried she'd bite her own tongue off. I got her inside and onto the thick pallet I'd made for her a few feet away from the stove. As soon as she was down, I covered her with layer after layer of blankets and sheets.

"I've got to get more firewood," I muttered, brushing the clumps of hair back from her face. "I'll be right back."

I ran outside, came back with all the firewood I could carry in one trip, added another log to the fire. Then I poured some water into the pot and set it on top of the stove to heat.

Someone came bursting into the house behind me while I was wringing out the first washcloth. A healer maybe. I didn't know, didn't care.

"Mr. Shepherd," the stout sounding woman began.

I ignored her, washing Tarah's face before folding the cloth and laying it over her forehead. Her lips were starting to crack. Maybe I had some chapstick somewhere in my truck? Once I got Tarah settled in, I'd go look.

Then I realized the woman was still standing there. "Shut the door. You're letting out all the heat."

"You can't just come barging in and steal a patient—"

"It's not a hospital. Tarah's not yours to keep. And it doesn't sound like you healers were doing any better than I can with her anyway. Now shut the damn door please." I stood up, my hands clenching at my sides, hoping the woman wouldn't keep pushing me. I'd been raised never to hit a woman, and I sure didn't want to start now.

She gasped, apparently at a loss for words as she took a nervous step backwards onto the porch.

Then I remembered they might need new herbs or something from town. But I wasn't going to be able to go that far away from Tarah. I dug the truck keys out of my jeans pocket and tossed them to her. She barely managed to catch them against her ample chest.

"There's my truck keys if anyone needs anything from town."

She was looking down at the keys as I slammed the door shut in front of her.

She had the nerve to start to open the door again. Without looking, I slammed it shut for the last time then locked it. Then I turned and checked the temperature of the water on the stove. After a few seconds, the sound of footsteps faded off my porch.

Good. I had work to do.

"Well, you sure told her," Tarah murmured, her teeth still chattering.

I crouched down beside her. "Had to. I wanted you all for myself." I forced a smile for her, even as her trembling tried its best to break my heart.

Tarah's eyes rolled around in their sockets. For a few seconds, I panicked, thinking she was going into convulsions or something. But then her gaze locked back onto mine and she smiled. "It's kind of dark in here. But f-from what I can see, it looks really g-good."

She'd been checking out her new home. I let the breath of relief ease out of me. "Not done with it yet. But it should be good enough for now. Get well for me and I might even let you do the interior decorating."

"Yeah?" She clutched the blankets up to her chin as a fresh round of shivering wracked her body. "Resorting to b-bribery now?"

I couldn't talk for a minute as my throat choked up. I took her hand, swallowed hard, and finally managed to say, "Whatever it takes. Now rest while I go see what meds I can find, all right?"

I waited for her nod before I rushed out, the cold burning my already stinging eyes.

I had to search the infirmary's kitchen cabinets to find the acetaminophen; the dragon ladies now running the show there refused to speak to me when I asked for some. Apparently they'd decided they couldn't fight me over Tarah, but they sure weren't going to help me none either.

They still had several bottles of meds, so I went ahead and took a mostly empty bottle plus a ceramic cup sitting on the drainboard. I also got some more firewood, which I left on my porch by the door for later. Finally, I found a tube of cherry flavored chapstick in the backseat of my truck.

Tarah's eyes were closed when I returned, and she was

murmuring something I couldn't make out.

"Hey, Tarah, I'm back," I told her, holding her hand. With my free hand I managed to twist and then pop the cap off the medicine. I shook out a few pills on the blanket by her.

She didn't respond.

CHAPTER 22

Fighting the rising panic, I dipped the cup from the infirmary into the water, now hot, on the stove. I had to blow it a little to cool it off. Then I slid a hand under Tarah's head, lifting her up as I pressed the cup to her lips. "Take a sip, Tarah. I need you to take some medicine now."

She seemed to hear me this time, dutifully swallowing the pills after I slid them past her lips. Then I applied the chapstick to her lips, doing a crap job of getting it on straight. Not that Tarah seemed to care about a little smeared lip product.

It was beyond nightmarish how quickly the virus gained a hold over her. She didn't speak again over the next few hours other than to make the occasional whimper, her head tossing and turning in her sleep like she was having bad dreams.

But they couldn't be nearly as bad as the real life memories I was making with her right now.

I alternated between washing her face and neck, getting her to take sips of water or more pills, and holding her hand, wanting her to know at all times that I was there. When she slept more peacefully, though her fever was still high, I ran out to the truck for the spellbook, waiting till I was back by her side before rereading the chapter on healing. I also tried to remember what Mike had told me about how to heal.

Again and again, I followed both his and the spellbook's instructions, trying to make my conscious mind relax and somehow mystically enter Tarah's body, hunt down the sickness and eradicate it.

Over and over again, I failed.

In frustration, I sat there on the floor, hands buried in my hair, tugging at it, using the pain on my scalp to keep me from going nuts. I stood up with the urge to pace then stopped myself just in time. I couldn't risk shaking the floor and disturbing Tarah. Her body probably needed this rest to help heal itself.

At least she was sleeping peacefully now. But her fever climbed ever higher with each passing hour.

She was like a flame, burning brighter and brighter, so beautiful and brilliant to look at even as her body tried to burn itself out as fast as it could.

And I was completely powerless to stop it.

"Please, Tarah," I whispered, sinking to my knees beside her, her hand limp and far too hot when I picked it up again. "Tarah, you've got to fight! I can't do it for you. You've got to do it. I know you can still hear me. Fight!"

Hot liquid scalded my eyes, my nose and cheeks as I kissed her hand, her body just a shell, her mind and soul so far out of my reach now.

Closing my eyes, I rested my forehead against her hand. I looked at her face, serene now, like that day when she'd seemed like an otherworldly queen, calm and accepting. She'd asked me to believe in the impossible that day. To have faith that the dark would end.

She wouldn't like my panicking like this.

"You've got to get well, Tarah," I whispered to her,

watching her face for some response, any response at all. "What about that story you wanted to finish writing about this place? Who's going to finish it if you don't? Not me. You know I can't write nothing worth crap."

No response from her, no flicker from her closed eyes.

She was the only person who really knew me, all of me, and still accepted me as I was. She wasn't just the first girl I'd fallen in love with. She was also my first and only true best friend other than my brother, and the only person I'd been completely honest with. If I lost her, there wasn't another person on this planet who would know who I really was.

I couldn't lose her.

I wouldn't. If she went, she'd have to take me with her.

I closed my eyes, pressed my lips to the back of her hand, and whispered, "Tell me what I have to do, and I swear I'll do it. Just please...don't die."

"You have to let go of yourself and what you want," Mike had told me during our one and only tutorial on healing. The useless spellbook said the same thing. "You have to learn how to let go of who you are."

Just let go, I could hear Tarah whisper to me.

And just like that, it clicked.

It was like falling asleep. Or maybe I really did fall asleep, because it sure seemed like a dream.

I was outside my body, a thin silver thread holding my spirit to my body at my stomach. I saw Tarah's body just below me, and my spirit growing smaller, floating down, the cord that bound me to my body stretching like infinite elastic as I seemed to sink right through Tarah's skin, through her tissues and muscles, into her veins that appeared all around me then like a maze of red tunnels. Beyond, I could feel her organs throbbing and pulsing.

Something bumped into me. I turned to look. It was a strangely shapeless black blob. And there, another black

MELISSA DARNELL

orb.

"Tarah, I'm yours," I whispered, embracing those evil shapes, not willing them to come to me, but simply allowing them to attack me if they wanted to. Because I didn't care if I got sick now. If that was what it took to save Tarah, if I had to take the virus out of her and into my own body, even if I got sick in the process, even if I died, it would be worth it. Up to now, my life on earth hadn't really been all that spectacular. But Tarah...she deserved to live. She had a story to tell. Hers. Mine. These people's. She had to live and tell that story so it wouldn't all be a big pointless waste.

But the black masses raced away.

"No!" I shouted. "No, it's me you want, not her!"

The virus didn't listen, and I could see it through the semi transparent walls of her veins, rushing off to attack her heart now, surrounding the desperately beating organ as if it were the last fortress in the virus's war on humanity and it must be brought down tonight.

And as always, I couldn't save her. I seemed destined to love her and lose her. I had no sword, no Clann skills, no medicine, no weapon at all to fight the virus with. Nothing. If only the virus would attack the both of us at once, then at least I could die with her and maybe it would be all right. But I could not face being the survivor. I didn't want to survive Tarah.

"Hayden," I heard Tarah murmur, her voice all around me at once.

"I'm failing you," I confessed in a whisper to her.

"No. Don't you see? This is not some ordinary virus. It thinks and reacts to us," she whispered back, her voice coaxing me not to give up. To have hope, as she always did, just one more time.

Somehow I found the strength to listen, to think about her words. "Then what is it? How do we beat it?"

"You must find its source."

Its source? What was she talking about?

As I began to get angry and frustrated, I felt myself slipping away, being pulled backward toward my own body again. And the more I fought it, the more strongly I was pulled away.

Because I was being negative?

I tried a different strategy, giving up resisting the pull. "Okay, Tarah. You win. What is its source?"

"Not what. Who."

My spirit eased back into my own body again, and I woke up, needing the deep breath of air I took as if I'd just surfaced after being underwater too long.

A dream? Or had I truly connected with Tarah's unconscious mind?

She was still asleep, her fever as high as before. And her pulse... I felt it beneath my fingertips at her wrist, its every beat more feeble than the last.

As if her heart really was now under attack. Just like in my dream.

She'd said the virus wasn't normal, that someone was creating it. But who? Who would want to hurt a bunch of outcasts hidden away in the woods?

The government? My dad?

I'd heard of experimental programs in the past where they'd used psychics to help them with government projects. And my father had said the government was working with scientists now, trying to suppress the genes that caused Clann abilities. What if they had changed tactics and were trying to wipe us out completely from a distance now, using Clann abilities to attack us with a fake illness that would cause us to die one by one?

If so, they sure were taking their time about it. Shouldn't the government have been killing us off much faster, if that was their intention?

What if they didn't want to kill all of us? What if they still wanted to capture us for some reason? The illness could be sent to try and flush us out of hiding and into nearby hospitals.

"Tarah, I'll be right back," I promised, kissing her burning cheek before I stumbled to my feet and out the door on wobbly legs to the infirmary.

"Hey, Tarah's got an idea," I said, only partially lying in order to get Mike and one of the healers to listen to me in the master bedroom. Once I had their attention, I told them the possibilities that I'd come up with.

"Tarah said this?" The older dragon lady I'd faced off with at the tiny house stood before me now, hands on her wide hips, her eyes squinting with suspicion.

"Yeah," I said, figuring Tarah wouldn't mind the half truth. If I'd really connected with Tarah's unconscious mind, then it was the truth. And if I hadn't and it was a lie, well, she'd lied about me being the one to suggest we all go to my grandma's in South Dakota. So she couldn't exactly mind my using her own tactics now. "Is it possible? Could someone use a spell to attack us and disguise it as a new strain of flu?"

Mike frowned. "Hey, didn't you healers say you couldn't pin the virus down in any of the patients in order to treat it?"

"That is true," Dragon Lady replied. I really needed to learn more people's names around here. "But why wouldn't they kill us off faster?"

They'd found the hole in my theory.

"Maybe because magic is harder to do from a distance?" Mike suggested.

I remembered how Steve had needed to come with me to the bus rental office in order to maintain the face altering spell on me. "Yeah, Steve talked about that too. But why couldn't they simply make more witches work together to help boost their spells to cover greater distances?" I was thinking out loud here. Surely the government could have put together a whole army of descendants and outcasts to work for them by now. All they would have to do is offer legal immunity and freedom from the internment camps to get the witches' cooperation. Some might still refuse to attack fellow magic users. But others would do whatever it took to protect their families.

What wouldn't a desperate magic user do in the name of saving their family?

Look at Steve. He hadn't hesitated to kill that cop. And he would have gladly dragged Cassie, and maybe Pamela too, right out of this village for their protection if we hadn't stopped him and convinced him they were happy here.

A guy like that wouldn't hesitate to take a deal from the government. Even if it meant having to attack a fellow outcast.

I looked past the healers and Mike, through the open bedroom door and kitchen area to the living room where Steve still sat at his wife's side. Steve looked like the walking dead. Almost as bad as the zombies in my nightmares a few weeks back.

"Attacking Clann people from a distance would take a lot of energy, wouldn't it?" I muttered.

Dragon Lady nodded. "Much easier to do it up close. Do you think they've tracked us to this area?"

I didn't answer her, still following my own train of thought. "Could you attack several people at once if you were physically close to them?" I couldn't seem to stop staring at Steve, my thoughts spiraling down into an ever darker abyss. But this idea had a problem too. Even if the government had somehow gotten to him and forced him to help them, he never would have used magic on his own wife.

Would he?

"Yes, you could attack multiple people close to you, but it would leave you constantly drained," she said.

Bud had gotten sick only minutes after Steve had...

After he had *tried and failed to convince his wife to leave the village with him and Cassie.*

What if the government had nothing to do with this? What if it was all Steve's doing just so he could get his way?

But surely Steve wouldn't make his own wife sick just to convince her that staying in the village wasn't safe for their family.

I remembered how at one point I'd been desperate enough to toss Tarah over my shoulder and nearly kidnap her for her own safety.

Mike frowned. He looked over his shoulder, following my line of sight. Then his head whipped back to face me, his eyes wide. "You're not thinking..."

"Get Cassie," I said.

Mike left, coming back a few minutes later with the little girl in tow. She nearly started crying when she saw her mother lying unconscious on a floor pallet. Her father seemed to be sleeping while still sitting upright. He never reacted to his daughter's presence or her soft whimpers.

Dragon Lady surprised me, pulling Cassie to her huge chest and patting her tiny back while murmuring soft sounds of comfort, promising the kid that her momma would be better soon. All lies if I was wrong and we couldn't figure this out.

After a few minutes, Cassie calmed down. I squatted in front of her so we could whisper without her dad hearing. "Cassie, you told me you can smell magic when someone near you is doing it, right?"

She nodded.

"Do you remember what your daddy's magic spells smell like?"

Her mouth turned up in a wobbly smile. "Like

Christmas!"

"You mean like Christmas cookies or pies?" I asked, needing her to be sure.

"No, like a Christmas tree." Her eyes darted up and around to each of us. "Why?"

I shook my head, everything inside me hardening. "Just curious, sweetie. Thank you. You want to go sit by your momma now?"

Cassie nodded and carefully made her way around the sleeping patients to her mother, sitting on the floor opposite her father.

"That's still not proof," Mike said. "Everything smells like pine trees around here. Outside, the logs, the fireplaces..."

"Which also makes it the perfect cover," I said, feeling a slow burn building in my stomach and chest.

"But why would he make his own wife sick?" Dragon Lady asked.

"Because trying to convince a hardheaded woman that she needs saving can make a man desperate."

I'd even sympathized with Steve's attempts to convince his wife. But unlike Steve, I'd turned to other ways to try and save the woman I loved, like building a place for Tarah to stay out of contact with possible carriers of the virus.

While at my grandma's house, Pamela had mentioned once that Steve was a Wiccan and for him magic was also a religion.

"What do Wiccans believe about karma and consequences to their actions?" I asked.

"They believe in the rule of three, that whatever magic they do will come back to them times three," Mike said. "Gary was a Wiccan. He was always talking about it. He also believed there are spells that can bind their abilities or enhance them."

Bingo. "Bind them how?"

He stuffed his hands in his pockets and rocked back on his heels with a frown. "Well, I remember him telling me something about mirrors to reflect a witch's actions back on themselves. And I think he said red yarn or cords wrapped around a photo of the target while saying something about binding them from harming themselves or others can also do the trick."

"Steve would probably know all of that too." I looked from Mike to the older woman with a grim smile. "Why don't we test him? If he believes his abilities can be bound with a spell and he's not the one behind this…"

"Then the patients won't show any change," Mike muttered with a slow nod.

And if he was behind the illness, Tarah should immediately start to improve.

"I'll get the supplies," I said. "You two keep him here."

I forced myself to walk slowly through the kitchen and living room to the front door. But the minute the door shut behind me, I leaped down the steps and over to the other houses, trying two before I found several handheld mirrors and a ball of red crochet yarn.

At my own house, I checked on Tarah, telling her to hold on a little longer for me but getting no response.

Then I ran back to the infirmary.

Steve woke up as Mike and I grabbed his upper arms. We hauled him off to the master bathroom so we could stand him in front of the large wall mirror mounted above the sink. We held him still, his bony skeletal body not making it much of an effort for us, while the older healer wrapped him from head to toe in the red yarn, leaving only his nose bare. Then we each held a mirror facing towards him and slowly began to chant, "We bind you, Steve, from doing any harm. Your spells reflect back at you now."

For several long minutes, he struggled against the bindings, his mouth working to free itself past the strings across his face. And I began to wonder if I was wrong, if I was so desperate to save Tarah that I'd finally snapped and wrongfully accused an innocent man, a man about to lose the woman he loved, just like me.

"What are you doing?" Pamela gasped, hugging the door jamb with both arms for support. Cassie clung to her mother's side, her eyes wide and bright. "Is that...is that *Steve* under there?"

"Daddy, you look silly!" Cassie giggled.

"How are you feeling?" I asked Pamela, reaching out to touch her forehead. It was cool to the touch.

"Better. Tired. Shaky. But better. I woke up and thought I should check on the worst of the patients in here, and heard you guys... Are you using a new healing method?" She gestured tiredly behind her as several people rose up on their elbows, murmuring and looking around in confusion.

Steve froze.

The older healer, Mike and I all exchanged looks.

"We tried something new, all right," Dragon Lady said, her lips forming a tight, thin line. "A binding spell on your husband."

Pamela turned pale again.

"I'll be right back." Handing the mirror to Pamela, I ran out of the bathroom, out of the infirmary, and over the now familiar minefield of tree stumps to my tiny house, the light from the wood stove making its windows flicker and glow. With every step, I prayed as hard as I could to find Tarah better when I opened that door.

CHAPTER 23

I leaped up onto the porch, yanked open the door...

She was still sleeping.

"Come on," I found myself muttering as I took the three steps through the house and over to her, stopping to kneel at her side.

I took her hand in mine. Then, with my free hand, I touched her cheek.

Her fever was gone.

Her eyelids fluttered open, and she smiled up at me. And it was the single best moment of my life.

"Hey beautiful," I murmured, smiling back. "How are you feeling?"

She sighed. "Tired. Sleepy. Really hopeful that you installed a shower in this thing and got the water hooked up too."

I'd tell her the bad news about that later. "But you're feeling better?"

"Mmm hmm. And thirsty. Can I have some water?"

I held her head up and helped her steady the cup as she eagerly sipped water from it. My hands shook as I took the cup from her when she'd finished. I added another log to the fire, covered her up again, and tried to hide my face as I used my shirt sleeves to wipe at my damp cheeks.

"All right. Sleep for awhile, and I'll be back with some soup or something. Okay?" I said.

But she was already asleep again. Which was strange. Pamela had been sick longer than her, yet was already back up on her feet. Most of the other patients had been sitting up already as I'd run out of the infirmary just now.

I felt Tarah's pulse at her wrist. It still wasn't strong, but at least it was steady now. Could the attack have caused permanent damage to her heart?

Steve better pray that it hadn't.

As I stalked back across the clearing to the infirmary, the weak-kneed relief quickly morphed into anger, then fury, then a near blinding rage. I knew exactly what I wanted to do to Steve in return for his nearly killing Tarah.

The answer was simple...I would kill him. With my bare hands, my fists, my feet, and my Clann abilities. It wasn't noble, but it was far less punishment than what he deserved. I would beat him until he felt the pain I'd felt while I'd thought Tarah was going to die. I would beat him over and over, letting him feel as helpless as I'd been while his spell had attacked Tarah's defenseless body over and over.

I would beat him until he was an empty shell, a meat carcass useful for nothing more than a quick and ugly burial in the ditch somewhere. Because a burial in this village's cemetery beside the others he'd killed would be too good for a murderer like him.

I ripped open the infirmary's storm door, then threw open its front door, revenge the only thought on my mind now.

Until I saw Cassie hugging her mother, the both of them surrounded by recovering patients who were sipping tea and quietly talking.

Pamela and Cassie had already gone through so much. And judging by the way Pamela was sobbing and rocking her daughter, they knew they were about to go through a lot more as they dealt with the truth of what their husband and father had done.

If I killed Steve, what would it do to them?

As I entered the living room, Pamela looked up at me then away. In shame? The thought of Pamela having to bear the burden of her husband's actions for the rest of her life renewed my fury. But it also honed it, compressing the fire inside me, giving me a measure of control. Steve would pay. He had to, for the sake of justice and righting his wrongs, to restore a sense of peace and hope and trust in this village. He'd made me, and no telling how many others, afraid of this place when it should have been a haven of peace and safety.

But I couldn't be the one to decide how he should be punished. This wasn't a dictatorship I was running here. In fact, for days now I hadn't been running anything, caught up in the selfish pursuit of trying to save Tarah while believing I was powerless to help anyone else. This was a community of people, and I wasn't the only one here that he'd hurt. Tarah had survived. What about the two families here who had lost loved ones?

I only wished Bud's family could weigh in on the judgement too.

I made my way past all the patients to the master bath, where the older healer and Mike still held watch over Steve.

"Can you two round up everyone outside?" I asked them. "I think it's time we held our first village meeting."

The older healer left without a word. I'd have to make a mental note to get her name later. She was one tough broad. Sort of reminded me of my grandma. I'd have to thank her later, too.

Mike hesitated, eying me with raised eyebrows, as if he

was wondering what I'd do while alone with Steve. I kept my face blank. After a half a minute, Mike seemed to decide he didn't care after all and left.

Once they were gone, I moved to stand in front of Steve.

His breaths started coming out fast and harsh through his nose. Then, after two long minutes, he held his breath and his shoulders dropped in resignation, as if he realized he couldn't stop me from hitting him, and maybe even agreed that I had the right to.

And that's when I realized even my beating up this guy would also be more than he deserved. Because he knew he was wrong. He knew what he'd done, to his own family and to everyone else's here. Deep down, part of him was probably even hoping I'd give him a beating or kill him. Because then he wouldn't have to feel guilty for getting away with his crimes.

But I didn't want his punishment to be quick or easy. I wanted him to live with what he'd done. Every day, I wanted him to have to see himself in the mirror and know he'd killed three people and attacked many others.

All out of fear and love for his family.

So while my hands literally ached with the need to smash up Steve's face and ribs, and while my imagination kept coming up with ever better ideas for exacting personal retribution on Tarah's attacker...

I simply led him past his victims and out the door to the infirmary's porch, around which the whole village now stood shivering.

"Hey, everyone, listen up. We found the source of the illness," I said, using those old debate skills my father had insisted I learn and speaking from my diaphragm so that my voice projected out over the crowd.

Silence. A few gasps. Someone called out, "Are you serious?"

"Very," I said. "Ask Mike. He helped me and..."

"And Wanda," the older healer yelled out from the crowd.

I nodded at her. "Wanda and Mike and I did a Wiccan binding spell on Steve here." I grabbed the trailing end of the red yarn and held it up. "Almost immediately after we did, everyone who was sick began to get well again. Including his wife Pamela."

I looked behind me through the infirmary's glass storm door. Pamela and Cassie stood behind the glass, huddled together as if worried the whole village would stone them to death.

"Pamela, why don't you join us? I think everyone here knows how hard you worked night and day to try and save everyone you could." I gave her a reassuring nod.

After a short hesitation, they both stepped out onto the porch, Cassie still clutching her mother's waist.

"But why'd he make his own wife sick?" someone asked from the crowd.

"Steve, why don't you explain in your own words?" I tugged the strings from over his mouth.

Absolute silence filled the clearing. In the distance, I saw the door to Tarah's and my house open and a tumble of dark hair above a sleeping bag moved to stand in the doorway. Tarah was obviously feeling better.

I wished I could go to her now. But being a leader seemed to mean personal sacrifice at times.

I just hoped I was handling this in a way she approved of. Of course, if I wasn't, she'd be sure to tell me about it later.

"I...wanted to take my wife and kid away from here," Steve finally confessed, his voice so quiet it never would have carried if I hadn't helped the wind catch his words and spread them around. "I was afraid it wasn't safe here for them. So I tried to show them that. And it got out of hand. I never meant to kill anyone—"

"But you did, Steve!" Pamela burst out on a sob, her hands gripping the porch railing. "Three people died because of you. How could you think I'd ever want to be with you after what you've done?"

"An eye for an eye!" someone yelled. "He's a murderer. He deserves to die."

Murmurs of agreement from the crowd. I glanced at Pamela, half expecting her to be afraid for her husband. But I should have known better. Pamela was made tougher than that. And she looked mad enough to kill him herself.

Unfortunately, their kid wasn't so tough. Tears poured down Cassie's face.

I made my way to the top step, raising my hands and letting the wind kick up everyone's hair and hats until they quieted down and paid attention. "I understand you're all mad, and rightfully so. I myself have good cause to beat the ever living crap out of Steve." I nodded at Tarah, and heads swiveled to glance her way. "But the truth of the matter is, there's only a few here who can really decide what's just punishment for Steve. And that's his wife and the families of those who died because of him."

"His wife?" someone yelled out, accompanied by loud mutters.

"That's right. Because she was also one of the people he attacked. And in every trial, the accused gets representation," I replied.

More mutterings as I slowly walked through the crowd toward Tarah. From what I overheard along the way, I could tell some people wanted to skip the trial and burn Steve alive. Still others didn't see how his death would bring any of his victims back.

Personally, I really didn't care what they decided. All I knew was that I'd managed to do something my father never would have, and that was to put my own feelings

aside and let justice have its way with Steve instead. My
father probably never would have let Steve reach a trial
alive. And even if he had, he never would have allowed his
voters to actually do the deciding as a group, at least not
without his "help". Instead, he would have stuck around,
instigating, whispering, or even blatantly yelling out
suggestions for what they should all do to the murderer.
One way or the other, my father would have had a hand in
the outcome, leading his people into fear and darkness and
distrust in both themselves, their community and their
world.

But I wanted to do things differently.

Was it possible to be a leader without becoming a
stereotypical politician, resorting to lies and manipulation
and destroying everyone around me in the process? Could a
true leader give the power to his people, instead of keeping
it all for himself? Could he build others up around himself
instead of tearing them down?

Tarah made me want to give it a try and see if I could
manage it.

Though it nearly took forever to accomplish it, I finally
got through the crowd and reached our porch where she
now stood.

"Hey, should you be up and about already?" I
murmured against the side of her cheek as I wrapped my
arms around her, blankets and all.

"Yuck, I'm all sweaty." Smiling, she tried to lean away
from me. But the effort left her gasping.

I pressed a hand to her neck, felt her pulse beating fast
and thin like a rabbit's, and cursed. Her heart still wasn't
beating right. How much damage had Steve done to her?
How long would it take to heal? Would it heal completely
someday? What if it didn't? Had he felt me trying to fight
him and gone extra hard after her heart, trying to kill her
even as I tried to save her from him?

Gritting my teeth, I turned around. Maybe I was wrong. Maybe Steve really did deserve to die.

His jury had gathered on the ground near the porch, huddled together as they tried to decide what to do. But they didn't have to deliberate any longer. I could end the debate right now, with my own two hands...

Cassie stood on the porch, her arms hugged around herself, sobbing. She was looking up at her father, her expression saying all the words her mouth couldn't manage to form. *Why, Daddy? Why were you so bad? Why did you try to hurt Mommy?*

I froze, grabbing my own porch's wooden railing with both hands to stop my forward momentum.

Cassie. She'd worried for hours that she was going to lose her mother. Now she was about to lose her father. And if we weren't careful, whatever scarring events she saw tonight would be our fault. Everyone's in this village.

Especially mine.

Maybe there were times when a leader did need to step in and guide things in the right direction after all.

I cleared my throat, letting the wind amplify it like a microphone through invisible speakers all around us. The crowd grew quiet and turned toward me.

"You know, I was just standing here thinking...well, thinking some not nice thoughts, to be honest. You see, someone I love very much became one of the newest patients at the infirmary today. She's better now, as you can all see for yourself. But just the thought of her being hurt... Well, I won't lie. I'd like to see some hard justice done just as much as everyone else here."

Tarah touched my back between my shoulder blades, as if to calm me. And her touch did ground me as always. But this time the effect wasn't necessary. I cleared my throat, unsure as always as to what I should say. But suddenly, it didn't matter that I didn't have a carefully prepared speech.

Maybe being a good leader started with leading from the heart and honesty. And if I spoke what I was really thinking and feeling, then I didn't have to have just the right words to say all figured out ahead of time.

"But the truth is, it's not just about who got sick, and who was most afraid for our loved ones," I continued. "Because there's someone else here that none of us have been considering much. His daughter." I nodded at Cassie, who turned and frowned in obvious fear of the crowd. "See, she knows what her daddy did was wrong. But she also loves him, same as we all probably love, or once loved, our parents. And as much as you and I would all like to see some old fashioned justice enacted here tonight, maybe we should also be thinking about her. And our own kids, and the future generations who'll grow up here. And what kind of history we want to create here tonight. And the kind of story we want to pass down to those future generations.

"Why did we come here in the first place? Because the rest of the world is afraid of us. And because they're thinking from a place of fear and darkness, they can't see us clearly anymore. They can't see with their hearts that we're still the same people we were before all this normal people versus Clann business got started. They're just acting out of fear.

"And right here, right now, we're tempted to do the exact same thing. We've all been afraid for weeks now, afraid we or someone we love would get sick and die. Now that we know the cause of that fear, we want to lash out, to take out our anger and fear on him. But if we do that, we become just like them." I gestured in the direction of the main road, hidden by our protective ring of forest. "We'll just be letting fear and anger and hatred eat us up from the inside out before we even gave this village a real chance to get off the ground."

"What are you saying?" someone yelled. "Are you saying

we should just forget what Steve did and let him go?"

I took a deep breath and shrugged, reminding myself that I didn't have to have all the answers here. "I'm not saying that. Personally, it'd be pretty hard for me to have to walk by him day in and day out and not give in to the urge to at least take a shot at him. All I'm saying is to try and think from your heart, not about what you personally want, but about what's good for everyone in the community. Including Cassie, and Pamela, and the families of those who died, and everyone else." I paused, considering, then understood. "It's like healing someone. You've got to let go of yourself, of what you personally want. Only then can the healing begin, for each of us individually and for our community as a whole."

Tarah leaned against my back, wrapping her arms around my waist. And that was the single best feedback on how I was doing that I could ever hope to receive.

Seeing the thoughtful looks on everyone's faces now, instead of the fear and anger that had burned there before, I finally took a deep breath and turned back toward my house and my girl.

"Nice speech," she whispered. "But you're turning into a politician; you already talk too much. Shut up and kiss me already."

"Yes ma'am." I bent my head and kissed her. And just like that, I was whole again.

A sudden wolf whistle pierced the kiss-induced fog, and I realized we had an audience.

"Get a room!" someone howled amid more than a few chuckles.

"Can't you see? He already built one!" someone else called out to even more laughter.

Tarah laughed against my lips, and I had to grin. "Sorry," I muttered. "Welcome to the public life of a leader." I turned, blocking their view of Tarah with my body. "Now why would I need a room when I built a whole house?"

"You call that thing a house?" Mike shouted. "It's nothing but a glorified shack on wheels."

More laughter from the village.

And that's when I knew that whatever the village decided tonight, it would be all right. Because even after weeks of fear, and running, and so many lives that had hung in the balance, we could all still joke and laugh together. We would survive this.

But I also knew that the quicker we could make our first decision as a community, the sooner we could get on with turning this place into what it could become...a place of dreams and legends.

"Well? Have y'all decided yet what to do with Steve there?" I asked, staying on the porch on purpose now to show the decision was up to them, not me.

The huddle of informal jurors grew tighter for a minute, then broke up.

Pamela slowly climbed the steps back up onto the infirmary's porch and to Cassie's side. She waited until she stood behind her daughter, her hands wrapped in comfort around the girl's shoulders, before she lifted her chin and spoke.

"We've reached a decision. Steve, your punishment is to be sent from this place, banished forever from our village. Before you will be sent away, you will be marked with a permanent tattoo containing a spell binding you from ever revealing the location of this village." Pamela swallowed, finally looking her husband in the eye. "You may never return."

The crowd surged forward, a hundred hands reaching for Steve. A blade glinted in the light from the porches and windows, and I started forward, thinking they were going to kill him after all. But then I saw the red string fall away and realized they'd only cut the yarn from around him.

Steve was resolute, accepting his punishment in silence, which seemed to keep things relatively calm. He walked down the steps off the porch, and Pamela guided the village into a giant, rough circle around him. Some merely watched; others actively chanted with her as she mixed herbs then applied them in a small tattoo of some kind behind Steve's right ear.

It was only when the crowd moved forward to take Steve away that he became visibly upset again, fighting for the chance to hug his daughter goodbye. Pamela hesitated then hugged him too, pressing a quick kiss to his cheek before the villagers swept him down the stump-littered avenue between the houses, past my house where Tarah and I had stood watching it all, and down the village road.

At the end of it, the villagers stopped and Steve continued on alone, a solitary figure, shoulders rounded in defeat as he walked through the moonlight towards the nearest town. Part of me wondered if we had all done the right thing. What if Steve somehow found a way to beat the binding spell and tell others where we were?

But I also knew the reality of our situation here...we would always run the risk of discovery. All we could do was try to keep our village as well hidden from the rest of the world as we could.

Which was why our second act as a community was for Mike to teach several others how to help him put up a shielding spell that deflected intruders and cloaked our village with the semblance of unbroken trees and treetops all around and above us. From that moment on, Mike and his aides worked in shifts to maintain the shield's spell, becoming our village's first official Guardians.

Once the shield was in place, I ventured out and up the nearest mountainside for a few minutes in the moonlight to make sure we were truly hidden. The shield was an amazing creation, completely hiding the clearing from view. From outside its boundaries, our land looked untouched for decades, nothing more than a thick forest that swayed correctly in both the gentlest of breezes and the strongest of winds that I could conjure up.

For now, we were safe.

That night, the village threw its first New Year's Eve party, not just to celebrate the end of probably the hardest year any of us had ever known and the beginning of a new year, but also to celebrate life and hope, remembering and honoring the dead, and sealing the communal bond that kicking out Steve and creating our village's protective shield had started. Our village had been tested and tried, challenged in ways both envisioned and unforeseen, and yet we'd emerged as survivors with a true appreciation for freedom, family, safety, and love.

As for Tarah and me, we spent the night in a much quieter way, asleep in each others' arms and thankful for life itself. And that was more than enough celebration for us.

THE END

THE CLANN

Out now from Harlequin Teen
in multiple languages in both
print and ebook formats in
Melissa Darnell's Clann Series

The Clann Series #1:

Savannah Colbert has never known why she's so hated by the kids of the Clann. Nor can she deny her instinct to get close to Clann golden boy Tristan Coleman. Especially when she recovers from a strange illness and the attraction becomes nearly irresistible. It's as if he's a magnet, pulling her gaze, her thoughts, even her dreams. Her family has warned her to have nothing to do with him, or any members of the Clann. But when Tristan is suddenly everywhere she goes, Savannah fears she's destined to fail.

For years, Tristan has been forbidden to even speak to Savannah Colbert. Then Savannah disappears from school for a week and comes back...different, and suddenly he can't stay away. Boys seem dangerously intoxicated just from looking at her. His own family becomes stricter than ever. And Tristan has to fight his own urge to protect her, to be near her no matter the consequences....

Also available in Melissa Darnell's Clann Series...

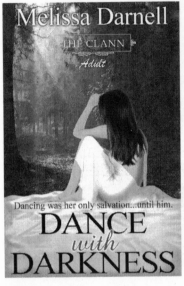

ABOUT THE AUTHOR

Melissa Darnell is the author of a growing list of adult, New Adult, and YA fiction and nonfiction books. Born in California, she grew up in East Texas, and as an adult has also called the following states home since then: Utah, West Virginia, Louisiana, Alabama, Kentucky, Iowa, and South Dakota. She currently lives in northeastern Nebraska with her awesome husband Tim and two amazingly cool children, Hunter and Alexander, where she enjoys watching TV shows as diverse as Newsroom, Being Human, Defiance, Game of Thrones, and True Blood, and of course writing her next book. Visit her website at www.MelissaDarnell.com for news about her upcoming books, author's notes about some of her novels, online playlists for each of her books, and more!

Made in the USA
Lexington, KY
19 June 2015